A Very Naughty Girl

This text was originally published in the UK in the year of 1901.
The text is in the public domain.
The edits and layout of this version are Copyright © 2022 by Wombrook Publishing

This publication has no affiliation with the original Author or publication company.

The publishers have made all reasonable efforts to ensure this book is indeed in the Public Domain in any and all territories it has been published, and apologise for any omissions or errors made. Corrections may be made to future printings or electronic publications.

www.wombrookpublishing.com

Printed or published to the highest ethical standard

A VERY NAUGHTY GIRL

L T Meade

United Kingdom
1901

CONTENTS

CHAPTER I.–SYLVIA AND AUDREY..1
CHAPTER II.–ARRIVAL OF EVELYN. 6
CHAPTER III.–THE CRADLE LIFE OF WILD EVE. 14
CHAPTER IV.–"I DRAW THE LINE AT UNCLE NED." 20
CHAPTER V.–FRANK'S EYES..24
CHAPTER VI.–THE HUNGRY GIRL..31
CHAPTER VII.–STAYING TO DINNER. 37
CHAPTER VIII.–EVENING-DRESS. 42
CHAPTER IX.–BREAKFAST IN BED...57
CHAPTER X.–JASPER WAS TO GO. 63
CHAPTER XI.–"I CANNOT ALTER MY PLANS." 68
CHAPTER XII.–HUNGER...77
CHAPTER XIII.–JASPER TO THE RESCUE. 87
CHAPTER XIV.–CHANGE OF PLANS. 90
CHAPTER XV.–SCHOOL..98
CHAPTER XVI.–SYLVIA'S DRIVE..105
CHAPTER XVII.–THE FALL IN THE SNOW. 113
CHAPTER XVIII.–A RED GIPSY CLOAK. 121
CHAPTER XIX.–"WHY DID YOU DO IT?" 128
CHAPTER XX.–"NOT GOOD NOR HONORABLE." 134
CHAPTER XXI.–THE TORN BOOK..140
CHAPTER XXII.–"STICK TO YOUR COLORS, EVELYN." 146
CHAPTER XXIII.–ONE WEEK OF GRACE..149
CHAPTER XXIV.–"WHO IS E. W.?" 157
CHAPTER XXV.–UNCLE EDWARD..166
CHAPTER XXVI.–TANGLES. 176
CHAPTER XXVII.–THE STRANGE VISITOR IN THE BACK BEDROOM..183
CHAPTER XXVIII.–THE ROOM WITH THE LIGHT THAT FLICKERED..193
CHAPTER XXIX.–WHAT COULD IT MEAN? 196
CHAPTER XXX.–THE LOADED GUN..201
CHAPTER XXXI.–FOR UNCLE EDWARD'S SAKE..........................209
A VERY NAUGHTY GIRL HISTORICAL CONTEXT 213

CHAPTER I.—SYLVIA AND AUDREY.

It was a day of great excitement, and Audrey Wynford stood by her schoolroom window and looked out. She was a tall girl of sixteen, with her hair hanging in a long, fair plait down her back. She stood with her hands folded behind her and an expectant expression on her face.

Up the avenue a stream of people were coming. Some came in cabs, some on bicycles; some walked. They all turned in the direction of the front entrance, and Audrey heard their voices rising and falling as they entered the house, walked down the hall, and disappeared into some region at the other end.

"It is all detestable," she muttered; "and just when Evelyn is coming, too. How strange she will think it! I wish father would drop this horrid custom. I do not approve of it at all."

Just then her governess, a bright-looking girl about six years Audrey's senior, came into the room.

"Well," she cried, "and what are you doing here? I thought you were going to ride this afternoon."

"How can I?" said Audrey, shrugging her shoulders. "I shall be met at every turn."

"And why not?" said Miss Sinclair. "You are not ashamed of being seen."

"It is quite detestable," said Audrey.

She crossed the room, flung herself into a deep straw armchair in front of a blazing log fire, and took up a magazine.

"It is all horrid," she continued as she rapidly turned the pages; "you know it, Miss Sinclair, as well as I do."

"If I were you," said Miss Sinclair, "I should be proud—very proud—to belong to an old family who had kept a custom like this in vogue."

"If you belonged to the old family you would not," said Audrey. "Every one laughs at us. I call it perfectly horrid. What possible good can it do that all the people of the neighborhood, and the strangers who come to stay in the town, should make free of Wynford Castle on New Year's Day? It makes me cross anyhow. I am sorry to be cross to you, Miss Sinclair; but I am, and that is a fact."

Miss Sinclair sat down on another chair.

"I like it," she said after a pause.

"Why?" asked Audrey.

"There were some quite hungry people passing through the hall as I came to you just now."

"Let them be hungry somewhere else, not here," said the angry girl. "It was all very well when some ancestor of mine first started the custom; but that father, a man of the present day, up-to-date in every sense of the word, should carry it on—that he should keep open house for every individual who chooses to come here on New Year's Day—is past endurance. Last year between two and three hundred people dined or supped or had tea at the Castle, and I believe, from the appearance of the avenue, there will be still more to-day. The house gets so dirty, for one thing, for half of them don't think of wiping their feet; and then we run a chance of being robbed, for how do we know that there are not adventurers in the throng? If I were the country-folk I would be too proud to come; but they are not—not a bit."

"I cannot agree with you," said Miss Sinclair. "It is a splendid old custom, and I hope it will not be abolished."

"Perhaps Evelyn will abolish it when she comes in for the property," said Audrey in a low tone. Her face looked scarcely amiable as she said the words.

Miss Sinclair regarded her with a puzzled expression.

"Audrey dear," she said after a pause, "I am very fond of you."

"And I of you," said Audrey a little unwillingly. "You are more friend than governess. I should like best to go to school, of course; but as father says that that is quite impossible, I have to put up with the next best; and you are a very good next best."

"Then if I am, may I just as a friend, and one who loves you very dearly, make a remark?"

"It is going to be something odious," said Audrey—"that goes without saying—but I suppose I'll listen."

"Don't you think you are just a wee bit in danger of becoming selfish, Audrey?" said her governess.

"Am I? Perhaps so; I am afraid I don't care."

"You would if you thought it over; and this is New Year's Day, and it is a lovely afternoon, and you might come for a ride—I wish you would."

"I will not run the chance of meeting those folks on any consideration whatever," said Audrey; "but I will go for a walk with you, if you like."

"Done," said Miss Sinclair. "I have to go on a message for Lady Wynford to the lodge; will you come by the shrubberies and meet me there?"

"All right," replied Audrey; "I will go and get ready."

She left the room.

After her pupil had left her, Miss Sinclair sat for a time gazing into the huge log fire.

She was a very pretty girl, with a high-bred look about her. She had received all the advantages which modern education could afford, and at the age of three-and-twenty had left Girton with the assurance from all her friends that she had a brilliant future before her. The first step in that future seemed bright enough to the handsome, high-spirited girl. Lady Wynford met her in town, took a fancy to her on the spot,

CHAPTER I.—SYLVIA AND AUDREY.

and asked her to conduct Audrey's education. Miss Sinclair received a liberal salary and every comfort and consideration. Audrey fell quickly in love with her, and a more delightful pupil governess never had. The girl was brimming over with intelligence, was keenly alive to the responsibilities of her own position, was absolutely original, and as a rule quite unselfish.

"Poor Audrey! she has her trials before her, all the same," thought the young governess now. "Well, I am very happy here, and I hope nothing will disturb our present arrangement for some time. As to Evelyn, we have yet to discover what sort of girl she is. She comes this evening. But there, I am forgetting all about Audrey, and she must be waiting for me."

It so happened that Audrey Wynford was doing nothing of the sort. She had hastily put on her warm jacket and fur cap and gone out into the grounds. The objectionable avenue, with its streams of people coming and going, was to be religiously avoided, and Audrey went in the direction of a copse of young trees, which led again through a long shrubbery in the direction of the lodge gates.

It was the custom from time immemorial in the Wynford family to keep open house on New Year's Day. Any wayfarer, gentle or simple, man or woman, boy or girl, could come up the avenue and ring the bell at the great front-door, and be received and fed and refreshed, and sent again on his or her way with words of cheer. The Squire himself as a rule received his guests, but where that was impossible the steward of the estate was present to conduct them to the huge hall which ran across the back of the house, where unlimited refreshments were provided. No one was sent away. No one was refused admission on this day of all days. The period of the reception was from sunrise to sundown. At sundown the hospitality came to an end; the doors of the house were shut and no more visitors were allowed admission. An extra staff of servants was generally secured for the occasion, and the one and only condition made by the Squire was, that as much food as possible might be eaten, that each male visitor might drink good wine or sound ale to his heart's content, that each might warm himself thoroughly by the huge log fires, but that no one should take any food away. This, in the case of so promiscuous an assemblage, was necessary. To Audrey, however, the whole thing was more or less a subject of dislike. She regarded the first day of each year as a penance; she shrank from the subject of the guests, and on this special New Year's Day was more aggrieved and put out than usual. More guests had arrived than had ever come before, for the people of the neighborhood enjoyed the good old custom, and there was not a villager, not a trades-person, nor even a landed proprietor near who did not make it a point of breaking bread at Wynford Castle on New Year's Day. The fact that a man of position sat down side by side with

A VERY NAUGHTY GIRL

a tramp or a laborer made no difference; there was no distinction of rank amongst the Squire's guests on this day.

Audrey heard the voices now as she disappeared into the shelter of the young trees. She heard also the rumble of wheels as the better class of guests arrived or went away again.

"It is horrid," she murmured for about the twentieth time to herself; and then she began to run in order to get away from what she called the disagreeable noise.

Audrey could run with the speed and grace of a young fawn, but she had not gone half-through the shrubbery before she stopped dead-short. A girl of about her own age was coming hurriedly to meet her. She was a very pretty girl, with black eyes and a quantity of black hair and a richly colored dark face. The girl was dressed somewhat fantastically in many colors. Peeping out from beneath her old-fashioned jacket was a scarf of deep yellow; the skirt of her dress was crimson, and in her hat she wore two long crimson feathers. Audrey regarded her with not only wonder but also disfavor. Who was she? What a vulgar, forward, insufferable young person!

"I say," cried the girl, coming up eagerly; "I have lost my way, and it is so important! Can you tell me how I can get to the front entrance of the Castle?"

"You ought not to have come by the shrubbery," said Audrey in a very haughty tone. "The visitors who come to the Castle to-day are expected to use the avenue. But now that you have come," she added, "if you will take this short cut you will find yourself in the right direction. You have then but to follow the stream of people and you will reach the hall door."

"Oh, thank you!" said the girl. "I am so awfully hungry! I do hope I shall get in before sunset. Good-by, and thank you so much! My name is Sylvia Leeson; who are you?"

"I am Audrey Wynford," replied Audrey, speaking more icily than ever.

"Then you are the young lady of the Castle?"

"I am Audrey Wynford."

"How strange! One would think to meet you here, and one would think to see me here, that we both belonged to Shakespeare's old play AS YOU LIKE IT. But I must not stay another minute. It is so sweet of your father to invite us all, and if I am not quick I shall lose the fun."

She nodded with a flash of bright eyes and white teeth at the amazed Audrey, and the next moment was lost to view.

"What a girl!" thought Audrey as she pursued her walk. "How dared she! She did not treat me with one scrap of respect, and she seemed to think—a girl of that sort!—that she was my equal; she absolutely spoke of us in the same breath. It was almost insulting. Sylvia and Audrey! We meet in a wood, and we might be characters out of AS

CHAPTER I.—SYLVIA AND AUDREY.

YOU LIKE IT. Well, she is awfully pretty, but—— Oh dear! what a creature she is when all is said and done—that wild dress, and those dancing eyes, and that free manner! And yet—and yet she was scarcely vulgar; she was only—only different from anybody else. Who is she, and where does she come from? Sylvia Leeson. Rather a pretty name; and certainly a pretty girl. But to think of her partaking of hospitality—all alone, too—with the CANAILLE of Wynford!"

CHAPTER II.—ARRIVAL OF EVELYN.

Audrey met her governess at the lodge gates, and the two plunged down a side-path, and were soon making for the wonderful moors about a mile away from Wynford Castle.

"What are you thinking about, Audrey?" said Miss Sinclair.

"Do you happen to know," said Audrey, "any people in the village or neighborhood of the name of Leeson?"

"No, dear, certainly not. I do not think any people of the name live here. Why do you ask?"

"For such a funny reason!" replied Audrey. "I met a girl who had come by mistake through the shrubberies. She was on her way to the Castle to get a good meal. She told me her name was Sylvia Leeson. She was pretty in an OUTRÉ sort of style; she was also very free. She had the cheek to compare herself with me, and said that as my name was Audrey and hers Sylvia we ought to be two of Shakespeare's heroines. There was something uncommon about her. Not that I liked her—very far from that. But I wonder who she is."

"I don't know," said Miss Sinclair. "I certainly have not the least idea that there is any one of that name living in our neighborhood, but one can never tell."

"Oh, but you know everybody round here," said Audrey. "Perhaps she is a stranger. I think on the whole I am glad."

"I heard a week ago that some people had taken The Priory," said Miss Sinclair.

"The Priory!" cried Audrey. "It has been uninhabited ever since I can remember."

"I heard the rumor," continued Miss Sinclair, "but I know no particulars, and it may not be true. It is just possible that this girl belongs to them."

"I should like to find out," replied Audrey. "She certainly interested me although——Oh, well, don't let us talk of her any more. Jenny dear"—Audrey in affectionate moments called her governess by her Christian name—"are you not anxious to know what Evelyn is like?"

"I suppose I am," replied Miss Sinclair.

"I think of her so much!" continued Audrey. "It seems so odd that she, a stranger, should be the heiress, and I, who have lived here all my days, should inherit nothing. Oh, of course, I shall have plenty of money, for mother had such a lot; but it does seem so unaccountable that all father's property should go to Evelyn. And now she is to live here, and of course take the precedence of me, I do not know that I quite like it. Sometimes I feel that she will rub me the wrong way; if she is very masterful, for instance. She can be—can't she, Jenny?"

"But why should we suppose that she will be?" replied Miss Sinclair. "There is no good in getting prejudiced beforehand."

CHAPTER II.—ARRIVAL OF EVELYN.

"I cannot help thinking about it," said Audrey. "You know I have never had any close companions before, and although you make up for everybody else, and I love you with all my heart and soul, yet it is somewhat exciting to think of a girl just my own age coming to live with me."

"Of course, dear; and I am so glad for your sake!"

"But then," continued Audrey, "she does not come quite as an ordinary guest; she comes to the home which is to be hers hereafter. I wonder what her ideas are, and what she will feel about things. It is very mysterious. I am excited; I own it. You may be quite sure, though, that I shall not show any of my excitement when Evelyn does come. Jenny, have you pictured her yet to yourself? Do you think she is tall or short, or pretty or ugly, or what?"

"I have thought of her, of course," replied Miss Sinclair; "but I have not formed the least idea. You will soon know, Audrey; she is to arrive in time for dinner."

"Yes," said Audrey; "mother is going in the carriage to meet her, and the train is due at six-thirty. She will arrive at the Castle a little before seven. Mother says she will probably bring a maid, and perhaps a French governess. Mother does not know herself what sort she is. It is odd her having lived away from England all this time."

Audrey chatted on with her governess a little longer, and presently they turned and went back to the house. The sun had already set, and the big front-door was shut; the family never used it except on this special day or when a wedding or a funeral left Wynford Castle. The pretty side-door, with its sheltered porch, was the mode of exit and ingress for the inhabitants of Wynford Castle. Audrey and her governess now entered, and Audrey stood for a few moments to warm her hands by the huge log fire on the hearth. Miss Sinclair went slowly up-stairs to her room; and Audrey, finding herself alone, gave a quick sigh.

"I wonder—I do wonder," she said half-aloud.

Her words were evidently heard, for some one stirred, and presently a tall man with a slight stoop came forward and stood where the light of the big fire fell all over him.

"Why, dad!" cried Audrey as she put her hand inside her father's arm. "Were you asleep?" she asked. "How was it that Miss Sinclair and I did not see you when we came in?"

"I was sound asleep in that big chair. I was somewhat tired. I had received three hundred guests; don't forget that," replied Squire Wynford.

"And they have gone. What a comfort!" said Audrey.

"My dear little Audrey, I have fed them and warmed them and sent them on their way rejoicing, and I am a more popular Squire Wynford of Castle Wynford than ever. Why should you grumble because your

A VERY NAUGHTY GIRL

neighbors, every mother's son of them, had as much to eat and drink as they could desire on New Year's Day?"

"I hate the custom," said Audrey. "It belongs to the Middle Ages; it ought to be exploded."

"What! and allow the people to go hungry?"

"Those who are likely to go hungry," continued Audrey, "might have money given to them. We do not want all the small squires everywhere round to come and feed at the Castle."

"But the small squires like it, and so do the poor people, and so do I," said Squire Wynford; and now he frowned very slightly, and Audrey gave another sigh.

"We must agree to differ, dad," she said.

"I am afraid so, my dear. Well, and how are you, my pet? I have not seen you until now. Very happy at the thought of your cousin's arrival?"

"No, dad, scarcely happy, but excited all the same. Are not you a little, wee bit excited too, father? It seems so strange her coming all the way from Tasmania to take possession of her estates. I wonder—I do wonder—what she will be like."

"She takes possession of no estates while I live," said the Squire, "but she is the next heiress."

"And you are sorry it is not I; are you not, father?"

"I don't think of it," said the Squire. "No," he added thoughtfully a moment later, "that is not the case. I do think of it. You are better off without the responsibility; you would never be suited to a great estate of this sort. Evelyn may be different. Anyhow, when the time comes it is her appointed work. Now, my dear"—he took out his watch—"your cousin will arrive in a moment. Your mother has gone to meet her. Do you intend to welcome her here or in one of the sitting-rooms?"

"I will stay in the hall, of course," said Audrey a little fretfully.

"I will leave you, then, my love. I have neglected a sheaf of correspondence, and would like to look through my letters before dinner."

The Squire moved away, walking slowly. He pushed aside some heavy curtains and vanished. Audrey still stood by the fire. Presently a restless fit seized her, and she too flitted up the winding white marble stairs and disappeared down a long corridor. She entered a pretty room daintily furnished in blue and silver. A large log fire burned in the grate; electric light shed its soft gleams over the furniture; there was a bouquet of flowers and a little pot of ivy on a small table, also a bookcase full of gaily-bound story-books. Nothing had been neglected, even to the big old Bible and the old-fashioned prayer-book.

"I wonder how she will like it," thought Audrey. "This is one of the prettiest rooms in the house. Mother said she must have it. I wonder if she will like it, and if I shall like her. Oh, and here is her dressing-

CHAPTER II.—ARRIVAL OF EVELYN.

room, and here is a little boudoir where she may sit and amuse herself and shut us out if she chooses. Lucky Evelyn! How strange it all seems! For the first time I begin to appreciate my darling, beloved home. Why should it pass away from me to her? Oh, of course I am not jealous; I would not be mean enough to entertain feelings of that sort, and— I hear the sound of wheels. She is coming; in a moment I shall see her. Oh, I do wonder—I do wonder! I wish Jenny were with me; I feel quite nervous."

Audrey dashed out of the room, rushed down the winding stairs, and had just entered the hall when a footman pushed aside the heavy curtains, and Lady Frances Wynford, a handsome, stately-looking woman, entered, accompanied by a small girl.

The girl was dragging in a great pile of rugs and wraps. Her hat was askew on her head, her jacket untidy. She flung the rugs down in the center of a rich Turkey carpet; said, "There, that is a relief;" and then looked full at Audrey.

Audrey was a head and shoulders taller than the heiress, who had thin and somewhat wispy flaxen hair, and a white face with insignificant features. Her eyes, however, were steady, brown, large, and intelligent. She came up to Audrey at once.

"Don't introduce me, please, Aunt Frances," she said. "I know this is Audrey.—I am Evelyn. You hate me, don't you?"

"No, I am sure I do not," said Audrey.

"Well, I should if I were you. It would be much more interesting to be hated. So this is the place. It looks jolly, does it not? Aunt Frances, do you know where my maid is? I must have her—I must have her at once. Please tell Jasper to come here," continued the girl, turning to a man-servant who lingered in the background.

"Desire Miss Wynford's maid to come into the hall," said Lady Frances in an imperious tone; "and bring tea, Davis. Be quick."

The man withdrew, and Evelyn, lifting her hand, took off her ugly felt hat and flung it on the pile of rugs and cushions.

"Don't touch them, please," she said as Audrey advanced. "That is Jasper's work.—By the way, Aunt Frances, may Jasper sleep in my room? I have never slept alone, not since I was born, and I could not survive it. I want a little bed just the ditto of my own for Jasper. I cannot live without Jasper. May she sleep close to me, please, Aunt Frances? And, oh! I do hope and trust this house is not haunted. It does look eerie. I am terrified at the thought of ghosts. I know I shall not be a very pleasant inmate, and I am sorry for you all—and for you in special, Audrey. What a grand, keep-your-distance sort of air you have! But I am not going to be afraid of you. I do not forget that the place will belong to me some day. Hullo, Jasper!"

Evelyn flitted in a curious, elf-like way across the hall, and went up to a dark woman who stood just by the velvet curtain.

"Don't be shy, Jasper," she said. "You have nothing to be afraid of here. It is all very grand, I know; but then it is to be mine some day, and you are never to leave me—never. I was speaking to my aunt, Lady Frances, and you are to have your little bed near mine. See that it is arranged for to-night. And now, please, pick up these rugs and cushions and my old hat, and take them to my room. Don't stare so, Jasper; do what I tell you."

Jasper somewhat sullenly obeyed. She was as graceful and deft in all her actions as Evelyn was the reverse. Evelyn stood and watched her. When she went slowly up the marble stairs, the heiress turned with a laugh to her two companions.

"How you stare!" she said; and she looked full at Audrey. "Do you regard me as barbarian, or a wild beast, or what?"

"I am interested in you," said Audrey in her low voice. "You are decidedly out of the common."

"Come," said Lady Frances, "we have no time for analyzing character just now. Audrey, take your cousin to her room, and then go yourself and get dressed for dinner."

"Will you come, Evelyn?" said Audrey.

She crossed the hall, Evelyn following her slowly. Once or twice the heiress stopped to examine a mailed figure in armor, or an old picture on which the firelight cast a fitful gleam. She said, "How ugly! A queer old thing, that!" to the figure in armor, and she scowled up at the picture.

"You are not going to frighten me, you old scarecrow," she said; and then she ran up-stairs by Audrey's side.

"So this is what they call English grandeur!" she remarked. "Is not this house centuries old?"

"Parts of the house are," answered Audrey.

"Is this part?"

"No; the hall and staircase were added about seventy years ago."

"Is my room in the old part or the new part?"

"Your room is in what is called the medium part. It is a lovely room; you will be charmed with it."

"I by no means know that I shall. But show it to me."

Audrey walked a little quicker. She began to feel a curious sense of irritation, and knew that there was something about Evelyn which might under certain conditions try her temper very much. They reached the lovely blue-and-silver room, and Audrey flung open the door, expecting a cry of delight from Evelyn. But the heiress was not one to give herself away; she cast cool and critical eyes round the chamber.

"Dear, dear!" she said—"dear, dear! So this is your idea of an English bedroom!"

"It is an English bedroom; there is no idea about it," said Audrey.

CHAPTER II.—ARRIVAL OF EVELYN.

"You are cross, are you not, Audrey?" was Evelyn's remark. "It is very trying for you my coming here. I know that, of course; Jasper has told me. I should be ignorant and quite lost were it not for Jasper, but Jasper puts me up to things. I do not think I could live without her. She has often described you—often and often. It would make you scream to listen to her. She has taken you off splendidly. Really, all things considered, you are very like what she has pictured you. I say, Audrey, would you like to come up here after your next meal, whatever you call it, and watch Jasper as she takes you off? She is the most splendid mimic in all the world. In a day or two she will be able to imitate Aunt Frances and every one in the house. Oh, it is killing to watch her and to listen to her! You would like to see yourself through Jasper's eyes, would you not, Audrey?"

"No, thank you," replied Audrey.

"How you kill me with that 'No, thank you,' of yours! Why, they are the very words Jasper said you would be certain to say. Oh dear! this is quite amusing." Evelyn laughed long and loud, wiping her eyes with her handkerchief as she did so. "Oh dear! oh dear!" she said. "Don't look any crosser, Audrey, or I shall die with laughing! Why, you will make me scream."

"That would be bad for you after your journey," said Audrey. "I see you have hot water, and your maid is in the dressing-room. I will leave you now. That is the dressing-bell; the bell for dinner will ring in half an hour. I must go and dress."

Audrey rushed out of the room, very nearly, but not quite, banging the door after her.

"If I stayed another moment I should lose my temper. I should say something terrible," thought the girl. Her heart was beating fast; she pressed her hand to her side. "If it were not for Jenny I do not believe I could endure the house with that girl," was her next ejaculation. "To think that she is a Wynford, and that the Castle—the lovely, beautiful Castle—is to belong to her some day. Oh, it is maddening! Our darling knight in armor—Sir Galahad I have always called him—and our Rembrandt: one is a scarecrow, and the other a queer old thing. Oh Evelyn, you are almost past bearing!"

Audrey ran away to her room, where her maid, Eleanor, was waiting to attend on her. Audrey was never in the habit of confiding in her maid; and the girl, who was brimful of importance, curiosity, and news, did not dare to express any of her feelings to Miss Audrey in her present mood.

"Put on my very prettiest frock to-night, please, Eleanor," said the young lady. "Dress my hair to the best advantage. My white dress, did you say? No, not white, but that pale, very pale, rose-colored silk with all the little trimmings and flounces."

"But that is one of your gayest dresses, Miss Audrey."

A VERY NAUGHTY GIRL

"Never mind; I choose to look gay and well dressed."

The girl proceeded with her young mistress's toilet, and a minute or two before the second bell rang Audrey was ready. She made a lovely and graceful picture as she looked at herself for a moment in the long mirror. Her figure was already beautifully formed; she was tall, graceful, dignified. The set of her young head on her stately neck was superb. Her white shoulders gleamed under the transparent folds of her lovely frock. Her rounded arms were white as alabaster. She slipped a small diamond ring on one of her fingers, looked for a moment longingly at a pearl necklace, but finally decided not to wear any more adornment, and ran lightly down-stairs.

The big drawing-room was lit with the softest light. The Squire stood by the hearth, on which a huge log blazed. Lady Frances, in full evening-dress, was carelessly turning the leaves of a novel.

"What a quiet evening we are likely to have!" she said, looking up at the Squire as she spoke. "To-morrow there are numbers of guests coming; we shall be a big party, and Audrey and Evelyn will, I trust, have a pleasant time.—My dear Audrey, why that dress this evening?"

"I took a fancy to wear it, mother," said Audrey in a light tone.

There was more color than usual in her cheeks, and her eyes were brighter than her mother had ever seen them. Lady Frances was not a woman of any special discernment. She was an excellent mother and a splendid hostess. She was good to look at, and was just the sort of GRANDE DAME to keep up all the dignity of Wynford Castle, but she never even pretended to understand her only child. The Squire, a sensitive man in many ways, was also more or less a stranger to Audrey's real character. He looked at her, it is true, a little anxiously now, and a slight curiosity stirred his breast as to the possible effect Evelyn's presence in the house might have on his beautiful young daughter. As to Evelyn herself, he had not seen her, and did not even care to inquire of his wife what sort of girl she was. He was deeply absorbed over the silver currency question, and was writing an exhaustive paper on it for the NINETEENTH CENTURY; he had not time, therefore, to worry about domestic matters. Just then the drawing-room door was flung open, and the footman announced, as though she were a stranger:

"Miss Evelyn Wynford."

If Audrey was, according to Lady Frances's ideas, slightly overdressed for so small a party, she was quite outshone by Evelyn, whose dress was altogether unsuitable for her age. She wore a very thick silk, bright blue in color, with a quantity of colored embroidery thrown over it. Her little fat neck was bare, and her sleeves were short. Her scanty fair hair was arranged on the top of her head, two diamond pins supporting it in position; a diamond necklace was clasped round her neck, and she had bracelets on her arms. She was evidently intensely pleased with herself, and looked with the utmost confidence from

CHAPTER II.–ARRIVAL OF EVELYN.

Lady Frances to her uncle. With a couple of long strides the Squire advanced to meet her. He looked into her queer little face and all his indifference vanished. She was his only brother's only child. He had loved his brother better than any one on earth, and, come what might, he would give that brother's child a welcome. So he took both of Evelyn's tiny hands, and suddenly stooping, he lifted her an inch or so from the ground and kissed her twice. Something in his manner made the little girl give a sort of gasp.

"Why, it is just as if you were father come to life," she said. "I am glad to see you, Uncle Ned."

Still holding her hand, the Squire walked up to the hearth and stood there facing Audrey and his wife.

"You have been introduced to Audrey, have you not, Evelyn?" he said.

"I did not need to be introduced. I saw a girl in the hall, and I guessed it must be Audrey. 'Cute of me, was it not? Do you know, Uncle Ned, I don't much like this place, but I like you. Yes, I am right-down smitten with you, but I don't think I like anything else. You don't mind if I am frank, Uncle Ned; it always was my way. We are brought up like that in Tasmania—Audrey, don't frown at me; you don't look pretty when you frown. But, oh! I say, the bell has gone, has it not?"

"Yes, my dear," said Lady Frances.

"And it means dinner, does it not?"

"Certainly, Evelyn," said her uncle, bending towards her with the most polished and stately grace. "Allow me, my niece, to conduct you to the dining-room."

"How droll you are, uncle!" said Evelyn. "But I like you all the same. You are a right-down good old sort. I am awfully peckish; I shall be glad of a round meal."

CHAPTER III.—THE CRADLE LIFE OF WILD EVE.

Eighteen years before the date of this story, two brothers had parted with angry words. They were both in love with the same woman, and the younger brother had won. The elder brother, only one year his senior, could not stand defeat.

"I cannot stay in the old place," he said. "You can occupy the Castle during my absence."

To this arrangement Edward Wynford agreed.

"Where are you going?" he said to his brother Frank.

"To the other side of the world—Australia probably. I don't know when I shall return. It does not much matter. I shall never marry. The estate will be yours. If Lady Frances has a son, it will belong to him."

"You must not think of that," said Edward. "I will live at the Castle for a few years in order to keep it warm for you, but you will come back; you will get over this. If she had loved you, old man, do you think I would have taken her from you? But she chose me from the very first."

"I don't blame you, Ned," said Frank. "You are as innocent of any intention of harm to me as the unborn babe, but I love her too well to stay in the old country. I am off. I don't want her ever to know. You will promise me, won't you, that you will never tell her why I have skulked off and dropped my responsibilities on to your shoulders? Promise me that, at least, will you not?"

Edward Wynford promised his brother, and the brother went away.

In the former generation father and son had agreed to break off the entail, and although there was no intention of carrying this action into effect, and Frank, as eldest son, inherited the great estates of Wynford Castle, yet at his father's death he was in the position of one who could leave the estates to any one he pleased.

During his last interview with his brother he said to him distinctly:

"Remember, if Lady Frances has a son I wish him to be, after yourself, the next heir to the property."

"But if she has not a son?" said Edward.

"In that case I have nothing to say. It is most unlikely that I shall marry. The property will come to you in the ordinary way, and as the entail is out off, you can leave it to whom you please."

"Do not forget that at present you can leave the estate and the Castle to whomever you please, even to an utter stranger," said Edward, with a slight smile.

To this remark Frank made no answer. The next day the brothers parted—as it turned out, for life. Edward married Lady Frances, and they went to live at Wynford Castle. Edward heard once from Frank

CHAPTER III.—THE CRADLE LIFE OF WILD EVE.

during the voyage, and then not at all, until he received a letter which must have been written a couple of months before his brother's death. It was forwarded to him in a strange hand, and was full of extraordinary and painful tidings. Frank Wynford had died suddenly of acute fever, but before his death he had arranged all his affairs. His letter ran as follows:

"MY DEAR EDWARD,—If I live you will never get this letter; if I die it reaches you all in good time. When last we parted I told you I should never marry. So much for man's proposals. When I got to Tasmania I went on a ranch, and now I am the husband of the farmer's daughter. Her name is Isabel. She is a handsome woman, and the mother of a daughter. Why I married her I can not tell you, except that I can honestly say it was not with any sense of affection. But she is my wife, and the mother of a little baby girl. Edward, when I last heard from you, you told me that you also had a daughter. If a son follows all in due course, what I have to say will not much signify; but if you have no son I should wish the estates eventually to come to my little girl. I do not believe in a woman's administration of large and important estates like mine, but what I say to myself now is, as well my girl as your girl. Therefore, Edward, my dear brother, I leave all my estates to you for your lifetime, and at your death all the property which came to me by my father's will goes to my little girl, to be hers when you are no longer there. I want you to receive my daughter, and to ask your wife to bring her up. I want her to have all the advantages that a home with Lady Frances must confer on her. I want my child and your child to be friends. I do no injustice to your daughter, Edward, when I make my will, for she inherits money on her mother's side. I will acquaint my wife with particulars of this letter, and in case I catch the fever which is raging here now she will know how to act. My lawyer in Hobart Town will forward this, and see that my will is carried into effect. There is a provision in it for the maintenance of my daughter until she joins you at Castle Wynford. Whenever that event takes place she is your care. I have only one thing to add. The child might go to you at once (I have a premonition that I am about to die very soon), and thus never know that she had an Australian mother, but the difficulty lies in the fact that the mother loves the child and will scarcely be induced to part with her. You must not receive my poor wife unless indeed a radical change takes place in her; and although I have begged of her to give up the child, I doubt

A VERY NAUGHTY GIRL

> if she will do it. I cannot add any more, for time presses. My will is legal in every respect, and there will be no difficulty in carrying it into effect."

This strange letter was discovered by Frank Wynford's widow a month after his death. It was sealed and directed to his brother in England. She longed to read it, but restrained herself. She sent it on to her husband's lawyer in Hobart Town, and in due course it arrived at Castle Wynford, causing a great deal of consternation and distress both in the minds of the Squire and Lady Frances.

Edward immediately went out to Tasmania. He saw the little baby who was all that was left of his brother, and he also saw that brother's wife. The coarse, loud-voiced woman received him with almost abuse. What was to be done? The mother refused to part with the child, and Edward Wynford, for his own wife's sake and his own baby daughter's sake, could not urge her to come to Castle Wynford.

"I do not care twopence," she remarked, "whether the child has grand relations or not. I loved her father, and I love her. She is my child, and so she has got to put up with me. As long as I live she stays with me here. I am accustomed to ranch life, and she will get accustomed to it too. I will not spare money on her, for there is plenty, and she will be a very rich woman some day. But while I live she stays with me; the only way out of it is, that you ask me to your fine place in England. Even if you do, I don't think I should be bothered to go to you, but you might have the civility to ask me."

Squire Wynford went away, however, without giving this invitation. He spoke to his wife on the subject. In that conversation he was careful to adhere to his brother's wish not to reveal to her that that brother's deep affection for herself had been the cause of his banishment. Lady Frances was an intensely just and upright woman. She had gone through a very bad quarter of an hour when she was told that her little girl was to be supplanted by the strange child of an objectionable mother, but she quickly recovered herself.

"I will not allow jealousy to enter into my life," she said; and she even went the length of writing herself to Mrs. Wynford in Tasmania, and invited her with the baby to come and stay at Wynford Castle. Mrs. Wynford in Tasmania, however, much to the relief of the good folks at home, declined the invitation.

"I have no taste for English grandeur," she said. "I was brought up in a wild state, and I would rather stay as I was reared. The child is well; you can have her when she is grown up or when I am dead."

Years passed after this letter and there was no communication between little Evelyn Wynford, in the wilds of Tasmania, and her rich and stately relatives at Castle Wynford. Lady Frances fervently hoped that God would give her a son, but this hope was not to be realized. Audrey was her only child, and soon it seemed almost like a dim, forgotten fact that the real heiress was in Tasmania, and that Audrey had no

CHAPTER III.—THE CRADLE LIFE OF WILD EVE.

more to do in the future with the stately home of her ancestors than she would have had had she possessed a brother. But when she was sixteen there suddenly came a change. Mrs. Wynford died suddenly. There was now no reason why Evelyn should not come home, and accordingly, untutored, uncared for, a passionate child with a curious, wilful strain in her, she arrived on New Year's Day at Castle Wynford. Evelyn Wynford's nature was very complex. She loved very few people, but those she did love she loved forever. No change, no absence, no circumstances could alter her regard. In her ranch life and during her baby days she had clung to her mother. Mrs. Wynford was fierce and passionate and wilful. Little Evelyn admired her, whatever she did. She trotted round the farm after her; she learnt to ride almost as soon as she could walk, and she followed her mother barebacked on the wildest horses on the ranch. She was fearless and stubborn, and gave way to terrible fits of passion, but with her mother she was gentle as a lamb. Mrs. Wynford was fond of the child in the careless, selfish, and yet fierce way which belonged to her nature. Mrs. Wynford's sole idea of affection was that her child should be with her morning, noon, and night; that for no education, for no advantages, should she be parted from her mother for a moment. Night after night the two slept in each other's arms; day after day they were together. The farmer's daughter was a very strong woman, and as her father died a year or two after her husband, she managed the ranch herself, keeping everything in order, and not allowing the slightest insubordination on the part of her servants. Little Evelyn, too, learnt her mother's masterful ways. She could reprimand; she could insist upon obedience; she could shake her tiny fists in the faces of those who dared to oppose her; and when she was disporting herself so Mrs. Wynford stood by and laughed.

"Hullo!" she used to cry. "See the spirit in the young un. She takes after me. A nice time her English relatives will have with her! But she will never go to them—never while I live."

Although Mrs. Wynford had long ago made up her mind that Evelyn was to have none of the immediate advantages of her birth and future prospects, she was fond of talking to the child about the grandeur which lay before her.

"If I die, Eve," she said, "you will have to go across the sea in a big ship to England. You would have a rough time of it, perhaps, on board, but you won't mind that, my beauty."

"I am not a beauty, mother," answered Evelyn. "You know I am not. You know I am a very plain girl."

"Hark to the child!" shrieked Mrs. Wynford. "It is as good as a play to hear her. If you are not beautiful in body, my darling, you are beautiful in your spirit. Yes, you have inherited from your proud English father lots of gold and a lovely castle, and all your relations will have to eat humble-pie to you; but you have got your spirit from me, Eve—don't forget that."

"Tell me about the Castle, mother, and about my father," said Evelyn, nestling up close to her parent, as they sat by the roaring fire in the winter evenings.

Mrs. Wynford knew very little, and what she did know she exaggerated. She gave Evelyn vivid pictures, however, in each and all of which the principal figure was Evelyn herself—Evelyn claiming her rights, mastering her relations, letting her unknown cousin know that she, Evelyn, was the heiress, and that the cousin was nobody. Only one person in the group of Evelyn's future relations did Mrs. Wynford counsel her to be civil to.

"The worst of it all is this, Eve," she said—"while your uncle lives you do not own a pennypiece of the estate; and he may hold out for many a long day, so you had best be agreeable to him. Besides, he is like your father. Your father was a very handsome man and a very fine man, and I loved him, child. I took a fancy to him from the day he arrived at the ranch, and when he asked me to marry him I thought myself in rare good luck. But he died soon after you were born. Had he lived I'd have been the lady of the Castle, but I'd not go there without him, and you shall never go while I live."

"I don't want to, mother. You are more to me than twenty castles," said the enthusiastic little girl.

Mrs. Wynford had one friend whom Evelyn tolerated and presently loved. That friend was a woman, partly of French extraction, who had come to stay at the ranch once during a severe illness of its owner. Her name was Jasper—Amelia Jasper; but she was known on the ranch by the title of Jasper alone. She was not a lady in any sense of the word, and did not pretend that she was one; but she was possessed of a certain strange fascination which she could exercise at will over those with whom she came in contact, and she made herself so useful to Mrs. Wynford and so necessary to Evelyn that she was never allowed to leave the ranch again. She soon obtained a great power over the curious, uneducated woman who was Evelyn's mother; and when at last Mrs. Wynford found that she was smitten with an incurable disease, and that at any moment death would come to fetch her, she asked her dear friend Jasper to take the child to England.

"I'll tell you what I'll do," said Jasper. "I'll take Evelyn to England, and stay with her there."

Mrs. Wynford laughed.

"You are clever enough, Jasper," she said; "but what a figure of fun you would look in the grand sort of imperial residence that my dear late husband has described to me! You are not a lady, you know, although you are smart and clever enough to beat half the ladies out of existence."

CHAPTER III.—THE CRADLE LIFE OF WILD EVE.

"I shall know how to manage," said Jasper. "I, too, have heard of the ways of English grandees. I'll be Evelyn's maid. She cannot do without a maid, can she? I'll take Evelyn back, and I will stay with her as her maid."

Mrs. Wynford hailed this idea as a splendid one, and she even wrote a very badly spelt letter to Lady Frances, which Jasper was to convey and deliver herself, if possible, to her proud ladyship, as the widow called her sister-in-law. In this letter Mrs. Wynford demanded that Jasper was to stay with Evelyn as long as Evelyn wished for her, and she finally added:

"I dare you, Lady Frances, fine lady as you are, to part the child from her maid."

When Mrs. Wynford died Evelyn gave way to the most terrible grief. She refused to eat; she refused to leave her mother's dead body. She shrieked herself into hysterics on the day of the funeral, and then the poor little girl was prostrated with nervous fever. Finally, she became so unwell that it was impossible for her to travel to England for some months. And so it happened that nearly a year elapsed between the death of the mother and the arrival of the child at Castle Wynford.

CHAPTER IV.—"I DRAW THE LINE AT UNCLE NED."

"Well, Jasper," said Evelyn in a very eager voice to her maid that first night, "and how do you like it all?"

"How do you like it, Evelyn?" was the response.

"That is so like you, Jasper!" replied the spoilt little girl. "When all is said and done, you are not a scrap original. You make me like you—I cannot help myself—but in some ways you are too cautious to please me. You don't want to say what you think of the place until you know my opinion. Well, I don't care; I'll tell you out plump what I think of everything. The place is horrid, and so are the people. I wish—oh! I wish I was back again on the ranch with mother."

Jasper looked down rather scornfully at the small girl, who, in a rich and elaborately embroidered dressing-gown, was kneeling by the fire. Evelyn's handsome eyes, the only really good feature she possessed, were fixed full upon her maid's face.

"The Castle is too stiff for me," she said, "and too—too airified and high and mighty. Mother was quite right when she spoke of Castle Wynford. I don't care for anybody in the place except Uncle Ned. I don't know how I shall live here. Oh Jasper, don't you remember the evenings at home? Cannot you recall that night when Whitefoot was ill, and you and mothery and I had to sit up all through the long hours nursing her, and how we thought the dear old moo-cow would die! Don't you remember the mulled cider and the gingerbread and the doughnuts and the apple-rings? How we toasted the apple-rings by the fire, and how they spluttered, and how good the hot cider was? And don't you remember how mothery sang, and how you and I caught each other's hands and danced, and dear old Whitefoot looked up at us with her big, sorrowful eyes? It is true that she died in the morning, but we had a jolly night. We'll never have such times any more. Oh, I do wish my own mothery had not died and gone to heaven! Oh, I do wish it—I do!"

Evelyn crossed her arms tightly on her breast and began to sway herself backwards and forwards. Tears streamed from her eyes; she did not attempt to wipe them away.

"Now then, it is my turn to speak," said Jasper. "I tell you what it is, Eve; you are about the biggest goose that was ever born in this world. Who would compare that stupid, rough old ranch with this lovely, magnificent house? And it is your own, Eve—or rather it will be your own. I took a good stare at the Squire, and I do not believe he will live to be very old; and whenever he dies you are to take possession—you and I together, Eve love—and out will go her ladyship, and out

CHAPTER IV.—"I DRAW THE LINE AT UNCLE NED."

will go proud Miss Audrey. That will be a fine day, darling—a day worth living for."

"Yes," said Evelyn slowly; "and then we'll alter things. We'll make the Castle something like the ranch. We'll get over some of our friends, and they shall live in the house. Mr. and Mrs. Petrie, who keep the egg-farm not a mile from the ranch, and Mr. Thomas Longchamp and Pete and Dick and Tom and Michael. I told them all when I was going away that when I was mistress of the Castle they should come, and we'll go on much as we went on at the ranch. If mothery up in heaven can see me she will be glad. But, Jasper, why do you speak in that scornful way of my cousin Audrey? I think she is very beautiful. I think she is quite the most beautiful girl I have ever looked at. As to her being stately, she cannot help being stately. I wish I could walk like her, and talk like her, and speak like her; I do, Jasper—I do really."

"Let me see," said Jasper in a contemplative tone. "You are learning to love her, ain't you?"

"I don't love easily. I love my own darling mothery, who is not dead at all, for she is in heaven with father; and I love you, Jasper, and my uncle Edward."

"My word! and why him?"

"I cannot help it; I love him already, and I'll love him more and more the longer I see him and the more I know him. My father must have been like that—a gentleman—a perfect gentleman. Oh! I was happy at the ranch, and mothery was like no one else on the wide earth, but it gave me a sort of quiver down my spine when Uncle Edward took my hand, and when he kissed me. He is like what father was. Had father lived I'd have spent all my days here, and I'd have been perhaps quite as graceful as Audrey, and nearly as beautiful."

"You will never be like her, so you need not think it. You are squat like your mother, and you ain't got a decent feature in your face except your eyes, and even they are only big, not dark; and your hair is skimpy and your face white. You are a sort of mix'um-gather'um—a sort of betwixt-and-between—neither very fair nor very dark, neither very short nor very tall. You are thick-set, just the very image of your mother, and you will always be thick-set and always mix'um-gather'um as long as you live. There! I have spoken. I ain't going to be afraid of you. You had better get into bed now, for it is late. You want your beauty-sleep, and you won't get it unless you are quick. Now march! Put on your night-dress and step into bed."

"I have got to say my prayers first," said Evelyn, "and——" She paused and looked full at her maid. "I have got to say something else. If you talk like that I won't love you any more. You are not to do it. I won't have it."

"Won't she, then?" said Jasper. Her whole manner changed. "And have I hurt her—have I—the little dear? Come to me, my darling.

- 21 -

A VERY NAUGHTY GIRL

Why, you are all trembling! Did you think I meant a word I said? Don't you know that you are the jewel of my eyes and the core of my heart and all the rest? Did your mother leave you to me for nothing, and would I ever leave you, sweetest and best? And if it is squat you are, there is no one like you for determination and fire of spirit. Eh, now, come to my arms and I'll rock the bitterness out of you, for it is puzzled you are, and fretted you are, and you shall not be—no, you shall not be either one or the other ever again while old Jasper lives."

Evelyn's eyes, which had flashed an almost ugly fire, now softened. She looked at Jasper as if she meant to resist her. Then she wavered, and came almost totteringly across the room, and the next moment the strange woman had clasped the girl to her embrace and was rocking her backwards and forwards, Evelyn's head lying on her breast just as if she were a baby.

"Now then, that's better," said Jasper. "I'll undress you as though we were back again on the ranch, and when you are snug and safe in your little white bed we'll have a bit of fun."

"Fun!" said Evelyn. "What?"

"Don't you know how you like a stolen supper? I have got chocolate here, and a little pot, and a jug of cream, and a saucepan, and I'll make a rich cup for you and another for myself; and here's a box of cakes, all sorts and very good. While you are sipping your chocolate I'll take off Miss Audrey and Lady Frances for you. The door is locked; no one can see us. We'll be as snug as snug can be, and we'll have our fun just as if we were back at the ranch."

Evelyn was now all laughter and high spirits. She had no idea of restraining herself. She called Jasper her honey and her honey-pot, and kissed the good woman several times. She superintended the making of the chocolate with eager words and many directions. Finally, a cup of the rich beverage was handed to her, and she sipped it, luxuriously curled up against her snowy pillows, and ate the sweet cakes, and watched Jasper with happy eyes.

"So it is Miss Audrey you'd like to take after?" said Jasper. "You think you are not a patch on her. To be sure not—wait and we'll see."

In an instant Jasper had transformed her features to a comical resemblance of Audrey's. She spoke in mincing tones, with just sufficient likeness to Audrey to cause Evelyn to scream with mirth. She took light, quick steps across the room, and imitated Audrey's very words. All of a sudden she changed her manner. She now resembled Miss Sinclair, putting on the slightly precise language of the governess, adjusting her shoulders and arranging her hands as she had seen Miss Sinclair do for a brief moment that evening. Her personation of Miss Sinclair was as good as her personation of Audrey, and Evelyn became so excited that she very nearly spilt her chocolate. But her crowning delight came when all of a sudden, without the slightest warning, Jasper became Lady Frances herself. She

CHAPTER IV.—"I DRAW THE LINE AT UNCLE NED."

now sailed rather than walked across the apartment; her tones were stately and slow; her manner was the sort which might inspire awe; her very words were those of Lady Frances. But the delighted maid believed that she had a further triumph in store, for, with a quick change of mien, she now had the audacity to personate the Squire himself; but in one instant, like a flash, Evelyn was out of bed. She put down her chocolate-cup and rushed towards Jasper.

"The others as much as you like," she said, "but not Uncle Ned. You dare not. You sha'n't. I'll turn you away if you do. I'll hate you if you do. The others over and over again—they are lovely, splendid, grand—it puts heart in me to see you—but not Uncle Ned."

Jasper looked in astonishment at the little girl.

"So you love him as much as that already?" she said. "Well, as you please, of course."

"Don't be cross, Jasper," said Evelyn. "I can stand all the others; I can even like them. I told Audrey to-night how splendidly you can mimic, and you shall mimic her to her face when I know her better. Oh, it is killing—it is killing! But I draw the line at Uncle Ned."

CHAPTER V.—FRANK'S EYES.

Evelyn did not get up to breakfast the following morning. Breakfast at the Castle was a rather stately affair. A loud, musical gong sounded to assemble the family at a quarter to nine; then all those who were not really ill were expected to appear in the small chapel, where the Squire read prayers morning after morning before the assembled household. After prayers, visitors and family alike trooped into the comfortable breakfast-room, where a merry and hearty meal ensued. To be absent from breakfast was to insure Lady Frances's displeasure; she had no patience with lazy people. And as to lazy girls, her horror of them was so great that Audrey would rather bear the worst cold possible than announce to her mother that she was too ill to appear. Evelyn's absence, therefore, was commented on with a very grave expression of face by both the Squire and his wife.

"I must speak to her," said Lady Frances. "It is the first morning, and she does not understand our ways, but it must not occur again."

"You will not be too hard on the child, dear," said her husband. "Remember she has never had the advantage of your training."

"Poor little creature!" said Lady Frances. "That, indeed, my dear Edward, is plain to be seen."

She bridled very slightly. Lady Frances knew that there was not a more correct trainer of youth in the length and breadth of the county than herself. Audrey, who looked very bright and handsome that morning, ventured to glance at her mother.

"Perhaps Evelyn is dressed and does not know that we are at breakfast," she said. "May I go to her room and find out?"

"No, Audrey, not this morning. I shall go to see Evelyn presently. By the way, I hope you are ready for your visitors?"

"I suppose so, mother. I don't really quite know who are coming."

"The Jervices, of course—Henrietta, Juliet, and their brothers; there are also the Claverings, Mary and Sophie. I think those are the only young people, but with six in addition to you and Evelyn, you will have your hands full, Audrey."

"Oh, I don't mind," replied Audrey. "It will be fun.—You will help me all you can, won't you, Jenny?"

"Certainly, dear," replied Miss Sinclair.

"It is the greatest possible comfort to me to have you in the house, Miss Sinclair," said Lady Frances, now turning to the pretty young governess. "You have not yet had an interview with Evelyn, have you?"

"I talked to her a little last night," replied Miss Sinclair. "She seems to me to be a child with a good deal of character."

"She is like no child I ever met before," said Lady Frances, with a shudder. "I must frankly say I never looked forward with any pleasure

CHAPTER V.—FRANK'S EYES.

to her arrival, but my worst fears did not picture so thoroughly objectionable a little girl."

"Oh, come, Frances—come!" said her husband.

"My dear Edward, I do not give myself away as a rule; but it is just as well that Miss Sinclair should see how much depends on her guidance of the poor little girl, and that Audrey should know how objectionable she is, and how necessary it is for us all to do what we can to alter her ways. The first step, of course, is to get rid of that terrible woman whom she calls Jasper."

"But, mother," said Audrey, "that would hurt Evelyn's feelings very much—she is so devoted to Jasper."

"You must leave the matter to me, Audrey," said Lady Frances, rising. "You may be sure that I will do nothing really cruel or unkind. But, my dear, it is as well that you should learn sooner or later that spoiling a person is never true kindness."

Lady Frances left the room as she spoke; and Audrey, turning to her governess, said a few words to her, and they also went slowly in the direction of the conservatory.

"What do you think of her, Jenny?" asked the girl.

"Just what I said, dear. The child is full of originality and strong feelings, but of course, brought up as she has been, she will be a trial to your mother."

"That is just it. Mother has never seen any one in the least like Evelyn. She won't understand her; and if she does not there will be mischief."

"Evelyn must learn to subdue her will to that of Lady Frances," said Miss Sinclair. "You and I, Audrey, will try to be very patient with her; we will put up with her small impertinences, knowing that she scarcely means them; and we will try to make things as happy for her as we can."

"I don't know about that," said Audrey. "I cannot see why she should be rude and chuff and disagreeable. I don't altogether dislike her. She certainly amuses me. But she will not have a very happy time at the Castle until she knows her place."

"That is it," said Miss Sinclair. "She has evidently been spoken to most injudiciously—told that she is practically mistress of the place, and that she may do as she likes here. Hence the result. But at the worst, Audrey, I am certain of one thing."

"What is that, Jenny? How wise you look, and how kind!"

"I believe your father will be able to manage her, whoever else fails. Did you not notice how her eyes followed him round the room last night, and how, whenever he spoke to her, her voice softened and she always replied in a gentle tone?"

"No, I did not," answered Audrey. "Oh dear! it is very puzzling, and I feel rather cross myself. I cannot imagine why that horrid little girl should ever own this lovely place. It is not that I am jealous of her—I

A VERY NAUGHTY GIRL

assure you I am anything but that—but it hurts me to think that one who can appreciate things so little should come in for our lovely property."

"Well, darling, let us hope she will be quite a middle-aged woman before she possesses Castle Wynford," said the governess. "And now, what about your young friends?"

Audrey slipped her hand inside Miss Sinclair's arm, and the two paced the conservatory, talking long and earnestly.

Meanwhile Evelyn, having partaken of a rich and unwholesome breakfast of pastry, game-pie, and chocolate, condescended slowly to rise. Jasper waited on her hand and foot. A large fire burned in the grate; no servant had been allowed into the apartment since Evelyn had taken possession of it the night before, and it already presented an untidy and run-to-seed appearance. White ashes were piled high in the untidy grate; dust had collected on the polished steel of the fire-irons; dust had also mounted to the white marble mantelpiece covered with velvet of turquoise-blue, but neither Evelyn nor Jasper minded these things in the least.

"And now, pet," said the maid, "what dress will you wear?"

"I had better assert myself as soon as possible," said Evelyn. "Mothery told me I must. So I had better put on something striking. I saw that horrid Audrey walking past just now with her governess; she had on a plain, dark-blue serge. Why, any dairymaid might dress like that. Don't you agree with me, Jasper?"

"There is your crimson velvet," said Jasper. "I bought it for you in Paris. You look very handsome in it."

"Oh, come, Jasper," said her little mistress, "you said I was squat last night."

"The rich velvet shows up your complexion," persisted Jasper. "Put it on, dear; you must make a good impression."

Accordingly Evelyn allowed herself to be arrayed in a dress of a curious shade between red and crimson. Jasper encircled her waist with a red silk sash; and being further decked with numerous rows of colored beads, varying in hue from the palest green to the deepest rose, the heiress pronounced herself ready to descend.

"And where will you go first, dear?" said Jasper.

"I am going straight to find my Uncle Edward. I have a good deal to say to him. And there is mother's note; I think it is all about you. I will give it to Uncle Edward to give to my Aunt Frances. I don't like my Aunt Frances at all, so I will see Uncle Edward first."

Accordingly Evelyn, in her heavy red dress, her feet encased in black shoes and white stockings, ran down-stairs, and having inquired in very haughty tones of a footman where the Squire was likely to be found, presently opened the door of his private sanctum and peeped in.

CHAPTER V.—FRANK'S EYES.

Even Lady Frances seldom cared to disturb the Squire when he was in his den, as he called it. When he raised his eyes, therefore, and saw Evelyn's pale face, her light flaxen hair falling in thin strands about her ears, her big, somewhat light-brown eyes staring at him, he could not help giving a start of annoyance.

"Oh, Uncle Ned, you are not going to be cross too?" said the little girl. She skipped gaily into the room, ran up to him, put one arm round his neck, and kissed him.

The Squire looked in a puzzled way at the queer little figure. Like most men, he knew little or nothing of the details of dress; he was only aware that his own wife always looked perfect, that Audrey was the soul of grace, and that Miss Sinclair presented a very pretty appearance. He was now, therefore, only uncomfortable in Evelyn's presence, not in the least aware of what was wrong with her, but being quite certain that Lady Frances would not approve of her at all.

"I have come first to you, Uncle Edward," said Evelyn, "because we must transact some business together."

"Transact some business!" repeated her uncle. "What long words you use, little girl!"

"I have heard my dear mothery talk about transacting business, so I have picked up the phrase," replied Evelyn in thoughtful tones. "Well, Uncle Edward, shall we transact? It is best to have things on a business footing; don't you think so—eh?"

"I think that you are a very strange little person," said her uncle. "You are too young to know anything of business matters; you must leave those things to your aunt and to me."

"But I am your heiress, don't forget. This room will be mine, and all that big estate outside, and the whole of this gloomy old house when you die. Is not that so?"

"It is so, my child." The Squire could not help wincing when Evelyn pronounced his house gloomy. "But at the same time, my dear Evelyn, things of that sort are not spoken about—at least not in England."

"Mothery and I spoke a lot about it; we used to sit for whole evenings by the fireside and discuss the time when I should come in for my property. I mean to make changes when my time comes. You don't mind my saying so, do you?"

"I object to the subject altogether, Evelyn." The Squire rose and faced his small heiress. "In England we don't talk of these things, and now that you have come to England you must do as an English girl and a lady would. On your father's side you are a lady, and you must allow your aunt and me to train you in the observances which constitute true ladyhood in England."

Evelyn's brown eyes flashed a very angry fire.

"I don't wish to be different from my mother," she said. "My mother was one of the most splendid women on earth. I wish to be exactly like her. I will not be a fine lady—not for anybody."

"Well, dear, I respect you for being fond of your mother."

"Fond of her!" said Evelyn; and a strange and intensely tragic look crossed the queer little face.

She was quite silent for nearly a minute, and Edward Wynford watched her with curiosity and pain mingled in his face. Her eyes reminded him of the brother whom he had so truly loved; in every other respect Evelyn was her mother over again.

"I suppose," she said after a pause, "although I may not speak about what lies before me in the future, and you must die some time, Uncle Edward, that I may at least ask you to supply me with the needful?"

"The what, dear?"

"The needful. Chink, you know—chink."

Squire Wynford sank slowly back again into his chair.

"You might ask me to sit down," said Evelyn, "seeing that the room and all it contains will be——" Here she broke off abruptly. "I beg your pardon," she continued. "I really and truly do not want you to die a minute before your rightful hour. We all have our hour—at least mothery said so—and then go we must, whether we like it or not; so, as you must go some day, and I must——Oh dear! I am always being drawn up now by that horrid wish of yours that I should try to be an English girl. I will try to be when I am in your presence, for I happen to like you; but as for the others, well, we shall see. But, Uncle Ned, what about the chink? Perhaps you call it money; anyhow, it means money. How much may I have out of what is to be all my own some day to spend now exactly as I like?"

"You can have a fair sum, Evelyn. But, first of all, tell me what you want it for and how you mean to spend it."

"I have all kinds of wants," began Evelyn. "Jasper had plenty of money to spend on me until I came here. She manages very well indeed, does Jasper. We bought lots of things in Paris—this dress, for instance. How do you like my dress, Uncle Ned?"

"I am not capable of giving an opinion."

"Aren't you really? I expect you are about stunned. You never thought a girl like me could dress with such taste. Do you mind my speaking to Audrey, Uncle Ned, about her dress? It does not seem to me to be correct."

"What is wrong with it?" asked the Squire.

"It is so awfully dowdy; it is not what a lady ought to wear. Ladies ought to dress in silks and satins and brocades and rich embroidered robes. Mothery always said so, and mothery surely knew. But there, I am idling you, and I suppose you are busy directing the management of your estates, which are to be——Oh, there! I am pulled up again. I

CHAPTER V.—FRANK'S EYES.

want my money for Jasper, for one thing. Jasper has got some poor relations, and she and I between us support them."

"She and you between you," said the Squire, "support your maid's relations!"

"Oh dear me, Uncle Ned, how stiffly you speak! But surely it does not matter; I can do what I like with my own."

"Listen to me, Evelyn," said her uncle. "You are only a very young girl; your mind may in some ways be older than your body, but you are nothing more than a child."

"I am not such a child as I look. I was sixteen a month ago. I am sixteen, and that is not very young."

"We must agree to differ," said her uncle. "You are young and you are not wise; and although there is some money which is absolutely your own coming from the ranch in Tasmania, yet I have the charge of it until you come of age."

"When I come of age I suppose I shall be very, very rich?"

"Not at all. You will be my care, and I will allow you what is proper, but as long as I live you will only have the small sum which will come to you yearly from the rent of the ranch. As the ranch may possibly be sold some day, we may be able to realize a nice little capital for you; but you are too young to know much of these things at present. The matter in hand, therefore, is all-sufficient. I will allow you as pocket-money five pounds a quarter. I give precisely the same sum to Audrey. Your aunt will buy your clothes, and you will live here and be treated in all respects as my daughter. Now, that is my side of the bargain."

Evelyn's face turned white.

"Five pounds a quarter!" she said. "Why, that is downright penury!"

"No, dear; for the use you require it for it is downright riches. But, be it riches or be it penury, you get no more."

Evelyn looked full at her uncle; her uncle looked back at her.

"Come here, little girl," he said.

Her heart was beating with furious anger, but there was something in his tone which subdued her. She went slowly to him, and he put his arm round her waist.

"Your eyes are like—very like—one whom I loved best on earth."

"You mean my father," said the girl.

"Your father. He left you to me to care for, and to love and to train—to train for a high position eventually."

"He left me to mothery; you are quite mistaken there. Mothery has trained me; father left me to her. She often and often and often told me so."

"That is true, dear. While your mother lived she had the prior claim over you, but now you belong to me."

"Yes," said Evelyn. She felt fascinated. She snuggled comfortably inside her uncle's arm; her strange brown eyes were fixed on his face.

"I give you," he continued, "the love and care of a father, but I expect a return."

"What? I don't mind. I have two diamonds—beauties. You shall have them to make into studs; you shall, because I—yes, I love you."

"I don't want your diamonds, my little girl, but I want other things—your love and your obedience. I want you, if you like me, and if you like your Aunt Frances, and if you like your cousin, to follow in our steps, for we have been brought up to approve of courteous manners and quiet dress and gentle speech; and I want that brain of yours, Evelyn, to be educated to high and lofty thoughts. I want you to be a grand woman, worthy of your father, and I expect this return from you for all that I am going to do for you."

"Are you going to teach me your own self?" asked Evelyn.

"You can come to me sometimes for a talk, but it is impossible for me to be your instructor. You will have a suitable governess."

"Jasper knows a lot of things. Perhaps she could teach both Audrey and me. She might if you paid her well. She has got some awfully poor relations; she must have lots of money, poor Jasper must."

"Well, dear, leave me now. We will talk of your education and who is to instruct you, and all about Jasper too, within a few days. You have got to see the place and to make Audrey's acquaintance; and there are some young friends coming to the Castle for a week. Altogether, you have arrived at a gay time. Now run away, find your cousin, and make yourself happy."

Squire Wynford rose as he spoke, and taking Evelyn's hand, he led her to the door. He opened the door wide for her, and saw her go out, and then he kissed his hand to her and closed the door again.

"Poor little mite!" he said to himself. "As strange a child as I ever saw, but with Frank's eyes."

CHAPTER VI.—THE HUNGRY GIRL.

Now, the Squire had produced a decidedly softening effect upon Evelyn, and if she had not had the misfortune to meet Lady Frances just as she left his room, much that followed need never taken place. But Lady Frances, who had never in the very least returned poor Frank Wynford's affection for her, and who had no sentimental feelings with regard to Evelyn—Lady Frances, who simply regarded the little girl as a troublesome and very tiresome member of the family—was not disposed to be too soothing in her manner.

"Come here, my dear," she said. "Come over here to the light. What have you got on?"

"My pretty red velvet dress," replied Evelyn, tossing her head. "A suitable dress for an heiress like myself."

"Come, this is quite beyond enduring. I want to speak to you, Evelyn. I have several things to say. Come into my boudoir."

"But, if you please," said Evelyn, "I have nothing to say to you, and I have a great deal to do in other directions. I am going back to Jasper; she wants me."

"Oh, that reminds me," began Lady Frances. "Come in here this moment, my dear."

She took Evelyn's hand and dragged the unwilling child into her private apartment. A bright fire burned in the grate. The room looked cozy, cheerful, orderly. Lady Frances was a woman of method. She had piles of papers lying neatly docketed on her writing-table; a sheaf of unanswered letters lay on one side. A Remington typewriter stood on a table near, and a slim-looking girl was standing by the typewriter.

"You will leave me for the present, Miss Andrews," she said, turning to her amanuensis. "I shall require you here again in a quarter of an hour."

Miss Andrews, with a low bow, instantly left the room.

"You see, Evelyn," said her aunt, "you are taking up the time of a very busy woman. I manage the financial part of several charities—in short, we are very busy people in this house—and in the morning I, as a rule, allow no one to interrupt me. When the afternoon comes I am ready and willing to be agreeable to my guests."

"But I am not your guest. The house belongs to me—or at least it will be mine," said Evelyn.

"You are quite right in saying you are not my guest. You are my husband's niece, and in the future you will inherit his property; but if I hear you speaking in that rude way again I shall be forced to punish you. I can see for myself that you are an ill-bred girl and will require a vast lot of breaking-in."

"And you think you can do it?" said Evelyn, her eyes flashing.

A VERY NAUGHTY GIRL

"I intend to do it. I am going to talk to you for a few minutes this morning, and after I have spoken I wish you to clearly understand that you are to do as I tell you. You will not be unhappy here; on the contrary, you will be happy. At first you may find the necessary rules of a house like this somewhat irksome, but you will get into the way of them before long. You need discipline, and you will have it here. I will not say much more on that subject this morning. You can find Audrey, and she and Miss Sinclair will take you round the grounds and amuse you, and you must be very much obliged to them for their attentions. Audrey is my daughter, and I think I may say without undue flattery that you will find her a most estimable companion. She is well brought up, and is a charming girl in every sense of the word. Miss Sinclair is her governess; she will also instruct you, but time enough for that in the future. Now, when you leave here go straight to your room and desire your servant—Jasper, I think, you call her—to dress you in a plain and suitable frock."

"A frock!" said Evelyn. "I wear dresses—long dresses. I am not a child; mothery said I had the sense of several grown-up people."

"The garment you are now in you are not to wear again; it is unsuitable, and I forbid you to be even seen in it. Do you understand?"

"I hear you," said Evelyn.

"Go up-stairs and do what I tell you, and then you can go into the grounds. Audrey is having holidays at present; you will find her with her governess in the shrubbery. Now go; the time I can devote to you for the present is up."

"I had better give you this first," said Evelyn.

She thrust her hand into her pocket and took out the ill-spelt and now exceedingly dirty note which poor Mrs. Wynford in Tasmania had written to Lady Frances before her death.

"This is from mothery, who is dead," continued the child. "It is for you. She wrote it to you. I expect she is watching you now; she told me that she would come back if she could and see how people treated me. I am going. Don't lose the note; it was written by mothery, and she is dead."

Evelyn laid the dirty letter on the blotting-pad on Lady Frances's table. It looked strangely out of keeping with the rest of her correspondence. The little girl left the room, banging the door behind her.

"A dreadful child!" thought Lady Frances. "How are we to endure her? My poor, sweet Audrey! I must get Edward to allow me to send Evelyn to school; she really is not a fit companion for my young daughter."

Miss Andrews came back.

"Please direct these envelopes, and answer some of these letters according to the notes which I have put down for you," said Lady Frances; and her secretary began to work. But Lady Frances did not ask Miss Andrews to read or reply to the dirty little note. She took it

CHAPTER VI.–THE HUNGRY GIRL.

up very much as though she would like to drop it into the fire, but finally she opened it and read the contents. The letter was rude and curt, and Lady Frances's fine black eyes flashed as she read the words. Finally, she locked the letter up in a private bureau, and sitting down, calmly proceeded with her morning's work.

Meanwhile Evelyn, choking with rage and utterly determined to disobey Lady Frances, left the room. She stood still for a moment in the long corridor and looked disconsolately to right and to left of her. "How ugly it all is!" she said to herself. "How I hate it! Mothery, why did you die? Why did I ever leave my darling, darling ranch in Tasmania?"

She turned and very slowly walked up the white marble staircase. Presently she reached her own luxurious room. It was in the hands of a maid, however, who was removing the dust and putting the chamber in order.

"Where is Jasper?" asked the little girl.

"Miss Jasper has gone out of doors, miss."

"Do you know how long she has been out?" asked Evelyn in a tone of keen interest.

"About half an hour, miss."

"Then I'll follow her."

Evelyn went to her wardrobe. Jasper had already unpacked her young lady's things and laid them higgledy-piggledy in the spacious wardrobe. It took the little girl a long time to find a tall velvet hat trimmed with plumes of crimson feathers. This she put on before the glass, arranging her hair to look as thick as possible, and smirking at her face while she arrayed herself.

"I would not wear this hat, for I got it quite for Sunday best, but I want her to see that she cannot master me," thought the child. She then wrapped a crimson silk scarf round her neck and shoulders, and so attired looked very much like a little lady of the time of Vandyck. Once more she went down-stairs.

Audrey she did not wish to meet; Miss Sinclair she intended to be hideously rude to; but Jasper—where was Jasper?

Evelyn looked all round. Suddenly she saw a figure on the other side of a small lake which adorned part of the grounds. The figure was too far off for her to see it distinctly. It must be Jasper, for it surely was not in the least like the tall, fair, and stately Aubrey, not like Miss Sinclair.

Picking up her skirts, which were too long for her to run comfortably, the small figure now skidded across the grass. She soon reached the side of the lake, and shouted:

"Jasper! Oh Jasper! Jasper, I have news for you! You never knew anything like the—"

A VERY NAUGHTY GIRL

The next instant she had rushed into the arms of Sylvia Leeson. Sylvia cried out eagerly:

"Who are you, and what are you doing here?"

Evelyn stared for a moment at the strange girl, then burst into a hearty laugh.

"Do tell me—quick, quick!—are you one of the Wynfords?" she asked.

"I a Wynford!" cried Sylvia. "I only wish I were. Are you a Wynford? Do you live at the Castle?"

"Do I live at the Castle!" cried Evelyn. "Why, the Castle is mine—I mean it will be when Uncle Ned dies. I came here yesterday; and, oh! I am miserable, and I want Jasper?"

"Who is Jasper?"

"My maid. Such a darling!—the only person here who cares in the least for me. Oh, please, please tell me your name! If you do not live at the Castle, and if you can assure me from the bottom of your heart that you do not love any one—any one who lives in the Castle—why, I will love you. You are sweetly pretty! What is your name?"

"Sylvia Leeson. I live three miles from here, but I adore the Castle. I should like to come here often."

"You adore it! Then that is because you know nothing about it. Do you adore Audrey?"

"Is Audrey the young lady of the Castle?"

"She is not the young lady of the Castle. I am the young lady of the Castle. But have you ever seen her?"

"Once; and then she was rude to me."

"Ah! I thought so. I don't think she could be very polite to anybody. Now, suppose you and I become friends? The Castle belongs to me—or will when Uncle Ned dies. I can order people to come or people to go; and I order you to come. You shall come up to the house with me. You shall have lunch with me; you shall really. I have got a lovely suite of rooms—a bedroom of blue-and-silver and a little sitting-room for my own use; and you shall come there, and Jasper shall serve us both. Do you know that you are sweetly pretty?—just like a gipsy. You are lovely! Will you come with me now? Do! come at once."

Sylvia laughed. She looked full at Evelyn; then she said abruptly:

"May I ask you a very straight question?"

"I love straight questions," replied Evelyn.

"Can you give me a right, good, big lunch? Do you know that I am very hungry? Were you ever very hungry?"

"Oh, sometimes," replied Evelyn, staring very hard at her. "I lived on a ranch, you know—or perhaps you don't know."

"I don't know what a ranch is."

"How funny! I thought everybody knew. You see, I am not English; I am Tasmanian. My father was an Englishman, but he died when I was a little baby, and I lived with mothery—the sweetest, the dearest, the darlingest woman on earth—on a ranch in Tasmania. Mothery is dead,

CHAPTER VI.—THE HUNGRY GIRL.

and I have come here, and all the place will belong to me—not to Audrey—some day. Yes, I was hungry when we went on long expeditions, which we used to do in fine weather, but there was always something handy to eat. I have heard of people who are hungry and there is nothing handy to eat. Do you belong to that sort?"

"Yes, to that sort," said Sylvia, nodding. "I will tell you about myself presently. Yes, take me to the house, please. I know HE will be angry when he knows it, but I am going all the same."

"Who is he?"

"I will tell you about him when you know the rest. Take me to the house, quick. I was there once before, on New Year's Day, when every one—every one has a right to come. I hope you will keep up that splendid custom when you get the property. I ate a lot then. I longed to take some for him, but it was the rule that I must not do that. I told him about it afterwards: game-pie, two helpings; venison pasty, two ditto."

"Oh, that is dull!" interrupted Evelyn. "Have you not forgotten yet about a lunch you had some days ago?"

"You would not if you were in my shoes," said Sylvia. "But come; if we stay talking much longer some one will see us and prevent me from going to the house with you."

"I should like to find the person who could prevent me from doing what I like to do!" replied Evelyn. "Come, Sylvia, come."

Evelyn took the tall, dark girl's hand, and they both set to running, and entered the house by the side entrance. They had the coast clear, as Evelyn expressed it, and ran up at once to her suite of rooms. Jasper was not in; the rooms were empty. They ran through the bedroom and found themselves in the beautifully furnished boudoir. A fire was blazing on the hearth; the windows were slightly open; the air, quite mild and fresh—for the day was like a spring one—came in at the open casement. Evelyn ran and shut it, and then turned and faced her companion.

"There!" she said. She came close up to Sylvia, and almost whispered, "Suppose Jasper brings lunch for both of us up here? She will if I command her. I will ring the bell and she'll come. Would you not like that?"

"Yes, I'd like it much—much the best," said Sylvia. "I am afraid of Lady Frances. And Miss Audrey can be very rude. She was very chuff with me on New Year's Day."

"She won't be chuff with you in my presence," said Evelyn. "Ah! here comes Jasper."

Jasper, looking slightly excited, now appeared on the scene.

"Well, my darling!" she said. She rushed up to Evelyn and clasped her in her arms. "Oh, my own sweet Eve, and how are you getting on?" she exclaimed. "I am thinking this is not the place for you."

A VERY NAUGHTY GIRL

"We will talk of that another time, please, Jasper," said Evelyn, with unwonted dignity. "I have brought a friend to lunch with me. This young lady is called Miss Sylvia Leeson, and she is awfully hungry, and we'd both like a big lunch in this room. Can you smuggle things up, Jasper?"

"Her ladyship will be mad," exclaimed Jasper. "I was told in the servants' hall that she was downright annoyed at your not going to breakfast; if you are not at lunch she will move heaven and earth."

"Let her; it will be fun," said Evelyn. "I am going to lunch here with my friend Sylvia Leeson. Bring a lot of things up, Jasper—good things, rich things, tempting things; you know what sort I like."

"I'll try if there is a bit of pork and some mincepies and plum-pudding and cream and such-like down-stairs. And you'd fancy your chocolate, would you not?"

"Rather! Get all you can, and be as quick as ever you can."

Jasper accordingly withdrew, and in a short time appeared with a laden tray in her hands.

"I had to run the gauntlet of the footman and the butler too; and what they will tell Lady Frances goodness knows, but I do not," answered Jasper. "But there, if things have to come to a crisis, why, they must. You will not forget me when the storm breaks, will you, Evelyn?"

"I'll never forget you," said Evelyn, with enthusiasm. "You are the dearest and darlingest thing left now that mothery is in heaven; and Sylvia will love you too. I have been telling her all about you.—Now, Sylvia, you will not be hungry long."

CHAPTER VII.—STAYING TO DINNER.

Again at luncheon that day Evelyn was missing. Lady Frances looked round: Audrey was in her place; Miss Sinclair was seated not far away; the Squire took the foot of the table; the servants handed round the different dishes; but still no Evelyn had put in an appearance.

"I wonder where she can be," said the Squire. "She looked a little wild and upset when she left me. Poor little girl! Do you know, Frances, I feel very sorry for her."

"More than I do," said Lady Frances, who at the same time had an uncomfortable remembrance of the look Evelyn had given her when she had left her presence. "Don't let us talk any more about her now, Edward," she said to her husband. "There is only one thing to be done for the child, and that I will tell you by and by."

The Squire was accustomed to attend to his wife's wishes on all occasions, and he said nothing further. Audrey felt constrained and uncomfortable. After a slight hesitation she said:

"Do let me find Evelyn, mother. I have been expecting her to join me the whole morning. She does not, of course, know about our rules yet."

"No, Audrey," said her mother; "I prefer that you should not leave the table.—Miss Sinclair, perhaps you will oblige me. Will you go to Evelyn's room and tell her that we are at lunch?"

Miss Sinclair rose at once. She was absent for about five minutes. When she came back there was a distressed look on her face.

"Well, Jenny, well?" said Audrey in a voice of suppressed excitement. "Is she coming?"

"I think not," said Miss Sinclair.—"I will explain matters to you, Lady Frances, afterwards."

"Dear, dear!" said the Squire. "What a lot of explanations seem to be necessary with regard to the conduct of one small girl!"

"But she is a very important small girl, is she not, father?" said Audrey.

"Well, yes, dear; and I should like to say now that I take an interest in her—in fact," he added, looking round him, for the servants had withdrawn, "I am prepared to love little Eve very much indeed."

Lady Frances's eyes flashed a somewhat indignant fire. Then she said slowly:

"As you speak so frankly, Edward, I must do likewise. I never saw a more hopeless child. There seems to be nothing whatever for it but to send her to school for a couple of years."

"No," said the Squire, "I will not allow that. We never sent Audrey to school, and I will have no difference made with regard to Evelyn's education. All that money can secure must be provided for her, but I do not care for school-life for girls."

- 37 -

Lady Frances said nothing further. She was a woman with tact, and would not on any consideration oppose her husband in public. All the same, she secretly made up her mind that if Evelyn proved unmanageable she was not to stay at Wynford Castle.

"And there is another thing," continued the Squire. "This is her first day in her future home. I do not wish her to be punished whatever she may have done. I should like her to have absolute freedom until to-morrow morning."

"It shall be exactly as you wish, Edward," said Lady Frances. "I did intend to seek Evelyn out; I did intend further to question Miss Sinclair as to the reason why Evelyn did not appear at lunch; but I will defer these things. It happens to be somewhat convenient, as I want to pay some calls this afternoon; and really, with that child on my brain, I should not enjoy my visits. You, Audrey dear, will see to your cousin's comforts, and when she is inclined to give you her society you will be ready to welcome her. Your young friends will not arrive until just before dinner. Please, at least use your influence, Audrey, to prevent Evelyn making a too extraordinary appearance to-night. Now I think that is all, and I must run off if I am to be in time to receive my guests."

Lady Frances left the room, and Audrey went to her governess's side. "What is it?" she said. "You did look strange, Jenny, when you came into the room just now. Where is Evelyn? Why did she not come to lunch?"

"It is the greatest possible mercy," said Miss Sinclair, "that Evelyn is allowed to have one free day, for perhaps—although I feel by no means sure—you and I may influence her for her own good to-night. But what do you think has happened? I went to her room and knocked at the door of the boudoir. I heard voices within. The door was immediately opened by the maid Jasper, and I saw Evelyn seated at a table, eating a most extraordinary kind of lunch, in the company of a girl whom I have never seen before."

"Oh Jenny," cried Audrey, "how frightfully exciting! A strange girl! Surely Evelyn did not bring a stranger with her and hide her somewhere last night?"

"No, dear, no," said Miss Sinclair, laughing; "she did nothing of that sort. I fancy the girl must live in the neighborhood, although her face is unfamiliar to me. She is rather a pretty girl, but by no means the sort that your mother would approve of as a companion for your cousin."

"What is she like?" asked Audrey in a grave voice.

Miss Sinclair proceeded to describe Sylvia's appearance. She was interrupted in the middle of her description by a cry from Audrey.

"Oh dear!" she exclaimed, "you must have seen that curious girl, Sylvia Leeson. Your description is exactly like her. Well, as this is a

CHAPTER VII.—STAYING TO DINNER.

free day, and we can do pretty much what we like, I will run straight up to Evelyn's room and look for myself."

"Do Audrey; I think on the whole it would be the best plan."

So Audrey ran up-stairs, and soon her tap was heard on Evelyn's door; the next moment she found herself in the presence of a very untidy, disheveled-looking cousin, and also in that of handsome Sylvia Leeson.

Sylvia dropped a sort of mock courtesy when she saw Audrey.

"My Shakespearian contemporary!" was her remark. "Well, Audrey, and how goes the Forest of Arden? And have you yet met Touchstone?"

Audrey colored very high at what she considered a direct impertinence.

"What are you doing here?" she said. "My mother does not know your mother."

Sylvia gave a ringing laugh.

"I met this lady," she said—and she pointed in Evelyn's direction—"and she invited me here. I have had lunch with her, and I am no longer hungry. This is her room, is it not?"

"I should just think it is," said Evelyn; "and I only invite those people whom I care about to come into it." She said the words in a very pointed way, but Audrey had now recovered both her dignity and good-nature.

She laughed.

"Really we three are too silly," she said. "Evelyn, you cannot mean the ridiculous words you say! As if any room in my father's house is not free to me when I choose to go there! Now, whether you like it or not, I am determined to be friends with you. I do not want to scold you or lecture you, for it is not my place, but I intend to sit down although you have not the civility to offer me a chair; and I intend to ask again why Miss Leeson is here."

"I came because Evelyn asked me," said Sylvia; and then, all of a sudden, an unexpected change came over her face. Her pretty, bright eyes, with a sort of robin-redbreast look in them, softened and melted, and then grew brighter than ever through tears. She went up to Audrey and knelt at her feet.

"Why should not I come? Why should not I be happy?" she said. "I am a very lonely girl; why should you grudge me a little happiness?"

Audrey looked at her in amazement; then a change came over her own face. She allowed her hand just for an instant to touch the hand of Sylvia, and her eyes looked into the wild eyes of the shabby girl who was kneeling before her.

"Get up," she said. "You have no right to take that attitude to me. As you are here, sit down. I do not want to be rude to you; far from that. I should like to make you happy."

"Should you really?" answered Sylvia. "You can do it, you know."

"Sylvia," interrupted Evelyn, "what does this mean? You and I have been talking in a very frank way about Audrey. We have neither of us been expressing any enthusiastic opinions with regard to her; and yet now—and yet now——"

"Oh, let me be, Eve," replied Sylvia. "I like Audrey. I liked her the other day. It is true I was afraid of her, and I was crushed by her, but I liked her; and I like her better now, and if she will be my friend I am quite determined to be hers."

"Then you do not care for me?" said Evelyn, getting up and strutting across the room.

Sylvia looked at Audrey, whose eyes, however, would not smile, and whose face was once more cold and haughty.

"Evelyn," she said, "I must ask you to try and remember that you are a lady, and not to talk in this way before anybody but me. I am your cousin, and when you are alone with me I give you leave to talk as you please. But now the question is this: I do not in the least care what Sylvia said of me behind my back. I hope I know better than to wish to find out what I was never meant to hear. This is a free country, and any girl in England can talk of me as she pleases—I am not afraid—that is, she can talk of me as she pleases when I am absent. But what I want to do now is to answer Sylvia's question. She is unhappy, and she has thrown herself on me.—What can I do, Sylvia, to make you happy?"

Sylvia was standing huddled up against the wall. Her pretty shoulders were hitched to her ears; her hair was disheveled and fell partly over her forehead; her eyes gleamed out under their thick thatch of black hair like wild birds in a nest; her coral lips trembled, there was just a gleam of snowy teeth, and then she said impulsively:

"You are a darling, and you can do one thing. Let me for to-day forget that I am poor and hungry and very lonely and very sad. Let me share your love and Evelyn's love for just one whole day."

"But there are people coming to-night, Sylvia," said Evelyn. "I heard Jasper speak of it. Lots of people—grandees, you know."

Sylvia shuddered slightly.

"We never say that sort of word now in England," she remarked; and she added: "I am well-born too. There was a time when I should not have been at all shy of Audrey Wynford."

"You are very queer," said Evelyn. "I do not know that I particularly want you for a friend."

"Well, never mind; I think I can get you to love me," said Sylvia. "But now the question is this: Will Audrey let me stay or will she not? Will you, Audrey—will you—just because my name is Sylvia and we have met in the Forest of Arden?"

CHAPTER VII.—STAYING TO DINNER.

"Oh dear," said Audrey, "what a difficult question you ask! And how can I answer it? I dare not give you leave all by myself, but I will go and inquire."

Audrey ran immediately out of the room.

"What a wonderful change has come into my life!" she said to herself as she flew down-stairs and looked into different rooms, but all in vain, for Miss Sinclair.

Her mother was out; it was hopeless to think of appealing to her. Without the permission of some one older than herself she could not possibly ask Sylvia to stay. Sylvia could be more or less lost in the crowd of children who would be at the Castle that evening, but her mother's eyes would quickly seek out the unfamiliar face, inquiries would be made, and—in short, Audrey did not dare to take this responsibility on herself. She was rushing up-stairs again, prepared to tell Sylvia that she could not grant her request, when she came plump up against her father.

"My dear girl, what a hurry you are in!" he exclaimed.

"Oh yes, father," replied Audrey. "I am excited. The house is full of life and almost mystery."

"Then you like your cousin to be here?" said the Squire, and his face brightened.

"Yes and no," answered Audrey truthfully. "But, father, I have a great request to make. You know you said that Evelyn was to have a free day to-day in which she could do as she pleased. She has a guest upstairs whom she would like to ask to stay. May she ask her, father? She is a girl, and lonely and pretty, and, I think, on the whole, a lady. May we both ask her to dinner and to spend the evening? And will you, father, take the responsibility?"

"Of course—of course," said the Squire.

"Will you explain to mother when she returns?"

"Yes, my dear—certainly. Ask anybody you please; I never restrain you with regard to your friends. Now do not keep me, my love; I am going out immediately."

CHAPTER VIII.—EVENING-DRESS.

When Audrey re-entered Evelyn's pretty boudoir she found the two girls standing close together and talking earnestly. Jasper also was joining in the conversation. Audrey felt her heart sink.

"How can Evelyn make free with Jasper as she does? And why does Sylvia talk to Evelyn as though they were having secrets together? Why, they only met to-day!" was the girl's thought. Her tone, therefore, was cold.

"I met father, and he says you may stay," she remarked in a careless voice. "And now, as doubtless you will be quite happy, I will run away and leave you, for I have much to do."

"No, no; not until I have thanked you and kissed you first," said Sylvia.

Audrey did not wish Sylvia to kiss her, but she could not make any open objection. She scarcely returned the girl's warm embrace, and the next moment had left the room.

"Is she not a horror?" said Evelyn. "I began by liking her—I mean I rather liked her. She had a grand sort of manner, and her eyes are handsome, but I hate her now. She is not half, nor quarter, as pretty as you are, Sylvia. And, oh, Sylvia, you will be my friend—my true, true friend—for I am so lonely now that mothery is dead!"

Sylvia was standing by the fire. There was a bright color in both her cheeks, and her eyes shone vividly.

"My mother died too," she said. "I was happy while she lived. Yes, Eve, I will be your friend if you like."

"It will be all the better for you," said Evelyn, who could never long forget her own importance. "If I take to you there is no saying what may happen, for, whatever lies before me in the future, I am my Uncle Edward's heiress; and Audrey, for all her pride, is nobody."

"Audrey looks much more suitable," said Sylvia, and then she stopped, partly amused and partly frightened by the look in Evelyn's light-brown eyes.

"How dare you!" she cried. "How horrid—how horrid of you! After all, I do not know that I want to see too much of you. You had better be careful what sort of things you say to me. And first of all, if I am to see any more of you, you must tell me why Audrey would make a better heiress than I shall."

"Oh, never mind," said Sylvia; but then she added: "Why should I not tell you? She is tall and graceful and very, very lovely, and she has the manners of a GRANDE DAME although she is such a young girl. Any one in all the world can see that Audrey is to the manner born, whereas you——"

Evelyn looked almost frightened while Sylvia was talking.

CHAPTER VIII.—EVENING-DRESS.

"Is that really so?" she answered. "I ought to be just mad with you, but I'm not. Before the year is out no one will compare Audrey and me. I shall be much, much the finest lady—much, much the grandest. I vow it; I declare it; I will do it; and you, Sylvia, shall help me."

"Oh, I have no objection," said Sylvia. "I am very glad indeed that you will want my help, and I am sure you are heartily welcome."

Evelyn looked full up at Sylvia. Jasper had left the two girls together. The only light in the room now was the firelight, for the short winter day was drawing to an end.

"You, I suppose," said Evelyn, "are a lady although you do wear such a shabby dress and you suffer so terribly from hunger?"

"How do you know?" asked Sylvia.

"First, because you are not afraid of anything; and second, because you are graceful and, although you are so very queer, your voice has a gentle sound. You are a lady by birth, are you not?"

"Yes," said Sylvia simply. She neither added to the word not took from it. She became very silent and thoughtful.

"Why do you live in such a funny way? Why are you not educated like other girls? And why will you tell me nothing about your home?"

"I have nothing to tell. My father and I came to live at The Priory three months ago. He does not care for society, and he does not wish me to leave him."

"And you are poor?"

"No," said Sylvia.

"Not poor! And yet, why are you almost in rags? And you did eat up your lunch so greedily!"

"I will answer nothing more, Evelyn. If you do not like me as I am, let me go now, and I will try to forget the beautiful, comfortable Castle, and the lovely meals, and you and your queer maid Jasper, and the beautiful girl Audrey; for if you do not want me as I am, you can never get me any other way. I am a lady, and we are not poor. Now are you satisfied?"

"I burn with curiosity," said Evelyn; "and if mothery were alive, would she not get it out of you! But if you wish it—and your eyes do look as if they were daggers—I will change the subject. What shall we do for the rest of the day? Shall we go out and take a walk in the dark?"

"Yes; that would be lovely," cried Sylvia.

Evelyn shouted in an imperious way to Jasper.

"Bring my fur cloak," she said, "and my goloshes. I won't wear anything over my head. I am going out with Miss Sylvia Leeson."

Jasper brought Evelyn's cloak, which was lined with the most lovely squirrel inside and covered with bright crimson outside, and put it over her shoulders. Sylvia in her very shabby black cloth jacket, much too short in the waist and in the arms, accompanied her. They ran down-stairs and went out into the grounds.

Now, if there was one thing more than another which would hopelessly displease Lady Frances, it was the idea of any of her relations wandering about after dusk. But luckily for Evelyn, and luckily also for poor Sylvia, Lady Frances was some miles from Wynford Castle at that moment. The girls rushed about, and soon Evelyn forgot all her restraints and shouted noisily. They played hide-and-seek amongst the trees in the plantation. Sylvia echoed Evelyn's shouts; and the Squire, who was returning to the house in time to meet his guests, paused and listened in much amazement to these unusual sounds of girlish laughter. There came a shrill shriek, and then the cry, "Here I am—seek and find," and then another ringing peal of girlish merriment.

"Surely that cannot be Audrey!" he said to himself. "What extraordinary noises!"

He went into the house. From his study window he saw the flash of a lantern, which lit up a red cloak, and for an instant he observed the very light hair and white face of his niece. But who was the girl with her—a tall, shabby-looking girl—about the height of his Audrey, too? It could not be Audrey! He sank down into a chair, and a look of perplexity crossed his face.

"What am I to do with that poor child?" he said to himself. "What extraordinary, unpardonable conduct! Well, I will not tell Lady Frances. I determined that the child should have one day of liberty, but I am glad I did not make it more than one."

After Evelyn and Sylvia had quite exhausted themselves they returned to the house.

Jasper was ready for them. She had laid out several dresses for Evelyn to select from.

"I have just had a message from her ladyship," she said when the girls came in with their cheeks glowing and eyes full of laughter. "All the young people are to dine with the family to-night. As a rule, when there is company the younger members of the house dine in the schoolroom, but to-night you are all to be together. I got the message from that stuck-up footman Scott. I hate the fellow; he had the impudence to say that he did not think I was suited to my post."

"He had better not say it again," cried Evelyn, "or he will catch it from me. I mean to have a talk with each of the servants in turn, and tell them quite openly that at any moment I may be mistress, and that they had better look sharp before they incur my displeasure."

"But, Eve, could you?" exclaimed Sylvia. "Why, that would mean——"

"Uncle Ned's death. I know that," said Evelyn. "I love Uncle Ned. I shall be awfully sorry when he does die. But however sorry I am, he will die when his turn comes; and then I shall be mistress. I was frightfully sorry when mothery died; but however broken-hearted I was, she did die just the same. It is so with every one. It is the height of folly to shirk subjects of that sort; one has to face them. I have no

CHAPTER VIII.—EVENING-DRESS.

one now to take my part except dear old Jasper, and so I shall have to take my own part, and the servants had better know.—You can tell them too, Jasper; I give you leave."

"Not I!" said Jasper. "I declare, Miss Evelyn, you are no end of a goose for all that you are the darling of my heart. But now, miss, what dress will you wear to-night? I should say the white satin embroidered with the seed pearls. It has a long train, and you will look like a bride in it, miss. It is cut low in the neck, and has those sleeves which open above the elbow, and a watteau back. It is a very elegant robe indeed; and I have a wreath of white stephanotis for your hair, miss. You will look regal in this dress, and like an heiress, I do assure you, Miss Eve."

"It is perfectly exquisite!" said Evelyn. "Come, Sylvia; come and look. Oh, those dear little bunches of chiffon, and white stephanotis in the middle of each bunch! And, oh, the lace! It is real lace, is it not, Jasper?"

"Brussels lace, and of the best quality; not too much, and yet enough. It cost a small fortune."

"Oh, here are the dear little shoes to match, and this petticoat with heaps of lace and embroidery! Well, when I wear this dress Audrey will have to respect me."

"That is why I bought it, miss. I thought you should have the best."

"Oh, you are a darling! What would not mothery say if she could look at me to-night!"

"Well, Miss Evelyn, I hope I do my duty. But you and Miss Sylvia have been very late out, so you must hurry, miss, if I am to do you justice."

"But, oh, I say!" cried Evelyn, looking for the first time at her friend. "What is Sylvia to wear?"

"I don't know, miss. None of your dresses will fit her; she is so much taller."

"I will not go down-stairs a fright," said Sylvia. "Audrey asked me, and she must lend me something. Please, Jasper, do go to Miss Wynford's room and ask her if she has a white dress she will lend me to wear to-night. Even a washing muslin will do. Anything that is long enough in the skirt and not too short in the waist. I will take it away and have it washed fresh for her. Do, please, please, ask her, Jasper!"

"I am very sorry, miss," answered Jasper. "I would do anything in reason to oblige, but to go to a young lady whom I don't know and to make a request of that sort is more than I can do, miss. Besides, she is occupied now. A whole lot of visitors have just arrived—fine young ladies and tall young gentlemen—and they are all chittering-chattering as though their lungs would burst. They are all in the hall, miss, chatting as hard as they can chat. No, I cannot ask her; I cannot really."

"Then I must stop up-stairs and lose all, all the fun," said Sylvia.

A VERY NAUGHTY GIRL

The gaiety left her face. She sat down on a chair.

"You will get me something to eat, at any rate, Jasper?" she said.

"Yes, of course, miss; you and I can have a cozy meal together."

"No, thank you," said Sylvia proudly. "I don't eat with servants."

Jasper's face turned an ugly green color. She looked at Evelyn, but Evelyn only laughed.

"You want to be put in your place, Jas," was her remark. "You are a little uppish, you know. I am quite pleased with Sylvia. I think she can teach me one or two things."

"Well," exclaimed Jasper, "if it is to be cruel and nasty to your own old Jasper, I wish you joy of your future, Miss Evelyn; that I do.—And I am sure, miss," she added, flashing angry eyes at the unconscious Sylvia, "I do not want to eat with you—not one bit. I am sure your dress ain't fit for any lady to wear."

Sylvia got up slowly.

"I am going to look for Audrey," she said; and before Evelyn could prevent her, she left the room.

"Ain't she a spiteful, nasty thing!" said the maid the moment Sylvia's back was turned. "Ain't she just the very sort that your mother would be mad at your knowing! And I willing to be kind to her and all, and to have a dull evening for her sake, and she ups and cries, 'I don't eat with servants.' Forsooth! I like her ways! I hope, Miss Evelyn, you won't have nothing more to do with her."

"Oh dear!" said Evelyn, lying back in her chair and going off into one peal of laughter after another. "You really kill me, Jas, with your silly ways. It was fun to see Sylvia when she spoke like that. And didn't she take a rise out of you! And was not your pecker up! Oh, it was killing—killing!"

"I am surprised to hear you talk, Miss Evelyn, as you do. You have already forgotten your poor mother and what she said I was to be to you."

"I have not forgotten her, Jas; but I mean to have great fun with Sylvia, and whether you like it or not you will have to lump it. Oh, I say, she has come back!—Well, Sylvia? Why, you have got a lovely dress hanging over your arm!"

"It is the best I could get," said Sylvia. "I went to Audrey's wardrobe and took it out. I did not ask her leave; she was not in the room. There were numbers of dresses, all hanging on pegs, and I took this one. See, it is only India muslin, and it can be washed and done up beautifully. I am determined to have my one happy evening without being docked of any of it, and I could not come down in my own frock. See, Evelyn; do you think it will do?"

"It looks rather raggy," said Evelyn, gazing at the white India muslin, with its lovely lace and chiffon and numerous little tucks, with small favor; "but I suppose it is better than nothing."

CHAPTER VIII.—EVENING-DRESS.

"I borrowed this white sash too," said Sylvia, "and those shoes and stockings. I am certain to be found out. I am certain never to be allowed to come to the Castle again; but I mean to have one really great evening of grand fun."

"And I won't help you to dress," said Jasper.

"But you will, Jasper, because I order it," cried the imperious little Evelyn. "Only," she added, "you must dress me first; and then, while you are helping Sylvia to look as smart as she can in that old rag, I will strut up and down before the glass and try to imagine myself a bride and the owner of Wynford Castle."

Jasper was, after all, too much afraid of Evelyn not to yield to her will, and the dressing of the extraordinary girl began. She was very particular about the arranging of her hair, and insisted on having a dash of powder on her face; finally, she found herself in the satin robe with its magnificent adornings. Her hair was once again piled on the top of her head, a wreath of stephanotis surrounding it, and she stood in silent ecstasy gazing at her image in the glass.

It was now Sylvia's turn to be appareled for the festive occasion, and Jasper at first felt cross and discontented as she took down the girl's masses of raven-black hair and began to brush them out; but soon the magnificence of the locks, which were tawny in places, and brightened here and there with threads of almost gold, interested her so completely that she could not rest until she had made what she called the best of Sylvia's head.

With all her faults, Jasper could on occasions have taste enough, and she soon made Sylvia look as she had seldom looked before. Her thick hair was piled high on her small and classical head; the white muslin dress fitted close to her slim young figure; and when she stood close to Evelyn, and they prepared to go down-stairs together, Sylvia, even in her borrowed plumes, even in the dress which was practically a stolen dress, looked fifty times more the heiress than the overdressed and awkward little real heiress.

When the girls reached the large central hall they both stopped. Audrey was standing near the log fire, and a group of bright and beautifully dressed children clustered round her. Two of the girls wore muslin frocks; their hair, bright in color and very thick in quantity, hung down below their waists. There were a couple of boys in the proverbial Eton jackets; and another pair of girls of ordinary appearance, but with intelligent faces and graceful figures. Audrey gave a perceptible start when she saw her cousin and Sylvia coming to meet her. Just for an instant Sylvia looked awkward. Audrey's eyes slightly dilated; then she came slowly forward.

"Evelyn," she said, "may I introduce my special friends? This is Henrietta Jervice, and this is Juliet; and here is Arthur, and here Robert. Can you remember so many names all at once? Oh, here are

A VERY NAUGHTY GIRL

Mary Clavering and Sophie.—Now, my dears," she added, turning and laughing back at the group, "you have all heard of Evelyn, have you not? This young lady is Miss Sylvia—"

"Sylvia Leeson," said Sylvia. A vivid color came into her cheeks; she drew herself up tall and erect; her black eyes flashed an angry fire.

Audrey looked at her with a slow and puzzled expression. She certainly was very handsome; but where had she got that dress? Sylvia seemed to read the thoughts in Audrey's heart. She bent towards her.

"I will send it back next week. You were not in your room. It was time to dress for dinner. I ran in and took it. If you cannot forgive me I will make an excuse to go up-stairs, and I will take it off and put it back again in your wardrobe, and I will slip home and no one will be the wiser. I know you meant to lend me a dress, for I could not come down in my old rags; but if I have offended you past forgiveness I will go quietly away and no one will miss me."

"Stay," said Audrey coldly. She turned round and began to talk to Henrietta Jervice.

Henrietta laughed and chatted incessantly. She was a merry girl, and very good-looking; she was tall for her age, which was between sixteen and seventeen. Both she and her sister were quite schoolgirls, however, and had frank, fresh manners, which made Sylvia's heart go out to them.

"How nice people in my own class of life really are!" she thought. "How dreadful—oh, how dreadful it is to have to live as I do! And I see by Audrey's face that she thinks that I have not the slightest idea how a lady ought to act. Oh, it is terrible! But there, I will enjoy myself for the nonce; I will—I vow it. Poor little Evelyn, however GAUCHE she is, and however ridiculous, has small chance against Audrey. Even if she is fifty times the heiress, Audrey has the manners of one born to rule. Oh, how I could love her! How happy she could make me!"

"Do you skate?" suddenly asked Arthur Jervice.

"Yes," replied Sylvia bluntly. She turned and looked at him. He looked back at her, and his eyes laughed.

"I wonder what you are thinking about?" he said. "You look as if—"

"As if what?" said Sylvia. She drew back a little, and Arthur did the same.

"As if you meant to run swords into us all. But, all the same, I like your look. Are you staying here?"

"No," said Sylvia. "I live not far away. I have come here just for the day."

"Well, we shall see you to-morrow, of course. Mr. Wynford says we can skate on the pond to-morrow, for the ice will be quite certain to bear. I hope you will come. I love good skating."

"And so do I," said Sylvia.

"Then will you come?"

CHAPTER VIII.—EVENING-DRESS.

"Probably not."

Arthur was silent for a moment. He was a tall boy for his age, and was a good half-head above Sylvia, tall as she also was.

"May I ask you about things?" he said. "Who is that very, very funny little girl?"

"Do you mean Eve Wynford?"

"Perhaps that is her name. I mean the girl in white satin—the girl who wears a grown-up dress."

"She is Audrey Wynford's cousin."

"What! the Tasmanian? The one who is to——"

"Yes. Hush! she will hear us," said Sylvia.

The rustle of silk was heard on the stairs. Sylvia turned her head, and instinctively hid just behind Arthur; and Lady Frances, accompanied by several other ladies, all looking very stately and beautiful, joined the group of young people. A great deal of chattering and laughter followed. Evelyn was in her element. She was not a scrap shy, and going up to her aunt, said in a confident way:

"I hope you like this dress, Aunt Frances. Jasper chose it for me in Paris. It is quite Parisian, is it not? Don't you think it stylish?"

"Hush, Evelyn!" said Lady Frances in a peremptory whisper. "We do not talk of dress except in our rooms."

Evelyn pouted and bit her lip. Then she saw Sylvia, whose eyes were watching Lady Frances. Lady Frances also looked up and saw the tall and beautiful girl at the same moment.

"Who is that girl?" she said, turning to Evelyn. "I don't know her face."

"Her name is Sylvia Leeson."

"Sylvia Leeson! Still I don't understand. Who is she?"

"A friend of mine," said Evelyn.

"My dear, how can you possibly have any friends in this place?"

"She is my friend, Aunt Frances. I found her wandering about out of doors, and I brought her in; and Audrey asked her to stay for the rest of the day, and she is happy. She is very nice, Aunt Frances," said Evelyn, looking up full in her aunt's face.

"That will do, dear."

Lady Frances went up to her daughter.

"Audrey," she said, "introduce me to Miss Leeson."

The introduction was made. Lady Frances held out her hand.

"I am glad to see you, Miss Leeson," she said.

A few minutes later the whole party found themselves clustered round the dinner-table. The children, by special request, sat all together. They chattered and laughed heartily, and seemed to have a world of things to say each to the other. Audrey, surrounded by her own special friends, looked her very best; she had a great deal of tact, and had long ago been trained in the observances of society. She managed now, helped by a warning glance from her mother, to divide Sylvia and Evelyn. She put Sylvia next to Arthur, who continued to chat to her, and to try to draw information from her. Evelyn sat between Robert and Sophie Clavering. Sophie was downright and blunt, and she made Evelyn laugh many times. Sylvia, too, was now quite at her ease. She contrived to fascinate Arthur, who thought her quite the most lovely girl he had ever met.

"I wish you would come and skate to-morrow," he said, as the dinner was coming to an end and the signal for the ladies to withdraw might be expected at any moment. "I wish you would, Sylvia. I cannot see why you should refuse. One has so little chance of skating in England that no one ought to be off the ice who knows how to skate when the weather is suitable. Cannot you come? Shall I ask Lady Frances if you may?"

"No, thank you," said Sylvia; then she added: "I long to skate just as much as you do, and I probably shall skate, although not on your pond; but there is a long reach of water just where the pond narrows and beyond where the stream rushes away towards the river. I may skate there. The water is nearly a mile in extent."

"Then I will meet you," said Arthur. "I will get Robert and Hennie to come with me; Juliet will never stir from Audrey's side when she comes to Castle Wynford; but I'll make up a party and we can meet at the narrow stretch. What do you call it?"

"The Yellow Danger," said Sylvia promptly.

"What a curious name! What does it mean?"

"I don't know; I have not been long enough in this neighborhood. Oh, there is Lady Frances rising from the table; I must go. If you do happen to come to the Yellow Danger to-morrow I shall probably be there."

She nodded to him, and followed the rest of the ladies and the girls to one of the drawing-rooms.

Soon afterwards games of all sorts were started, and the children, and their elders as well, had a right merry time. There was no one smarter at guessing conundrums and proposing vigorous games of chance than Sylvia. The party was sufficiently large to divide itself into two groups, and "clumps," amongst other games, was played with much laughter and vigor. Finally, the whole party wandered into the hall, where an impromptu dance was struck up, and in this also Sylvia managed to excel herself.

"Who is that remarkably graceful and handsome girl?" said Mrs. Jervice to Lady Frances.

"My dear Agnes," was the answer, "I have not the slightest idea. She is a girl from the neighborhood; that terrible aborigine Evelyn picked her up. She certainly is handsome, and clever too; and she is well dressed. That dress she has on reminds me of one which I bought for Audrey in Paris last year. I suppose the girl's people are very well off,

CHAPTER VIII.—EVENING-DRESS.

for that special kind of muslin, with its quantities of real lace, would not be in the possession of a poor girl. On the whole, I like the girl, but the way in which Evelyn has brought her into the house is beyond enduring."

"My Arthur has quite lost his heart to her," said Mrs. Jervice, with a laugh. "He said something to me about asking her to join our skating party to-morrow."

"Well, dear, I will make inquiries, and if she belongs to any nice people I will call on her mother if she happens to have one; but I make it a rule to be very particular what girls Audrey becomes acquainted with."

"And you are quite right," said Mrs. Jervice. "Any one can see how very carefully your Audrey has been brought up."

"She is a sweet girl," said the mother, "and repays me for all the trouble I have taken with her; but what I shall do with Evelyn is a problem, for her uncle has put down his foot and declares that go to school she shall not."

The ladies moved away, chatting as they did so. The music kept up its merry sounds; the young feet tripped happily over the polished floor; all went on gaily, and Sylvia felt herself in paradise. Warmed and fed, petted and surrounded by luxury, she looked a totally different creature from the wild, defiant girl who had pushed past Audrey in order to have a hearty meal on New Year's Day.

But by and by the happy evening came to an end, and Sylvia ran up to Evelyn.

"It is time for me to go," she said. "I must say good night to Lady Frances; and then will you take me to your room just to change my dress, Evelyn?"

"Oh, what a nuisance you are!" said Evelyn. "I am not thinking of going to bed yet."

"Yes; but you are at home, remember. I have to go to my home."

"Well, I do not see why I should go to bed an hour before I wish to. Do go if you wish, Sylvia; I will see you another time. You will find Jasper up-stairs, and she will do anything for you you want."

Sylvia said nothing more. She stood silent for a minute; then noticing Lady Frances in the distance, she ran up to her.

"Good night, Lady Frances," she said; "and thank you very much."

"I am glad you have enjoyed yourself, Miss Leeson," said the lady. She looked full into the sparkling eyes, and suddenly felt a curious drawing towards the girl. "Tell me where you live," she said, "and who your mother is; I should like to have the pleasure of calling on her."

Sylvia's face suddenly became white. Her eyes took on a wild and startled glance.

"I have no mother," she said slowly; "and please do not call, Lady Frances—please don't."

- 51 -

"As you please, of course," said Lady Frances in a very stiff tone. "I only thought—"

"I cannot explain. I cannot help what you think of me. I know I shall not see you, perhaps, ever again—I mean, ever again like this," said Sylvia; "but thank you all the same."

She made a low courtesy, but did not even see the hand which Lady Frances was prepared to hold out. The next instant she was skimming lightly up-stairs.

"Audrey," said Lady Frances, turning to her daughter, "who is that girl?"

"I cannot tell you, mother. Her name is Sylvia Leeson. She lives somewhere near, I suppose."

"She is fairly well-bred, and undoubtedly handsome," said Lady Frances. "I was attracted by her appearance, but when I asked her if I might call on her mother she seemed distressed. She said her mother was dead, and that I was not to call."

"Poor girl!" said Audrey. "You upset her by talking about her mother, perhaps."

"I do not think that was it. Do you know anything at all about her, Audrey?"

"Nothing at all, mother, except that I suppose she lives in the neighborhood, and I am sure she is desperately poor."

"Poor, with that dress!" said Lady Frances. "My dear, you talk rubbish."

Audrey opened her lips as if to speak; then she shut them again.

"I think she is poor notwithstanding the dress," she said in a low voice. "But where is she? Has she gone?"

"She bade me good-night a minute ago and ran up-stairs."

"But Evelyn has not gone up-stairs. Has she let her go alone?"

"Just what I should expect of your cousin," said Lady Frances.

Audrey crossed the hall and went up to Evelyn's side.

"Do you notice that Sylvia has gone up-stairs?" she said. "Have you let her go alone?"

"Yes. Don't bother," said Evelyn.—"What are you saying, Bob?—that you can cut the figure eight in—"

Audrey turned away with an expression of disgust. A moment later she said something to her friend Juliet and ran up-stairs herself.

"What are we to do with Evelyn?" was her thought.

The same thought was passing through the minds of almost all the matrons present; but Evelyn herself imagined that she was most fascinating.

Audrey went to Evelyn's bedroom. There she saw Sylvia already arrayed in her ugly, tattered, and untidy dress. She looked like a different girl. She was pinning her battered sailor-hat on her head; the color had left her cheeks, and her eyes were no longer bright. When

CHAPTER VIII.—EVENING-DRESS.

she saw Audrey she pointed to the muslin dress, which was lying neatly folded on a chair.
"I am going to take it home; it shall be washed, and you shall have it back again."
"Never mind about that," answered Audrey; "I would rather you did not trouble."
"Very well—as you like; and thank you, Miss Wynford, a hundred times. I have had a heavenly evening—something to live for. I shall live on the thoughts of it for many and many a day. Good night, Miss Wynford."
"But stay!" cried Audrey—"stay! It is nearly midnight. How are you going to get home?"
"I shall get home all right," said Sylvia.
"You cannot go alone."
"Nonsense! Don't keep me, please."
Before Audrey had time to say a word Sylvia had rushed down-stairs. A side-door was open, she ran out into the night. Audrey stood still for a moment; then she saw Jasper, who had come silently into the room.
"Follow that young lady immediately," she said. "Or, stay! Send one of the servants. The servant must find her and go home with her. I do not know where she lives, but she cannot be allowed to go out by herself at this hour of night."
Jasper ran down-stairs, and Audrey waited in Evelyn's pretty bedroom. Already there were symptoms all over the room of its new owner's presence; a marked disarrangement of the furniture had already taken place. The room, from being the very soul of order, seemed now to represent the very spirit of unrest. Jasper came back, panting slightly.
"I sent a man after the young lady, miss, but she is nowhere to be seen. I suppose she knows how to find her way home."
Audrey was silent for a minute or two; then taking up the dress which Sylvia had worn, she hung it over her arm.
"Shall I take that back to your room, miss?"
"No, thank you; I will take it myself," replied the girl.
She walked slowly down the passage, descended some steps, and entered her own pretty room in a distant wing. She opened her wardrobe and hung up the dress.
"I do hope one thing," thought Audrey. "Yes, I earnestly hope that mother will never, never discover that poor Sylvia wore my dress. Poor Sylvia! Who is she? Where does she live? What is she?"
Meanwhile Sylvia Leeson was walking fast through the dark and silent night. She was not at all afraid; nor did she choose the frequented paths. On the contrary, after plunging through the shrubbery, she mounted a stile, got into a field, crossed it, squeezed through a hedge at the farther end, and so, by devious paths and many unexpected

A VERY NAUGHTY GIRL

windings, found herself at the entrance of a curious, old-fashioned house. The house was surrounded by thick yew-trees, which grew up almost to the windows. There was a wall round it, and the enclosed space within was evidently very confined. In the gleam of light which came now and then through wintry, driving clouds, a stray flower-bed or a thick holly-bush was visible, but the entire aspect of the place was gloomy, neglected, and disagreeable in the extreme. Sylvia pushed a certain spring in the gate; it immediately opened, and she let herself in. She closed the gate softly and silently behind her, and then, looking eagerly around, began to approach the house. The house stood not thirty yards from the gate. Sylvia now for the first time showed symptoms of fear. Suddenly a big dog in a kennel near uttered a bay. She called his name.

"Pilot, it is I," she said.

The dog ambled towards her; she put her hand on his neck, bent down, and kissed him on the forehead. He wagged his tail, and thrust his cold nose into her hand. She then stood in a listening attitude, her head thrown back; presently, still holding the dog by the collar, she went softly—very softly—round the house. She came to a low window, which was protected by some iron bars.

"Good night, Pilot," she said then. "Good night, darling; go back and guard the house."

The dog trotted swiftly and silently away. When he was quite out of sight Sylvia put up her hand and removed one bar from the six which stood in front of the window. A moment later the window had been opened and the girl had crept within. When inside she pushed the bar which had been previously loosened back into its place, shut the window softly, and crossing the room into which she had entered, stole up-stairs, trembling as she did so. Suddenly a door from above was opened, a light streamed across the passage, and a man's voice said:

"Who goes there?"

There was an instant's silence on the part of Sylvia. The voice repeated the question in a louder key.

"It is I, father," she answered. "I am going to bed. It is all right."

"You impertinent girl!" said the man. "Where have you been all this time? I missed you at dinner; I missed you at supper. Where have you been?"

"Doing no harm, father. It is all right; it is really. Good night, father."

The light, however, did not recede from the passage. A man stood in the entrance to a room. Sylvia had to pass this man to get to her own bedroom. She was thoroughly frightened now. She was shaking all over. As she approached, the man took up the candle he held and let its light fall full on her face.

"Where have you been?" he said roughly.

"Out, father—out; doing no harm."

CHAPTER VIII.—EVENING-DRESS.

"What, my daughter—at this time of night! You know I cannot afford a servant; you know all about me, and yet you desert me for hours and hours. Aren't you ashamed of yourself? You have been out of doors all this long time and supper ready for you on the table! Oatmeal and skimmed milk—an excellent meal; a princess could not desire better. I am keeping it for your breakfast. You shall have no supper now; you deserve to go to bed supper-less, and you shall. What a disgraceful mess your dress is in!"

"There has been snow, and it is wintry and cold outside," replied Sylvia; "and I am not hungry. Good night, father."

"You think to get over me like that! You have no pity for me; you are a most heartless girl. You shall not stir from here until you tell me where you have been."

"Then I will tell you, father. I know you'll be angry, but I cannot help it. There is such a thing as dying for want of—oh, not for want of food, and not for want of clothes—for want of pleasure, fun, life, the joy of being alive. I did go, and I am not ashamed."

"Where?" asked the man.

"I went to Wynford Castle. I have spent the evening there. Now, you may be as angry as you please, but you shall not scold me; no, not a word until the morning."

With a sudden movement the girl flitted past the angry man. The next instant she had reached her room. She opened the door, shut it behind her, and locked herself in. When she was quite alone she pulled off her hat, and got with frantic speed out of her wet jacket; then she clasped her hands high above her head.

"How am I to bear it! What have I done that I should be so miserable?" she thought.

She flung herself across the bare, uninviting bed, and lay there for some time sobbing heavily. All the joy and animation had left her young frame; all the gaiety had departed from her. But presently her passionate sobs came to an end; she undressed and got into bed.

She was bitterly—most bitterly—cold, and it was a long time before the meager clothes which covered her brought any degree of warmth to her frame. But by-and-by she did doze off into a troubled slumber. In her sleep she dreamt of her mother—her mother who was dead.

She awoke presently, and opening her eyes in the midst of the darkness, the thought of her dream came back to her. She remembered a certain night in her life when she had been awakened suddenly to say good-by to her mother. The mother had asked the father to leave the child alone with her.

"You will be always good to him, Sylvia?" she said then. "You will humor him and be patient. I hand my work on to you. It was too much for me, and God is taking me away, but I pass it on to you. If you promise to take the burden and carry it, and not to fail, I shall die happy. Will you, Sylvia—will you?"

"What am I to do, mother?" asked the child. She was a girl of fourteen then.

"This," said the mother: "do not leave him whatever happens."

"Do you mean it, mother? He may go away from here; he may go into the country; he may—do anything. He may become worse—not better. Am I never to be educated? Am I never to be happy? Do you mean it?"

The dying woman looked solemnly at the eager child.

"I mean it," she said; "and you must promise me that you will not leave him whatever happens."

"Then I promise you, mother," Sylvia had said.

CHAPTER IX.–BREAKFAST IN BED.

The day of Evelyn's freedom came to an end. No remark had been made with regard to her extraordinary dress; no comments when she declined to accompany her own special guest to her bedroom. She was allowed to have her own sweet will. She went up-stairs very late, and, on the whole, not discontented. She had enjoyed her chat with some of the strange children who had arrived that afternoon. Lady Frances had scarcely looked at her. That fact did not worry her in the least. She had said good-night in quite a patronizing tone to both her aunt and uncle, she did not trouble even to seek for Audrey, and went up to her room singing gaily to herself. She had a fine, strong contralto voice, and she had not the slightest idea of keeping it in suppression. She sang the chorus of a common-place song which had been popular on the ranch. Lady Frances quite shuddered as she heard her. Presently Evelyn reached her own room, where Jasper was awaiting her. Jasper knew her young mistress thoroughly. She had not the slightest idea of putting herself out too much with regard to Evelyn, but at the same time she knew that Evelyn would be very cross and disagreeable if she had not her comforts; accordingly, the fire burned clear and bright, and there were preparations for the young girl's favorite meal of chocolate and biscuits already going on.

"Oh dear!" said Evelyn, "I am tired; but we have had quite a good time. Of course when the Castle belongs to me I shall always keep it packed with company. There is no fun in a big place like this unless you have heaps of guests. Aunt Frances was quite harmless to-night."

"Harmless!" cried Jasper.

"Yes; that is the word. She took no notice of me at all. I do not mind that. Of course she is jealous, poor thing! And perhaps I can scarcely wonder. But if she leaves me alone I will leave her alone."

"You are conceited, Evelyn," said Jasper. "How could that grand and stately lady be jealous of a little girl like yourself?"

"I think she is, all the same," replied Evelyn. "And, by the way, Jasper, I do not care for that tone of yours. Why do you call me a little girl and speak as though you had no respect for me?"

"I love you too well to respect you, darling," replied Jasper.

"Love me too well! But I thought people never loved others unless they respected them."

"Yes, but they do," answered Jasper, with a short laugh. "How should I love you if that was not the case?"

Evelyn grew red and a puzzled expression flitted across her face.

"I should like my chocolate," she said, sinking into a chair by the fire. "Make it for me, please."

A VERY NAUGHTY GIRL

Jasper did so without any comment. It was long past midnight; the little clock on the mantelpiece pointed with its jeweled hands to twenty minutes to one.

"I shall not get up early," said Evelyn. "Aunt Frances was annoyed at my not being down this morning, but she will have to bear it. You will get me a very nice breakfast, won't you, dear old Jasper? When I wake you will have things very cozy, won't you, Jas?"

"Yes, darling; I'll do what I can. By the way, Evelyn, you ought not to have let that poor Miss Sylvia come up here and go off by herself."

Evelyn pouted.

"I won't be scolded," she said. "You forget your place, Jasper. If you go on like this it might really be best for you to go."

"Oh, I meant nothing," said Jasper, in some alarm; "only it did seem—you will forgive my saying it—not too kind."

"I like Sylvia," said Evelyn; "she is handsome and she says funny things. I mean to see a good deal more of her. Now I am sleepy, so you may help me to get into bed."

The spoilt child slept in unconscious bliss, and the next morning, awaking late, desired Jasper to fetch her breakfast. Jasper rang the bell. After a time a servant appeared.

"Will you send Miss Wynford's breakfast up immediately?" said Jasper.

The girl, a neat-looking housemaid, withdrew. She tapped at the door again in a few minutes.

"If you please, Miss Jasper," she said, "Lady Frances's orders are that Miss Evelyn is to get up to breakfast."

Jasper, with a slight smirk on her face, went into Evelyn's bedroom to retail this message. Evelyn's face turned the color of chalk with intense anger.

"Impertinent woman!" she murmured. "Go down immediately yourself, Jasper, and bring me up some breakfast. Go—do you hear? I will not be ruled by Lady Frances."

Jasper very unwillingly went down-stairs. She returned in about ten minutes to inform Evelyn that it was quite useless, that Lady Frances had given most positive orders, and that there was not a servant in the house who would dare to disobey her.

"But you would dare," said the angry child. "Why did you not go into the larder and fetch the things yourself?"

"The cook took care of that, Miss Evelyn; the larder door was locked."

"Oh, dear me!" said Evelyn; "and I am so hungry." She began to cry.

"Had you not better get up, Evelyn?" said the maid. "The servants told me down-stairs that breakfast would be served in the breakfast-room to-day up to ten o'clock."

"Do you think I am going to let her have the victory over me?" said Evelyn. "No; I shall not stir. I won't go to meals at all if this sort of

CHAPTER IX.–BREAKFAST IN BED.

thing goes on. Oh, I am cruelly treated! I am–I am! And I am so desperately hungry! Is not there even any chocolate left, Jasper?"

"I am sorry to say there is not, dear–you finished it all, to the last drop, last night; and the tin with the biscuits is empty also. There is nothing to eat in this room. I am afraid you will have to hurry and dress yourself–that is, if you want breakfast."

"I won't stir," said Evelyn–"not if she comes to drag me out of bed with cart-ropes."

Jasper stood and stared at her young charge.

"You are very silly, Miss Evelyn," she said. "You will have to submit to her ladyship. You are only a very young girl, and you will find that you cannot fight against her."

Evelyn now covered her face with her handkerchief, and her sobs became distressful.

"Come, dear, come!" said Jasper not unkindly; "let me help you to get into your clothes."

But Evelyn pushed her devoted maid away with vigorous hands.

"Don't touch me. I hate you!" she said.–"Oh mothery, mothery, why did you die and leave me? Oh, your own little Evelyn is so wretched!"

"Now, really, Miss Evelyn, I am angry with you. You are a silly child! You can dress and go down-stairs and have as nice a breakfast as you please. I heard them talking in the breakfast-room as I went by. They were such a merry party!"

"Much they care for me!" said Evelyn.

"Well, they don't naturally unless you go and make yourself pleasant. But there, Miss Evelyn! if you don't get up, I cannot do without my breakfast, so I am going down to the servants' hall."

"Oh! could not you bring me up a little bit of something, Jasper– even bread–even dry bread? I don't mind how stale it is, for I am quite desperately hungry."

"Well, I'll try if I can smuggle something," said Jasper; "but I do not believe I can, all the same."

The woman departed, anxious for her meal.

She came back in a little over half an hour, to find Evelyn sitting up in bed, her eyes red from all the tears she had shed, and her face pale.

"Well," she said, "have you brought up anything?"

"Only hot water for your bath, my dear. I was not allowed to go off even with a biscuit."

"Oh dear! then I'll die–I really shall. You don't know how weak I am! Aunt Frances will have killed me! Oh, this is too awful!"

"You had better get up now, Miss Evelyn. You are very fat and stout, my dear, and missing one meal will not kill you, so don't think it."

"I know what I do think, Jasper, and that is that you are horrid!" said Evelyn.

A VERY NAUGHTY GIRL

But she had scarcely uttered the words before there came a low but very distinct knock on the door. Jasper went to open it. Evelyn's heart began to beat with a mixture of alarm and triumph. Of course this was some one coming with her breakfast. Or could it be, possibly— But no; even Lady Frances would not go so far as to come to gloat over her victim's miseries.

Nevertheless, it was Lady Frances. She walked boldly into the room.

"You can go, Jasper," she said. "I have something I wish to say to Miss Wynford."

Jasper, in considerable annoyance, withdrew, but returned after a minute and placed her ear to the keyhole. Lady Frances did not greatly mind, however, whether she was overheard or not.

"Get up, Evelyn," she said. "Get up at once and dress yourself."

"I—I don't want to get up," murmured Evelyn.

"Come! I am waiting."

Lady Frances sat down on a chair. Her eyes traveled slowly round the disorderly room; displeasure grew greater in her face.

"Get up, my dear—get up," she said. "I am waiting."

"But I don't want to."

"I am afraid your wanting to or not wanting to makes little or no difference, Evelyn. I stay here until you get up. You need not hurry yourself; I will give you until lunch-time if necessary, but until you get up I stay here."

"And if," said Evelyn in a tremulous voice, "I don't get up until after lunch?"

"Then you do without food; you have nothing to eat until you get up. Now, do not let us discuss this point any longer; I want to be busy over my accounts."

Lady Frances drew a small table towards her, took a note-book and a Letts's Diary from a bag at her side, and became absorbed in the irritating task of counting up petty expenses. Lady Frances no more looked at Evelyn than if she had not existed. The angry little girl in the bed even ventured to make faces in the direction of the tyrannical lady; but the tyrannical lady saw nothing. Jasper outside the door found it no longer interesting to press her ear to the keyhole. She retired in some trepidation, and presently made herself busy in Evelyn's boudoir. For half an hour the conflict went on; then, as might be expected, Evelyn gingerly and with intense dislike put one foot out of bed.

Lady Frances saw nothing. She was now murmuring softly to herself. She had long—very long—accounts to add up.

Evelyn drew the foot back again.

"Nasty, horrid, horrid thing!" she said to herself. "She shall not have the victory. But, oh, I am so hungry!" was her next thought; "and she does mean to conquer me. Oh, if only mothery were alive!"

CHAPTER IX.—BREAKFAST IN BED.

At the thought of her mother Evelyn burst into loud sobs. Surely these would draw pity from that heart of stone! Not at all. Lady Frances went calmly on with her occupation.
Finally, Evelyn did get up. She was not accustomed to dressing herself, and she did so very badly. Lady Frances did not take the slightest notice. In about half an hour the untidy toilet was complete. Evelyn had once more donned her crimson velvet dress.
"I am ready," she said then, and she came up to Lady Frances's side.
Lady Frances dropped her pencil, raised her eyes, and fixed them on Evelyn's face.
"Where do you keep your dresses?" she said.
"I don't know. Jasper knows."
"Is Jasper in the next room?"
"Yes."
"Go and fetch her."
Evelyn obeyed. She imagined her head was giddy and that her legs were too weak to enable her to walk steadily.
"Jasper, come," she said in a tremulous voice.
"Poor darling! Poor pet!" muttered Jasper in an injudicious undertone to her afflicted charge.
Lady Frances was now standing up.
"Come here, Jasper," she said. "In which wardrobe do you keep Miss Wynford's dresses?"
"In this one, madam."
"Open it and let me see."
The maid obeyed. Lady Frances went to the wardrobe and felt amongst skirts of different colors, different materials, and different degrees of respectability. Without exception they were all unsuitable; but presently she chose the least objectionable, an ugly drab frieze, and lifting it herself from its hook, laid it on the bed.
"Is there a bodice for this dress?" she asked of the maid.
"Yes, madam. Miss Evelyn used to wear that on the ranch. She has outgrown it rather."
"Put it on your young mistress and let me see her."
"I won't wear that horrid thing!" said Evelyn.
"You will wear what I choose."
Again Evelyn submitted. The dress was put on. It was not becoming, but was at least quiet in appearance.
"You will wear that to-day," said her aunt. "I will myself take you into town this afternoon to get some suitable clothes.—Jasper, I wish Miss Evelyn's present wardrobe to be neatly packed in her trunks."
"Yes, madam."
"No, no, Aunt Frances; you cannot mean it," said Evelyn.
"My dear, I do.—Before you go, Jasper, I have one thing to say. I am sorry, but I cannot help myself. Your late mistress wished you to

remain with Miss Wynford. I grieve to say that you are not the kind of person I should wish to have the charge of her. I will myself get a suitable maid to look after the young lady, and you can go this afternoon. I will pay you well. I am sorry for this; it sounds cruel, but it is really cruel to be kind.—Now, Evelyn, what is the matter?"

"Only I hate you! Oh, how I hate you!" said Evelyn. "I wish mothery were alive that she might fight you! Oh, you are a horrid woman! How I hate you!"

"When you come to yourself, Evelyn, and you are inclined to apologize for your intemperate words, you can come down-stairs, where your belated breakfast awaits you."

CHAPTER X.–JASPER WAS TO GO.

What will not hunger—real, healthy hunger—effect? Lady Frances, after her last words, swept out of the room; and Jasper, her bosom heaving, her black eyes flashing angry fire, looked full at her little charge. What would Evelyn do now? The spoilt child, who could scarcely brook the smallest contradiction, who had declined to get up even to breakfast, to do without Jasper! To allow her friend Jasper to be torn from her arms—Jasper, who had been her mother's dearest companion, who had sworn to that mother that she would not leave Evelyn come what might, that she would protect her against the tyrant aunt and the tyrant uncle, that if necessary she would fight for her with the power which the law bestows! Oh, what an awful moment had arrived! Jasper was to go. What would Evelyn do now?
Evelyn's first impulse had been all that was satisfactory. Her fury had burst forth in wild, indignant words. But now, when the child and the maid found themselves alone, Jasper waited in expectancy which was almost certainty. Evelyn would not submit to this? She and her charge would leave Castle Wynford together that very day. If they were eventually parted, the law should part them.
Still Evelyn was silent.
"Oh Eve—my dear Miss Evelyn—my treasure!" said the afflicted woman.
"Yes, Jasper?" said Evelyn then. "It is an awful nuisance."
"A nuisance! Is that all you have got to say?"
Evelyn rubbed her eyes.
"I won't submit, of course," she said. "No, I won't submit for a minute. But, Jasper, I must have some breakfast; I am too hungry for anything. Perhaps you had better take all my darling, lovely clothes; and if you have to go, Jasper, I'll—I'll never forget you; but I'll talk to you more about it when I have had something to eat."
Evelyn turned and left the room. She was in an ugly dress, beyond doubt, but in her neat black shoes and stockings, and with her fair hair tied back according to Lady Frances's directions, she looked rather more presentable than she had done the previous day. She entered the breakfast-room. The remains of a meal still lay upon the table. Evelyn looked impatiently round. Surely some one ought to appear—a servant at the very least! Hot tea she required, hot coffee, dishes nicely cooked and tempting and fresh. The little girl went to the bell and rang it. A footman appeared.
"Get my breakfast immediately," said Evelyn.
The man withdrew, endeavoring to hide a smile. Evelyn's conduct in daring to defy Lady Frances had been the amusement of the servants'

hall that morning. The man went to the kitchen premises now with the announcement that "miss" had come to her senses.

"She is as white as a sheet, and looks as mad as a hatter," said the man; "but her spirit ain't broke. My word! she 'ave got a will of her own. 'My breakfast, immediate,' says she, as though she were the lady of the manor."

"Which she will be some day," said cook; "and I 'ates to think of it. Our beautiful Miss Audrey supplanted by the like of her. There, Johnson! my missus said that Miss Wynford was to have quite a plain breakfast, so take it up—do."

Toast, fresh tea, and one solitary new-laid egg were placed on a tray and brought up to the breakfast-room.

Evelyn sat down without a word, poured herself out some tea, ate every crumb of toast, finished her egg, and felt refreshed. She had just concluded her meal when Audrey, accompanied by Arthur Jervice, ran into the room.

"Oh, I say, Evelyn," cried Audrey, "you are the very person that we want. We are getting up charades for to-night; will you join us?"

"Yes, do, please," said Arthur. "And we are most anxious that Sylvia should join too."

"I wish I knew her address," said Audrey. "She is such a mystery! Mother is rather disturbed about her. I am afraid, Arthur, we cannot have her to-night; we must manage without.—But will you join us, Evelyn? Do you know anything about acting?"

"I have never acted, but I have seen plays," said Evelyn. "I am sure I can manage all right. I'll do my best if you will give me a big part. I won't take a little part, for it would not be suitable."

Audrey colored and laughed.

"Well, come, anyway, and we will do our best for you," she said. "Have you finished your breakfast? The rest of us are in my schoolroom. You have not been introduced to it yet. Come if you are ready; we are all waiting."

After her miserable morning, Evelyn considered this an agreeable change. She had intended to go up-stairs to comfort Jasper, but really and truly Jasper must wait. She accordingly went with her cousin, and was welcomed by all the children, who pitied her and wanted to make her as much at home as possible. A couple of charades were discussed, and Evelyn was thoroughly satisfied with the RÔLE assigned her. She was a clever child enough, and had some powers of mimicry. As the different arrangements were being made she suddenly remembered something, and uttered a cry.

"Oh dear!" she said—"oh dear! What a pity!"

"What is it now, Evelyn?" asked her cousin.

"Why, your mother is so—I suppose I ought not to say it—your mother—I—— There! I must not say that either. Your mother——"

CHAPTER X.—JASPER WAS TO GO.

"Oh, for goodness' sake speak out!" said Audrey. "What has poor, dear mother done?"

"She is sending Jasper away; she is—she is. Oh, can I bear it? Don't you think it is awful of her?"

"I am sorry for you," said Audrey.

"Jasper would be so useful," continued Evelyn. "She is such a splendid actress; she could help me tremendously. I do wish she could stay even till to-morrow. Cannot you ask Aunt Frances—cannot you, Audrey? I wish you would."

"I must not, Evelyn; mother cannot brook interference. She would not dream of altering her plans just for a play.—Well," she added, looking round at the rest of her guests, "I think we have arranged everything now; we must meet here not later than three o'clock for rehearsal. Who would like to go out?" she added. "The morning is lovely."

The boys and girls picked up hats and cloaks and ran out immediately into the grounds. Evelyn took the first covering she could find, and joined the others.

"They ought to consult me more," she said to herself. "I see there is no help for it; I must live here for a bit and put Audrey down—that at least is due to me. But when next there are people here I shall be arranging the charades, and I shall invite them to go out into the grounds. It is a great bother about Jasper; but there! she must bear it, poor dear. She will be all right when I tell her that I will get her back when the Castle belongs to me."

Meanwhile Arthur, remembering his promise to Sylvia, ran away from where the others were standing. The boy ran fast, hoping to see Sylvia. He had taken a great fancy to her bright, dark eyes and her vivacious ways.

"She promised to meet me," he said to himself. "She is certain to keep her word."

By and by he uttered a loud "Hullo!" and a slim young figure, in a shabby crimson cloak, turned and came towards him.

"Oh, it is you, Arthur!" said Sylvia. "Well, and how are they all?"

"Quite well," replied the boy. "We are going to have charades to-night, and I am to be the doctor in one. It is rather a difficult part, and I hope I shall do it right. I never played in a charade before. That little monkey Evelyn is to be the patient. I do hope she will behave properly and not spoil everything. She is such an extraordinary child! And of course she ought to have had quite one of the most unimportant parts, but she would not hear of it. I wish you were going to play in the charade, Sylvia."

"I have often played in charades," said Sylvia, with a quick sigh.

"Have you? How strange! You seem to have done everything."

"I have done most things that girls of my age have done."

A VERY NAUGHTY GIRL

Arthur looked at her with curiosity. There was—he could not help noticing it, and he blushed very vividly as he did see—a very roughly executed patch on the side of her shoe. On the other shoe, too, the toes were worn white. They were shabby shoes, although the little feet they encased were neat enough, with high insteps and narrow, tapering toes. Sylvia knew quite well what was passing in Arthur's mind. After a moment she spoke.

"You wonder why I look poor," she said. "Sometimes, Arthur, appearances deceive. I am not poor. It is my pleasure to wear very simple clothes, and to eat very plain food, and——"

"Not pleasure!" said Arthur. "You don't look as if it were your pleasure. Why, Sylvia, I do believe you are hungry now!"

Poor Sylvia was groaning inwardly, so keen was her hunger.

"And I am as peckish as I can be," said the boy, a rapid thought flashing through his mind. "The village is only a quarter of a mile from here, and I know there are tuck-shops. Why should we not go and have a lark all by ourselves? Who's to know, and who's to care? Will you come, Sylvia?"

"No, I cannot," replied Sylvia; "it is impossible. Thank you very much indeed, Arthur. I am so glad to have seen you! I must go home, however, in a minute or two. I was out all day yesterday, and there is a great deal to be done."

"But may I not come with you? Cannot I help you?"

"No, thank you; indeed I could not possibly have you. It is very good of you to offer, but I cannot have you, and I must not tell you why."

"You do look so sad! Are you sure you cannot join the charades to-night?"

"Sure—certain," said Sylvia, with a little gasp. "And I am not sad," she added; "there never was any one more merry. Listen to me now; I am going to laugh the echoes up."

They were standing where a defile of rocks stretched away to their left. The stream ran straight between the narrow opening. The girl slightly changed her position, raised her hand, and called out a clear "Hullo!" It was echoed back from many points, growing fainter and fainter as it died away.

"And now you say I am not merry!" she exclaimed. "Listen."

She laughed a ringing laugh. There never was anything more musical than the way that laughter was taken up, as if there were a thousand sprites laughing too. Sylvia turned her white face and looked full at Arthur.

"Oh, I am such a merry girl!" she said, "and such a glad one! and such a thankful one! And I am rich—not poor—but I like simple things. Good-by, Arthur, for the present."

"I will come and see you again. You are quite wonderful!" he said. "I wish mother knew you. And I wish my sister Moss were here; I wish she knew you."

CHAPTER X.—JASPER WAS TO GO.

"Moss! What a curious name!" said Sylvia.
"We have always called her that. She is just like moss, so soft and yet so springy; so comfortable, and yet you dare not take too much liberty with her. She is fragile, too, and mother had to take great care of her. I should like you to see her; she would——"
"What would she do?" asked Sylvia.
"She would understand you; she would draw part at least of the trouble away."
"Oh! don't, Arthur—don't, don't read me like that," said the girl.
The tears just dimmed her eyes. She dashed them away, laughed again merrily, and the next moment had turned the corner and was lost to view.

CHAPTER XI.—"I CANNOT ALTER MY PLANS."

Immediately after lunch Lady Frances beckoned Evelyn to her side.
"Go up-stairs and ask Jasper to dress you," she said. "The carriage will be round in a few minutes."
Evelyn wanted to expostulate. She looked full at Audrey. Surely Audrey would protect her from the terrible infliction of a long drive alone with Lady Frances! Audrey did catch Evelyn's beseeching glance; she took a step forward.
"Do you particularly want Evelyn this afternoon, mother?" she asked.
"Yes, dear; if I did not want her I should not ask her to come with me."
Lady Frances's words were very impressive; Audrey stood silent.
"Please tell her—please tell her!" interrupted Evelyn in a voice tremulous with passion.
"We are going to have charades to-night, mother, and Evelyn's part is somewhat important; we are all to rehearse in the schoolroom at three o'clock."
"And my part is very important," interrupted Evelyn again.
"I am sorry," said Lady Frances, "but Evelyn must come with me. Is there no one else to take the part, Audrey?"
"Yes, mother; Sophie could do it. She has a very small part, and she is a good actress, and Evelyn could easily do Sophie's part; but, all the same, it will disappoint Eve."
"I am sorry for that," said Lady Frances; "but I cannot alter my plans. Give Sophie the part that Evelyn would have taken; Evelyn can take her part.—You will have plenty of time, Evelyn, when you return to coach for the small part."
"Yes, you will, Evelyn; but I am sorry, all the same," said Audrey, and she turned away.
Evelyn's lips trembled. She stood motionless; then she slowly revolved round, intending to fire some very angry words into Lady Frances's face; but, lo and behold! there was no Lady Frances there. She had gone up-stairs while Evelyn was lost in thought.
Very quietly the little girl went up to her own room. Jasper, her eyes almost swollen out of her head with crying, was there to wait on her.
"I have been packing up, Miss Evelyn," she said. "I am to go this afternoon. Her ladyship has made all arrangements, and a cab is to come from the 'Green Man' in the village to fetch me and my luggage at half-past three. It is almost past belief, Miss Eve, that you and me should be parted like this."

CHAPTER XI.—"I CANNOT ALTER MY PLANS."

"You look horrid, Jasper, when you cry so hard!" said Evelyn. "Oh, of course I am awfully sorry; I do not know how I shall live without you."

"You will miss me a good bit," said the woman. "I am surprised, though, that you should take it as you do. If you raised your voice and started the whole place in an uproar you would be bound to have your own way. But as it is, you are mum as you please; never a word out of you either of sorrow or anything else, but off you go larking with those children and forgetting the one who has made you, mended you, and done everything on earth for you since long before your mother died."

"Don't remind me of mothery now," said the girl, and her lips trembled; then she added in a changed voice: "I cannot help it, Jasper. I have been fighting ever since I came here, and I want to fight—oh, most badly, most desperately!—but somehow the courage has gone out of me. I am ever so sorry for you, Jasper, but I cannot help myself; I really cannot."

Jasper was silent. After a time she said slowly:

"And your mother wrote a letter on her deathbed asking Lady Frances to let me stay with you whatever happened."

"I know," said Evelyn. "It is awful of her; it really is."

"And do you think," continued the woman, "I am going to submit?"

"Why, you must, Jasper. You cannot stay if they do not wish for you. And you have got all your wages, have you not?"

"I have, my dear; I have. Yes," continued the woman; "she thinks, of course, that I am satisfied, and that I am going as mum as a mouse and as quiet as the grave, but she is fine and mistook; I ain't doing nothing of the sort. Go I must, but not far. I have a plan in my head. It may come to nothing; but if it does come to something, as I hope to goodness it will, then you will hear of me again, my pet, and I won't be far off to protect you if the time should come that you need me. And now, what do you want of me, my little lamb, for your face is piteous to see?"

"I am a miserable girl," said Evelyn. "I could cry for hours, but there is no time. Dress me, then, for the last time, Jasper. Oh, Jasper darling, I am fond of you!"

Evelyn's stoical, hard sort of nature seemed to give way at this juncture; she flung her arms round her maid's neck and kissed her many times passionately. The woman kissed her, too, in a hungry sort of way.

"You are really not going far away, Jasper?" said Evelyn when, dressed in her coat and hat, she was ready to start.

"My plans are laid but not made yet," said the woman. "You will hear from me likely to-morrow, my love. And now, good-by. I have packed all your things in the trunks they came in, and the wardrobe is empty.

A VERY NAUGHTY GIRL

Oh, my pet, my pet, good-by! Who will look after you to-night, and who will sleep in the little white bed alongside of you? Oh, my darling, the spirit of your Jasper is broke, that it is!"

"Evelyn!" called her aunt, who was passing her room at that moment, "the carriage is at the door. Come at once."

Evelyn ran down-stairs. She wore a showy, unsuitable hat and a showy, unsuitable jacket. She got quickly into the carriage, and flopped down by the side of the stately Lady Frances.

Lady Frances was a very judicious woman in her way. She reprimanded whenever in her opinion it was necessary to reprimand, but she never nagged. It needed but a glance to show her that Evelyn required to be educated in every form of good-breeding, and that education the good woman fully intended to take in hand without a moment's delay, but she did not intend to find fault moment by moment. She said nothing, therefore, either in praise or blame to the small, awkward, conceited little girl by her side; but she gave orders to stop at Simpson's in the High Street, and the carriage started briskly forward. Wynford Castle was within half a mile of the village which was called after it, and five miles away from a large and very important cathedral town—the cathedral town of Easterly. During the drive Lady Frances chatted in the sort of tone she would use to a small girl, and Evelyn gave short and sulky replies. Finding that her conversation was not interesting to her small guest, the good lady became silent and wrapped up in her own thoughts. Presently they arrived at Simpson's, and there the lady and the child got out and entered the shop. Evelyn was absolutely bewildered by the amount of things which her aunt ordered for her. It is true that she had had, as Jasper expressed it, quite a small trousseau when in Paris; but during her mother's lifetime her dresses had come to her slowly and with long intervals between. Mrs. Wynford had been a showy but by no means a good dresser; she loved the gayest, most bizarre colors, and she delighted in adorning her child with bits of feathers, scraps of shabby lace, beads, and such-like decorations. After her mother's death, when Evelyn, considered herself rich, she and Jasper purchased the same sort of things, only using better materials. Thus the thin silk was exchanged for thick silk, cotton-back satin for the real article, velveteen for velvet, cheap lace for real lace, and the gaily colored beads for gold chains and strings of pearls. Nothing in Evelyn's opinion and nothing in Jasper's opinion could be more exquisitely beautiful than the toilet which Evelyn brought to Castle Wynford; but Lady Frances evidently thought otherwise. She ordered a dark-blue serge, with a jacket to match, to be put in hand immediately for the little girl; she bought a dark-gray dress, ready made, which was to be sent home that same evening. She got a neat black hat to wear with the dress, and a thick black pilot-cloth jacket to cover the small person of the heiress. As to her evening-dresses, she chose them of fine, soft white silk and fine,

CHAPTER XI.—"I CANNOT ALTER MY PLANS."

soft muslin; and then, having added a large store of underclothing, all of the best quality, and one or two pale-pink and pale-blue evening-frocks, all severely plain, she got once more into her carriage, and, accompanied by Evelyn, drove home. On the seat in front of the pair reposed a box which contained a very simple white muslin frock for Evelyn to wear that evening.

"I suppose Jasper will have gone when I get back?" said the little girl to Lady Frances.

"Certainly," said Lady Frances. "I ordered her to be out of the house by half-past three; it is now past five o'clock."

"What am I to do for a maid?"

"My servant Read shall wait on you to-night and every evening and morning until our guests have gone; then Audrey's maid Louisa will attend on you."

"But I want a maid all to myself."

"You cannot have one. Louisa will give you what assistance is necessary. I presume you do not want to be absolutely dependent; you would like to be able to do things for yourself."

"In mother's time I did everything for myself, but now it is different. I am a very, very rich girl now."

Lady Frances was silent when Evelyn made this remark.

"I am rich, am I not, Aunt Frances?" said the little heiress almost timidly.

"I cannot see where the riches come in, Evelyn. At the present moment you depend on your uncle for every penny that is spent upon you."

"But I am the heiress!"

"Let the future take care of itself. You are a little girl—small, insignificant, and ignorant. You require to be trained and looked after, and to have your character moulded, and for all these things you depend on the kindness of your relations. The fact is this, Evelyn: at present you have not the slightest idea of your true position. When you find your level I shall have hopes of you—not before."

Evelyn leant back hopelessly in the carriage and began to sob. After a time she said:

"I wish you would let me keep Jasper."

Lady Frances was silent.

"Why won't you let me keep Jasper?"

"I do not consider it good for you."

"But mothery asked you to."

"It gives me pain, Evelyn, under the circumstances to refuse your mother's request; but I have consulted your uncle, and we both feel that the steps I have taken are the only ones to take."

"Who will sleep in my room to-night?"

"Are you such a baby as to need anybody?"

A VERY NAUGHTY GIRL

"I never slept alone in my life. I am quite terrified. I suppose your big, ancient house is haunted?"

"Oh, what a silly child you are! Very well, for a night or two I will humor you, and Read shall sleep in the room; but now clearly understand I allow no bedroom suppers and no gossip—but Read will see to that. Now, make up your mind to be happy and contented—in short, to submit to the life which Providence has ordered for you. Think first of others and last of yourself and you may be happy. Consult Audrey and Miss Sinclair and you will gain wisdom. Obey me whether you like it or not, or you will certainly be a very wretched girl. Ah! and here we are. You would like to go to the schoolroom; they are having tea there, I believe. Run off, dear; that will do for the present."

When Evelyn reached the schoolroom she found a busy and animated group all seated about in different parts of it. They were eagerly discussing the charade, and when Evelyn arrived she was welcomed.

"I am ever so sorry, Evelyn," said Audrey, "that you cannot have the part you wanted; but we mean to get up some other charades later on in the week, and then you shall help us and have a very good part. You do not mind our arrangement for to-night, do you?"

Evelyn replied somewhat sulkily. Audrey determined to take no notice. She sat down by her little cousin, told Sophie to fetch some hot tea, and soon coaxed Evelyn into a fairly good-humor. The small part she was to undertake was read over to her, and she was obliged to get certain words by heart. She had little or no idea of acting, but there was a certain calm assurance about her which would carry her through many difficulties. The children, incited by Audrey's example, were determined to pet her and make the best of her; and when she did leave the schoolroom she felt almost as happy and important as she thought she ought to be.

"What a horrid girl she is!" said Sophie as soon as the door had closed behind Evelyn.

"I wish you would not say that," remarked Audrey; and a look of distress visited her pretty face.

"Oh, we do not mind for ourselves," remarked Juliet; "it is on your account, Audrey. You know what great friends we have always been, and now to have you associated every day, and all day long with a girl of that sort—it really seems almost past bearing."

"I shall get used to it," said Audrey. "And remember that I pity her, and am sorry—very sorry—for her. I dare say we shall win her over by being kind."

"Well," said Henrietta, rising as she spoke and slowly crossing the room, "I have promised to be civil to her for your sake for a day or two, but I vow it will not last long if she gives herself such ridiculous airs. The idea of her ever having a place like this!"

CHAPTER XI.—"I CANNOT ALTER MY PLANS."

She said the last words below her breath, and Audrey did not hear them. Presently her mother called her, and the young girl ran off. The others looked at each other.

"Well, Arthur, and what is filling your mind?" said his sister Henrietta, looking into the face of the handsome boy.

"I am thinking of Sylvia," he answered. "I wish she were here instead of Evelyn. Don't you like her very much, Hennie? Don't you think she is a very handsome and very interesting girl?"

"I hardly spoke to her," replied Henrietta. "I saw you were taken with her."

"She was mysterious; that is one reason why I like her," he replied. Then he added abruptly: "I wish you would make friends with her, Henrietta. I wish you, and Juliet too, could be specially kind to her; she looks so very sad."

"I never saw a merrier girl," was Juliet's reply. "But then, I don't see people with your eyes; you are always a good one at guessing people's secrets."

"I take after Moss in that," he replied.

"There never was any one like her," said Juliet. "Well, I am going to dress now. I hope the charade will go off well. What a blessing Lady Frances came to the rescue and delivered us from Evelyn's spoiling everything by taking a good part!"

Meanwhile Evelyn had gone up to her room. It was neat and in perfect order once more. Jasper's brief reign had passed and left no sign. The fire burned brightly on the carefully swept-up hearth; the electric light made the room bright as day. A neat, grave-looking woman was standing by the fire, and when Evelyn appeared she came forward to meet her.

"My name is Mrs. Read," she said. "I am my mistress's own special maid, but she has asked me to see to your toilet this evening, Miss Wynford; and this, I understand, is the dress her ladyship wishes you to wear."

Evelyn pouted; then she tossed off her hat and looked full up at Read. Her lips quivered, and a troubled, pathetic light for the first time filled her brown eyes.

"Where is Jasper?" she asked abruptly.

"Miss Jasper has left, my dear young lady."

"Then I hate you, and I don't want you to dress me. You can go away," said Evelyn.

"I am sorry, Miss Wynford, but her ladyship's orders are that I am to attend to your wardrobe. Perhaps you will allow me to do your hair and put on your dress at once, as her ladyship wants me to go to her a little later."

"You will do nothing of the kind. I will dress myself now that Jasper has gone."

"And a good thing too, miss. Young ladies ought always to make themselves useful. The more you know, the better off you will be; that is my opinion."

Evelyn looked full up at Read. Read had a kindly face, calm blue eyes, a firm, imperturbable sort of mouth. She wore her hair very neatly banded on each side of her head. Her dress was perfectly immaculate. There was nothing out of place; she looked, in short, like the very soul of order.

"Do you know who I am?" was Evelyn's remark.

"Certainly I do, Miss Wynford."

"Please tell me."

The glimmer of a smile flitted across Read's calm mouth.

"You are a young lady from Tasmania, niece to the Squire, and you have come over here to be educated with Miss Audrey—bless her!"

"Is that all you know!" said Evelyn. "Then I will tell you more. There will come a day when your Miss Audrey will have nothing to do with the Castle, and when I shall have everything to do with it. I am to be mistress here any day, whenever my uncle dies."

"My dear Miss Wynford, don't speak like that! The Squire is safe to live, Providence permitting, for many a long year."

Evelyn sat down again.

"I think my aunt, Lady Frances, one of the cruellest women in the world," she continued. "Now you know what I think, and you can tell her, you nasty cross-patch. You can go away and tell her at once. I longed to say so to her face when I was out driving to-day, but she has got the upper hand of me, although she is not going to keep it. I don't want you to help me; I hate you nearly as much as I hate her!"

Read looked as though she did not hear a single remark that Evelyn made. She crossed the room, and presently returned with a can of hot water and poured some into a basin.

"Now, miss," she said, "if you will wash your face and hands, I will arrange your hair."

There was something in her tone which reduced Evelyn to silence.

"Did you not hear what I said?" she remarked after a minute.

"No, miss; it may be more truthful to say I did not. When young ladies talk silly, naughty words I have a 'abit of shutting up my ears; so it ain't no manner of use to talk on to me, miss, for I don't hear, and I won't hear, and that is flat. If you will come now, like a good little lady, and allow yourself to be dressed, I have a bit of a surprise for you; but you will not know about it before your toilet is complete."

"A bit of a surprise!" said Evelyn, who was intensely curious. "What in the world can it be?"

"I will tell you when you are dressed, miss; and I must ask you to hurry, for my mistress is waiting for me."

CHAPTER XI.—"I CANNOT ALTER MY PLANS."

If Evelyn had one overweening failing more than another, it was inordinate curiosity. She rose, therefore, and submitted with a very bad grace to Read's manipulations. Her face and hands were washed, and Read proceeded to brush out the scanty flaxen locks.

"Are you not going to pile my hair on the top of my head?" asked the little girl.

"Oh dear, no, Miss Wynford; that ain't at all the way little ladies of your age wear their hair."

"I always wore it like that when I was in Tasmania with mothery!"

"Tasmania is not England, miss. It would not suit her ladyship for you to wear your hair so."

"Then I won't wear it any other way."

"As you please, miss. I can put on your dress, and you can arrange your hair yourself, but I won't give you what will be a bit of a surprise to you."

"Oh, do it as you please," said Evelyn.

Her hair, very pretty in itself, although far too thin to make much show, was accordingly arranged in childish fashion; and when Evelyn presently found herself arrayed in her high-bodied and long-sleeved white muslin dress, with white silk stockings and little silk shoes to match, and a white sash round her waist, she gazed at herself in the glass in puzzled wonder.

Read stood for a moment watching her face.

"I am pretty, am I not?" said Evelyn, turning and looking full at her maid.

"It is best not to think of looks, and it is downright sinful to talk of them," was Read's somewhat severe answer.

Evelyn's eyes twinkled.

"I feel like a very good, pretty little girl," she said. "Last night I was a charming grown-up young lady. Very soon again I shall be a charming grown-up young lady, and whether Aunt Frances likes it or not, I shall be much, much better-looking than Audrey. Now, please, I have been good, and I want what you said you had for me."

"It is a letter from Jasper," replied Read. "She told me I was to give it to you. Now, please, miss, don't make yourself untidy. You look very nice and suitable. When the gong rings you can go down-stairs, or sooner if your fancy takes you. I am going off now to attend to my mistress."

When alone, Evelyn tore open the letter which Jasper had left for her. It was short, and ran as follows:

> MY DARLING, PRECIOUS LAMB,—The best friends must part, but, oh, it is a black, black heart that makes it necessary! My heart is bleeding to think that you won't have me to make your chocolate, and to lie down in the little white bed by your side this evening. Yes, it is bleeding,

A VERY NAUGHTY GIRL

and bleeding badly, and there will be no blessing on her who has tried to part us. But, Miss Evelyn, my dear, don't you fret, for though I am away I do not mean to be far away, and when you want me I will still be there. I have a plan in my head, and I will let you know about it when it is properly laid. No more at present, but if you think of me every minute to-night, so will I think of you, my dear little white Eve; and don't forget, darling, that whatever they may do to you, the time will come when they will all, the Squire excepted, be under your thumb.

—Your loving
"JASPER."

The morsel of content and satisfaction which Evelyn had felt when she saw herself looking like a nice, ordinary little girl, and when she had sat in the schoolroom surrounded by all the gay young folks of her cousin's station in life, vanished completely as she read Jasper's injudicious words. Tears flowed from her eyes; she clenched her hands. She danced passionately about the room. She longed to tear from her locks the white ribbons which Read had arranged there; she longed to get into the white satin dress which she had worn on the previous occasion; she longed to do anything on earth to defy Lady Frances; but, alack and alas! what good were longings when the means of yielding to them were denied?—for all that precious and fascinating wardrobe had been put into Evelyn's traveling-trunks, and those trunks had been conveyed from the blue-and-silver bedroom. The little girl found that she had to submit.

"Well, I do—I do," she thought—"but only outwardly. Oh, she will never break me in! Mothery darling, she will never break me in. I am going to be naughty always, always, because she is so cruel, and because I hate her, and because she has parted me from Jasper—your friend, my darling mothery, your friend!"

CHAPTER XII.—HUNGER.

When Jasper was conveyed from Wynford Castle she drove to the "Green Man" in the village. There she asked the landlady if she could give her a small bedroom for the night. The landlady, a certain Mrs. Simpson, was quite willing to oblige Miss Jasper. She was accommodated with a bedroom, and having seen her boxes deposited there, wandered about the village. She took the bearings of the place, which was small and unimportant, and altogether devoted to the interests of the great folks at Castle Wynford. Wynford village lived, indeed, for the Castle; without the big house, as they called it, the villagers would have little or no existence. The village received its patronage from the Squire and his family. Every house in the village belonged to Squire Wynford. The inhabitants regarded him as if he were their feudal lord. He was kindly to all, sympathetic in sorrow, ready to rejoice when bright moments visited each or any of his tenants. Lady Frances was an admirable almoner of the different charities which came from the great house. There was not a poor woman in the length and breadth of Wynford village who was not perfectly well aware that her ladyship knew all about her, even to her little sins and her small transgressions; all about her struggles as well as her falls, her temptations as well as her moments of victory. Lady Frances was loved and feared; the Squire was loved and respected; Audrey was loved in the sort of passionate way in which people will regard the girl who always has been to them more or less a little princess. Therefore now, as Jasper walked slowly through the village with the fading light falling all over her, she knew she was a person of interest. Beyond doubt that was the case; but although the villagers were interested in her, and peeped outside their houses to watch her (even the grocer, who did a roaring trade, and took the tenor solo on Sunday in the church choir, peered round his doorstep with the others), she knew that she was favored with no admiring looks, and that the villagers one and all were prepared to fight her. That was indeed the case, for secrets are no secrets where a great family are concerned, and the villagers knew that Jasper had come over from the other side of the world with the real heiress.

"A dowdy, ill-favored girl," they said one to the other; "but nevertheless, when the Squire—bless him!—is gathered to his fathers, she will reign in his stead, and sweet, darling, beautiful Miss Audrey will be nowhere."

They said this, repeating the disagreeable news one to the other, and vowing each and all that they would never care for the Australian girl, and never give her a welcome.

A VERY NAUGHTY GIRL

As Jasper slowly walked she was conscious of the feeling of hostility which surrounded her.

"It won't do," she said to herself. "I meant to take up my abode at the 'Green Man,' and I meant that no one in the place should turn me out, but I do not believe I shall be able to continue there; and yet, to go far away from my sweet little Eve is not to be thought of. I have money of my own. Her mother was a wise woman when she said to me, 'Jasper, the time may come when you will need it; and although it belongs to Eve, you must spend it as you think best in her service.'

"It ain't much," thought Jasper to herself, "but it is sixty pounds, and I have it in gold sovereigns, scattered here and there in my big black trunk, and I mean to spend it in watching over the dear angel lamb. Mrs. Simpson of the 'Green Man' would be the better of it, but she sha'n't have much of it—of that I am resolved."

So Jasper presently left the village and began strolling in the direction where the river Earn flows between dark rocks until it loses itself in a narrow stream among the peaceful hills. In that direction lay The Priory, with its thick yew hedge and its shut-in appearance.

As Jasper continued her walk she knew nothing of the near neighborhood of The Priory, and no one in all the world was farther from her thoughts than the pretty, tall slip of a girl who lived there.

Now, it so happened that Sylvia was taking her walks abroad also in the hour of dusk. It was one of her peculiarities never to spend an hour that she could help indoors. She had to sleep indoors, and she had to take what food she could manage to secure also under the roof which she so hated; but, come rain or shine, storm or calm, every scrap of the rest of her time was spent wandering about. To the amount of fresh air which she breathed she owed her health and a good deal of her beauty. She was out now as usual, her big mastiff, Pilot, bearing her company. She was never afraid where she wandered with this protection, for Pilot was a dog of sagacity, and would soon make matters too hot for any one who meant harm to his young mistress.

Sylvia walked slowly. She was thinking hard. "What a delightful time she was having twenty-four hours ago! What a good dinner she was about to eat! How pleasant it was to wear Audrey's pretty dress! How delightful to dance in the hall and talk to Arthur Jervice! She wondered what his sister with the curious name was like. How beautiful his face looked when he spoke of her!

"She must be lovely too," thought Sylvia. "And so restful! There is nothing so cool and comfortable and peaceful as a mossy bank. I suppose she is called Moss because she comforts people."

Sylvia hurried a little. Presently she stood and looked around her to be sure that no one was by. She then deliberately tightened her belt.

"It makes me feel the pangs less," she thought. "Oh dear, how delightful, how happy those must be who are never, never hungry!

CHAPTER XII.—HUNGER.

Sometimes I can scarcely bear it; I almost feel that I could steal something to have a big, big meal. What a lot I ate last night, and how I longed to pocket even that great hunch of bread which was placed near my plate! But I did not dare. I thought my big meal would keep off my hunger to-day, but I believe it has made it worse than ever. I must have a straight talk with father to-night. I must tell him plainly that, however coarse the food, I must at least have enough of it. Oh dear, I ache—I ACHE for a good meal!"

The poor girl stood still. Footsteps were heard approaching. They were now close by. Pilot pricked up his ears and listened. A moment later Jasper appeared on the scene.

When she saw Sylvia she stopped, dropped a little courtesy, and said in a semi-familiar tone:

"And how are you this evening, Miss Leeson?"

Sylvia had not seen her as she approached. The girl started now and turned quickly round.

"You are Jasper?" she said. "What are you doing here?"

"Taking the air, miss. Have you any objection?"

"None, of course," replied Sylvia.

Had there been light enough to see, Jasper would have noticed that the girl's face took on a cheerful expression. She laid her hand on Pilot's forehead. Pilot growled. Sylvia said to him:

"Be quiet; this is a friend."

Pilot evidently understood the words. He wagged his bushy tail and looked in Jasper's direction. Jasper came boldly up and laid her hand beside Sylvia's on the dog's forehead. The tail wagged more demonstratively.

"You have won him," said Sylvia in a tone of delight. "Do you know, I am glad, although I cannot tell why I should be."

"He looks as if he could be very formidable," said Jasper.—"Ah, good dog—good dog! Noble creature! So I am your friend? Good dog!"

"But it must be rather unpleasant for visitors to come to call on you, Miss Sylvia, with such a dog as that loose about the place. Now, I, for instance——"

"If you had a message from Evelyn for me," said Sylvia, "you could call now with impunity. Strangers cannot; that is why father keeps Pilot. He is trained never to touch any one, but he is also trained to keep every one out. He does that in the best manner possible. He stands right in the person's path and shows his big fangs and growls. Nobody would dream of going past him; but you would be safe."

Jasper stood silent.

"It may be useful," she repeated.

"You have not come now with a message from Evelyn?" said Sylvia, a pathetic tone in her voice.

"No, miss, I have not; but do you know, miss—do you know what has happened to me?"

"How should I?" replied Sylvia.

"I am turned out, miss—turned out by her ladyship—I who had a letter from Mrs. Wynford in Tasmania asking her ladyship to keep me always as my little Evelyn's friend and nurse and guardian. Yes, Miss Sylvia, I am turned away as though I were dirt. I am turned away, miss, although it was only yesterday that her ladyship got the letter which the dying mother wrote. It is hard, is it not, Miss Leeson? It is cruel, is it not?"

"Hard and cruel!" echoed Sylvia. "It is worse. It is a horrible sin. I wonder you stand it!"

"Now, miss, for such a pretty young lady I wonder you have not more sense. Do you think I'd go if I could help it?"

"What does Evelyn say?" asked Sylvia, intensely excited.

"What does she say? Nothing. She is stunned, I take it; but she will wake up and know what it means. No chocolate, and no one to sleep in the little white bed by her side."

"Oh, how she must enjoy her chocolate!" said poor Sylvia, a sigh of longing in her voice.

"I am grand at making it," said Jasper. "I have spent my life in many out-of-the-way places. It was in Madrid I learnt to make chocolate; no one can excel me with it. I'd like well to make a cup for you."

"And I'd like to drink it," said Sylvia.

"As well as I can see you in this light," continued Jasper, "you look as if a cup of my chocolate would do you good. Chocolate made all of milk, with plenty of bread and butter, is a meal which no one need despise. I say, miss, shall we go back to the "Green Man," and shall you and me have a bit of supper together? You would not be too proud to take it with me although I am only my young lady's maid?"

"I wish I could," said Sylvia. There was a wild desire in her heart, a sort of passion of hunger. "But," she continued, "I cannot; I must go home now."

"Is your home near, miss?"

"Oh yes; it is just at the other side of that wall. But please do not talk of it—father hates people knowing. He likes us to live quite solitary."

"And it is a big house. Yes, I can see that," continued Jasper, peering through the trees.

Just then a young crescent moon showed its face, a bank of clouds swept away to the left, and Jasper could distinctly see the square outline of an ugly house. She saw something else also—the very white face of the hungry Sylvia, the look which was almost starvation in her eyes. Jasper was clever; she might not be highly educated in the ordinary sense, but she had been taught to use her brains, and she had excellent brains to use. Now, as she looked at the girl, an idea flashed through her mind.

CHAPTER XII.–HUNGER.

"For some extraordinary reason that child is downright hungry," she said to herself. "Now, nothing would suit my purpose better."

She came close to Sylvia and laid her hand on her arm.

"I have taken a great fancy to you, miss," she said.

"Have you?" answered Sylvia.

"Yes, miss; and I am very lonely, and I don't mean to stay far away from my dear young lady."

"Are you going to live in the village?" asked Sylvia.

"I have a room now at the 'Green Man,' Miss Leeson, but I don't mean to stay there; I don't care for the landlady. And I don't want to be, so to speak, under her ladyship's nose. Her ladyship has took a mortal hatred to me, and as the village, so to speak, belongs to the Castle, if the Castle was to inform the 'Green Man' that my absence was more to be desired than my company, why, out I'd have to go. You can understand that, can you not, miss?"

"Yes—of course."

"And it is the way with all the houses round here," continued Jasper; "they are all under the thumb of the Castle—under the thumb of her ladyship—and I cannot possibly stay near my dear young lady unless——"

"Unless?" questioned Sylvia.

"You was to give me shelter, miss, in your house."

Sylvia backed away, absolute terror creeping over her face.

"Oh! I could not," she said. "You do not know what you are asking. We never have any one at The Priory. I could not possibly do it."

"I'd pay you a pound a week," said Jasper, throwing down her trump card—"a pound a week," she continued—"twenty whole shillings put in the palm of that pretty little hand of yours, paid regularly in advance; and you might have me in a big house like that without anybody knowing. I heard you speak of the gentleman, your father; he need never know. Is there not a room at The Priory which no one goes into, and could not I sleep there? And you'd have money, miss—twenty shillings; and I'd feed you up with chocolate, miss, and bread and butter, and—oh! lots of other things. I have not been on a ranch in Tasmania for nothing. You could hide me at The Priory, and you could keep me acquainted with all that happened to my little Eve, and I'd pay for it, miss, and not a soul on earth would be the wiser."

"Oh, don't!" said Sylvia—"don't!" She covered her face with her hands; she shook all over. "Don't tempt me!" she said. "Go away; do go away! Of course I cannot have you. To deceive him—to shock him—why—— Oh, I dare not—I dare not! It would not be safe. There are times when he is scarcely—yes, scarcely himself; and I must not try him too far. Oh, what have I said?"

"Nothing, my dear—nothing. You are a bit overcome. And now, shall I tell you why?"

"No, don't tell me anything more. Go; do go—do go!"

"I will go," said Jasper, "after I have spoken. You are trembling, and you are cold, and you are frightened—you who ought never to tremble; you who under ordinary circumstances ought to know no fear; you who are beautiful—yes, beautiful! But you tremble because that poor young body of yours needs food and warmth—poor child!—I know."

"Go!" said Sylvia. They were her only words.

"I will go," answered Jasper after a pause; "but I will come again to this same spot to-morrow night, and then you can answer me. Her ladyship cannot turn me out between now and to-morrow night, and I will come then for my answer."

She turned and left Sylvia and went straight back to the village.

Sylvia stood still for a minute after she had gone. She then turned very slowly and re-entered The Priory grounds. A moment later she was in the ugly, ill-furnished house. The hall into which she had admitted herself was perfectly dark. There were no carpets on the floor, and the wind whistled through the ill-fitting casements. The young girl fumbled about until she found a box of matches. She struck one and lit a candle which stood in a brass candlestick on a shelf. She then drearily mounted the uncarpeted stairs. She went to her own room, and opening a box, looked quickly and furtively around her. The box contained some crusts of bread and a few dried figs. Sylvia counted the crusts with fingers that shook. There were five. The crusts were not large, and they were dry.

"I will eat one to-night," she said to herself, "and—yes, two of the figs. I will not eat anything now. I wish Jasper had not tempted me. Twenty shillings, and paid in advance; and father need never know! Lots of room in the house! Yes; I know the one she could have, and I could make it comfortable; and father never goes there—never. It is away beyond the kitchen. I could make it very comfortable. She should have a fire, and we could have our chocolate there. We must never, never have any cooking that smells; we must never have anything fried; we must just have plain things. Oh! I dare not think any more. Mother once said to me, 'If your father ever, ever finds out, Sylvia, that you have deceived him, all, all will be up.' I won't yield to temptation; it would be an awful act of deceit. I cannot—I will not do it! If he will only give me enough I will resist Jasper; but it is hard on a girl to be so frightfully hungry."

She sighed, pulled herself together, walked to the window, and looked up at the watery moon.

"My own mother," she whispered, "can you see me, and are you sorry for me, and are you helping me?"

Then she washed her hands, combed out her pretty, curly black hair, and ran down-stairs. When she got half-way down she burst into a cheerful song, and as she bounded into a room where a man sat

CHAPTER XII.—HUNGER.

crouching over a few embers on the hearth her voice rose to positive gaiety.
"Where have you been all this time?" said the querulous tones.
"Learning a new song for you, dad. Come now; supper is ready."
"Supper!" said the man. He rose, and turned and faced his daughter. He was a very thin man, with hair which must once have been as black as Sylvia's own; his eyes, dark as the young girl's, were sunk so far back in his head that they gleamed like half-burnt-out coals; his cheeks were very hollow, and he gave a pathetic laugh as he turned and faced the girl.
"I have been making a calculation," he said, "and it is my firm impression that we are spending a great deal more than is necessary. There are further reductions which it is quite possible to make. But come, child—come. How fat and well and strong you look, and how hearty your voice is! You are a merry creature, Sylvia, and the joy of my life. Were it not for you I should never hold out. And you are so good at pinching and contriving, dear! But there, I give you too many luxuries don't I, my little one? I spoil you, don't I? What did you say was ready?"
"Supper, father—supper."
"Supper!" said Mr. Leeson. "Why, it seems only a moment ago that we dined."
"It is six hours ago, father."
"Now, Sylvia, if there is one thing I dislike more than another, it is that habit of yours of counting the hours between your meals. It is a distinct trace of greediness and of the lower nature. Ah, my child, when will you live high above your mere bodily desires? Supper, you say? I shall not be able to eat a morsel, but I will go with you, dear, if you like. Come, lead the way, my singing-bird; lead the way."
Sylvia took a candle and lighted it. She then went on in front of her father. They traversed a long and dark passage, and presently she threw open the door of as melancholy and desolate a room as could be found anywhere in England.
The paper on the wall was scarcely perceptible, so worn was it by the long passage of time. The floor was bare of any carpet; there was a deal table at one end of the room; on the table a small white cloth had been placed. A piece of bread was on a wooden platter on this table. There was also a jug of water and a couple of baked potatoes. Sylvia had put these potatoes into the oven before she went out, otherwise there would not have been anything hot at all for the meager repast. The grate was destitute of any fire; and although there were blinds to the windows, there were no curtains. The night was a bitterly cold one, and the girl, insufficiently clothed as well as unfed, shivered as she went into the room.

- 83 -

"What a palatial room this is!" said Mr. Leeson. "I really often think I did wrong to come to this house. I have not the slightest doubt that my neighbors imagine that I am a man of means. It is extremely wrong to encourage that impression, and I trust, Sylvia, that you never by word or action do so. A lady you are, my dear, and a lady you will look whatever you wear; but that beautiful simplicity which rises above mere dress and mere food is what I should like to inculcate in your nature, my sweet child. Ah! potatoes—and hot! My dear Sylvia, was this necessary?"

"There are only two, father—one for you and one for me."

"Well, well! I suppose the young must have their dainties as long as the world lasts," said Mr. Leeson. "Sit down, my dear, and eat. I will stand and watch you."

"Won't you eat anything, father?" said the girl. A curious expression filled her dark eyes. She longed for him to eat, and yet she could not help thinking how supporting and soothing and satisfying both those potatoes would be, and all that hunch of dry bread.

Mr. Leeson paused before replying:

"It would be impossible for you to eat more than one potato, and it would be a sin that the other should be wasted. I may as well have it." He dropped into a chair. "Not that I am the least hungry," he added as he took the largest potato and put it on his plate. "Still, anything is preferable to waste. What a pity it is that no one has discovered a use for the skins, for these as a rule have absolutely to be wasted! When I have gone through some abstruse calculations over which I am at present engaged, I shall turn my attention to the matter. Quantities of nourishing food are doubtless wasted every year by the manner in which potato-skins are thrown away. Ah! and this bread, Sylvia—how long has it been in the house?"

"I got it exactly a week ago," said Sylvia. "It is quite the ordinary kind."

"It is too fresh, my dear. In future we must not eat new bread."

"It is a week old, father."

"Don't take me up in that captious way. I say we must not eat new bread. It was only to-day I came across a book which said that bread when turning slightly—very slightly—moldy satisfies the appetite far more readily than new bread. Then you will see for yourself, Sylvia, that a loaf of such bread may be made to go nearly as far as two loaves of the ordinary kind. You follow me, do you not, singing-bird?"

"Yes, father—yes. But may I eat my potato now while it is hot?"

"How the young do crave for unnecessary indulgences!" said Mr. Leeson; but he broke his own potato in half, and Sylvia seized the opportunity to demolish hers.

Alack and alas! when it was finished, every scrap of it, scarcely any even of the skin being left, she felt almost more hungry than ever. She

CHAPTER XII.–HUNGER.

stretched out her hand for the bread. Mr. Leeson raised his eyes as she did so and gave her a reproachful glance.

"You will be ill," he said. "You will suffer from a bilious attack. Take it—take it if you want it; I am the last to interfere with your natural appetite."

Sylvia ate; she ate although her father's displeased eyes were fixed on her face. She helped herself twice to the stale and untempting loaf. Delicious it tasted. She could even have demolished every scrap of it and still have felt half-wild with hunger. But she was eating it now to give herself courage, for she had made up her mind—speak she must. The meal came to an end. Mr. Leeson had finished his potato; Sylvia had very nearly consumed the bread.

"There will be a very small breakfast to-morrow," he said in a mournful tone; "but you, Sylvia, after your enormous supper, will scarcely require a large one."

Sylvia made no answer. She took her father's hand and walked back with him through the passage. The fire was out now in the sitting-room; Sylvia brought her father's greatcoat.

"Put it on," she said. "I want to sit close to you, and I want to talk."

He smiled at her and wrapped himself obediently in his coat. It was lined with fur, a relic of bygone and happier days. Sylvia turned the big fur collar up round his ears; then she drew herself close to him. She seated herself on his lap.

"Put your arm round me; I am cold," she said.

"Cold, my dear little girl!" he said. "Why, so you are! How very strange! It is doubtless from overeating."

"No, father."

"Why that 'No, father'? What a curious expression is in your voice, Sylvia, my dear! Since your mother's death you have been my one comfort. Heart and soul you have gone with me through the painful life which I am obliged to lead. I know that I am doing the right thing. I am no longer lavishly wasting that which has been entrusted to me, but am, on the contrary, saving for the day of need. My dear girl, you and I have planned our life of retrenchment. How much does our food cost us for a week?"

"Very, very little, father. Too little."

"What do you mean by that?"

"Father, forgive me; I must speak."

"What is wrong?"

Mr. Leeson pushed his daughter away. His eyes, which had been full of kindness, grew sharp and became slightly narrowed; a watchful expression came into his face.

"Beware, Sylvia, how you agitate me; you know the consequences."

"Since mother died," answered the girl, "I have never agitated you; I have always tried to do exactly as you wished."

A VERY NAUGHTY GIRL

"On the whole you have been a good girl; your one and only fault has been your greediness. Last night, it is true, you displeased me very deeply, but on your promise never to transgress so again I have forgiven you."

"Father," said Sylvia in a tremulous tone, "I must speak, and now. You must not be angry, father; but you say that we spend too much on housekeeping. We do not; we spend too little."

"Sylvia!"

"Yes; I am not going to be afraid," continued the girl. "You were displeased with me to-night—yes, I know you were—because I nearly finished the bread. I finished it because—because I was hungry; yes, hungry. And, father, I do not mind how stale the bread is, nor how poor the food, but I must—I must have enough. You do not give me enough. No, you do not. I cannot bear the pain. I cannot bear the neuralgia. I cannot bear the cold of this house. I want warmth, and I want food, and I want clothes that will keep the chill away. That is all—just physical things. I do not ask for fun, nor for companions of my own age, nor for anything of that sort, but I do ask you, father, not to oblige me to lead this miserable, starved life in the future."

Sylvia paused; her courage, after all, was short-lived. The look on her father's face arrested her words. He wore a stony look. His face, which had been fairly animated, had lost almost all expression. The pupils of his eyes were narrowed to a pin's point. Those eyes fixed themselves on the girl's face as though they were gimlets, as though they meant to pierce right into her very soul. Alarm now took the place of beseeching.

"Never mind," she said—"never mind; it was just your wild little rebellious Sylvia. Don't look at me like that. Don't—don't! Oh, I will bear it—I will bear it! Don't look at me like that!"

"Go to your room," was his answer, "at once. Go to your room."

She was a spirited girl, but she crept out of the room as though some one had beaten her.

CHAPTER XIII.—JASPER TO THE RESCUE.

The next evening, at the hour which she had named, Jasper walked down the road which led to The Priory. She walked with a confident step; she had very little doubt that Sylvia would be waiting for her. She was not far wrong in her expectations. A girl, wrapped in a cloak, was standing by a hedge. By the girl stood the mastiff Pilot. Pilot was not too well fed, but he was better fed than Sylvia. It was necessary, according to Mr. Leeson's ideas, that Pilot should be strong enough to guard The Priory against thieves, against unwelcome, prying visitors—against the whole of the human race. But even Pilot could be caught by guile, and Sylvia was determined that he should be friends with Jasper. As Jasper came up the road Sylvia advanced a step or two to meet her.

"Well, dear," said Jasper in a cheerful tone, "am I to come in, and am I to be welcome?"

"You are to come in," said Sylvia. "I have made up my mind. I have been preparing your room all day. If he finds it out I dare not think what will happen. But come—do come; I am ready and waiting for you."

"I thought you would be. I can fetch the rest of my things to-morrow. Can we slip into my room now?"

"We can. Come at once.—Pilot, remember that this lady is our friend.—One moment, please, Jasper; I must be quite certain that Pilot does not do you an injury.—Pilot, give your right paw to this lady."

Pilot looked anxiously from Jasper to Sylvia; then, with a deliberate movement, and a great expression of condescension on his face, he did extend his right paw. Jasper took it.

"Kiss him now just between his eyes," said Sylvia.

"Good gracious, child! I never kissed a dog in my life."

"Kiss him as you value your future safety. You surely do not want to be a prisoner at The Priory!"

"Heaven forbid!" said Jasper. "What I want to do, and what I mean to do, is to parade before her ladyship just where her ladyship cannot touch me. She could turn me out of every house in the place, but not from here. I do not want to keep it any secret from her ladyship that I am staying with you, Miss Sylvia."

"We can talk of that afterwards," said Sylvia. "Come into the house now."

The two turned, the dog accompanying them. They passed through the heavy iron gates and walked softly up the avenue.

"What a close, dismal sort of place!" said Jasper.

"Please—please do not speak so loud; father may overhear us."

"Then mum's the word," said the woman.

A VERY NAUGHTY GIRL

"Step on the grass here, please."

Jasper did exactly as Sylvia directed her, and the result was that soon the two found themselves in as empty a kitchen as Jasper had ever beheld in the whole course of her life.

"Sakes, child!" she cried, "is this where you cook your meals?"

"The kitchen does quite well enough for our requirements," said Sylvia in a low tone.

"And where are you going to put me?"

"In this room. I think in the happy days when the house was full this room must have been used as the servants' hall. See, there is a nice fireplace, with a good fire in it. I have drawn down the blinds, and I have put thick curtains—the only thick curtains we possess—across the windows. There are shutters too. If my father does walk abroad he cannot see any light through this window. But I am sorry to say you can have a fire only at night, for he would be very angry if he saw the smoke ascending in the daytime."

"Hard lines! But I suppose, as I made the offer, I must abide by it," said Jasper. "The room looks bare but well enough. It is clean, I suppose?"

"It is about as clean as I can make it," said Sylvia, with a dreary sigh.

"As clean as you can make it? Have you not a servant, my dear?"

"Oh no; we do not keep a servant."

"Then I expect my work is cut out for me," said Jasper, who was thoroughly good-natured, and had taken an immense fancy to Sylvia.

"Please," said the girl earnestly, "you must not attempt to make the place look the least bit better; if you do, father will find out, and then—"

"Find out!" said Jasper. "If I were you, you poor little thing, I would let him. But there! I am in, and possession is everything. I have brought my supper with me, and I thought maybe you would not mind sharing it. I have it in this basket. This basket contains what I require for the night and our supper as well. I pay you twenty shillings a week, and buy my own coals, so I suppose at night at least I may have a big fire."

Here Jasper went to a large, old-fashioned wooden hod, and taking big lumps of coal, put them on the fire. It blazed right merrily, and the heat filled the room. Sylvia stole close to it and stretched out her thin, white hands for the warmth.

"How delicious!" she said.

"You poor girl! Can you spend the rest of the evening with me?"

"I must go to father. But, do you know, he has prohibited anything but bread for supper."

"What!"

"He does not want it himself, and he says that I can do with bread. Oh, I could if there were enough bread!"

CHAPTER XIII.—JASPER TO THE RESCUE.

"You poor, poor child! Why, it was Providence which sent me all the way from Tasmania to make you comfortable and to save the bit of life in your body."

"Oh, I cannot—I cannot!" said Sylvia. Her composure gave way; she sank into a chair and burst into tears.

"You cannot what, you poor child?"

"Take everything from you. I—I am a lady. In reality we are rich—yes, quite rich—only father has a craze, and he won't spend money. He hoards instead of spending. It began in mother's lifetime, and he has got worse and worse and worse. They say it is in the family, and his father had it, and his father before him. When father was young he was extravagant, and people thought that he would never inherit the craze of a miser; but it has grown with his middle life, and if mother were alive now she would not know him."

"And you are the sufferer, you poor lamb!"

"Yes; I get very hungry at times."

"But, my dear, with twenty shillings a week you need not be hungry."

"Oh no. I cannot realize it. But I have to be careful; father must not see any difference."

"We will have our meals here," said Jasper.

"But we must not light a fire by day," said the girl.

"Never mind; I can manage. Are there not such things as spirit-lamps? Oh yes, I am a born cook. Now then, go away, my dear; have your meal of bread with your father, say good-night to him, and then slip back to me."

Sylvia ran off almost joyfully. In about an hour she returned. During that time Jasper had contrived to make a considerable change in the room. The warmth of the fire filled every corner now the thick curtains at the window looked almost cheerful; the heavy door tightly shut allowed no cold air to penetrate. On the little table she had spread a white cloth, and now that table was graced by a great jug of steaming chocolate, a loaf of crisp white bread, and a little pat of butter; and besides these things there were a small tongue and a tiny pot of jam.

"Things look better, don't they?" said Jasper. "And now, my dearie, you shall not only eat in this room, but you shall sleep in that warm bed in which I have just put my own favorite hot-water bag."

"But you—you?" said Sylvia.

"I either lie down by your side or I stay in the chair by the fire. I am going to warm you up and pet you, for you need it, you poor, brave little girl!"

CHAPTER XIV.—CHANGE OF PLANS.

A whole month had gone by since Jasper had left Evelyn, and Evelyn after a fashion had grown accustomed to her absence. Considerable changes had taken place in the little girl during that time. She was no longer dressed in an OUTRÉ style. She wore her hair as any other very young girl of her age would. She had ceased to consider herself grown-up; and although she knew deep down in her heart that she was the heiress—that by and by all the fine property would belong to her—and although she still gloried in the fact, either fear, or perhaps the dawnings of a better nature prevented her talking so much about it as she had done during the early days of her stay at Castle Wynford. The guests had all departed, and schoolroom life held sway over both the girls. Miss Sinclair was the very soul of order; she insisted on meals being served in the schoolroom to the minute, and schoolroom work being pursued with regularity and method. There were so many hours for work and so many hours for amusement. There were times when the girls might be present with the Squire and Lady Frances, and times when they only enjoyed the society of Miss Sinclair. There were masters for several accomplishments, and the girls had horses to ride, and a pony-carriage was placed at their disposal, and the hours were so full of occupation that they went by on wings. Evelyn looked fifty times better and happier than she had done when she first arrived at Castle Wynford, and even Lady Frances was forced to own that the child was turning out better than she expected. How long this comparatively happy state of things might have lasted it is hard to say, but it was brought to an abrupt conclusion by an event which occurred just then. This was no less than the departure of kind Miss Sinclair. Her mother had died quite suddenly; her father needed her at home. She could not even stay for the customary period after giving notice of her intention to leave. Lady Frances, under the circumstances, did not press her; and now the subject of how the two girls were best to be educated was ceaselessly discussed. Lady Frances was a born educationist; she had the greatest love for subjects dealing with the education of the young. She had her own theories with regard to this important matter, and when Miss Sinclair went away she was for a time puzzled how to act. To get another governess was, of course, the only thing to be done; but for a time she wavered much as to the advisability of sending Evelyn to school.

"I really think she ought to go," said Lady Frances to the Squire. "Even now she does not half know her place. She has improved, I grant you, but the thorough discipline of school would do her good."

"You have never sent Audrey to school," was the Squire's answer.

"I have not, certainly; but Audrey is so different."

CHAPTER XIV.—CHANGE OF PLANS.

"I should not like anything to be done in Evelyn's case which has not been done in Audrey's," was the Squire's reply.

"But surely you cannot compare the girls!"

"I do not intend to compare them. They are absolutely different. Audrey is all that the heart of the proudest father could desire, and Evelyn is still—"

"A little savage at heart," interrupted Lady Frances.

"Yes; but she is taming, and I think she has some fine points in her—indeed, I am sure of it. She is, for instance, very affectionate."

Lady Frances looked somewhat indignant.

"I am tired of hearing of Evelyn's good qualities. When I perceive them for myself I shall be the first to acknowledge them. But now, my dear Edward, the point to be considered is this: What are we to do at once? It is nearly the middle of the term. To give those two girls holidays would be ruinous. There is an excellent school of a very superior sort kept by the Misses Henderson in that large house just outside the village. What do you say to their both going there until we can look round us and find a suitable governess to take Miss Sinclair's place?"

"If they both go it does not so much matter," said the Squire. "You can arrange it in that way if you like, my dear Frances."

Lady Frances gave a sigh of relief. She was much interested in the Misses Henderson; she herself had helped them to start their school. Accordingly, that very afternoon she ordered the carriage and drove to Chepstow House. The Misses Henderson were expecting her, and received her in state in their drawing-room.

"You know what I have come about?" she said. "Now, the thing is this—can you do it?"

"I am quite certain of one thing," said the elder Miss Henderson—"that there will be no stone left unturned on our parts to make the experiment satisfactory."

"Poor, dear Miss Sinclair—it is too terrible her having to leave!" said Lady Frances. "We shall never get her like again. To find exactly the governess for girls like my daughter and niece is no easy matter."

"As to your dear daughter, she certainly will not be hard to manage," said the younger Miss Henderson.

"You are right, Miss Lucy," said Lady Frances, turning to her and speaking with decision. "I have always endeavored to train Audrey in those nice observances, those moral principles, and that high tone which befits a girl who is a lady and who in the future will occupy a high position."

"But your niece—your niece; she is the real problem," said the elder Miss Henderson.

"Yes," answered Lady Frances, with a sigh. "When she came to me she was little less than a savage. She has improved. I do not like her—I do not pretend for a moment that I do—but I wish to give the poor child every possible advantage, and I am anxious, if possible, that my prejudice shall not weigh with me in any sense in my dealings with her; but she requires very firm treatment."

"She shall have it," said the elder Miss Henderson; and a look of distinct pleasure crossed her face. "I have had refractory girls before now," she said, "and I may add with confidence, Lady Frances, that I have always broken them in. I do not expect to fail in the case of Miss Wynford."

"Firm discipline is essential," replied Lady Frances. "I told Miss Sinclair so, and she agreed with me. I do not exactly know what her method was, nor how she managed, but the child seemed happy, she learnt her lessons correctly, and, in short, she has improved. I trust the improvement will continue under your management."

Here the good lady, after adding a few more words with regard to hours, etc., took her leave. The girls were to go to Chepstow House as day-pupils, and the work of their education at that distinguished school was to begin on the following morning.

Evelyn was rather pleased than otherwise when she heard that she was to be sent to school. She had cried and flung her arms round Miss Sinclair's neck when that lady was taking leave of her. Audrey, on the contrary, had scarcely spoken; her face looked a little whiter than usual, and her eyes a little darker. She took the governess's hand and wrung it, and as she bent forward to kiss her again on the cheek, Miss Sinclair kissed her and whispered something to her. But it was poor Evelyn who cried. The carriage took the governess away, and the girls looked at each other.

"I did not know you could be so stony-hearted," said Evelyn. She took out her handkerchief as she spoke and mopped her eyes. "Oh dear!" she added, "I am quite broken-hearted without her. I am SUCH an affectionate girl."

"We had better prepare for school," said Audrey. "We are to go there to-morrow morning, remember."

"Yes," answered Evelyn, her eyes brightening; "and do you know, although I am terribly sorry to part with dear Miss Sinclair, I am glad about school. Mothery always wished me to go; she said that talents like mine could never find a proper vent except in school-life. I wonder what sort of girls there are at Chepstow House?"

"I don't know anything about it," said Audrey.

"Are you sorry to go, Audrey?"

"Yes—rather. I have never been to school."

"How funny it will be to see you looking shy and awkward! Will you be shy and awkward?"

"I don't think so. I hope not."

"It would be fun to see it, all the same," said Evelyn. "But there, I am going for a race; my legs are quite stiff for want of running. I used to

CHAPTER XIV.—CHANGE OF PLANS.

run such a lot in Tasmania on the ranch! Often and often I ran a whole mile without stopping. Good-by for the present. I suppose I may do what I like to-day."

Evelyn rushed off into the grounds. She was running at full speed through the shrubbery on her way to a big field, which was known as the ten-acre field, on the other side of the turnstile, when she came full tilt against her uncle. He stopped, took her hand, and looked kindly at her.

"Do you know, Uncle Edward," she said, "that I am going to school to-morrow?"

"So I hear, my dear little girl; and I hope you will be happy there."

Evelyn made no reply. Her eyes sparkled. After a time she said slowly: "I am glad; mother wished me to go."

"You love your mother's memory very much, do you not, Eve?"

"Yes," she said; and tears came into her big, strange-looking eyes. "I love her just as much as if she were alive," she continued—"better, I think. Whenever I am sad she seems near to me."

"You would do anything to please her, would you not, Eve?"

"Yes," answered the child.

"Well, I wish to say something to you. You had a great fight when you came here, but I think to a certain extent you have conquered. Our ways were not your ways—everything was strange—and at first, my dear little girl, you rebelled, and were not very happy."

"I was miserable—miserable!"

"But you have done, on the whole, well; and if your mother could come back again she would be pleased. I thought I should like to tell you."

"But, please, Uncle Edward, why would mothery be pleased? She often told me that I was not to submit; that I was to hold my own; that——"

"My dear, she told you those things when she was on earth; but now, in the presence of God, she has learnt many new lessons, and I am sure, could she now speak to you, she would tell you that you did right to submit, and were doing well when you tried to please me, for instance."

"Why you, Uncle Edward?"

"Because I am your father's brother, and because I loved your father better than any one on earth."

"Better than Aunt Frances?" said Evelyn, with a sparkle of pleasure in her eyes.

"In a different, quite a different way. Ay, I loved him well, and I would do my utmost to promote the happiness of his child."

"I love you," said the little girl. "I am glad—I am GLAD that you are my uncle."

A VERY NAUGHTY GIRL

She raised his hand, pressed it to her lips, and the next moment was lost to view.

"Queer, erratic little soul!" thought Squire Wynford to himself. "If only we can train her aright! I often feel that Frank is watching me, and wondering how I am dealing with the child. It seems almost cruel that Frances should dislike her, but I trust in the end all will be well." Meanwhile Evelyn, having tired herself racing round the ten-acre field, suddenly conceived a daring idea. She had known long ere this that her beloved Jasper was not in reality out of reach. More than once the maid and the little girl had met. These meetings were by no means conducive to Evelyn's best interests, but they added a great spice of excitement to her life; and the thought of seeing her now, and telling her of the change which was about to take place with regard to her education, was too great a temptation to be resisted. Evelyn accordingly, skirting the high-roads and making many detours through fields and lanes, presently arrived close to The Priory. She had never ventured yet into The Priory; she had as a rule sent a message to Jasper, and Jasper had waited for her outside. She knew now that she must be quick or she would be late for lunch. She did not want on this day of all days to seriously displease Lady Frances. She went, therefore, boldly up to the gate, pushed it open, and entered. Here she was immediately confronted by Pilot. Pilot walked down the path, uttered one or two deep bays, growled audibly, and showed his strong white teeth. Whatever Evelyn's faults were, she was no coward. An angry dog standing in her path was not going to deter her. But she was afraid of something else. Jasper had told her how insecure her tenure at The Priory was—how it all absolutely depended on Mr. Leeson never finding out that she was there. Evelyn therefore did not want to bring Mr. Leeson to her rescue. Were there no means by which she could induce Pilot to let her pass? She went boldly up to the dog. The dog growled more fiercely, and put himself in an attitude which the little girl knew well meant that he was going to spring. She did not want him to bound upon her; she knew he was much stronger than herself.

"Good, good dog—good, good," she said.

But Pilot, exasperated beyond measure, began to bark savagely.

Who was this small girl who dared to defy him? His custom was to stand as he stood to-day and terrify every one off the premises. But this small person did not mean to go. He therefore really lost his temper, and became decidedly dangerous.

Mr. Leeson, in his study, was busily engaged over some of that abstruse work which occupied all his time. He was annoyed at Pilot's barking, and went to the window to ascertain the cause. He saw a stumpy, stout-looking little girl standing on the path, and Pilot barring her way. He opened the window and called out:

CHAPTER XIV.—CHANGE OF PLANS.

"Go away, child; go away. We don't have visitors here. Go away immediately, and shut the gate firmly after you."

"But, if you please," said Evelyn, "I cannot go away. I want to see Sylvia."

"You cannot see her. Go away."

"No, I won't," said Evelyn, her courage coming now boldly to her aid. "I have come here on business, and I must see Sylvia. You dare not let your horrid dog spring on me; and I am going to stand just where I am till Sylvia comes."

These very independent words astonished Mr. Leeson so much that he absolutely went out of the house and came down the avenue to meet Evelyn.

"Who are you, child?" he said, as the bold light eyes were fixed on his face.

"I am Evelyn Wynford, the heiress of Wynford Castle."

A twinkle of mirth came into Mr. Leeson's eyes.

"And so you want Sylvia, heiress of Wynford Castle?"

"Yes; I want to speak to her."

"She is not in at present. She is never in at this hour. Sylvia likes an open-air life, and I am glad to encourage her in her taste. May I show you to the gate?"

"Thank you," replied Evelyn, who felt considerably crestfallen.

Mr. Leeson, with his very best manners, accompanied the little girl to the high iron gates. These he opened, bowed to her as she passed through them, and then shut them in her face, drawing a big bar inside as he did so.

"Good Pilot—excellent, brave, admirable dog!" Evelyn heard him say; and she ground her small white teeth in anger.

A moment or two later, to her infinite delight, she saw Jasper coming up the road to meet her. In an instant the child and maid were in each other's arms. Evelyn was petting Jasper, and kissing her over and over again on her dark cheek.

"Oh Jasper," said the little girl, "I got such a fright! I came here to see you, and I was met by that horrible dog; and then a dreadful-looking old man came out and told me I was to go right away, and he petted the dog for trying to attack me. I was not frightened, of course—it is not likely that mothery's little girl would be easily afraid—but, all the same, it was not pleasant. Why do you live in such a horrid, horrid place, Jasper darling?"

"Why do I live there?" answered Jasper. "Now, look at me—look me full in the face. I live in that house because Providence wills it, because—because—— Oh, I need not waste time telling you the reason. I live there because I am near to you, and for another reason; and I hope to goodness that you have not gone and made mischief, for if

A VERY NAUGHTY GIRL

that dreadful old man, as you call him, finds out for a single moment that I am there, good-by to poor Miss Sylvia's chance of life."

"You are quite silly about Sylvia," said Evelyn in a jealous tone.

"She is a very fine, brave young lady," was Jasper's answer.

"I wish you would not talk of her like that; you make me feel quite cross."

"You always were a jealous little piece," said Jasper, giving her former charge a look of admiration; "but you need not be, Eve, for no one—no one shall come inside my little white Eve. But there, now; do tell me. You did not say anything about me to Mr. Leeson?"

"No, I did not," said Evelyn. "I only told him I had come to see Sylvia. Was it not good of me, Jasper? Was it not clever and smart?"

"It was like you, pet," said Jasper. "You always were the canniest little thing—always, always."

Evelyn was delighted at these words of praise.

"But how did you get here, my pet? Does her ladyship know you are out?"

"No, her ladyship does not," replied Evelyn, with a laugh. "I should be very sorry to let her know, either. I came here all by myself because I wanted to see you, Jasper. I have got news for you."

"Indeed, pet; and what is that?"

"Cannot you guess?"

"Oh, how can I? Perhaps that you have got courage and are sleeping by yourself. You cannot stand that horrid old Read; you would rather be alone than have her near you."

"Read has not slept in my room for over three weeks," said Evelyn proudly. "I am not at all nervous now. It was Miss Sinclair who told me how silly I was to want any one to sleep close to me."

"But you would like your old Jasper again?"

"Yes—oh yes; you are different."

"Well, and what is the change, dear?"

"It is this: poor Miss Sinclair—dear, nice Miss Sinclair—has been obliged to leave."

"Oh, well, I am not sorry for that," said Jasper. "I was getting a bit jealous of her. You seemed to be getting on so well with her."

"So I was. I quite loved her; she made my lessons so interesting. But what do you think, Jasper? Although I am very sorry she has gone, I am glad about the other thing. Audrey and I are going to school, as daily boarders, just outside the village; Chepstow House it is called. We are going to-morrow morning. Mothery would like that; she always did want me to go to school. I am glad. Are you not glad too, Jasper?"

"That depends," said Jasper in an oracular voice.

"What does it all depend on? Why do you speak in that funny way?"

"It depends on you, my dear. I have heard a great deal about schools. Some are nice and some are not. In some they give you a lot of

CHAPTER XIV.—CHANGE OF PLANS.

freedom, and you are petted and fussed over; in others they discipline you. When you are disciplined you don't like it. If I were you—"
"Yes—what?"
"I would stay there if I liked it, and if I did not I would not stay. I would not have my spirit broke. They often break your spirit at school. I would not put up with that if I were you."
"I am sure they won't break my spirit," said Evelyn in a tone of alarm. "Why do you speak so dismally, Jasper? Do you know, I am almost sorry I told you. I was so happy at the thought of going, and now you have made me miserable. No, there is not the slightest fear that they will break my spirit."
"Then that is all right, dear. Don't forget that you are the heiress."
"I could let them know at school, could I not?"
"I would if I were you," said the injudicious woman. "I would tell the girls if I were you."
"Oh yes; so I can. I wonder if they will be nice girls at Chepstow House?"
"You let them feel your power, and don't knock under to any of them," said Jasper. "And now, my dear, I must really send you home. There, I'll walk a bit of the way back with you. You are looking very bonny, my little white Eve; you have got quite a nice color in your cheeks. I am glad you are well; and I am glad, too, that the governess has gone, for I don't want her to get the better of me. Remember what I said about school."
"That I will, Jasper; I'll be sure to remember."
"It would please her ladyship if you got on well there," continued Jasper.
"I don't want to please Aunt Frances."
"Of course you don't. Nasty, horrid thing! I shall never forgive her for turning me off. Now then, dear, you had best run home. I don't want her to see us talking together. Good-by, pet; good-by."

CHAPTER XV.—SCHOOL.

The girls at Chepstow House were quite excited at the advent of Audrey and Evelyn. They were nice girls, nearly all of them; they were ladies, too, of a good class; but they had not been at Chepstow House long without coming under the influence of what dominated the entire place—that big house on the hill, with its castellated roof and its tower, its moat too, and its big, big gardens, its spacious park, and all its surroundings. It was a place to talk to their friends at home about, and to think of and wonder over when at school. The girls at Chepstow House had often looked with envy at Audrey as she rode by on her pretty Arab pony. They talked of her to each other; they criticised her appearance; they praised her actions. She was a sort of princess to them. Then there appeared on the scene another little princess—a strange child, without style, without manners, without any personal attractions; and this child, it was whispered, was the real heiress. By and by pretty Audrey would cease to live at Castle Wynford, and the little girl with the extraordinary face would be monarch of all she surveyed. The girls commented over this story amongst each other, as girls will; and when the younger Miss Henderson—Miss Lucy, as they called her—told them that Audrey Wynford and her cousin Evelyn were coming as schoolgirls to Chepstow House their excitement knew no bounds.

"They are coming here," said Miss Lucy, "and I trust that all you girls who belong to the house will treat them as they ought to be treated."

"And how is that, Miss Lucy?" said Brenda Fox, the tallest and most important girl in the school.

"You must treat them as ladies, but at the same time as absolutely your equals in every respect," said Miss Lucy. "They are coming to school partly to find their level; we must be kind to them, but there is to be no difference made between them and the rest of you. Now, Brenda, go with the other girls into the Blue Parlor and attend to your preparation for Signor Forre."

Brenda and her companions went away, and during the rest of the day, whenever they had a spare moment, the girls talked over Audrey and Evelyn.

The next morning the cousins arrived. They came in Audrey's pretty governess-cart, and Audrey drove the fat pony herself. A groom took it back to the Castle, with orders to come for his young ladies at six in the evening, for Lady Frances had arranged that the girls were to have both early dinner and tea at school.

They both entered the house, and even Audrey just for a moment felt slightly nervous. The elder Miss Henderson took them into her private sitting-room, asked them a few questions, and then, desiring them to follow her, went down a long passage which led into the large

CHAPTER XV.—SCHOOL.

schoolroom. Here the girls, about forty in number, were all assembled. Miss Henderson introduced the new pupils with a few brief words. She then went up to Miss Lucy and asked her, as soon as prayers were over, to question both Audrey and Evelyn with regard to their attainments, and to put them into suitable classes.

The Misses Wynford sat side by side during prayers, and immediately afterwards were taken into Miss Lucy's private sitting-room. Here a very vigorous examination ensued, with the result that Audrey was promoted to take her place with the head girls, and Evelyn was conducted to the Fourth Form. Her companions received her with smiling eyes and beaming looks. She felt rather cross, however; and was even more so when the English teacher, Miss Thompson, set her some work to do. Evelyn was extremely backward with regard to her general education. But Miss Sinclair had such marvelous tact, that, while she instructed the little girl and gave her lessons which were calculated to bring out her best abilities, she never let her feel her real ignorance. At school, however, all this state of things was reversed. Audrey, calm and dignified, took a high position in the school; and Evelyn was simply, in her own opinion, nowhere. A sulky expression clouded her face. She thought of Jasper's words, and determined that no one should break her spirit.

"You will read over the reign of Edward I., and I will question you about it when morning school is over," said Miss Thompson in a pleasant tone. "After recreation I will give you your lessons to prepare for to-morrow. Now, please attend to your book. You will be able to take your proper place in class to-morrow."

Miss Thompson as she spoke handed a History of England to the little girl. The History was dry, and the reign, in Evelyn's opinion, not worth reading. She glanced at it, then turned the book, open as it was, upside down on her desk, rested her elbows on it, and looked calmly around her.

"Take up your book, Miss Wynford, and read it," said Miss Thompson.

Evelyn smiled quietly.

"I know all about the reign," she said. "I need not read the history any more."

The other girls smiled. Miss Thompson thought it best to take no notice. The work of the school proceeded; and at last, when recess came, the English teacher called the little girl to her.

"Now I must question you," she said. "You say you know the reign of Edward I. Let me hear what you do know. Stand in front of me, please; put your hands behind your back. So."

"I prefer to keep my hands where they are," said Evelyn.

"Do what I say. Stand upright. Now then!"

A VERY NAUGHTY GIRL

Miss Thompson began catechizing. Evelyn's crass ignorance instantly appeared. She knew nothing whatever of that special period of English history; indeed, at that time her knowledge of any history was practically NIL.

"I am sorry you told me what was not true with regard to the reign of Edward I.," said the governess. "In this school we are very strict and particular. I will say nothing further on the matter to-day; but you will stay here and read over the history during recess."

"What!" cried Evelyn, her face turning white. "Am I not to have my recreation?"

"Recess only lasts for twenty minutes; you will have to do without your amusement in the playground this morning. To-morrow I hope you will have got through your lessons well and be privileged to enjoy your pastime with the other pupils."

"Do you know who I am?" began Evelyn.

"Yes—perfectly. You are little Evelyn Wynford. Now be a good girl, Evelyn, and attend to your work."

Miss Thompson left the room. Evelyn found herself alone. A wild fury consumed her. She jumped up.

"Does she think for a single moment that I am going to obey her?" thought the naughty child. "Oh, if only Jasper were here! Oh Jasper! you were right; they are trying to break me in, but they won't succeed."

A book which the governess had laid upon a table near attracted the little girl's attention. It was not an ordinary lesson-book, but a very beautiful copy of Ruskin's SESAME AND LILIES. Evelyn took up the book, opened it, and read the following words on the title-page:

"To dear Agnes, from her affectionate brother Walter. Christmas Day, 1896."

Quick as thought the angry child tore out the title-page and two or three other pages at the beginning, scattered them into little bits, and then, going up to the fire which burned at one end of the long room, flung the scattered fragments into the blaze. She had no sooner done so than a curious sense of dismay stole over her. She shut up the book hastily, and being really alarmed, began to look over her English history. Miss Thompson came back just before recess was over, picked up Evelyn's book, asked her one or two questions, and gave her an approving nod.

"That is better," she said. "You have done as much as I could expect in the time. Now then, come here, please. These are your English lessons for to-morrow."

Evelyn walked quite meekly across the room. Miss Thompson set her several lessons in the ordinary English subjects.

"And now," she said, "you are to go to mademoiselle. She is waiting to find out what French you know, and to give you your lesson for to-morrow."

CHAPTER XV.—SCHOOL.

The rest of the school hours passed quickly. Evelyn was given what she considered a disgraceful amount of work to do; but a dull fear sat at her heart, and she felt a sense of regret at having torn the pages out of the volume of Ruskin. Immediately after morning school the girls went for a short walk, then dinner was announced, and after dinner there was a brief period of freedom. Evelyn, Audrey, and the rest all found themselves walking in the grounds. Brenda Fox immediately went up to Audrey, and introduced her to a few of the nicest girls in the head form, and they all began to pace slowly up and down. Evelyn stood just for an instant forlorn; then she dashed into the midst of a circle of little girls who were playing noisily together.

"Stop!" she said. "Look at me, all of you."

The children stopped playing, and looked in wonder at Evelyn.

"I am Evelyn Wynford. Who is going to be my friend? I shall only take up with the one I really like. I am not afraid of any of you. I have come to school to find out if I like it; if I don't like it I shall not stay. You had best, all of you, know what sort I am. It was very mean and horrid to put me into the Fourth Form with a number of ignorant little babies; but as I am there, I suppose I shall have to stay for a week or so."

"You were put into the Fourth Form," said little Sophie Jenner, "because, I suppose, you did not know enough to be put into the Fifth Form."

"You are a cheeky little thing," said Evelyn, "and I am not going to trouble myself to reply to you.—Well, now, who is going to be my friend? I can tell you all numbers of stories; I have heaps of pocket-money, and I can bring chocolate-creams and ginger-pop and all sorts of good things to the school."

These last remarks were decidedly calculated to ensure Evelyn's popularity. Two or three of the girls ran up to her, and she was soon marching up and down the playground relating some of her grievances, and informing them, one and all, of the high position which lay before her.

"You are all very much impressed with Audrey, I can see, but she is really nobody," cried Eve. "By and by Wynford Castle will be mine, and won't you like to say you knew me when I am mistress of the Castle—won't you just! I do not at all know that I shall stay long at school, but you had better make it pleasant for me."

Some of the girls were much impressed, and a few of them swore eternal fealty to Evelyn. One or two began to flatter her, and on the whole the little girl considered that she had a fairly good time during play-hour. When she got back to her work she was relieved to see that Ruskin's SESAME AND LILIES no longer lay in its place on the small table where Miss Thompson had left it.

"She will not open it, perhaps, for years," thought Evelyn. "I need not worry any more about that. And if she did like the book I am glad I tore it. Horrid, horrid thing!"

Lessons went on, and by and by Audrey and Evelyn's first day at school came to an end. The governess-cart came to fetch them, and they drove off under the admiring gaze of several of their fellow-pupils.

"Well, Evelyn, and how did you like school?" said Audrey when the two were alone together.

"You could not expect me to like it very much," replied Evelyn. "I was put into such a horrid low class. I am angry with Miss Thompson."

"Miss Thompson! That nice, intelligent girl?"

"Not much of a girl about her!" said Evelyn. "Why, she is quite old."

"Do you think so? She struck me as young, pretty, and very nice."

"It is all very well for you, Audrey; you are so tame. I really believe you never think a bad thought of anybody."

"I try not to, of course," replied Audrey. "Do you imagine it is a fine trait in one's character to think bad thoughts of people?"

"Mothery always said that if you did not dislike people, you were made of cotton-wool," replied Evelyn.

"Then you really do dislike people?"

"Oh! some I dislike awfully. Now, there is one at the Castle—but there! I won't say any more about HER; and there is one at school whom I hate. It is that horrid Thompson woman. And she had the cheek to call me Evelyn."

"Of course she calls you Evelyn; you are her pupil."

"Well, I think it is awful cheek, all the same. I hate her, and—oh, Audrey, such fun—such fun! I have revenged myself on her; I really have."

"Oh Evelyn! don't get into mischief, I beseech of you."

"I sha'n't say any more, but I do believe that I have revenged myself. Oh, such fun—such fun!"

Evelyn laughed several times during the rest of her drive home, and arrived at the Castle in high spirits. The girls were to dine with Lady Frances and the Squire that evening, as they happened to be alone; and the Squire was quite interested in the account which Evelyn gave him of her class.

"The only reason why I could read the dull, dull life of Edward I.," she said, "is because Edward is your name, Uncle Ned, and because I love you so much."

"On the whole, my dear," said the Squire later on to his wife, "the school experiment seems to work well. Little Evelyn was in high spirits to-night."

"You think of no one but Evelyn!" said Lady Frances. "What about Audrey?"

CHAPTER XV.–SCHOOL.

"I am not afraid about Audrey; you have trained her, and she is by nature most amiable," said the Squire.

"I am glad you paid me a compliment, my dear," answered his wife. "Audrey certainly does credit to my training. But I trust Miss Henderson will break that naughty girl in; she certainly needs it."

The next morning the girls went back to school; and Evelyn, who had quite forgotten what she had done to the book, and who had provided herself secretly with a great packet of delicious sweetmeats which she intended to distribute amongst her favorites, was still in high spirits. School began, the girls went to their different classes, Evelyn stumbled badly through her lessons, and at last the hour of recess came. The girls were all preparing to leave the schoolroom when Miss Thompson asked them to wait a moment.

"Something most painful has occurred," she said, "and I trust whichever girl has done the mischief will at once confess it."

Evelyn's face did not change color. A curious, numb feeling got round her heart; then an obstinate spirit took possession of her.

"Not for worlds will I tell," she thought. "Of course Miss Thompson is alluding to the book."

Yes, Miss Thompson was. She held the beautifully bound copy of Ruskin in her hand, opened it where the title-page used to be, and with tears in her eyes looked at the girls.

"Some one has torn four pages out of the beginning of this book," she said. "I left it here by mistake yesterday. I took it up this morning to continue a lecture which I was preparing for the afternoon, and found what terrible mischief had been done. I trust whoever has done this will at least have the honor to confess her wrong-doing."

Silence and expressions of intense dismay were seen on all the young faces.

"If it were my own book I should not mind so much," said the governess; "but it happens to belong to Miss Henderson, and was given to her by her favorite brother, who died two months afterwards. I had some difficulty in getting her to allow me to use it for this lecture. Nothing can replace to her the loss of the inscription written in her brother's own hand. The only possible chance for the guilty person is to tell all at once. But, oh! who could have been so cruel?"

Still the girls were silent, although tears had risen to many of their eyes. Miss Thompson could hear the words "Oh, what a shame!" coming from more than one pair of lips.

She waited for an instant, and then said:

"I must put a question to each and all of you. I had hoped the guilty person would confess; but as it is, I am obliged to ask who has done this mischief."

She then began to question one girl after another in the class. There were twelve in all in this special class, and each as her turn came replied in the negative. Certainly she had not done the mischief; certainly she had not torn the book. Evelyn's turn came last. She replied quietly:

"I have not done it. I have not seen the book, and I have not torn out the inscription."

No one had any reason to doubt her words; and Miss Thompson, looking very sorrowful, paused for a minute and then said:

"I have asked each of you, and you have all denied it. I must now question every one else in the school. When I have done all that I can I shall have to submit the matter to Miss Henderson, but I did not want to grieve her with the news of this terrible loss until I could at least assure her that the girl who had done the mischief had repented."

Still there was silence, and Miss Thompson left the schoolroom. The moment she did so the buzz of eager voices began, and during the recess that followed nothing was talked of in the Fourth Form but the loss which poor Miss Henderson had sustained.

"Poor dear!" said Sophie Jenner; "and she did love her brother so much! His name was Walter; he was very handsome. He came once to the school when first it was started. My sister Rose was here then, and she said how kind he was, and how he asked for a holiday for the girls; and Miss Henderson and Miss Lucy were quite wrapped up in him. Oh, who could have been so cruel?"

"I never heard of such a fuss about a trifle before," here came from Evelyn's lips. "Why, it is only a book when all is said and done."

"Don't you understand?" said Sophie, looking at her in some astonishment. "It is not a common book; it is one given to Miss Henderson by the brother she loved. He is dead now; he can never give her any other book. That was the very last present he ever made her."

"Have some lollipops, and try to think of cheerful things," said Evelyn; but Sophie turned almost petulantly away.

"Do you know," Sophie said to her special friend, Cherry Wynne, "I don't think I like Evelyn. How funnily she spoke! I wonder, Cherry, if she had anything to do with the book?"

"Of course not," answered Cherry. "She would not have dared to utter such a lie. Poor Miss Henderson! How sorry I am for her!"

CHAPTER XVI.–SYLVIA'S DRIVE.

"I have something very delightful to tell you, Sylvia," said her father. He was standing in his cold and desolate sitting-room. The fire was burning low in the grate. Sylvia shivered slightly, and bending down, took up a pair of tongs to put some more coals on the expiring fire.

"No, no, my dear–don't," said her father. "There is nothing more disagreeable than a person who always needs coddling. The night is quite hot for the time of year. Do you know, Sylvia, that I made during the last week a distinct saving. I allowed you, as I always do, ten shillings for the household expenses. You managed capitally on eight shillings. We really lived like fighting-cocks; and what is nicest of all, my dear daughter, you look the better in consequence."

Sylvia did not speak.

"I notice, too," continued Mr. Leeson, a still more satisfied smile playing round his lips, "that you eat less than you did before. Last night I was pleased to observe how truly abstemious you were at supper."

"Father," said Sylvia suddenly, "you eat less and less; how can you keep up your strength at this rate? Cannot you see, clever man that you are, that you need food and warmth to keep you alive?"

"It depends absolutely," replied Mr. Leeson, "on how we accustom ourselves to certain habits. Habits, my dear daughter, are the chains which link us to life, and we forge them ourselves. With good habits we lead good lives. With pernicious habits we sink: the chains of those habits are too thick, too rusty, too heavy; we cannot soar. I am glad to see that you, my dear little girl, are no longer the victim of habits of greediness and desire for unnecessary luxuries."

"Well, father, dinner is ready now. Won't you come and eat it?"

"Always harping on food," said Mr. Leeson. "It is really sad."

"You must come and eat while the things are hot," answered Sylvia.

Mr. Leeson followed his daughter. He was, notwithstanding all his words to the contrary, slightly hungry that morning; the intense cold–although he spoke of the heat–made him so. He sat down, therefore, and removed the cover from a dish on which reposed a tiny chop.

"Ah," he said, "how tempting it looks! We will divide it, dear. I will take the bone; far be it from me to wish to starve you, my sweet child."

He took up his knife to cut the chop. As he did so Sylvia's face turned white.

"No, thank you," she said. "It really so happens that I don't want it. Please eat it all. And see," she continued, with a little pride, lifting the cover of a dish which stood in front of her own plate; "I have been teaching myself to cook; you cannot blame me for making the best of

A VERY NAUGHTY GIRL

my materials. How nice these fried potatoes look! Have some, won't you, father?"

"You must have used something to fry them in," said Mr. Leeson, an angry frown on his face. "Well, well," he added, mollified by the delicious smell, which could not but gratify his hungry feelings—"all right; I will take a few."

Sylvia piled his plate. She played with a few potatoes herself, and Mr. Leeson ate in satisfied silence.

"Really they are nice," he said. "I have enjoyed my dinner. I do not know when I made such a luxurious meal. I shall not need any supper to-night."

"But I shall," said Sylvia stoutly. "There will be supper at nine o'clock as usual, and I hope you will be present, father."

"Well, my dear, have something very plain. I am absolutely satisfied for twenty-four hours. And you, darling—did you make a good meal?"

"Yes, thank you, father."

"There were a great many potatoes cooked. I see they are all finished."

"Yes, father."

"I am now going back to my sitting-room. I shall be engaged for some hours. What are you going to do, Sylvia?"

"I shall go out presently for a walk."

"Is it not rather dangerous for you to wander about in such deep snow?"

"Oh, I like it, father; I enjoy it. I could not possibly stay at home."

"Very well, my dear child. You are a good girl. But, Sylvia dear, it strikes me that we had better not have any more frying done; it must consume a great quantity of fuel. Now, that chop might have been boiled in a small saucepan, and it really would have been quite as nutritious. And, my dear, there would have been the broth—the liquor, I mean—that it had been boiled in; it would have made an excellent soup with rice in it. I have been lately compiling some recipes for living what is called the unluxurious life. When I have completed my little recipes I will hand them down to posterity. I shall publish them. I quite imagine that they will have a large sale, and may bring me in some trifling returns—eh, Sylvia?"

Sylvia made no answer.

"My dear," said her father suddenly, "I have noticed of late that you are a little extravagant in the amount of coals you use. It is your only extravagance, my dear child, so I will not say much about it."

"But, father, I don't understand. What do you mean?"

"There is smoke—SMOKE issuing from the kitchen chimney at times when there ought to be none," said Mr. Leeson in a severe voice. "But there, dear, I won't keep you now. I expect to have a busy afternoon. I am feeling so nicely after our simple little lunch, my dear daughter."

Mr. Leeson touched Sylvia's smooth cheek with his lips, went into the sitting-room, and shut the door.

CHAPTER XVI.—SYLVIA'S DRIVE.

"The fire must be quite out by now," she said to herself. "Poor, poor father! Oh dear! oh dear! if he discovers that Jasper is here I shall be done for. Now that I know the difference which Jasper's presence makes, I really could not live without her."

She listened for a moment, noticed that all was still in the big sitting-room (as likely as not her father had dropped asleep), and then, turning to her left, went quickly away in the direction of the kitchen. When she entered the kitchen she locked the door. There was a clear and almost smokeless fire in the range, and drawn up close to it was a table covered with a white cloth; on the table were preparations for a meal.

"Well, Sylvia," said Jasper, "and how did he enjoy his chop? How much of it did he give to you, my dear?"

"Oh, none at all, Jasper. I pretended I was not hungry. It was such a pleasure to see him eat it!"

"And what about the fried potatoes, love?"

"He ate them too with such an appetite—I just took a few to satisfy him. Do you know, Jasper, he says that he thinks an abstemious life agrees with me. He says that I am looking very well, and that he is quite sure no one needs big fires and plenty of food in cold weather— it is simply and entirely a matter of habit."

"Oh! don't talk to me of him any more," said Jasper. "He is the sort of man to give me the dismals. I cannot tell you how often I dream of him at night. You are a great deal too good to him, Sylvia, and that is the truth. But here—here is our dinner, you poor frozen lamb. Eat now and satisfy yourself."

Sylvia sat down and ate with considerable appetite the good and nourishing food which Jasper had provided. As she did so her bright, clear, dark eyes grew brighter than ever, and her young cheeks became full of the lovely color of the damask rose. She pushed her hair from her forehead, and looked thoughtfully into the fire.

"You feel better, dear, don't you?" asked Jasper.

"Better!" said the young girl. "I feel alive. I wonder, Jasper, how long it will last."

"Why should it not go on for some time, dear? I have money—enough, that is, for the present."

"But you are spending your money on me."

"Not at all. You are keeping me and feeding me. I give you twenty shillings a week, and out of that you feed me as well as yourself."

"Oh, that twenty shillings!" cried Sylvia. "What riches it seems! The first week I got it I really felt that I should never, never be able to come to the end of it. I quite trembled when I was in father's presence. I dreaded that he might see the money lying in my pocket. It seemed impossible that he, who loves money so much, would not notice it;

but he did not, and now I am almost accustomed to it. Oh Jasper, you have saved my life!"

"It is well to have lived for some good purpose," said Jasper in a guarded tone. She looked at the young girl, and a quick sigh came to her lips.

"Do you know," she said abruptly, "that I mean to do more than feed you and warm you?"

"But what more could you do?"

"Why, clothe you, love—clothe you."

"No, Jasper; you must not."

"But I must and will," said Jasper. "I have smuggled in all my belongings, and the dear old gentleman does not know a single bit about it. Bless you! notwithstanding that Pilot of his, and the way he himself sneaks about and watches—notwithstanding all these things, I, Amelia Jasper, am a match for him. Yes, my dear, my belongings are in this house, and one of the trunks contains little Evelyn's clothes—the clothes she is not allowed to wear. I mean to alter them, and add to them, and rearrange them, and make them fit for you, my bonny girl."

"It is a temptation," said Sylvia; "but, Jasper dear, I dare not allow you to do it. If I were to appear in anything but the very plainest clothes father would discover there was something up; he would get into a state of terror, and my life would not be worth living. When mother was alive she sometimes tried to dress me as I ought to be dressed, and I remember now a terrible scene and mother's tears. There was an occasion when mother gave me a little crimson velvet frock, and I ran into the dining-room to father. I was quite small then, and the frock suited me, and mother was, oh, so proud! But half an hour later I was in my room, drowned in tears, and ordered to bed immediately, and the frock had been torn off my back by father himself."

"The man is a maniac," said Jasper. "Don't let us talk of him. You can dress fine when you are with me. I mean to have a gay time; I don't mean to let the grass grow under my feet. What do you say to my smuggling in little Eve some day and letting her have a right jolly time with us two in this old kitchen?"

"But father will certainly, certainly discover it."

"No; I can manage that. The kitchen is far away from the rest of the house, and with this new sort of coal there is scarcely any smoke. At night—at any rate on dark nights—he cannot see even if there is smoke; and in the daytime I burn this special coal. Oh, we are safe enough, my dear; you need have no fear."

Sylvia talked a little longer with Jasper, and then she ran to her own room to put on her very threadbare garments preparatory to going out. Yes, she certainly felt much, much better. The air was keen and crisp; she was no longer hungry—that gnawing pain in her side had absolutely ceased; she was warm, too, and she longed for exercise. A

CHAPTER XVI.–SYLVIA'S DRIVE.

moment or two later, accompanied by Pilot, she was racing along the snow-covered roads. The splendid color in her cheeks could not but draw the attention of any chance passer-by.

"What a handsome—what a very handsome girl!" more than one person said; and it so happened that as Sylvia was flying round a corner, her great mastiff gamboling in front of her, she came face to face with Lady Frances, who was driving to make some calls in the neighborhood.

Lady Frances Wynford was never proof against a pretty face, and she had seldom seen a more lovely vision than those dark eyes and glowing cheeks presented at that moment. She desired her coachman to stop, and bending forward, greeted Sylvia in quite an affectionate way.

"How do you do, Miss Leeson?" she said. "You never came to see me after I invited you to do so. I meant to call on your mother, but you did not greet my proposal with enthusiasm. How is she, by the way?"

"Mother is dead," replied Sylvia in a low tone. The rich color faded slowly from her cheeks, but she would not cry. She looked full up at Lady Frances.

"Poor child!" said that lady kindly; "you must miss her. How old are you, Miss Leeson?"

"I am just sixteen," was the reply.

"Would you like to come for a drive with me?"

"May I?" said the girl in an almost incredulous voice.

"You certainly may; I should like to have you.—Johnson, get down and open the carriage door for Miss Leeson.—But, oh, my dear, what is to be done with the dog?"

"Pilot will go home if I speak to him," said Sylvia.—"Come here, Pilot."

The mastiff strode slowly up.

"Go home, dear," said Sylvia. "Go, and knock as you know how at the gates, and father will let you in. Be quick, dear dog; go at once."

Pilot put on a shrewd and wonderfully knowing expression, cocked one ear a little, wagged his tail a trifle, glanced at Lady Frances, seemed on the whole to approve of her, and then turning on his heel, trotted off in the direction of The Priory.

"What a wonderfully intelligent dog, and how you have trained him!" said Lady Frances.

"Yes; he is almost human," replied Sylvia. "How nice this is!" she continued as the carriage began to roll smoothly away. She leant back against her comfortable cushions.

"But you will soon be cold, my dear, in that very thin jacket," said Lady Frances. "Let me wrap this warm fur cloak round you. Oh, yes, I insist; it would never do for you to catch cold while driving with me."

A VERY NAUGHTY GIRL

Sylvia submitted to the warm and comforting touch of the fur, and the smile on her young face grew brighter than ever.

"And now you must tell me all about yourself," said Lady Frances. "Do you know, I am quite curious about you—a girl like you living such a strange and lonely life!"

"Lady Frances," said Sylvia.

"Yes my dear; what?"

"I am going to say something which may not be quite polite, but I am obliged to say it. I cannot answer any of your questions; I cannot tell you anything about myself."

"Really?"

"Not because I mean to be rude, for in many ways I should like to confide in you; but it would not be honorable. Do you understand?"

"I certainly understand what honor means," said Lady Frances; "but whether a child like you is acting wisely in keeping up an unnecessary mystery is more than I can tell."

"I would much rather tell you everything about myself than keep silence, but I cannot speak," said Sylvia simply.

Lady Frances looked at her in some wonder.

"She is a lady when all is said and done," she said to herself. "As to poverty, I do not know that I ever saw any one so badly dressed; the child has not sufficient clothing to keep her warm. When last I saw her she was painfully thin, too; she has more color in her cheeks now, and more flesh on her poor young bones, so perhaps whoever she lives with is taking better care of her. I am curious, and I will not pretend to deny it, but of course I can question the child no further."

No one could make herself more agreeable than Lady Frances Wynford when she chose. She chatted now on many matters, and Sylvia soon felt perfectly at home.

"Why, the child, young as she is, knows some of the ways of society," thought the great lady. "I only wish that that miserable little Evelyn was half as refined and nice as this poor, neglected girl."

Presently the drive came to an end. Sylvia had not enjoyed herself so much for many a day.

"Now, listen, Sylvia," said Lady Frances: "I am a very plain-spoken woman; when I say a thing I mean it, and when I think a thing, as a rule, I say it. I like you. That I am curious about you, and very much inclined to wonder who you are and what you are doing in this place, goes without saying; but of course I do not want to pry into what you do not wish to tell me. Your secret is your own, my dear, and not my affair; but, at the same time, I should like to befriend you. Can you come to the Castle sometimes? When you do come it will be as a welcome guest."

"I do not know how I can come," replied Sylvia. She colored, looked down, and her face turned rather white. "I have not a proper dress," she added. "Oh, not that I am poor, but——"

CHAPTER XVI.—SYLVIA'S DRIVE.

Lady Frances looked puzzled. She longed to say, "I will give you the dress you need," but there was something about Sylvia's face which forbade her.

"Well," she said, "if you can manage the dress will you come? This, let me see, is Thursday. The girls are to have a whole holiday on Saturday. Will you spend Saturday with us? Now you must say yes; I will take no refusal."

Sylvia's heart gave a bound of pleasure.

"Is it right; is it wrong?" she said to herself. "But I cannot help it," was her next thought; "I must have my fun—I must. I do like Audrey so much! And I like Evelyn too—not, of course, like Audrey; but I like them both."

"You will come, dear?" said Lady Frances. "We shall be very pleased to see you. By the way, your address is——"

"The Priory," said Sylvia hastily. "Oh, please, Lady Frances, don't send any message there! If you do I shall not be allowed to come to you. Yes, I will come—perhaps never again, but I will come on Saturday. It is a great pleasure; I do not feel able to refuse."

"That is right. Then I shall expect you."

Lady Frances nodded to the young girl, told the coachman to drive home, and the next moment had turned the corner and was lost to view.

"What fun this is!" said Sylvia to herself. "I wish Pilot were here. I should like to have a race with him over the snow. Oh, how beautiful is the world when all is said and done! Now, if only I had a proper dress to go to the Castle in!"

She ran home. Her father was standing on the steps of the house. His face looked pinched, blue, and cold; the nourishment of the chop and the fried potatoes had evidently passed away.

"Why, father, you want your tea!" said the girl. "How sorry I am I was not in sooner to get it for you!"

"Tea, tea!" he said irritably. "Always the same cry—food, nothing but food; the world is becoming impossible. My dear Sylvia, I told you that I should not want to eat again to-day. The fact is, you overfed me at lunch, and I am suffering from a sort of indigestion—I am really. There is nothing better for indigestion than hot water; I have been drinking it sparingly during the afternoon. But where have you been, dear, and why did you send Pilot home? The dog made such a noise at the gate that I went myself to find out what was the matter."

"I did not want Pilot, so I sent him home," was Sylvia's low reply.

"But why so?"

She was silent for a moment; then she looked up into her father's face. "We agreed, did we not," she said, "that we both were to go our own way. You must not question me too closely. I have done nothing wrong—nothing; I am always faithful to you and to my mother's memory. You must not expect me to tell you everything, father, for you know you do not tell me everything."

"Silly child!" he answered. "But there, Sylvia, I do trust you. And, my dear little girl, know this, that you are the great—the very greatest—comfort of my life. I will come in; it is somewhat chilly this evening."

Sylvia rushed before her father into his sitting-room, dashed up to the fire, flung on some bits of wood and what scraps of coal were left in the coal-hod, thrust in a torn newspaper, set a match to the fire she had hastily laid, and before Mr. Leeson strolled languidly into the room, a cheerful fire was crackling and blazing up the chimney.

"How extravagant——" he began, but when he saw Sylvia's pretty face as she knelt on the hearth the words were arrested on his lips.

"The child is very like her mother, and her mother was the most beautiful woman on earth when I married her," he thought. "Poor little Sylvia! I wonder will she have a happier fate!"

He sat down by the fire. The girl knelt by him, took his cold hands, and rubbed them softly. Her heart was full; there were tears in her eyes.

CHAPTER XVII.—THE FALL IN THE SNOW.

The next morning, when the meager breakfast which Mr. Leeson and his daughter enjoyed together had come to an end, Sylvia ran off to find Jasper. She had stayed with her father during most of the preceding evening, and although she had gone as usual to drink her chocolate and eat her bread before going to bed, she had said very little to Jasper. But she wanted to speak to her this morning, for she had thoughts in the night, and those thoughts were driving her to decisive action. Jasper was standing in the kitchen. She had made up the fire with the smokeless coal, and it was burning slowly but steadily. A little, plump chicken lay on the table; a small piece of bacon was close at hand. There was also a pile of large and mealy-looking potatoes and some green vegetables.

"Our dinner for to-day," said Jasper briefly.

"Oh Jasper!" answered the girl—"oh, if only father could have some of that chicken! Do you know, I do not think he is at all well; he looked so cold and feeble last night. He really is starving himself—very much as I starved myself before you came; but he is old and cannot bear it quite so well. What am I to do to keep him alive?"

Jasper looked full at Sylvia.

"Do!" she said. "How can a fool be cured of his folly? That is the question I ask myself. If he denies himself the necessaries of life, how are you to give them to him?"

"Well," said Sylvia, "I manage as best I can by hardly ever eating in his presence; he does not notice, particularly at breakfast. He enjoyed his egg and toast this morning, and really said nothing about my unwonted extravagance."

"I have a plan in my head," said Jasper, "which may or may not come to anything. You know those few miserable barn-door fowls which your father keeps just by the shrubbery in that old hen-house?"

"Yes," replied Sylvia.

"Do they ever lay any eggs?"

"No."

"I thought not. I wonder a prudent, careful man like Mr. Leeson should keep them eating their heads off, so to speak."

"Oh, they don't eat much," replied Sylvia. "I got them when father spoke so much about the wasted potato-skins. I bought them from a gipsy. I did not know they were so old."

"We must get rid of those fowls," said Jasper. "You must tell your father that it is a great waste of money to keep them; and, my dear, we will give him fowl to eat for his dinner as long as the old fowls in the shrubbery last. There are ten of them. I shall sell them—very little indeed we shall get for them—and he will imagine he is eating them

- 113 -

when he really is consuming a delicate little bird like the one you and I are going to enjoy for our dinner to-day."

"What fun!" said Sylvia, the color coming into her cheeks and her eyes sparkling. "You do not think it is wrong to deceive him, do you?"

"Wrong! Bless you! no," replied Jasper. "And now, my dear, what is the matter with you? You look——"

"How?" replied Sylvia.

"Just as if you were bursting to tell me something."

"I am—I am," answered Sylvia. "Oh Jasper, you must help me!"

"Of course I will, dear."

"I have resolved to accept your most kind offer. I will pay you somehow, in some fashion, but if you could make just one of Evelyn's frocks fit for me to wear!"

"Ah!" replied Jasper. "Now, I am as pleased about this as I could be about anything. We will have more than one, my pretty young miss. But what do you want it for?"

"I am going to do a great, big, dangerous thing," replied Sylvia. "If father discovers, things will be very bad, I am sure; but perhaps he will not discover. Anyhow, I am not proof against temptation. I met Lady Frances Wynford."

"And how does her ladyship look?" asked Jasper—"as proud as ever?"

"She was not proud to me, Jasper; she was quite nice. She asked me to take a drive with her."

"You took a drive with her ladyship!"

"I did indeed; you must treat me with great respect after this."

Jasper put her arms akimbo and burst into a loud laugh.

"I guess," she said after a pause, "you looked just as fine and aristocratic as her ladyship's own self."

"I drove in a luxurious carriage, and had a lovely fur cloak wrapped round me," replied the girl; "and Lady Frances was very, very kind, and she has asked me to spend Saturday at the Castle."

"Saturday! Why, that is to-morrow."

"Yes, I know it is."

"You are going?"

"Yes, I am going."

"You will see my little Eve to-morrow?"

"Yes, Jasper."

Jasper's black eyes grew suspiciously bright; she raised her hand to dash away something which seemed to dim them for a second, then she said in a brisk tone:

"We have our work cut out for us, for you shall not go shabby, my pretty, pretty maid. I will soon have the dinner in order, and——"

"But what have you got for father's dinner?"

"A little soup. You can tell him that you boiled his chop in it. It is really good, and I am putting in lots of pearl barley and rice and potatoes. He will be ever so pleased, for he will think it cost next to

CHAPTER XVII.–THE FALL IN THE SNOW.

nothing; but there is a good piece of solid meat boiled down in that soup, nevertheless."

"Oh, thank you, Jasper; you are a comfort to me."

"Well," replied Jasper, "I always like to do my best for those who are brave and young and put upon. You are a very silly girl in some ways, Miss Sylvia; but you have been good to me, and I mean to be good to you. Now then, dinner is well forward, and we will go and search out the dress."

The rest of the day passed quickly, and with intense enjoyment as far as Sylvia was concerned. She had sufficiently good taste to choose the least remarkable of Evelyn's many costumes. There was a rich darkbrown costume, trimmed with velvet of the same shade, which could be lengthened in the skirt and let out in the bodice, and which the young girl would look very nice in. A brown velvet hat accompanied the costume, with a little tuft of ostrich feathers placed on one side, and a pearl buckle to keep all in place. There were muffs and furs in quantities to choose from. Sylvia would for once in her life be richly appareled. Jasper exerted herself to the utmost, and the pretty dress was all in order by the time night came.

It was quite late evening when Sylvia sought the room where her father lived. A very plain but at the same time nourishing supper had been provided for Mr. Leeson. Sylvia's own supper she would take as usual with Jasper. Sylvia dashed into her father's room, her eyes bright and her cheeks glowing. She was surprised and distressed to see the room empty. She wondered if her father had gone to his bedroom. Quickly she rushed up-stairs and knocked at the door; there was no response. She opened the door softly and went in. All was cold and icy desolation within the large, badly furnished room. Sylvia shivered slightly, and rushed down-stairs again. She peeped out of the window. The snow was falling heavily in great big flakes.

"Oh, I hope it will not snow too much to-night!" thought the young girl. "But no matter; however deep it is, I shall find my way to Castle Wynford to-morrow."

She wondered if her father would miss her, if he would grow restless and anxious; but nevertheless she was determined to enjoy her pleasure. Still, where was he now? She glanced at the fire in the big grate; she ventured to put on some more coals and to tidy up the hearth; then she drew down the blinds of the windows, pulled her father's armchair in front of the fire, sat down herself by the hearth, and waited. She waited for over half an hour. During that time the warmth of the fire made her drowsy. She found herself nodding. Suddenly she sat up wide awake. A queer sense of uneasiness stole over her; she must go and seek her father. Where could he be? How she longed to call Jasper to her aid! But that, she knew, would be impossible. She wrapped a threadbare cloak, which hung on a peg in the hall, round her shoulders, slipped her feet into goloshes, and set out into the wintry night. She had not gone a dozen yards before she saw the object of her search. Mr. Leeson was lying full length on the snow; he was not moving. Sylvia had a wild horror that he was dead; she bent over him.

"Father! father!" she cried.

There was no answer. She touched his face with her lips; it was icy cold. Oh, was he dead? Oh, terror! oh, horror! All her accustomed prudence flew to the winds. Get succor for him at once she must. She dashed into the kitchen. Jasper was standing by the fire.

"Come at once, Jasper!" she said. "Bring brandy, and come at once."

"What has happened, my darling?"

"Come at once and you will see. Bring brandy—brandy."

Jasper in an emergency was all that was admirable. She followed Sylvia out into the snow, and between them they dragged Mr. Leeson back to the house.

"Now, dear," said Jasper, "I will give him the brandy, and I'll stand behind him. When he comes to I will slip out of the room. Oh, the poor gentleman! He is as cold as ice. Hold that blanket and warm it, will you, Sylvia? We must put it round him. Oh, bless you, child! heap some coals on the fire. What matter the expense? There! you cannot lift that great hod; I'll do it."

Jasper piled coals on the grate; the fire crackled and blazed merrily. Mr. Leeson lay like one dead.

"He is dead—he is dead!" gasped Sylvia.

"No, love, not a bit of it; but he slipped in the cold and the fall stunned him a bit, and the cold is so strong he could not come to himself again. He will soon be all right; we must get this brandy between his lips."

That they managed to do, and a minute or two later the poor man opened his eyes. Just for a second it seemed to him that he saw a strange woman, stout and large and determined-looking, bending over him; but the next instant, his consciousness more wholly returning, he saw Sylvia. Sylvia's little face, white with fear, her eyes, large with love and anxiety, were close to his. He smiled into the sweet little face, and holding out his thin hand, allowed her to clasp it. There was a rustle as though somebody was going away, and Sylvia and her father were alone. A moment later the young girl raised her eyes and saw Jasper in the background making mysterious signs to her. She got up. Jasper was holding a cup of very strong soup in her hand. Sylvia took it with thankfulness, and brought it to her father.

"Do you know," she said, trying to speak as cheerfully as she could, "that you have behaved very badly? You went out into the snow when you should have been in your warm room, and you fell down and you fainted or something. Anyhow, I found you in time; and now you are to drink this."

CHAPTER XVII.—THE FALL IN THE SNOW.

"I won't; hot water will do—not that expensive stuff," said Mr. Leeson, true to the tragedy of his life even at this crucial moment.

"Drink this and nothing else," said Sylvia, speaking as hardly and firmly as she dared.

Mr. Leeson was too weak to withstand her. She fed him by spoonfuls, and presently he was well enough to sit up again.

"Child, what a fire!" he said.

"Yes, father; and if it means our very last sixpence, or our very last penny even, it is going to be a big fire to-night: and you are going to be nursed and petted and comforted. Oh, father, father, you gave me such a fright!"

As Sylvia spoke her composure gave way; her tense feelings were relieved by a flood of tears. She pressed her face against her father's hand and sobbed unrestrainedly.

"You do not mean to say you are really fond of me?" he said; and a queer moisture came into his own eyes. He said nothing more about the coals, and Sylvia insisted on his having more food, and, in short, having a really good time.

"Dare I leave him to-morrow?" she said to herself. "He may be very weak after this; and yet—and yet I cannot give up my great, great fun. My lovely dress, too, ready and all! Oh! I must go. I am sure he will be all right in the morning."

Presently, much to Sylvia's relief, Mr. Leeson suggested that he should sleep on the sofa, in the neighborhood of the big fire.

"For you have been so reckless, my dear little girl," he said, "that really you have provided a fire to last for hours and hours. It would be a sad pity to waste it; I think, therefore, that I shall spend the night on this sofa, well wrapped up, enjoying the heat."

"Nothing could be better, father," said Sylvia, "except a big, very big, fire in your own room, and you in your own bed well warmed with hot bottles."

"We should soon be in the workhouse," was Mr. Leeson's rejoinder.

"No, no; I will enjoy the fire here now that you have been so extravagant; and you had better go to bed if you have had your supper."

Sylvia had had no supper, but Mr. Leeson was far too self-absorbed to notice that fact. Presently she left him, and he lay on the sofa, blinking into the fire, and occasionally half-dozing. After a time he dropped off to sleep, and the young girl, who stole in to look at him, went out with a satisfied expression on her face.

"He is quite well again," she said to Jasper, "and he is sleeping sweetly.

"Now, look here," said Jasper. "What is fretting you?"

"I don't think I ought to leave him to-morrow."

"But I shall be here. I will manage to let him have his meals comfortable without his knowing it. Do you suppose I have not done

A VERY NAUGHTY GIRL

more difficult things than that in my day? Now, my love, you go to bed and sleep sound, and I will have a plan all mature to give you your happy day with an undisturbed conscience in the morning."

Sylvia was really very tired—dead tired. She went up-stairs, and as soon as she laid her head on her pillow was sound asleep.

Meanwhile Mr. Leeson slept on for two or three hours; it was past the middle of the night when he awoke. He woke wide awake, as elderly people will, and looked round him. The fire had burnt itself down to a great red mass; the room looked cheery and comfortable in the warm rays. Mr. Leeson stirred himself luxuriously and wrapped the blanket, which Jasper had brought from her own stores, tightly round his person. After a time, however, its very softness and fluffiness and warmth attracted his attention. He began to feel it between his fingers and thumb; then he roused himself, sat up, and looked at it. A suspicious look came into his eyes.

"What is the matter?" he said to himself. "Is Sylvia spending money that I know nothing about? Why, this is a new blanket! I have an inventory of every single thing that this house possesses. Surely new blankets are not included in that inventory! I can soon see."

He rose, lit a pair of candles, went to a secretary which stood against the wall, opened it, and took out a book marked "Exact Inventory of all the Furniture at The Priory." He turned up the portion devoted to house linen, and read the description of the different blankets which the meager establishment contained. There was certainly a lack of these valuable necessaries; the blankets at The Priory had seen much service, and were worn thin with use and washing. But this blanket was new—oh, delicious, of course—but what was the man worth who needed such luxuries! Mr. Leeson pushed it aside with a disturbed look on his face.

"Sylvia must be spending money," he said to himself. "I have observed it of late. She looks better, and she decidedly gives me extravagant meals. The bread is not as stale as it might be, and there is too much meat used. This soup——"

He took up the empty cup from which he had drained the soup a few hours back, and looked at a drop or two which still remained at the bottom.

"Positively it jellies," he said to himself—"jellies! Then, too, in my rambles round this evening I noticed that smoke again—that smoke coming from the kitchen. There is too much fuel used here, and these blankets are disgraceful, and the food is reckless—there is no other word for it."

He sank back on his sofa and gazed at the fire.

"Ah!" he said as he looked full at the flames, "out you go presently; and for some time the warmth will remain in the room, and I shall not dream of lighting any other fire here until that warmth is gone. Sylvia takes after her mother. There was never a better woman than

CHAPTER XVII.–THE FALL IN THE SNOW.

my dear wife, but she was madly, disgracefully extravagant. What shall I do if this goes on?—and pretty girls like Sylvia are apt to be so thoughtless. I wish I could send her away for a bit; it will be quite terrible if she develops her mother's tastes. I could not be cruel to my pretty little girl, but she certainly will be a fearful thorn in my side if she buys blankets of this sort, and feeds me with soup that jellies, forsooth! What am I to do? I have not saved quite so much as I ought during the last week. Ah! the house is silent as the grave. I shall just count out the money I have put into that last canvas bag."

A stealthy, queer light came into Mr. Leeson's eyes. He crossed the room on tiptoe and turned the key in the lock. As he did so he seemed to be assailed by a memory.

"Was I alone with Sylvia when I awoke out of unconsciousness," he said to himself, "or was there some one else by? I cannot quite make out. Was it a dream that I saw an ugly, large woman bending over me? People do dream things of that sort when they sink from exhaustion. I have read of it in stories of misers. Misers! I am nothing of that kind; I am just a prudent man who will not spend too much—a prudent man who tries to save. It must have been a dream that a stranger was in the house; my little girl might take after her mother, but she is not so bad as that. Yes, I will take the opportunity; I will count what is in the canvas bag. I was too weak to-night to attempt the work of burying my treasure, but to-morrow night I must be stronger. I believe I ate too much, and that is what ails me—in fact, I am certain of it. The cold took me and brought on an acute attack of indigestion, and I stumbled and fell. Poor dear little Sylvia! But I won't leave her penniless; that is one comfort."

Putting out one candle carefully, Mr. Leeson now laid the other on a table. He then went to his secretary and opened it. He pushed in his hand far, and brought out from its innermost depths a small bag made of rough canvas. The bag was tied with coarse string. He glanced round him, a strange expression on his face, and loosening the string of the bag, poured its contents upon the table. He poured them out slowly, and as he did so a look of distinct delight visited his face. There lay on the table in front of him a pile of money—gold, silver, copper. He spent some time dividing the three species of coin into different heaps. The gold coins were put in piles one on top of the other at his right hand, the silver lying in still larger heaps in the middle; the coppers, up to farthings, lay on his left hand. He bent his head and touched the gold with his lips.

"Beautiful! blessed! lovely!" he muttered. "I have saved all this out of the money which my dear wife would have spent on food and dress and luxuries. The solid, tangible, precious thing is here, and there is more like it—much more like it—many bags larger than these, full, full to the brim, all buried down deep in the fowl-house. No one would

A VERY NAUGHTY GIRL

guess where I bank my spoils. They are as safe as can be. I dare not keep much treasure in the house, but no one will know where it really lies."

He counted his gold carefully; he also counted his silver; finally he counted his copper. He wrote down the different sums on a piece of paper, which he slipped into the canvas bag; he put back the coins, tied the bag with the string, and returned it to its hiding-place.

"To-morrow night I must bury it," he said to himself. "I had hoped that I would have saved a little more, but by dint of great additional economy I may succeed next month. Well, I must begin to be very careful, and I must speak plainly on the subject to Sylvia."

CHAPTER XVIII.—A RED GIPSY CLOAK.

Mr. Leeson looked quite well the next morning, and Sylvia ate her scanty breakfast with a happy heart; she no longer felt any qualms at leaving her father for the day. Jasper assured Sylvia over and over again that all would be well; that without in the least betraying the secret of her residence in the house, she would see to Mr. Leeson's comforts. The difficulty now was for Sylvia to dress in her smart clothes and slip away without her father seeing her. She did not want to get to Castle Wynford much before one o'clock, but she would leave The Priory long before that hour and wander about in her usual fashion. No outdoor exercise tired this energetic girl. She looked forward to a whole long day of unalloyed bliss, to the society of other girls, to congenial warmth and comfort and luxury. She even looked forward with a pleasure, that her father would put down to distinct greediness, to nice, temptingly served meals. Oh yes, she meant to enjoy everything. She meant to drink this cup of bliss to the bottom, not to leave one drop untasted. Jasper seemed to share her pleasure. Jasper burdened her with many messages to Evelyn; she got Sylvia to promise that she would contrive a meeting between Evelyn and her old maid on the following day. Jasper selected the rendezvous, and told Sylvia exactly what she was to say to Evelyn.

"Whatever happens, I must see her," said the woman. "Tell her there are many reasons; and tell her too that I am hungry for a sight of her—hungry, hungry."

"Because you love her so much," said Sylvia, a soft light in her eyes.

"Yes, my darling, that is it—I love her."

"And she must love you very much," said Sylvia.

Jasper uttered a quick sigh.

"It is not Evelyn's way to love to extremities," she said slowly. "You must not blame her, my dear; we are all made according to the will of the Almighty; and Evelyn—oh yes, she is as the apple of the eye to me, but I am nothing of that sort to her. You see, dear, her head is a bit turned with the lofty future that lies before her. In some ways it does not suit her; it would suit you, Miss Sylvia, or it would suit Miss Audrey, but it does not suit little Eve. It is too much for my little Eve; she would do better in a less exalted sphere."

"Well, I do hope and trust she will be glad to see you and glad to hear about you," said Sylvia. "I will be sure to tell her what a dear old thing you are. But, oh, Jasper, do you think she will notice the smart dress made out of her dress?"

"You can give her this note, dear; I am sending her a word of warning not to draw attention to your dress. And now, don't you think you had better get into it, and let me see you out by the back premises?"

"I must go and see father just for a minute first," said Sylvia.
She ran off, saw her father, as usual busily writing letters, and bent down to kiss him.
"Don't disturb me," he said in a querulous tone. "I am particularly busy. The post this morning has brought me some gratifying news. A little investment I made a short time ago in great fear and trembling has turned up trumps. I mean to put a trifle more money—oh, my dear! I only possess a trifle—into the same admirable undertaking (gold-mines, my dear), and if all that the prospectus says is true I shall be in very truth a rich man. Not yet, Sylvia—don't you think it—but some day."
"Oh father! and if you are——"
"Why, you may spend a little more then, dear—a little more; but it is wrong to squander gold. Gold is a beautiful and precious thing, my dear; very beautiful, very precious, very hard to get."
"Yes, father; and I hope you will have a great deal of it, and I hope you will put plenty—plenty of money into the—into the——"
"Investment," said Mr. Leeson. "The investment that sounds so promising. Don't keep me now, love."
"I am going out for a long walk, father; it is such a bright, sunshiny day. Good-by for the present."
Mr. Leeson did not hear; he again bent over the letter which he was writing. Sylvia ran back to Jasper.
"He seems quite well," she said, "and very much interested in what the post brought him this morning. I think I can leave him quite safely. You will be sure to see that he has his food."
"Bless you, child!—yes."
"And you will on no account betray that you live here?"
"Bless you, child! again—not I."
"Well then, I will get into my finery. How grand and important I shall feel!"
So Sylvia was dressed in the brown costume and the pretty brown velvet hat, and she wore a little sable collar and a sable muff; and then she kissed Jasper, and telling her she would remember all the messages, started on her day of pleasure. Jasper saw her out by the back entrance. This entrance had been securely closed before Jasper's advent, but between them the woman and the girl had managed to open the rusty gate, although Mr. Leeson was unaware that it had moved on its hinges for many a long day. It opened now to admit of Sylvia's exit, and Jasper went slowly back to the house, meditating as she did so. Whatever her meditations were, they roused her to action. She engaged herself busily in her bedroom and kitchen. She opened her trunk and took out a small bag which contained her money. She had plenty of money, still, but it would not last always. Without Sylvia's knowing it, she had often spent more than a pound a week on this establishment. It had been absolutely necessary for her to provide

CHAPTER XVIII.—A RED GIPSY CLOAK.

herself with warm bedclothes, and to add to the store of coals by purchasing anthracite coal, which is almost smokeless. In one way or another her hoard was diminished by twenty pounds; she had therefore only forty more. When this sum was spent she would be penniless.

"Not that I am afraid," thought Jasper, "for Evelyn will have to give me more money—she must. I could not leave my dear little Sylvia now that I find the dreadful plight she is in; and I cannot stay far from my dear Evelyn, for although she does not love me as I love her, still, I should suffer great pain if I could not be, so to speak, within call. I wonder if my plan will succeed. I must have a try."

Jasper, having fulfilled her small duties, sat for a time gazing straight before her. The hours went on. The little carriage clock which she kept in her bedroom struck eleven, then twelve.

"Time for him to have something," thought Jasper. "Now, can I possibly manage? Yes, I think so."

She took a saucepan, which held something mysterious, out into the open air. It was an old, shabby saucepan. She hid it in the shrubbery. She then went back to her room and changed her dress. She was some little time over her toilet, and when she once more emerged into view, the old Jasper, to all appearance, had vanished.

A dark, somewhat handsome woman, in a faded red gipsy cloak, now stood before the looking-glass. Jasper slipped out the back way, pushed aside the rusty gate, said a friendly word to Pilot, who wagged his tail with approbation, and carrying a basket on her arm, walked slowly down the road. She met one or two people, and accosted them in the true Romany style.

"May I tell your fortune, my pretty miss? May I cross your hand with silver and tell you of the fine gentleman who is going to ride by presently? Let me, my dear—let me."

And when the young girl she addressed ran away giggling, little suspecting that Jasper was not a real gipsy, Jasper knew that her scheme had succeeded. She even induced a village boy to submit to her fortune-telling, and half-turned his head by telling him of a treasure to be found, and a wife in an upper class who would raise him once for all to a position of luxury. She presently pounded loudly on The Priory gates. Mr. Leeson had an acute ear; he always sat within view of these gates. His one desire was to keep all strangers from the premises; he had trained Pilot for the purpose. Accordingly Jasper's knocks were not heeded. Sylvia was always desired to go to the village to get the necessary food; trades-people were not allowed on the premises. His letter occupied him intently; he was busy, too, looking over files of accounts and different prospectuses; he was engaged over that most fascinating pastime, counting up his riches. But, ah! ah! how poor he was! Oh, what a poverty-stricken man! He sighed and

A VERY NAUGHTY GIRL

grumbled as he thought over these things. Jasper gave another furious knock, and finding that no attention was paid to her imperious summons, she pushed open the gate. Pilot immediately, as his custom was, appeared on guard. He stood in front of Jasper and just for a moment barked at her, but she gave him a mysterious sign, and he wagged his tail gently, went up to her, and let her pat him on the head. The next instant, to Mr. Leeson's disgust, the gipsy and the dog were walking side by side up to the door. He sprang to his feet, and in a moment was standing on the steps.

"Go away, my good woman; go away at once. I cannot have you on the premises. I will set the dog on you if you don't go away."

"One minute, kind sir," whined Jasper. "I have come to know if you have any fowls to sell. I want some fowls; old hens and cocks—not young pullets or anything of that sort. I want to buy them, sir, and I am prepared to give a good price."

These extraordinary remarks aroused Mr. Leeson's thoughtful attention. He had long been annoyed by the barn-door fowls, and they were decidedly old. He had often wished to dispose of them; they were too tough to eat, and they no longer laid eggs.

"If you will promise to take the fowls right away with you now, I do not mind selling them for a good price," he said. "Are you prepared to give a good price? I wonder where my daughter is; she would know better than I what they are worth. Stand where you are, my good woman; do not attempt to move or the dog Pilot will fly at your throat. I will call my daughter."

Mr. Leeson went into the house and shouted for Sylvia. Of course there was no answer.

"I forgot," muttered Mr. Leeson. "Sylvia is out. Really that child over-exercises; such devotion to the open air must provoke unnecessary appetite. I wish that horrid gipsy would go away! How extraordinary that Pilot did not fly at her! But they say gipsies have great power over men and animals. Well, if she does give a fair price for the birds I may as well be quit of them; they annoy me a good deal, and some time, in consequence of them, some one may discover my treasure. Good heavens, how awful! The thought almost unmans me."

Mr. Leeson therefore came out and spoke in quite a civil tone for him.

"If you will accompany me to the fowl-house I will show you the birds, but I may as well say at once that I won't give them for a mere nothing, old as they are—and I should be the last to deceive you as to their age. They are of a rare kind, and interesting from a scientific point of view."

"I do not know about scientific fowls," replied the gipsy, "but I want to buy a few old hens to put into my pot."

"Eh?" cried Mr. Leeson in a tone of interrogation. "Have you a recipe for boiling down old fowls?"

CHAPTER XVIII.—A RED GIPSY CLOAK.

"Have not I, your honor! And soon they are done, too—in a jiffy, so to speak. But let me look at them, your honor, and I will pay you far more than any one else would give for them."

"You won't get them unless you give a very good sum. You gipsies, if the truth were known, are all enormously rich."

He walked round to the hen-house, accompanied by the supposed gipsy and Pilot. The fowls, about a dozen in number, were strutting up and down their run. They were hungry, poor creatures, for they had had but a slight meal that morning. The gipsy pretended to bargain for them, keeping a sharp eye all the time on Mr. Leeson.

"This one," she said, catching the most disreputable-looking of the birds, "is the one I want for the gipsies' stew. There, I will give you ninepence for this bird."

"Ninepence!" cried Mr. Leeson, almost shrieking out the word. "Do you think I would sell a valuable hen like that for ninepence? And you say it can be boiled down to eat tender!"

"Boiled down to eat tender!" said the supposed gipsy. "Why, it can be made delicious. There is broth in it, soup in it, and meat in it. There is dinner for four, and supper for four, and soup for four in this old hen!"

"And you offer me ninepence for such a valuable bird! I tell you what: I wish you would show me that recipe. I will give you sixpence for it. I do not know how to make an old hen tender."

"Give me a quarter of an hour, your honor, and you will not know that you are not eating the youngest chicken in the land."

"But how are you to cook it?"

"I will make a bit of fire in the shrubbery, and do it by a recipe of my own."

"You are sure you will not go near the house?"

"No, your honor."

"But how can a fowl that is now alive be fit to eat in a quarter of an hour?"

"It is a recipe of my grandmother's, your honor, and I am not going to give it until you taste what the bird is like. Now, if you will go away I will get it ready for you."

Mr. Leeson really felt interested.

"What a sensible woman!" he said to himself. "I shall try and get that recipe out of her for threepence; it will be valuable for my little book of cheap recipes; it would probably sell the book. How to make four dinners, four lunches, and four plates of soup out of an old hen. A most taking recipe—most taking!"

He walked up and down while the pretended gipsy heated up the stew she had already made out of a really tender chicken. The poor old hen was tied up so that she could not cackle or make any sound, and put into the bottom of the supposed gipsy's basket; and presently Jasper appeared carrying the stew in a cracked basin.

"Here, your honor, eat it up before me, and tell me afterwards if a better or a more tender fowl ever existed."

It was in this way that Mr. Leeson made an excellent repast. He was highly pleased, for decidedly the boniest and most scraggy of the fowls had been selected, and nothing could be more delicious than this stew. He fetched a plate and knife and fork from his sitting-room, where he always kept a certain amount of useful kitchen utensils, ate his dinner, pronounced it to be the best of the best, and desired the gipsy to leave the balance in the porch.

"Thank you," he said; "it is admirable. And so you really made that out of my old hen in a few minutes? I will give you threepence if you will give me the recipe."

"I could not sell it for threepence, sir—no, not for sixpence; no, not for a shilling. But I should like to make a bargain for the rest of the fowls."

"How much will you give for each?"

"Taking them all in a heap, I will give sixpence apiece," replied the gipsy.

Mr. Leeson uttered a scream.

"You have outdone yourself, my good woman," he said. "Do you think I am going to give fowls that will make such delicious and nourishing food away for that trivial sum? My little daughter is a very clever cook, and I shall instruct her with regard to the serving up of the remainder of my poultry. If you will not give me the recipe I must ask you to go."

The gipsy pretended to be extremely angry.

"I won't go," she said, "unless you allow me to tell you your fortune; I won't stir, and that's flat."

"I do not believe in gipsy fortune-tellers. I shall have to call the police if you do not leave my establishment immediately."

"And how will you manage when you don't ever leave your own grounds? I am thinking it may be you are a bit afraid. People who stick so close to home often have a reason."

This remark frightened Mr. Leeson very much. He was always in terror lest some one would guess that he kept his treasure on the premises.

"Look here," he said, raising his voice. "You see before you the poorest man for my position in the whole of England; it is with the utmost difficulty that I can keep soul and body together. Observe the place; observe the house. Do you think I should care for a recipe to make old fowls tender if I were not in very truth a most poverty-stricken person?"

"I will tell you if you show me your palm," said the gipsy.

Now, Mr. Leeson was superstitious. It was the last thing he credited himself with, but nevertheless he was. The gipsy, with her dancing

CHAPTER XVIII.—A RED GIPSY CLOAK.

black eyes, looked full at him. He had a shadowy, almost a fearful idea that he had seen that face before—he could not make out when. Then it occurred to him that this was the very face that had bent over him for an instant the night before when he was coming back from his fit of unconsciousness. Oh, it was impossible that the gipsy could have been here then! Had he seen her in a sort of vision? He felt startled and alarmed. The gipsy kept watching him; she seemed to be reading him through and through.

"I saw you in a dream," she said. "And I know you will show your hand; and I know I have things to tell you, both good and bad."

"Well, well!" said Mr. Leeson, "here is sixpence. Tell me your gibberish, and then go."

The gipsy looked twice at the coin.

"It is a poor one," she said. "But them who is rich always give the smallest."

"I am not rich, I tell you."

"They who are rich find it hardest to part with their pelf. But I will take it."

"I will give you a shilling if you'll go. But it is hard for a very poor man to part with it."

"Sixpence will do," said the gipsy, with a laugh. "Give it me. Now show me your palm."

She pretended to look steadily into the wrinkled palm of the miser's hand, and then spoke.

"I see here," she said, "much wealth. Yes, just where this cross lies is gold. I also see poverty. I also see a very great loss and a judgment."

"Go!" screamed the angry man. "Do not tell me another word."

He dashed into the house in absolute terror, and banged the hall door after him.

"I said I would give him a fright," said Jasper to herself. "Well, if he don't touch another morsel till Miss Sylvia comes home late to-night, he won't die after my dinner. Ah, the poor old hen! I must get her out of the basket now or she will be suffocated."

The gipsy walked slowly down the path, let herself out by the front entrance, walked round to the back, got in once more, and handed the old hen to a boy who was standing by the hedge.

"There," she said. "There's a present for you. Take it at once and go."

"What do I want with it?" he asked in astonishment. "Why, it belongs to old Mr. Leeson, the miser!"

"Go—go!" she said. "You can sell it for sixpence, or a shilling, or whatever it will fetch, only take it away."

The boy ran off laughing, the hen tucked under his arm.

CHAPTER XIX.—"WHY DID YOU DO IT?"

Meanwhile Sylvia was thoroughly enjoying herself. She started for the Castle in the highest spirits. Her walk during the morning hours had not fatigued her; and when, soon after twelve o'clock, she walked slowly and thoughtfully up the avenue, a happier, prettier girl could scarcely be seen. The good food she had enjoyed since Jasper had appeared on the scene had already begun to tell. Her cheeks were plump, her eyes bright; her somewhat pale complexion was creamy in tint and thoroughly healthy. Her dress, too, effected wonders. Sylvia would look well in a cotton frock; she would look well as a milkmaid, as a cottage girl; but she also had that indescribable grace which would enable her to fill a loftier station. And now, in her rich furs and dark-brown costume, she looked fit to move in any society. She held Evelyn's letter in her hand. Her one fear was that Evelyn would remark on her own costume transmogrified for Sylvia's benefit.

"Well, if she does, I don't much care," thought the happy girl. "After all, truth is best. Why should I deceive? I deceived when I was here last, when I wore Audrey's dress. I had not the courage then that I have now. Somehow to-day I feel happy and not afraid of anything."

She was met, just before she reached the front entrance, by Audrey and Evelyn.

"Here, Evelyn," she cried—"here is a note for you."

Evelyn took it quickly. She did not want Audrey to know that Jasper was living at The Priory. She turned aside and read her note, and Audrey devoted herself to Sylvia. Audrey had liked Sylvia before; she liked her better than ever now. She was far too polite to glance at her improved dress; that somehow seemed to tell her that happier circumstances had dawned for Sylvia, and a sense of rejoicing visited her.

"I am so very glad you have come!" she said. "Evelyn and I have been planning how we are to spend the day. We want to give you, and ourselves also, a right good time. Do you know that Evelyn and I are schoolgirls now? Is it not strange? Dear Miss Sinclair has left us. We miss her terribly; but I think we shall like school-life—eh, Eve?"

Evelyn had finished Jasper's letter, and had thrust it into her pocket.

"I hate school-life!" she said emphatically.

"Oh Eve! but why?" asked Audrey. "I thought you were making a great many friends at school."

"Wherever I go I shall make friends," replied Evelyn in a careless tone. "That, of course, is due to my position. But I do not know, after all," she continued, "that I like fair-weather friends. Mothery used to tell me that I must be careful when with them. She said they would, one and all, expect me to do something for them. Now, I hate people

CHAPTER XIX.—"WHY DID YOU DO IT?"

who want you to do things for them. For my part, I shall soon let my so-called friends know that I am not that sort of girl."

"Let us walk about now," said Audrey. "It will be lunch-time before long; afterwards I thought we might go for a ride. Can you ride, Sylvia?"

"I used to ride once," she answered, coloring high with pleasure.

"I can lend you a habit; and we have a very nice horse—quite quiet, and at the same time spirited."

"I am not afraid of any horses," answered the girl. "I should like a ride immensely."

"We will have lunch, then a ride, then a good cozy chat together by the schoolroom fire, then dinner; and then, what do you say to a dance? We have asked some young friends to come to the Castle to-night for the purpose."

"I must not be too late in going home," said Sylvia. "And," she added, "I have not brought a dress for the evening."

"Oh, we must manage that," said Audrey. "What a good thing that you and I are the same height! Now, shall we walk round the shrubbery?"

"The shrubbery always reminds me," said Sylvia, "of the first day we met."

"Yes. I was very angry with you that day," said Audrey, with a laugh. "You must know that I always hated that old custom of throwing the Castle open to every one on New Year's Day."

"But I am too glad of it," said Sylvia. "It made me know you, and Evelyn too."

"Don't forget, Audrey," said Evelyn at that moment, "that Sylvia is really my friend. It was I who first brought her to the Castle.—You do not forget that, do you, Sylvia?"

"No," said Sylvia, smiling. "And I like you both awfully. But do tell me about your school—do, please."

"Well," said Audrey, "there is a rather exciting thing to tell—something unpleasant, too. Perhaps you ought not to know."

"Please—please tell me. I am quite dying to hear about it."

Audrey then described the mysterious damage done to SESAME AND LILIES.

"Miss Henderson was told," she said, "and yesterday morning she spoke to the entire school. She is going to punish the person who did it very severely if she can find her; and if that person does not confess, I believe the whole school is to be put more or less into Coventry."

"But how does she know that any of the girls did it?" was Sylvia's answer. "There are servants in the house. Has she questioned them?"

"She has; but it so happens that the servants are quite placed above suspicion, for the book was whole at a certain hour the very first day we came to school, and that evening it was found in its mutilated

A VERY NAUGHTY GIRL

condition. During all those hours it happened to be in the Fourth Form schoolroom."

"Yes," said Evelyn in a careless tone. "It is quite horrid for me, you know, for I am a Fourth Form girl. I ought not to be. I ought to be in the Sixth Form with Audrey. But there! those unpleasant mistresses have no penetration."

"But why should you wish to be in a higher form than your acquirements warrant?" replied Sylvia. "Oh," she added, with enthusiasm, "don't I envy you both your luck! Should I not love to be at school in order to work hard!"

"By the way, Sylvia," said Audrey suddenly, "how have you been educated?"

"Why, anyhow," said the girl. "I have taught myself mostly. But please do not ask me any questions. I don't want to think of my own life at all to-day; I am so very happy at being with you two."

Audrey immediately turned the conversation; but soon, by a sort of instinct, it crept back again to the curious occurrence which had taken place at Miss Henderson's school.

"Please do not speak of it at lunch," said Audrey, "for we have not told mother or father anything about it. We hope that this disgraceful thing will not be made public, but that the culprit will confess."

"Much chance of that!" said Evelyn; and she nudged Sylvia's arm, on which she happened to be leaning.

The girls presently went into the house. Lunch followed. Lady Frances was extremely kind to Sylvia—in fact, she made a pet of her. She looked with admiration at the pretty and suitable costume, and wondered in her own heart what she could do for the little girl.

"I like her," she said to herself. "She suits me better than any girl I have ever met except my own dear Audrey. Oh, how I wish she were the heiress instead of Evelyn!"

Evelyn was fairly well behaved; she had learnt to suppress herself. She was now outwardly dutiful to Lady Frances, and was, without any seeming in the matter, affectionate to her uncle. The Squire was always specially kind to Evelyn; but he liked young girls, and took notice of Sylvia also, trying to draw her out. He spoke to her about her father. He told her that he had once known a distinguished man of the name, and wondered if it could be the same. Sylvia colored painfully, and showed by many signs that the conversation distressed her.

"It cannot be the same, of course," said the Squire lightly, "for my friend Robert Leeson was a man who was likely to rise to the very top of his profession. He was a barrister of extreme eminence. I shall never forget the brilliant way he spoke in a CAUSE CÉLÈBRE which occupied public attention not long ago. He won the case for his clients, and covered himself with well-earned glory."

CHAPTER XIX.—"WHY DID YOU DO IT?"

Sylvia's eyes sparkled; then they grew dim with unshed tears. She lowered her eyes and looked on her plate. Lady Frances nodded softly to herself.

"The same—doubtless the same," she said to herself. "A most distinguished man. How terribly sad! I must inquire into this; Edward has unexpectedly given me the clue."

The girls went for a ride after lunch, and the rest of the delightful day passed swiftly. Sylvia counted the hours. Whenever she looked at the clock her face grew a little sadder. Half-hour after half-hour of the precious time was going by. When should she have such a grand treat again? At last it was time to go up-stairs to dress for dinner.

"Now, you must come to my room, Sylvia," said Evelyn. "Yes, I insist," she added, "for I was in reality your first friend."

Sylvia was quite willing to comply. She soon found herself in Evelyn's extremely pretty blue-and-silver room. How comfortable it looked— how luxurious, how sweet, how refreshing to the eyes! The cleanliness and perfect order of the room, the brightness of the fire, the calm, proper look of Read as she stood by waiting to dress Evelyn for dinner, all impressed Sylvia.

"I like this life," she said suddenly. "Perhaps it is bad for me even to see it, but I like it; I confess as much."

"Perhaps, Miss Leeson," said Read just then in a very courteous voice, "you will not object to Miss Audrey lending you the same dress you wore the last time you were here? It has been nicely made up, and looks very fresh and new."

As Read spoke she pointed to the lovely Indian muslin robe which lay across Evelyn's bed.

"Please, Read," said Evelyn suddenly, "don't stay to help me to dress to-night; Sylvia will do that. I want to have a chat with her; I have a lot to say."

"I will certainly help Evelyn if I can," replied Sylvia.

"Very well, miss," replied Read. "To tell you the truth, I shall be rather relieved; my mistress requires a fresh tucker to be put into the dress she means to wear this evening, and I have not quite finished it. Then you will excuse me, young ladies. If you want anything, will you have the goodness to ring?"

The next moment Read had departed.

"Now, that is right," said Evelyn. "Now we shall have a cozy time; there is nearly an hour before we need go down-stairs. How do you like my room, Sylvia?"

"Very much indeed. I see the second bed has gone."

"Oh yes. I do not mind a scrap sleeping alone now; in fact, I rather prefer it. Sylvia, I want so badly to confide in you!"

"To confide in me! How? Why?"

"I want to ask you about Jasper. Oh yes, she wants to see me. I can manage to slip out about nine o'clock on Tuesday next; we are not to dine down-stairs on Tuesday night, for there is a big dinner party. She can come to meet me then; I shall be standing by the stile in the shrubbery."

"But surely Lady Frances will not like you to be out so late!"

"As if I minded her! Sylvia, for goodness' sake don't tell me that you are growing goody-goody."

"No; I never was that," replied Sylvia. "I don't think I could be; it is not in me, I am afraid."

"I hope not; I don't think Jasper would encourage that sort of thing. Yes, I have a lot to tell her, and you may say from me that I don't care for school."

"Oh, I am so sorry! It is incomprehensible to me, for I should think that you would love it."

"For some reasons I might have endured it; but then, you see, there is that awkward thing about the Ruskin book."

"The Ruskin book!" said Sylvia. She turned white, and her heart began to beat. "Surely—surely, Evelyn, you have had nothing to do with the tearing out of the first pages of SESAME AND LILIES!"

"You won't tell—you promise you won't tell?" said Evelyn, nodding her head, and her eyes looking very bright.

"Oh! I don't know. This is dreadful; please relieve my anxiety."

"You will not tell; you dare not!" said Evelyn, with passion. "If you did I would tell about Jasper—I would. Oh! I would not leave a stone unturned to make your life miserable. There, Sylvia, forgive me; I did not mean to scold. I like you so much, dear Sylvia; and I am so glad you have Jasper with you, and it suits me to perfection. But I did tear the leaves out of the book; yes, I did, and I am glad I did; and you must never, never tell."

"But, Eve—oh, Eve! why did you do such a dreadful thing?"

"I did it in a fit of temper, to spite that horrid Miss Thompson; I hate her so! She was so intolerably cheeky; she made me stay in during recreation on the very first day, and she accused me of telling lies, and when she had left the room I saw the odious book lying on the table. I had seen her reading it before, and I thought it was her book; and almost before I had time to think, the pages were out and torn up and in the fire. If I had known it was Miss Henderson's book, of course, I should not have done it. But I did not know. I meant to punish horrid old Thompson, and it seems I have succeeded better than I expected."

"But, Eve—Eve, the whole school is suspected now. What are you going to do?"

"Do!" replied Evelyn. "Nothing."

"But you have been asked, have you not, whether you knew anything about the injury to the book?"

CHAPTER XIX.–"WHY DID YOU DO IT?"

"I have, and I told a nice little whopper—a nice pretty little whopper—a dear, charming little whopper—and I mean to stick to it."

"Eve!"

"You look shocked. Well, cheer up; it has not been your fault. I must confide in some one, so I have told you, and you may tell Jasper if you like. Dear old Jasper! she will applaud me for my spirit. Oh dear! do you know, Sylvia, I think you are rather a tiresome girl. I thought you too would have admired the plucky way I have acted."

"How can I admire deceit and lies?" replied Sylvia in a low tone.

"You dare say those words to me!"

"Yes, I dare. Oh, you have made me unhappy! Oh, you have destroyed my day! Oh Eve, Eve, why did you do it?"

"You won't tell on me, please, Sylvia? You have promised that, have you not?"

"Oh, why should I tell? It is not my place. But why did you do it?"

"If you will not tell, nothing matters. I have done it, and it is not your affair."

"Yes, it is, now that you have confided in me. Oh, you have made me unhappy!"

"You are a goose! But you may tell dear Jasper; and tell her too that her little Eve will wait for her at the turnstile on Tuesday night at nine o'clock. Now then, let's get ready or we shall be late for dinner."

CHAPTER XX.—"NOT GOOD NOR HONORABLE."

It was very late indeed when Sylvia got home. On this occasion she was not allowed to return to The Priory unaccompanied; Lady Frances insisted on Read going with her. Read said very little as the two walked over the roads together; but she was ever a woman of few words. Sylvia longed to question her, as she wanted to take as much news as possible to Jasper, but Read's face was decidedly uninviting. As soon as the woman had gone, Sylvia slipped round to the back entrance, where Jasper was waiting for her. Jasper had the gate ajar, and Pilot was standing by her side.

"Come, darling—come right in," she said. "The coast is clear, and, oh! I have a lot to tell you."

She fastened the back gate, making it look as though it had not been disturbed for years, and a moment later the woman and the girl were standing in the warm kitchen.

"The door is locked, and he will not come," said Jasper. "He is quite well, and I heard him go up-stairs to his bed an hour ago."

"And did he eat anything, Jasper?"

"Oh, did he not, my love? Oh, I am fit to die with laughter when I think of it! He imagines that he has demolished one quarter of the scraggiest hen in the hen-house."

"What! old Wallaroo?" replied Sylvia, a smile breaking over her face.

"Wallaroo, or whatever outlandish name you like to call the bird."

"Please tell me all about it."

Sylvia sank down as she spoke into a chair. Jasper related her morning's adventure, and the two laughed heartily.

"Only it seems a shame to deceive him," said Sylvia at last. "And so Wallaroo has really gone! Do you know, I shall miss her; I have stood and watched her antics for so many long days. She was the most outrageous flirt of any bird I have ever come across, and so indignant when old Roger paid the least attention to any of his other wives."

"She has passed her flirting days," replied Jasper, "and is now the property of little Tim Donovan in the village; perhaps, however, she will get more food there. My dear Miss Sylvia, you must make up your mind that each one of those birds has to be disposed of in secret, and that I in exchange get in sleek and fat young fowls for your father's benefit. But now, that is enough on the subject for the present. Tell me all about Miss Evelyn; I am just dying to hear."

"She will meet you on Tuesday evening at nine o'clock by the turnstile in the shrubbery," replied Sylvia.

"That is right. What a brave, dear, plucky pet she is!"

Sylvia was silent.

CHAPTER XX.–"NOT GOOD NOR HONORABLE."

"What is the matter with you, Miss Sylvia? Had you not a happy day?"
"I had—very, very happy until just before dinner."
"And what happened then?"
"I will tell you in the morning, Jasper—not to-night. Something happened then. I am sorry and sad, but I will tell you in the morning. I must slip up to bed now without father knowing it."
"Your father thinks that you are in bed, for I went up, just imitating your step to perfection, an hour before he did, and I went into your room and shut the door; and when he went up he knocked at the door, and I answered in your voice that I had a bit of a headache and had gone to bed. He asked me if I had had any supper, and I said no; and he said the best thing for a headache was to rest the stomach. Bless you! he is keen on that, whatever else he is not keen on. He went off to his bed thinking you were snug in yours. When I made sure that he was well in his bed, which I could tell by the creaking of the bedstead, I let myself out. I had oiled the lock previously. I shut the door without making a sound loud enough to wake a mouse, and crept down-stairs; and here I am. You must not go up to-night or you will give me away, and there will be a fine to-do. You must sleep in my cozy room to-night."
"Well, I do not mind that," replied Sylvia. "How clever you are, Jasper! You really did manage most wonderfully; only again I must say it seems a shame to deceive my dear old father."
"It is a question of dying in the cause of your dear old father or deceiving him," replied Jasper in blunt tones. "Now then, come to bed, my love, for if you are not dead with sleep I am."
The next morning Mr. Leeson was in admirable spirits. He met Sylvia at breakfast, and congratulated her on the long day she had spent in the open air.
"And you look all the better for it," he said. "I was too busy to think about you at tea-time; indeed, I did not have any tea, having consumed a most admirable luncheon some time before one o'clock. I was so very busy attending to my accounts all the afternoon that I quite forgot my dear little girl. Well, I have made arrangements, dearest, to buy shares in the Kilcolman Gold-mines. The thing may or may not turn up trumps, but in any case I have made an effort to spare a little money to buy some of the shares. That means that we must be extra prudent and careful for the next year or so. You will aid me in that, will you not, Sylvia? You will solemnly promise me, my dear and only child, that you will not give way to recklessness; when you see a penny you will look at it two or three times before you spend it. You have not the least idea how careful it makes you to keep what I call close and accurate accounts, every farthing made to produce its utmost value, and, if possible—if possible, my dear Sylvia— saved. It is surprising how little man really wants here below; the

luxuries of the present day are disgusting, enervating, unnecessary. I speak to you very seriously, for now and then, I grieve to say, I have seen traces in you of what rendered my married life unhappy."

"Father, you must not speak against mother," said Sylvia. Her face was pale and her voice trembled. "There was no one like mother," she continued, "and for her sake I——"

"Yes, Sylvia, what do you do for her sake?"

"I put up with this death in life. Oh father, father, do you think I really—really like it?"

Mr. Leeson looked with some alarm at his child. Sylvia's eyes were full of tears; she laid her hands on the table, bent forward, and looked full across at her father.

"For mother's sake I bear it; you cannot think that I like it!" she repeated.

Mr. Leeson's first amazement now gave place to cold displeasure.

"We will not pursue this topic," he said. "I have something more to tell you. I made a pleasant discovery yesterday. During your absence a strange thing occurred. A gipsy woman entered the avenue and walked up to the front door, unmolested by Pilot. She seemed to have a strange power over Pilot, for the dog did not bar her entrance in the least. I naturally went to see what she wanted, and she told me that she had come, thinking I might have some fowls for sale. Now, you know, my dear, those old birds in the hen-house have long been eating their heads off, and I rather hailed an opportunity of getting rid of them; they only lay eggs—and that but a few—in the warm weather, and during the winter we are at a loss by our efforts to keep them alive."

"I know plenty about fowls," said Sylvia then. "They need hot suppers and all sorts of good things to make them lay eggs in cold weather."

"We can do without eggs, but we cannot afford to give the fowls hot suppers," said Mr. Leeson in a tone of great dignity. "But now, Sylvia, to the point. The woman offered a ludicrous price for the birds, and of course I would not part with them; at the same time she incidentally—silly person—gave herself away. She let me understand that she wanted the fowls to stew down in the gipsy pot. Now, of late, when arranging my recipes for publication, I have often thought of the gipsies and the delicious stews they make out of all sorts of things which other people would throw away. It occurred to me, therefore, to question her; and the result was, dear, not to go too much into particulars, that she killed one of the fowls, and in a very short time brought me a delicious stew made out of the bird, really as tasty and succulent as anything I have ever swallowed. I paid her a trifle for her services, and the remainder of the fowl is at the present moment lying in the cupboard in our sitting-room. I should like it to be warmed up for our midday repast; there is a great deal more there than we can by any possibility consume, but we can have a dainty meal out of part of

CHAPTER XX.—"NOT GOOD NOR HONORABLE."

the stew, and the rest can be saved for supper. I have further decided that we must get some one to kill the rest of the birds, and we will have them one by one on the table. Do you ever, my dear Sylvia, in your perambulations abroad, go near any of the gipsies?—for, if so, I should not mind giving you a shilling to purchase that woman's recipe."

Sylvia at this juncture rose from the table. She had with the utmost difficulty kept her composure while her father was so innocently talking about the gipsy's stew.

"I will see—I will see, father. I quite understand," she said; and the next instant she ran out of the room.

"Really," thought Mr. Leeson when she had gone, "Sylvia talks a little strangely at times. Just think how she spoke just now of her happy home! Death in life, she called it—a most wrong and exaggerated term; and exaggeration of speech leads to extravagance of mind, and extravagance of mind means most reckless expenditure. If I am not very careful my poor child will soon be on the road to ruin. I doubt if I ought to feed her up with dainties—and really that stewed fowl made a rare and delicious dish—but it is the most saving thing I can do; there are enough birds in the hen-house to last Sylvia and me for several weeks to come."

Meanwhile Sylvia had rushed off to Jasper.

"Oh Jasper!" she said, "I nearly died with laughter, and yet it is horrid to deceive him. Oh! please do not kill any more of the birds for a long time; it is more than I can stand. Father is so delighted; and he has offered me a shilling to buy the recipe from you."

"Bless you, dear!" replied Jasper, "and I think what I am doing for your father is well worth a shilling, so you had better give it to me."

"I have not got it yet," replied Sylvia. "You must live on trust, Jasper; but, oh, it is quite too funny!"

"Now, you sit down just there," said Jasper, "and tell me what troubled you last night."

Sylvia's face changed utterly when Jasper spoke.

"It is about Eve," she said. "She has done very wrong—very wrong indeed." And then Sylvia related exactly what had occurred at school. Jasper stood and listened with her arms akimbo; her face more than once underwent a curious expression.

"And so you blame my little Eve very much?" she said when Sylvia had ceased speaking.

"How can I help it? To get the whole school accused—to tell a lie to do it! Oh Jasper, how can I help myself?"

"You were brought up so differently," said Jasper. "Maybe if I had had the rearing of you and the loving of you from your earliest days I might have thought with you; as it is, I think with Eve. I could not

A VERY NAUGHTY GIRL

counsel her to tell. I cannot but admire her spirit when she did what she did."

"Jasper! Jasper!" said Sylvia in a tone of horror, "you cannot—cannot mean what you are saying! Oh, please unsay those dreadful words! I was hoping—hoping—hoping that you might put things right. What is to be done? There is going to be a great fuss—a great commotion—a great trouble at Miss Henderson's school. Evelyn can put it right by confessing; are you not going to urge her to confess?"

"I urge my darling to lower herself! Miss Sylvia, if you say that kind of thing to me again, you and I can scarcely be friends."

"Jasper! Jasper!"

"We won't talk about it," said Jasper, with decision. "I love you, miss, and what is more, I respect and admire you, but I cannot rise as high as you, Miss Sylvia; I was not reared so. I do not think that my little Eve could have done other than she did when she was so tempted."

"Then, Jasper, you are a bad friend to Evelyn—a very bad friend; and what is more, if there is great trouble at the school, and if Audrey gets into it, and if Evelyn herself will never tell, why, I must."

"Oh, good gracious! you would not be so mean as that; and the poor, dear little innocent confided in you!"

"I do not want to be so mean, and I will not tell for a long, long time; but I will tell—I will—if no one else can put it right, for it is quite too cruel."

Jasper looked long and full at Sylvia.

"This may mean a good deal," she said—"more than you think. And have you no sense of honor, miss? What you are told in confidence, have you any right to give to the world?"

"I will not tell if I can help myself, but this matter has made me very unhappy indeed."

Then Sylvia put on her shabby hat and went out. She passed the fowl-house, and stood for a moment, a sad smile on her face, looking down at the ill-fed birds. Then she went along the tiny shrubbery to the front entrance, and, accompanied as usual by her beloved Pilot, started forth. She was in her very shabbiest and oldest dress to-day, and the joy and brightness of her appearance of twenty-four hours ago had absolutely left her young face. It was Sunday morning, but Sylvia never went to church. She heard the bells ringing now. Sweetly they pealed across the valley, and one little church on the top of the hill sent forth a low and yet joyful chime. Sylvia longed to press her hands to her ears; she did not want to listen to the church bells. Those who went to church did right, not wrong; those who went to church listened to God's Word, and followed the ways—the good and holy ways—of religion.

"And I cannot go because of my shabby, shabby dress," she thought. "But why should I not wear the beautiful dress I had yesterday and venture to church?"

CHAPTER XX.–"NOT GOOD NOR HONORABLE."

No sooner had the thought come to her than she returned, dashed in by the back entrance, desired Pilot to stay where he was, flew up-stairs, dressed herself recklessly in her rich finery of yesterday, and started off for church. She had a fancy to go to the church on the top of the hill, but she had to walk fast to reach it. She did arrive there a little late. The verger showed her into a pew half-way up the church. One or two people turned to stare at the handsome girl. The brilliant color was in her cheeks from the quickness of her walk. She dropped on her knees and covered her face; all was confusion in her mind. In the Squire's pew, a very short distance away, sat Audrey and Evelyn. Could Evelyn indeed mean to pray? Of what sort of nature was Evelyn made? Sylvia felt that she could not meet her eyes.

"Some people who are not good, who are not honorable, go to church," she thought to herself. "It is very sad and very puzzling."

CHAPTER XXI.—THE TORN BOOK.

On the following morning Audrey and Evelyn started off for school. On the way Audrey turned to her companion.

"I wonder if anything has been discovered with regard to the injured book?" she said.

"Oh, I wish you would not talk so continually about that stupid old fuss!" said Evelyn in her crossest voice.

"It is useless to shirk it," was Audrey's reply. "You do not suppose for a single moment that Miss Henderson will not get to the bottom of the mischief? For my part, I think I could understand a girl doing it just for a moment in a spirit of revenge, although I have never yet felt revengeful to any one—but how any one could keep it up and allow the school to get into trouble is what puzzles me."

"Were you ever at school before, Audrey?" was Evelyn's remark.

"No; were you?"

"I wish I had been; I have always longed for school."

"Well, you have your wish at last. How do you like it?"

"I should like it fairly well if I were put into a higher form, and if this stupid fuss were not going on."

"Why do you dislike the subject being mentioned so much?"

Evelyn colored slightly. Audrey looked at her. There was no suspicion in Audrey's eyes; it was absolutely impossible for her to connect her cousin with anything so mean and low. Evelyn had a great many objectionable habits, but that she could commit what was in Audrey's opinion a very grave sin, and then tell lies about it, was more than the young girl could either imagine or realize.

The pretty governess-cart took them to school in good time, and the usual routine of the morning began. It was immediately after prayers, however, that Miss Henderson spoke from her desk to the assembled school.

"I am sorry to tell you all," she began, "that up to the present I have not got the slightest clue to the mystery of the injured book. I have questioned, I have gone carefully into every particular, and all I can find out is that the book was left in classroom No. 4 (which is usually occupied by the girls of the Fourth Form); that it was placed there at nine o'clock in the morning, and was not used again by Miss Thompson until school was over—namely, between five and six o'clock in the evening. During that time, as far as I can make out, only one girl was alone in the room. That girl was Evelyn Wynford. I do not in any way accuse Evelyn Wynford of having committed the sin—for sin it was—but I have to mention the fact that she was alone in the room during recess, having failed to learn a lesson which had been set her. During the afternoon the room was, as far as I can tell, empty for a couple of hours, and of course some one may have come

CHAPTER XXI.–THE TORN BOOK.

in then and done the mischief. I therefore have not the slightest intention of suspecting a girl who only arrived that morning; but I mention the fact, all the same, that Evelyn Wynford was ALONE IN THE ROOM FOR THE SPACE OF TWENTY MINUTES."

While Miss Henderson was speaking all eyes were turned in Evelyn's direction; all eyes saw a white and stubborn face, and two angry brown eyes that flashed almost wildly round the room and then looked down. Just for an instant a few of the girls said to themselves, "That is a guilty face." But again they thought, "How could she do it? Why should she do it? No, it certainly cannot be Evelyn Wynford."

As to Audrey, she pitied Evelyn very much. She thought it extremely hard on her that Miss Henderson should have singled her out for individual notice on this most painful occasion, and out of pity for her she would not once glance in her direction.

Miss Henderson paused for a moment; then she continued:

"Whoever the sinner may be, I am determined to sift this crime to the bottom. I shall severely punish the girl who tore the book unless she makes up her mind to confess to me between now and to-morrow evening. If she confesses before school is over to-morrow evening, I shall not only not punish but I shall forgive her. It will be my painful duty, however, to oblige her to confess her sin before the entire school, as in no other way can the rest of the girls be exonerated. I give her till to-morrow evening to make up her mind. I hope she will ask for strength from above to enable her to make this very painful confession. I myself shall pray that she may be guided aright. If no one comes forward by that time, I must again assemble the school to suggest a very terrible alternative."

Here Miss Henderson left the room, and the different members of the school went off to their respective duties.

School went on much as usual. The girls were forced to attend to their numerous duties; the all-absorbing theme was therefore held more or less in abeyance for the time being. At recess, however, knots of girls might be seen talking to one another in agitated whispers. The subject of the injured book was the one topic on every one's tongue. Evelyn produced chocolates, crystallized fruits, and other dainties from a richly embroidered bag which she wore at her side, and soon had her own little coterie of followers. To these she imparted her opinion that Miss Henderson was not only a fuss, but a dragon; that probably a servant had torn the book—or perhaps, she added, Miss Thompson herself.

"Why," said Evelyn, "should not Miss Thompson greatly dislike Miss Henderson, and tear the outside page out of the book just to spite her?"

But this theory was not received as possible by any one to whom she imparted it. Miss Thompson was a favorite; Miss Thompson hated no one; Miss Thompson was the last person on earth to do such a shabby thing.

"Well," said Evelyn crossly, "I don't know who did it; and what is more, I don't care. Come and walk with me, Alice," she said to a pretty little curly-headed girl who sat next to her at class. "Come and let me tell you about all the grandeur which will be mine by and by. I shall be queen by and by. It is a shame—a downright shame—to worry a girl in my position with such a trifle as a torn book. The best thing we can all do is to subscribe amongst ourselves and give the old dragon another SESAME AND LILIES. I don't mind subscribing. Is it not a good thought?"

"But that will not help her," said Alice; while Cherry, who stood near, solemnly shook her head.

"Why will it not help her?" asked Evelyn.

"Because it was the inscription she valued—the inscription in her brother's writing; her brother who is dead, you know."

Evelyn was about to make another pert remark when a memory assailed her. Naughty, heartless, rude as she was, she had somewhere a spark of feeling. If she had loved any one it was the excitable and strange woman she had called "mothery."

"If mothery gave me something and wrote my name in it I'd be fond of it," she thought; and just for a moment a prick of remorse visited her hard little heart.

No other girl in the whole school could confess the crime which Evelyn had committed, and the evening came in considerable gloom and excitement. Audrey could talk of nothing else on their way home.

"It is terrible," said Audrey. "I am really sorry we are both at the school; it makes things so unpleasant for us. And you, Evelyn—I did pity you when Miss Henderson said to-day that you were alone in the room. Did you not feel awful?"

"No, I did not," replied Evelyn. "At least, perhaps I did just for a minute."

"Well, it was very brave of you. I should not have liked to be in your position."

Evelyn turned the conversation.

"I wonder whether any one will confess to-morrow," said Audrey again.

"Perhaps it was one of the servants," remarked Evelyn. Then she said abruptly, "Oh, do let us change the subject!"

"There is something fine about Evelyn after all," thought Audrey; "And I am so glad! She took that speech of Miss Henderson's very well indeed. Now, I scarcely thought it fair to have her name singled out in the way it was. Surely Miss Henderson could not have suspected my little cousin!"

At dinner Audrey mentioned the whole circumstance of the torn book to her parents. The girls were again dining with the Squire and Lady

CHAPTER XXI.–THE TORN BOOK.

Frances. The Squire was interested for a short time; he then began to chat with Evelyn, who was fast, in her curious fashion, becoming a favorite of his. She was always at her best in his society, and now nestled up close to him, and said in an almost winsome manner:
"Don't let us talk about the old fuss at school."
"Whom do you call the old fuss, Evelyn?"
"Miss Henderson. I don't like her a bit, Uncle Edward."
"That is very naughty, Evelyn. Remember, I want you to like her."
"Why?"
"Because for the present, at least, she is your instructress."
"But why should I like my instructress?"
"She cannot influence you unless you like her."
"Then she will never influence me, because I shall never like her," cried the reckless girl. "I wish you would teach me, Uncle Edward. I should learn from you; you would influence me because I love you."
"I do try to influence you, Evelyn, and I want you to do a great many things for me."
"I would do anything in all the world for him," thought Evelyn, "except confess that I tore that book; but that I would not do even for him. Of course, now that there has been such an awful fuss, I am sorry I did it, but for no other reason. It is one comfort, however, they cannot possibly suspect me."
Lady Frances, however, took Audrey's information in a very different spirit from what her husband did. She felt indignant at Evelyn's having been singled out for special and undoubtedly unfavorable notice by Miss Henderson, and resolved to call at the school the next day to have an interview with the head-mistress. She said nothing to Audrey about her intention, and the girls went off to school without the least idea of what Lady Frances was about to do. Her carriage stopped before Chepstow House a little before noon. She inquired for Miss Henderson, and was immediately admitted into the head-mistress's private sitting-room. There Miss Henderson a moment or two later joined her.
"I am sorry to trouble you," began Lady Frances at once, "but I have come on a matter which occasioned me a little distress. I allude to the mystery of the torn book. Audrey has told me all about it, so I am in possession of full particulars. Of course I am extremely sorry for you, and can quite understand your feelings with regard to the injury of a book you value so much; but, at the same time, you will excuse my saying, Miss Henderson, that I think your mentioning Evelyn's name in the way you did was a little too obvious. It was uncomfortable for the poor child, although I understand from my daughter that she took it extremely well."
"In a case of this kind," replied Miss Henderson quietly, "one has to be just, and not to allow any favoritism to appear."

A VERY NAUGHTY GIRL

"Oh, certainly," said Lady Frances; "it was my wish in sending both girls to school that they should find their level."

"And I regret to say," answered Miss Henderson, "that your niece's level is not a high one."

"Alas! I am aware of it. I have been terribly pained since Evelyn came home by her recklessness and want of obedience; but this is a very different matter. This shows a most depraved nature; and of course you cannot for a moment have suspected my niece when you spoke of her being alone in the room."

"Had any other girl been alone in the room I should equally have mentioned her name," said Miss Henderson. "I certainly did not at the time suspect Miss Wynford."

"What do you mean by 'did not at the time'? Have you changed your opinion?"

Lady Frances's face turned very white.

"I am sorry to say that I have."

"What do you mean?"

"If you will pardon me for a moment I will explain."

Miss Henderson left the room.

While she was absent Lady Frances felt a cold dew breaking out on her forehead.

"This is beyond everything," she thought. "But it is impossible; the child could never have done it. What motive would she have? She is not as bad as that; and it was her very first day at school."

Miss Henderson re-entered the room, accompanied by Miss Thompson. In Miss Thompson's hand was a copy of the History of England that Evelyn had been using.

"Will you kindly open that book," said Miss Henderson, "and show Lady Frances what you have found there?"

Miss Thompson did so. She opened the History at the reign of Edward I. Between the leaves were to be seen two fragments of torn paper. Miss Thompson removed them carefully and laid them upon Lady Frances's hand. Lady Frances glanced at them, and saw that they were beyond doubt torn from a copy of Ruskin's SESAME AND LILIES. She let them drop back again on to the open page of the book.

"I accuse no one," said Miss Henderson. "Even now I accuse no one; but I grieve to tell you, Lady Frances, that this book was in the hands of your niece, Evelyn Wynford, on that afternoon.—Miss Thompson, will you relate the entire circumstances to Lady Frances?"

"I am very, very sorry," said Miss Thompson. "I wish with all my heart I had understood the child better, but of course she was a stranger to me. The circumstance was this: I gave her the history of the reign of Edward I. to look over during class, as of course on her first day at school she had no regular lessons ready. She glanced at it, told me she knew the reign, and amused herself looking about during the

CHAPTER XXI.—THE TORN BOOK.

remainder of the time. At recess I called her to me and questioned her. She seemed to be totally ignorant of anything relating to Edward I. I reproved her for having made an incorrect statement——"

"For having told a lie, you mean," snapped Lady Frances.

Miss Thompson bowed.

"I reproved her, and as a punishment desired her to look over the reign while the other girls were in the playground."

"And quite right," said Lady Frances.

"She was very much annoyed, but I was firm. I left her with the book in her hand. I have nothing more to say. At six o'clock that evening I removed SESAME AND LILIES from its place in the classroom, and took it away to continue the preparation of a lecture. I then found that several pages had been removed. This morning, early, I happened to take this very copy of the History, and found these fragments in the part of the book which contains the reign of Edward I."

"Suspicion undoubtedly now points to Evelyn," said Miss Henderson; "and I must say, Lady Frances, that although a matter of this kind pertains entirely to the school, and must be dealt with absolutely by the head-mistress, yet your having called, and in a measure taken the matter up, relieves me of a certain responsibility."

"Suspicion does undoubtedly point to the unhappy child," said Lady Frances; "but still, I can scarcely believe it. What do you mean to do?"

"I shall to-morrow morning have to state before the entire school what I have now stated to you."

"It might be best for me to remove Evelyn, and let her confess to you in writing."

"I do not think that would be either right or fair. If the girl is taken away now she is practically injured for life. Give her a chance, I beseech you, Lady Frances, of retrieving her character."

"Oh, what is to be done?" said Lady Frances. "To think that my daughter should have a girl like that for a companion! You do not know how we are all to be pitied."

"I do indeed; you have my sincere sympathy," said Miss Henderson.

"And what do you advise?"

"I think, as she is a member of the school, you must leave her to me. She committed this offense on the very first day of her school-life, and if possible we must not be too severe on her. She has not been brought up as an English girl."

Lady Frances talked a little longer with the head-mistress, and went away; she felt terribly miserable and unhappy.

CHAPTER XXII.—"STICK TO YOUR COLORS, EVELYN."

Evelyn met Jasper, as arranged, on Tuesday evening. She found it quite easy to slip away unnoticed, for in truth Lady Frances was too unhappy to watch her movements particularly. The girls had been dining alone. Audrey had a headache, and had gone to bed early. Evelyn rushed up to her room, put on a dark shawl, which completely covered her fair hair and white-robed little figure, and rushed out by a side entrance. She wore thin shoes, however, being utterly reckless with regard to her health. Jasper was waiting for her. It took but an instant for Jasper to clasp her in her arms, lifting her off the ground as she did so.

"Oh, my little darling," cried the affectionate woman—"my sweet little white Eve! Oh, let me hug you; let me kiss you! Oh, my pet! it is like cold water to a thirsty person to clasp you in my arms again."

"Do not squeeze me quite so tight, Jasper," said Evelyn. "Yes, of course, I am glad to see you—very glad."

"But let me feel your feet, pet. Oh, to think of your running out like this in your house-shoes! You will catch your death! Here, I will sit down on this step and keep you in my arms. Now, is not that cozy, my fur cloak wrapped round you, feet and all? Is not that nice, little Eve?"

"Yes, very nice," said Evelyn. "It is almost as good as if I were back again on the ranch with mothery and you."

"Ah, the happy old days!" sighed Jasper.

"Yes, they were very happy, Jasper. I almost wish I was back again. I am worried a good bit; things are not what I thought they would be in England. There is no fuss made about me, and at school they treat me so horribly."

"You bide your time, my love; you bide your time."

"I don't like school, Jas."

"And why not, my beauty? You know you must be taught, my dear Miss Evelyn; an ignorant young lady has no chance at all in these enlightened days."

"Oh! please, Jas, do not talk so much like a horrid book; be your true old self. What does learning matter?"

"Everything, love; I assure you it does."

"Well, I shall never be learned; it is too much trouble."

"But why don't you like school, pet?"

"I will tell you. I have got into a scrape; I did not mean to, but I have."

"Oh, you mean about that book. Sylvia told me. Why did you tell Sylvia, Evelyn?"

"I had to tell some one, and she is not a schoolgirl."

CHAPTER XXII.—"STICK TO YOUR COLORS, EVELYN."

"She is not your sort, Evelyn."

"Is she not? I like her very much."

"But she is not your sort; for instance, she could not do a thing of that kind."

"Oh, I do not suppose many people would have spirit enough," said Evelyn in the voice of one who had done a very fine act.

"She could not do it," repeated Jasper; "and I expect she is in the right, and that you, my little love, are in the wrong. You were differently trained. Well, my dear Eve, the long and short of it is that I admire what you did, only somehow Sylvia does not, and you will have to be very careful or she may——"

"What—what, Jasper?"

"She may not regard it as a secret that she will always keep."

"Is she that sort? Oh, the horrid, horrid thing!" said Evelyn. "Oh, to think that I should have told her! But you cannot mean it; it is impossible that you can mean it, Jasper!"

"Don't you fret, love, for I will not let her. If she dares to tell on you, why, I will leave her, and then it is pretty near starvation for the poor little miss."

"You are sure you will not let her tell? I really am in rather a nasty scrape. They are making such a horrid fuss at school. This evening was the limit given for the guilty person—I should not say the guilty person, but the spirited person—to tell, and the spirited person has not told; and to-morrow morning goodness knows what will happen. Miss Henderson has a rod in pickle for us all, I expect. I declare it is quite exciting. None of the girls suspect me, and I talk so openly, and sometimes they laugh, too. I suppose we shall all be punished. I do not really know what is going to be done."

"You hold your tongue and let the whole matter slide. That is my advice," said Jasper. "I would either do that or I would out with it boldly—one or the other. Say you did it, and that you are not ashamed to have done it."

"I could not—I could not," said Evelyn. "I may be brave after a fashion, but I am not brave enough for that. Besides, you know, Jasper, I did say already that I had not done it."

"Oh, to be sure," answered Jasper. "I forgot that. Well, you must stick to your colors now, Eve; and at the worst, my darling, you have but to come to me and I will shield you."

"At the worst—yes, at the worst," said Evelyn. "I will remember that. But if I want to come to you very badly how can I?"

"I will come every night to this stile at nine o'clock, and if you want me you will find me. I will stay here for exactly five minutes, and any message you may like to give you can put under this stone. Now, is not that a 'cute thought of your dear old Jasper's?"

A VERY NAUGHTY GIRL

"It is—it is," said the little girl. "Perhaps, Jasper, I had better be going back now."

"In a minute, darling—in a minute."

"And how are you getting on with Sylvia, Jasper?"

"Oh, such fun, dear! I am having quite an exciting time—hidden from the old gentleman, and acting the gipsy, and pretending I am feeding him with old fowls when I am giving him the tenderest chicken. You have not, darling, a little scrap of money to spare that you can help old Jasper with?"

"Oh! you are so greedy, Jasper; you are always asking for things. Uncle Edward makes me an allowance, but not much; no one would suppose I was the heiress of everything."

"Well dear, the money don't matter. I will come here again to-morrow night. Now, keep up your pecker, little Eve, and all will be well."

Evelyn kissed Jasper, and was about to run back to the house when the good woman remembered the light shoes in which she had come out.

"I'll carry you back," she said. "Those precious little feet shall not touch the frosty ground."

Jasper was very strong, and Evelyn was all too willing. She was carried to within fifty yards of the side entrance in Jasper's strong arms; then she dashed back to the house, kissed her hand to the dark shadow under a tree, and returned to her own room. Read had seen her, but Evelyn knew nothing of that. Read had had her suspicions before now, and determined, as she said, to keep a sharp lookout on young miss in future.

CHAPTER XXIII.—ONE WEEK OF GRACE.

There never was a woman more distressed and puzzled than Miss Henderson. She consulted with her sister, Miss Lucy; she consulted with her favorite teacher, Miss Thompson. They talked into the small hours of the night, and finally it was resolved that Evelyn should have another chance.

"I must appeal to her honor; it is impossible that any girl could be quite destitute of that quality," said Miss Henderson.

"I am sure you are doing right, sister," said Miss Lucy. "Once you harden a girl you do for her. Whatever Evelyn Wynford's faults may be, she will hold a high position one day. It would be terrible—more than terrible—if she grew up a wicked woman. How awful to have power and not to use it aright! My dear Maria, whatever you are, be merciful."

"I must pray to God to guide me aright," answered Miss Maria. "This is a case for a right judgment in all things. Poor child! I pity her from my heart; but how to bring her to the necessary confession is the question."

Miss Henderson went to bed, but not to sleep. Early in the morning she arose, having made up her mind what to do.

Accordingly, when Audrey and Evelyn arrived in the pretty little governess-cart—Audrey with a high color in her cheeks, looking as sweet and fresh and good and nice as English girl could look, and Evelyn tripping after her with a certain defiance on her white face and a look of hostility in her brown eyes—they were both greeted by Miss Henderson herself.

"Ah, Audrey dear," she said in a cheerful and friendly tone, "how are you this morning?—How do you do, Evelyn?—No, Audrey, you are not late; you are quite in nice time. Will you go to the schoolroom, my dear? I will join you presently for prayers.—Evelyn, can I have a word with you?"

"Why so?" asked Evelyn, backing a little.

"Because I have something I want to say to you."

Audrey also stood still. She cast a hostile glance at Miss Henderson, saying to herself:

"After all, my head-mistress is horribly unfair; she is doubtless going to tell Evelyn that she suspects her."

"Evelyn," said Audrey, "I will wait for you in the dressing-room if Miss Henderson has no objection."

"But I have, for it may be necessary for me to detain your cousin for a short time," said Miss Henderson. "Go, Audrey; do not keep me any longer."

A VERY NAUGHTY GIRL

Evelyn stood sullenly and perfectly still in the hall; Audrey disappeared in the direction of the schoolrooms. Miss Henderson now took Evelyn's hand and led her into her private sitting-room.

"What do you want me for?" asked the little girl.

"I want to say something to you, Evelyn."

"Then say it, please."

"You must not be pert."

"I do not know what 'pert' is."

"What you are now. But there, my dear child, please control yourself; believe me, I am truly sorry for you."

"Then you need not be," said Evelyn, with a toss of her head. "I do not want anybody to be sorry for me. I am one of the most lucky girls in the world. Sorry for me! Please don't. Mothery could never bear to be pitied, and I won't be pitied; I have nothing to be pitied for."

"Who did you say never cared to be pitied?" asked Miss Henderson.

"Never you mind."

"And yet, Evelyn, I think I have heard the words. You allude to your mother. I understand from Lady Frances that your mother is dead. You loved her, did you not?"

Evelyn gave a quick nod; her face seemed to say, "That is nothing to you."

"I see you did, and she was fond of you."

In spite of herself Evelyn gave another nod.

"Poor little girl; how sad to be without her!"

"Don't," said Evelyn in a strained voice.

"You lived all your early days in Tasmania, and your mother was good to you because she loved you, and you loved her back; you tried to please her because you loved her."

"Oh, bother!" said Evelyn.

"Come here, dear."

Evelyn did not budge an inch.

"Come over to me," said Miss Henderson.

Miss Henderson was not accustomed to being disobeyed. Her tone was not loud, but it was quiet and determined. She looked full at Evelyn. Her eyes were kind. Evelyn felt as if they mesmerized her. Step by step, very unwillingly, she approached the side of the head-mistress.

"I love girls like you," said Miss Henderson then.

"Bother!" said Evelyn again.

"And I do not mind even when they are sulky and rude and naughty, as you are now; still, I love them—I love them because I am sorry for them."

"You need not be sorry for me; I won't have you sorry for me," said Evelyn.

"If I must not be sorry for you I must be something else."

"What?"

"Angry with you."

CHAPTER XXIII.—ONE WEEK OF GRACE.

"Why so? I never! What do you mean now?"

"I must be angry with you, Evelyn—very angry. But I will say no more by way of excusing my own conduct. I will say nothing of either sorrow or anger. I want to state a fact to you."

"Get it over," said Evelyn.

Miss Henderson now approached the table; she opened the History at the reign of Edward I., and taking two tiny fragments of torn paper from the pages of the book, she laid them in her open palm. In her other hand she held the mutilated copy of SESAME AND LILIES. The print on the torn scrap exactly corresponded with the print in the injured volume. Miss Henderson glanced from Evelyn to the scraps of paper, and from Evelyn to the copy of Ruskin.

"You have intelligence," she said; "you must see what this means."

She then carefully replaced the bits of paper in the History and laid it on the table by her side.

"Between now," she said, "and this time yesterday Miss Thompson discovered these scraps of paper in the copy of the History which you had to read on the morning of the day when you first came to school. The scraps are evidently part of the pages torn from the injured book. Have you anything to say with regard to them?"

Evelyn shook her head; her face was white and her eyes bright. But there was a small red spot on each cheek—a spot about the size of a farthing. It did not grow any larger. It gave a curious effect to the pallid face. The obstinacy of the mouth was very apparent. The cleft in the chin still further showed the curious bias of the girl's character.

"Have you anything to say—any remark to make?"

Again the head was slowly shaken.

"Is there any reason why I should not immediately after prayers to-day explain these circumstances to the whole school, and allow the school to draw its own conclusions?"

Evelyn now raised her eyes and fixed them on Miss Henderson's face.

"You will not do that, will you?" she asked.

"Have you ever, Evelyn, heard of such a thing as circumstantial evidence?"

"No. What is it?"

"You are very ignorant, my dear child—ignorant as well as wilful; wilful as well as wicked."

"No, I am not wicked; you shall not say it!"

"Tell me, is there any reason why I should not show what I have now shown you to the rest of the school, and allow the school to draw its own conclusion?"

"You won't—will you?"

"Must I explain to you, Evelyn, what this means?"

"You can say anything you like."

"These scraps of paper prove beyond doubt that you, for some extraordinary reason, were the person who tore the book. Why you did it is beyond my conception, is beyond Miss Thompson's conception, is beyond the conception of my sister Lucy; but that you did do it we none of us for a moment doubt."

"Oh, you are wicked! How dare you think such things of me?"

"Tell me, Evelyn—tell me why you did it. Come here and tell me. I will not be unkind to you, my poor little girl. I am sorry for one so ignorant, so wanting in all conceptions of right or wrong. Tell me, dear, and as there is a God in heaven, Evelyn, I will forgive you."

"I will not tell you what I did not do," said the angry child.

"You are vexed now and do not know what you are saying. I will go away, and come back again at the end of half an hour; perhaps you will tell me then."

Evelyn stood silent. Miss Henderson, taking the History with her, left the room. She turned the key in the lock. Evelyn rushed to the window. Could she get out by it? She rushed to the door and tried to open it. Window and door defied her efforts. She was locked in. She was like a wild creature in a trap. To scream would do no good. Never before had the spoilt child found herself in such a position. A wild agony seized her; even now she did not repent.

If only mothery were alive! If only she were back on the ranch! If only Jasper were by her side!

"Oh mothery! oh Jasper!" she cried; and then a sob rose to her throat, tears burst from her eyes. The tension for the time was relieved; she huddled up in a chair, and sobbed as if her heart would break.

Miss Henderson came back again in half an hour. Evelyn was still sobbing.

"Well, Evelyn," she said, "I am just going into the schoolroom now for prayers. Have you made up your mind? Will you tell me why you did it, and how you did it, and why you denied it? Just three questions, dear; answer truthfully, and you will have got over the most painful and terrible crisis of your life. Be brave, little girl; ask God to help you."

"I cannot tell you what I do not know," burst now from the angry child. "Think what you like. Do what you like. I am at your mercy; but I hate you, and I will never be a good girl—never, never! I will be a bad girl always—always; and I hate you—I hate you!"

Miss Henderson did not speak a word. The most violent passion cannot long retain its hold when the person on whom its rage is spent makes no reply. Even Evelyn cooled down a little. Miss Henderson stood quite still; then she said gently:

"I am deeply sorry. I was prepared for this. It will take more than this to subdue you."

"Are you going into the schoolroom with those scraps of paper, and are you going to tell all the girls I am guilty?" said Evelyn.

CHAPTER XXIII.—ONE WEEK OF GRACE.

"No, I shall not do that; I will give you another chance. There was to have been a holiday to-day, but because of that sin of yours there will be no holiday. There was to be a visit on Saturday to the museum at Chisfield, which the girls were all looking forward to; they are not to go on account of you. There were to be prizes at the break-up; they will not be given on account of you. The girls will not know that you are the cause of this deprivation, but they will know that the deprivation is theirs because there is a guilty person in the school, and because she will not confess. Evelyn, I give you a week from now to think this matter over. Remember, my dear, that I know you are guilty; remember that my sister Lucy knows it, and Miss Thompson; but before you are publicly disgraced we wish to give you a chance. We will treat you during the week that has yet to run as we would any other girl in the school. You will be treated until the week is up as though you were innocent. Think well whether you will indeed doom your companions to so much disappointment as will be theirs during the next week, to so dark a suspicion. During the next week the school will practically be sent to Coventry. Those who care for the girls will have to hold aloof from them. All the parents will have to be written to and told that there is an ugly suspicion hanging over the school. Think well before you put your companions, your schoolfellows, into this cruel position."

"It is you who are cruel," said Evelyn.

"I must ask God to melt your hard heart, Evelyn."

"And are you really going to do all this?"

"Certainly."

"And at the end of the week?"

"If you have not confessed before then I shall be obliged to confess for you before all the school. But, my poor child, you will; you must make amends. God could not have made so hard a heart!"

Evelyn wiped away her tears. She scarcely knew what she felt; she scarcely comprehended what was going to happen.

"May I bathe my eyes," she said, "before I go with you into the schoolroom?"

"You may. I will wait for you here."

The little girl left the room.

"I never met such a character," said Miss Henderson to herself. "God help me, what am I to do with her? If at the end of a week she has not confessed her sin, I shall be obliged to ask Lady Frances to remove her. Poor child—poor child!"

Evelyn came back looking pale but serene. She held out her hand to Miss Henderson.

"I do not want your hand, Evelyn."

"You said you would treat me for a week as if I were innocent."

"Very well, then; I will take your hand."

A VERY NAUGHTY GIRL

Miss Henderson entered the schoolroom holding Evelyn's hand. Evelyn was looking as if nothing had happened; the traces of her tears had vanished. She sat down on her form; the other girls glanced at her in some wonder. Prayers were read as usual; the head-mistress knelt to pray. As her voice rose on the wings of prayer it trembled slightly. She prayed for those whose hearts were hard, that God would soften them. She prayed that wrong might be set right, that good might come out of evil, and that she herself might be guided to have a right judgment in all things. There was a great solemnity in her prayer, and it was felt throughout the hush in the big room. When she rose from her knees she ascended to her desk and faced the assembled girls.

"You know," she said, "what an unpleasant task lies before me. The allotted time for the confession of the guilty person who injured my book, SESAME AND LILIES, has gone by. The guilty person has not confessed, but I may as well say that the injury has been traced home to one of your number—but to whom, I am at present resolved not to tell. I give that person one week in order to make her confession. I do this for reasons which my sister and I consider all-sufficient; but during that week, I am sorry to say, my dear girls, you must all bear with her and for her the penalty of her wrong-doing. I must withhold indulgences, holidays, half-holidays, visits from friends; all that makes life pleasant and bright and home-like will have to be withdrawn. Work will have to be the order of the hour—work without the impetus of reward—work for the sake of work. I am sorry to have to do this, but I feel that such a course of conduct is due to myself. In a week's time from now, if the girl has not confessed, I must take further steps; but I can assure the school that the cloud of my displeasure will then alone visit the guilty person, on whom it will fall with great severity."

There was a long, significant pause when Miss Henderson ceased speaking. She was about to descend from her seat when Brenda Fox spoke.

"Is this quite fair?" she said. "I hope I am not asking an impertinent question, but is it fair that the innocent should suffer for the guilty?"

"I must ask you all to do so. Think of the history of the past, girls. Take courage; it is not the first time."

"I think," said Brenda Fox later on that same day to Audrey, "that Miss Henderson is right."

"Then I think her wrong," answered Audrey. "Of course I do not know her as well as you do, Brenda, and I am also ignorant with regard to the ordinary rules of school-life, but I cannot but feel it would be much better, if the guilty girl will not confess, to punish her at once and put an end to the thing."

"It would be pleasanter for us," replied Brenda Fox; "but then, Miss Henderson never thinks of that."

"What do you mean?"

CHAPTER XXIII.—ONE WEEK OF GRACE.

"I mean that Miss Henderson is the sort of woman who would think very little of small personal pain and inconvenience compared with the injury which might be permanently inflicted on a girl who was harshly dealt with."

"Still I do not quite understand. If any girl in the school did such a disgraceful thing it ought to be known at once."

"Miss Henderson evidently does know, but for some reason she hopes the girl will repent."

"And we are to be punished?"

"Is it not worth having a little discomfort if the girl's character can be saved?"

"Yes, of course; if it does save her."

"We must hope for that. For my part," said Brenda in a reverent tone, "I shall pray about it. I believe in prayer."

"And so do I," answered Audrey. "But do you know, Brenda, that I think Miss Henderson was greatly wanting in tact when she mentioned my poor little cousin's name two days ago."

"Why so? Your cousin did happen to be alone in the room."

"But it seemed to draw a very unworthy suspicion upon her head."

"Oh no, no, Audrey!" answered Brenda. "Who could think that your cousin would do it? Besides, she is quite a stranger; it was her first day at school."

"Then have you the least idea who did it?"

"None; no one has. We are all very fond of Miss Thompson. We are all fond of Miss Henderson; we respect her and Miss Lucy as most able and worthy mistresses. We enjoy our school-life. Who could have been so unkind?"

Audrey had an uncomfortable sensation at her heart that Evelyn at least did not enjoy her school-life; that Evelyn disliked Miss Thompson, and openly said that she hated Miss Henderson. Still, that Evelyn could really be guilty did not for an instant visit her brain.

Meanwhile Evelyn went recklessly on her way. The DÉNOUEMENT, of whatever nature, was still a week off. For a week she could be gay or impertinent or rude or defiant or good, just as the mood took her; at the end of the week, or towards the end, she would run away. She would go to Jasper and tell her she must hide her. This was her resolve. She was as inconsequent as an infant. To save herself trouble and pain was her one paramount idea; even her schoolfellows' annoyance and distress scarcely worried her. As she and Audrey always spent their evenings at home, the dulness of the school, the increase of lessons and the absence of play, the walks two and two in absolute silence, scarcely depressed her; she could laugh and play at home, and talk to her uncle and draw him out to tell her stories of her father. The one redeeming trait in her character was her love for Uncle Edward. She was certainly going downhill very rapidly at this time.

- 155 -

A VERY NAUGHTY GIRL

Poor child! who was there to understand her, to bring her to a standstill, to help her to choose right?

CHAPTER XXIV.—"WHO IS E. W.?"

The one person who might have helped Evelyn was too busy with her own troubles just then to think a great deal about her. Poor Sylvia was visited with a very great dread. Her father's manner was strange; she began to fear that he suspected Jasper's presence in the house. If Jasper left, Sylvia felt that things must come to a crisis; she could not stand the life she had lived before the comfortable advent of this kindly but ill-informed woman. Sylvia was really very much attached to Jasper, and although she argued much over Evelyn, and disagreed strongly with her with regard to the best way to treat this unruly little member of society, Sylvia's very life depended on Jasper's purse and Jasper's tact.

One by one the fowls disappeared, the same boy receiving them over the hedge day by day from Jasper. The boy sold each of the old hens for sixpence, and reaped quite a harvest in consequence. He was all too willing to keep Jasper's secret. Jasper bought tender young cockerels from a neighbor in the village, conveyed them home under her arm, killed them, and dressed them in various and dainty manners for Mr. Leeson's meals. He was loud in his praise of Sylvia, and told her that if the worst came to the worst she could go out as a lady cook.

"Nothing could give me such horror, my dear child," he said, "as to think that a Leeson, and a member of one of the proudest families in the kingdom, should ever demean herself to earn money; but, my dear girl, in these days of chance and change one must be prepared for the worst—there never is any telling. Sylvia, I go through anxious moments—very, very anxious moments."

"You do, father," answered the girl. "You watch the post too much. I cannot imagine," she continued, "why you are so fretted and so miserable, for surely we must spend very, very little indeed."

"We spend more than we ought, Sylvia—far more. But there, dear, I am not complaining; I suppose a young girl must have dainties and fine dress."

"Fine dress!" said Sylvia. She looked down at her shabby garment and colored painfully.

Mr. Leeson faced her with his bright and sunken dark eyes.

"Come here," he said.

She went up to him, trembling and her head hanging.

"I saw you two days ago; it was Sunday, and you went to church. I was standing in the shrubbery. I was lost—yes, lost—in painful thoughts. Those recipes which I was about to give to the world were occupying my mind, and other things as well. You rushed by in your shabby dress; you went into the house by the back entrance. Sylvia dear, I sometimes think it would be wise to lock that door. With you and me alone in the house it might be safest to have only one mode of ingress."

"But I always lock it when I go out," said Sylvia; "and it saves so much time to be able to use the back entrance."

"It is just like you, Sylvia; you argue about every thing I say. However, to proceed. You went in; I wondered at your speed. You came out again in a quarter of an hour transformed. Where did you get that dress?"

"What dress, father?"

"Do not prevaricate. Look me straight in the face and tell me. You were dressed in brown of rich shade and good material. You had a stylish and fanciful and hideous hat upon your head; it had feathers. My very breath was arrested when I saw the merry-andrew you made of yourself. You had furs, too—doubtless imitations, but still, to all appearance, rich furs—round neck and wrist. Sylvia, have you during these months and years been secretly saving money?"

"No, father."

"You say 'No, father,' in a very strange tone. If you had no money to buy the dress, how did you get it?"

"It was—given to me."

"By whom?"

"I would rather not say."

"But you must say."

Here Mr. Leeson took Sylvia by both her wrists; he held them tightly in his bony hands. He was seated, and he pulled her down towards him.

"Tell me at once. I insist upon knowing."

"I cannot—there! I will not."

"You defy me?"

"If that is defying you, father, yes. The dress was given to me."

"You refuse to say by whom?"

"Yes, father."

"Then leave my presence. I am angry, hurt. Sylvia, you must return it."

"Again, no, father."

"Sylvia, have you ever heard of the Fifth Commandment?"

"I have, father; but I will break it rather than return the dress. I have been a good daughter to you, but there are limits. You have no right to interfere. The dress was given to me; I did not steal it."

"Now you are intolerable. I will not be agitated by you; I have enough to bear. Leave me this minute."

Sylvia left the room. She did not go to Jasper; she felt that she could not expose her father in the eyes of this woman. She ran up to her own bedroom, locked the door, and flung herself on her bed. Of late she had not done this quite so often. Circumstances had been happier

CHAPTER XXIV.—"WHO IS E. W.?"

for her of late: her father had been strange, but at the same time affectionate; she had been fed, too, and warmed; and, oh! the pretty dress—the pretty dress—she had liked it. She was determined that she would not give it up; she would not submit to what she deemed tyranny. She wept for a little; then she got up, dried her tears, put on her cloak (sadly thin from wear), and went out. Pilot came, looked into her face, and begged for her company. She shook her head.

"No, darling; stay at home—guard him," she whispered.

Pilot understood, and turned away. Sylvia found herself on the highroad. As she approached the gate, and as she spoke to Pilot, eager eyes watched her over the wire screen which protected the lower part of Mr. Leeson's sitting-room.

"What can all this mean?" he said to himself. "There is a mystery about Sylvia. Sometimes I feel that there is a mystery about this house. Sylvia used to be a shocking cook; now the most dainty chef who has ever condescended to cook meals for my pampered palate can scarcely excel her. She confessed that she did not get the recipe from the gipsy; the gipsies had left the common, so she could not get what I gave her a shilling to obtain. Or, did I give her the shilling? I think not—I hope not. Oh, good gracious! if I did, and she lost it! I did not; I must have it here."

He fumbled anxiously in his waistcoat pocket.

"Yes, yes," he said, with a sigh of relief. "I put it here for her, but she did not need it. Thank goodness, it is safe!"

He looked at it affectionately, replaced it in its harbor of refuge, and thought on.

"Now, who gave her those rich and extravagant clothes? Can she possibly have been ransacking her mother's trunks? I was under the impression that I had sold all my poor wife's things, but it is possible I may have overlooked something. I will go and have a look now in the attics. I had her trunks conveyed there. I will go and have a look."

When Mr. Leeson was engaged in what he was pleased to call a voyage of discovery, he, as a rule, stepped on tiptoe. As he wore, for purposes of economy, felt slippers when in the house, his steps made no noise. Now, it so happened that when Jasper arrived at The Priory she brought not only her own luggage, which was pretty considerable, but two or three boxes of Evelyn's finery. These trunks having filled up Jasper's bedroom and the kitchens to an unnecessary extent, she and Sylvia had contrived to drag them up to the attics in a distant part of the house without Mr. Leeson hearing. The trunks, therefore, mostly empty, which had contained the late Mrs. Leeson's wardrobe and Evelyn's trunks were now all together, in what was known as the back attic—that attic which stood, with Sylvia's room between, exactly over the kitchen.

A VERY NAUGHTY GIRL

Mr. Leeson knew, as he imagined, every corner of the house. He was well aware of the room where his wife's trunks were kept, and he went there now, determined, as he expressed it, to ferret out the mystery which was unsettling his life.

He reached the attic in question, and stared about him. There were the trunks which he remembered so well. Many marks of travel were on them—names of foreign hotels, names of distant places. Here was a trophy of a good time at Florence; here a remembrance of a delightful fortnight at Rome; here, again, of a week in Cairo; here, yet more, of a never-to-be-forgotten visit to Constantinople. He stared at the hall-marks of his past life as he gazed at his wife's trunks, and for a time memory overpowered the lonely man, and he stood with his hands clasped and his head slightly bent, thinking—thinking of the days that were no more. No remorse, it is true, seized his conscience. He did not recognize how, step by step, the demon of his life had gained more and more power over him; how the trunks became too shabby for use, but the desire for money prevented his buying new ones. Those labels were old, and the places he and his wife had visited were much changed, and the hotels where they had stayed had many of them ceased to exist, but the labels put on by the hall porters remained on the trunks and bore witness against Mr. Leeson. He turned quickly from the sight.

"This brings back old times," he said to himself, "and old times create old feelings. I never knew then that she would be cursed by the demon of extravagance, and that her child—her only child—would inherit her failing. Well, it is my bounden duty to nip it in the bud, or Sylvia will end her days in the workhouse. I thought I had sold most of the clothes, but doubtless she found some materials to make up that unsuitable costume."

He dragged the trunks forward. They were unlocked, being supposed to contain nothing of value. He pulled them open and went on his knees to examine them. Most of them were empty; some contained old bundles of letters; there was one in the corner which still had a couple of muslin dresses and an old-fashioned black lace mantilla. Mr. Leeson remembered the mantilla and the day when he bought it, and how pretty his handsome wife had looked in it. He flung it from him now as if it distressed him.

"Faugh!" he said. "I remember I gave ten guineas for it. Think of any man being such a fool!"

He was about to leave the attic, more mystified than ever, when his eyes suddenly fell upon the two trunks which contained that portion of Evelyn Wynford's wardrobe which Lady Frances had discarded. The trunks were comparatively new. They were handsome and good, being made of crushed cane. They bore the initials E. W. in large white letters on their arched roofs.

CHAPTER XXIV.—"WHO IS E. W.?"

"But who in the name of fortune is E. W.?" thought Mr. Leeson; and now his heart beat in ungovernable excitement. "E. W.! What can those initials stand for?"

He came close to the trunks as though they fascinated him. They were unlocked, and he pulled them open. Soon Evelyn's gay and useless wardrobe was lying helter-skelter on the attic floor—silk dresses, evening dresses, morning dresses, afternoon dresses, furs, hats, cloaks, costumes. He kicked them about in his rage; his anger reached white-heat. What was the meaning of this?

E. W. and E. W.'s clothes took such an effect on his brain that he could scarcely speak or think. He left the attic with all the things scattered about, and stumbled rather than walked down-stairs. He had nearly got to his own part of the house when he remembered something. He went back, turned the key in the attic door, and put it in his pocket. He then breathed a sigh of relief, and went back to his sitting-room. The fire was nearly out; the day was colder than ever—a keen north wind was blowing. It came in at the badly fitting windows and shook the old panes of glass. The attic in which Mr. Leeson had stood so long had also been icy-cold. He shivered and crept close to the remains of the fire. Then a thought came to him, and he deliberately took up the poker and poked out the remaining embers. They flamed up feebly on the hearth and died out.

"No more fires for me," he said to himself; "I cannot afford it. She is ruining—ruining me. Who is E. W.? Where did she get all those clothes? Oh, I shall go mad!"

He stood shivering and frowning and muttering. Then a change came over him.

"There is a secret, and I mean to discover it," he said to himself; "and until I do I shall say nothing. I shall find out who E. W. is, where those trunks came from, what money Sylvia stole to purchase those awful and ridiculous and terrible garments. I shall find out before I act. Sylvia thinks that she can make a fool of her old father; she will discover her mistake."

The postman's ring was heard at the gate. The postman was never allowed to go up the avenue. Mr. Leeson kept a box locked in the gate, with a little slit for the postman to drop in the letters. He allowed no one to open this box but himself. Without even putting on his greatcoat, he went down the snowy path now, unlocked the box, and took out a letter. He returned with it to the house; it was addressed to himself, and was from his broker in London. The letter contained news which affected him pretty considerably. The gold mine in which he had invested nearly the whole of his available capital was discovered to be by no means so rich in ore as was at first anticipated. Prices were going down steadily, and the shares which Mr. Leeson had bought were now worth only half their value.

A VERY NAUGHTY GIRL

"I'll sell out—I'll sell out this minute," thought the wretched man; "if I don't I shall lose all."

But then he paused, for there was a postscript to the letter.

"It would be madness to sell now," wrote the broker. "Doubtless the present scare is a passing one; the moment the shares are likely to go up then sell."

Mr. Leeson flung the letter from him and tore his gray hair. He paced up and down the room.

"Disaster after disaster," he murmured. "I am like Job; all these things are against me. But nothing cuts me like Sylvia. To buy those things—two trunks full of useless finery! Oh yes, I have money on the premises—money which I saved and never invested; I wonder if that is safe. For all I can tell——But, oh, no, no, no! I will not think that. That way madness lies. I will bury the canvas bag to-night; I have delayed too long. No one can discover that hiding-place. I will bury the canvas bag, come what may, to-night."

Mr. Leeson wrote to his broker, telling him to seize the first propitious moment to sell out from the gold-mine, and then sat moodily, getting colder and colder, in front of the empty grate.

Sylvia came in presently.

"Dinner is ready, father," she said.

"I don't want dinner," he muttered.

She went up to him and laid her hand on his arm.

"Why are you like ice?" she said.

He pushed her away.

"The fire is out," she continued; "let me light it."

"No!" he thundered. "Leave it alone; I wish for no fire. I tell you I am a beggar, and worse; and I wish for no fire!"

"Oh father—father darling!" said the girl.

"Don't 'darling' me; don't come near me. I am displeased with you. You have cut me to the quick. I am angry with you. Leave me."

"You may be angry," she answered, "but I will not leave you ; and if you are cold—cold to death—and cannot afford a fire, you will warm yourself with me. Let me put my arms round you; let me lay my cheek against yours. Feel how my cheek glows. There, is not that better?"

He struggled, but she insisted. She sat on his knee now and put the cloak she was wearing, thin and poor enough in itself, round his neck. Inside the cloak she circled him with her arms. Her dark luxuriant hair fell against his white and scanty locks; she pressed her face close to his.

"You may hate me, but I am going to stay with you," she said. "How cold you are!"

Just for a minute or two Mr. Leeson bore the loving caress and the endearing words. She was very sweet, and she was his—his only child—bone of his bone. Yes, it was nicer to be warm than cold, nicer to be

CHAPTER XXIV.—"WHO IS E. W.?"

loved than to be hated, nicer to——But was he loved? Those trunks upstairs; that costly, useless finery; those initials which were not Sylvia's! "Oh that I could tell her!" he said to himself. "She pretends; she is untrue—untrue as our first mother. What woman was ever yet to be trusted?"

"Go, Sylvia," he replied vehemently; and he started up and shook her off cruelly, so that she fell and hurt herself.

She rose, pushed her hair back from her forehead and gazed at him in bewilderment. Was he going mad?

"Come and eat your dinner before it gets cold," she said. "It is extravagant to waste good food; come and eat it."

"Made from some of those old fowls?" he queried; and a scornful smile curled his lips.

"Come and eat it; it costs you practically nothing," she added. "Come, it is extravagant to waste it."

He pondered in his own mind; there were still about three fowls left. He would not take her hand but he followed her into the dining-room. He sat down before the dainty dish, helped her to a small portion, and ate the rest.

"Now you are better," she said cheerfully.

He gave her a glance which seemed to her to be one of almost venom. "I am going into my sitting-room," he said; "do not disturb me again to-day."

"But you must have a fire!"

"I decline to have a fire."

"You will die of cold."

"Much you care."

"Father!"

"Yes, Sylvia, much you care; you are like the one who gave you being. I will not say any more."

She started away at this; he knew she would. She was patient with him almost beyond the limits of human patience, but she could not stand having her mother abused.

He went down the passage, and locked himself in his sitting-room.

"Now I can think," he thought; "and to-night when Sylvia is in bed I will bury the last canvas bag."

When Sylvia went into the kitchen Jasper asked her at once what was the matter. She stood for a moment without speaking; then she said in a low, broken-hearted voice:

"Father sometimes gets these moods, but I never saw him as bad before. He refuses to have a fire in the parlor; he will die of this cold."

"Let him," muttered Jasper under her breath. She did not say these words aloud; she knew Sylvia too well by this time.

"What has put him into this state of mind?" she asked as she dished up a hot dinner for Sylvia and herself.

A VERY NAUGHTY GIRL

"It was my dress, Jasper; I ought not to have allowed you to make it for me. I ran in to put it on to go to church on Sunday; and he saw me and drew his own conclusions, as he said. He asked me where I got it, and I refused to tell him."

"Now, if I were you, dear," said Jasper, "I would just up and tell him the whole story. I would tell him that I am here, and that I mean to stay, and that he has been living on me for some time now. I would tell him everything. He would rage and fume, but not more than he has raged and fumed. Things are past bearing, darling. Why, your pretty, young, and brave heart will be broken. I would not bear it. It is best for him too, dear; he must learn to know you, and if necessary to fear you. He cannot go on killing himself and every one else with impunity. It is past bearing, Sylvia, my love—past bearing."

"I know, Jasper—I know—but I dare not tell him. You cannot imagine what he is when he is really roused. He would turn you out."

"Well, darling, and you would come with me. Why should we not go out?"

"In the first place, Jasper, you have no money to support us both. Why, poor, dear old thing, you are using up all your little savings to keep me going! And in the next place, even if you could afford it, I promised mother that I would never leave him. I could not break my word to her. Oh! it hurt much; but the pain is over. I will never leave him while he lives, Jasper."

"Dear, dear!" said Jasper, "what a power of love is wasted on worthless people! It is the most extraordinary fact on earth."

Sylvia half-smiled. She thought of Evelyn, who was also in her opinion more or less worthless, and how Jasper was wasting both substance and heart on her.

"Well," she said, "I can eat if I can do nothing else ; but the thought of father dying of cold does come between me and all peace."

She finished her dinner, and then went and stood by the window.

"It is a perfect miracle he has not found me out before," said Jasper; "and, by the same token," she added, "I heard footsteps in the attic up-stairs while I was preparing his fowl for dinner. My heart stood still. It must have been he; and I thought he would see the smoke curling up through that stack of chimneys just alongside of the attics. What was he doing up stairs?"

"Oh, I know—I know!" said Sylvia; and her face turned very white, and her eyes seemed to start from her head. "He went to look in mother's trunks; he thought that I had got my brown dress from there."

"And he will discover Evelyn's trunks as sure as fate," said Jasper; "and what a state he will be in! That accounts for it, Sylvia. Well, darling, discovery is imminent now; and for my part the sooner it is over the better."

CHAPTER XXIV.—"WHO IS E. W.?"

"I wonder if he did discover! Something has put him into a terrible rage," thought the girl.
She went out of the kitchen, and stole softly up-stairs to the attic where the trunks were kept. It was locked. Doubt was now, of course, at an end. Sylvia went back and told her discovery to Jasper.

CHAPTER XXV.—UNCLE EDWARD.

According to her promise, Jasper went that evening to meet Evelyn at the stile. Evelyn was there, and the news she had for her faithful nurse was the reverse of soothing.

"You cannot stand it," said Jasper; "you cannot demean yourself. I don't know that I'd have done it—yes, perhaps I would—but having done it, you must stick to your guns."

"Yes," said Evelyn in a mournful tone; "I must run away. I have quite, quite, absolutely made up my mind."

"And when, darling?" said Jasper, trembling a good deal.

"The night before the week is up. I will come to you here, Jasper, and you must take me."

"Of course, love; you will come back with me to The Priory. I can hide you there as well as anywhere on earth—yes, love, as well as anywhere on earth."

"Oh, I'd be so frightened! It would be so close to them all!"

"The closer the better, dear. If you went into any village or any town near you would be discovered; but they'd never think of looking for you at The Priory. Why, darling, I have lived there unsuspected for some time now—weeks, I might say. Sylvia will not tell. You shall sleep in my bed, and I will keep you safe. Only you must bring some money, Evelyn, for mine is getting sadly short."

"Yes," said Evelyn. "I will ask Uncle Edward; he will not refuse me. He is very kind to me, and I love him better than any one on earth—better even than Jasper, because he is father's very own brother, and because I am his heiress. He likes to talk to me about the place and what I am to do when it belongs to me. He is not angry with me when I am quite alone with him and I talk of these things; only he has taught me to say nothing about it in public. If I could be sorry for having got into this scrape it would be on his account; but there, I was not brought up with his thoughts, and I cannot think things wrong that he thinks wrong. Can you, Jasper?"

"No, my little wild honey-bird—not I. Well, dearie, I will meet you again to-morrow night; and now I must be going back."

Evelyn returned to the house. She went up to her room, changed her shoes, tidied her hair, and came down to the drawing-room. Lady Frances was leaning back in a chair, turning over the pages of a new magazine. She called Evelyn to her side.

"How do you like school?" she said. Her tones were abrupt; the eyes she fixed on the child were hard.

Evelyn's worst feelings were always awakened by Lady Frances's manner to her.

"I do not like it at all," she said. "I wish to leave."

CHAPTER XXV.—UNCLE EDWARD.

"Your wishes, I am afraid, are not to be considered; all the same, you may have to leave."
"Why?" asked Evelyn, turning white. She wondered if Lady Frances knew.
Her aunt's eyes were fixed, as though they were gimlets, on her face.
"Sit down," said Lady Frances, "and tell me how you spend your day. What class are you in? What lessons are you learning?"
"I am in a very low class indeed?" said Evelyn. "Mothery always said I was clever."
"I do not suppose your mother knew."
"Why should she not know, she who was so very clever herself? She taught me all sorts of things, and so did poor Jasper."
"Ah! I am glad at least that I have removed that dreadful woman out of your path," said Lady Frances.
Evelyn smiled and lowered her eyes. Her manner irritated her aunt extremely.
"Well," she said, "go on; we will not discuss the fact of the form you ought to be in. What lessons do you do?"
"Oh, history, grammar; I suppose, the usual English subjects."
"Yes, yes; but history—that is interesting. English history?"
"Yes, Aunt Frances."
"What part of the history?"
"We are doing the reigns of the Edwards now."
"Ah! can you tell me anything with regard to the reign of Edward I.?"
Evelyn colored. Lady Frances watched her.
"I am certain she knows," thought the little girl. "But, oh, this is terrible! Has that awful Miss Henderson told her? What shall I do? I do not think I will wait until the week is up; I think I will run away at once."
"Answer my question, Evelyn," said her aunt.
Evelyn did mutter a tiny piece of information with regard to the said reign.
"I shall question you on your history from time to time," said Lady Frances. "I take an interest in this school experiment. Whether it will last or not I cannot say; but I may as well say one thing—if for any reason your presence is not found suitable in the school where I have now sent you, you will go to a very different order of establishment and to a much stricter RÉGIME elsewhere."
"What is a RÉGIME?" asked Evelyn.
"I am too tired to answer your silly questions. Now go and read your book in that corner. Do not make a noise; I have a headache."
Evelyn slouched away, looking as cross and ill-tempered as a little girl could look.

"Audrey darling," called her mother in a totally different tone of voice, "play me that pretty thing of Chopin's which you know I am so fond of."

Audrey approached the piano and began to play.

Evelyn read her book for a time without attending much to the meaning of the words. Then she observed that her uncle, who had been asleep behind his newspaper, had risen and left the room. Here was the very opportunity that she sought. If she could only get her Uncle Edward quite by himself, and when he was in the best of good humors, he might give her some money. She could not run away without money to go with. Jasper, she knew, had not a large supply. Evelyn, with all her ignorance of many things, had early in her life come into contact with the want of money. Her mother had often and often been short of funds. When Mrs. Wynford was short, the ranch did without even, at times, the necessaries of life. Evelyn had a painful remembrance of butterless breakfasts and meatless dinners; of shoes which were patched so often that they would scarcely keep out the winter snows; of little garments turned and turned again. Then money had come back, and life became smooth and pleasant; there was an abundance of good food for the various meals, and Evelyn had shoes to her heart's content, and the sort of gay-colored garments which her mother delighted in. Yes, she understood Jasper's appeal for money, and determined on no account to go to that good woman's protection without a sufficient sum in hand.

Therefore, as Audrey was playing some of the most seductive music of that past master of the art, Chopin, and Lady Frances lay back in her chair with closed eyes and listened, Evelyn left the room. She knew where to find her uncle, and going down a corridor, opened the door of his smoking-room without knocking. He was seated by the fire smoking. A newspaper lay by his side; a pile of letters which had come by the evening post were waiting to be opened. When Evelyn quietly opened the door he looked round and said:

"Ah, it is you, Eve. Do you want anything, my dear?"

"May I speak to you for a minute or two, Uncle Edward?"

"Certainly, my dear Evelyn; come in. What is the matter, dear?"

"Oh, nothing much."

Evelyn went and leant up against her uncle. She had never a scrap of fear of him, which was one reason why he liked her, and thought her far more tolerable than did his wife or Audrey. Even Audrey, who was his own child, held him in a certain awe; but Evelyn leant comfortably now against his side, and presently she took his arm of her own accord and passed it securely round her waist.

"Now, that is nice," she said; "when I lean up against you I always remember that you are father's brother."

"I am glad that you should remember that fact, Evelyn."

CHAPTER XXV.—UNCLE EDWARD.

"You are pleased with me on the whole, aren't you, Uncle Edward?" asked the little girl. Evelyn backed her head against his shoulder as she spoke, and looked into his face with her big and curious eyes.

"On the whole, yes."

"But Aunt Frances does not like me."

"You must try to win her affection, Evelyn; it will all come in good time."

"It is not pleasant to be in the house with a person who does not like you, is it, Uncle Edward?"

"I can understand you, Evelyn; it is not pleasant."

"And Audrey only half-likes me."

"My dear little girl," said her uncle, rousing himself to talk in a more serious strain, "would it not be wisest for you to give over thinking of who likes you and who does not, and to devote all your time to doing what is right?"

Evelyn made a wry face.

"I don't care about doing what is right," she said; "I don't like it."

Her uncle smiled.

"You are a strange girl; but I believe you have improved," he said.

"You would be sorry if I did anything very, very naughty, Uncle Edward?"

"I certainly should."

Evelyn lowered her eyes.

"He must not know. I must keep him from knowing somehow, but I wonder how I shall," she thought.

"And perhaps you would be sorry," she continued, "if I were not here—if your naughty, naughty Eve was no longer in the house?"

"I should. I often think of you. I——"

"What, Uncle Edward?"

"Love you, little girl."

"Love me! Do you?" she asked in a tone of affection. "Do you really? Please say that again."

"I love you, Evelyn."

"Uncle Edward, may I give you just the tiniest kiss?"

"Yes, dear."

Evelyn raised her soft face and pressed a light kiss on her uncle's cheek. She was quite silent then for a minute; truth to tell, her heart was expanding and opening out and softening, and great thrills of pure love were filling it, so that soon, soon that heart might have melted utterly and been no longer a hard heart of stone. But, alas! as these good thoughts visited her, there came also the remembrance of the sin she had committed, and of the desperate measures she was about to take to save herself—for she had by no means come to the stage of confessing that sin, and by so doing getting rid of her naughtiness.

A VERY NAUGHTY GIRL

"Uncle Edward," she said abruptly, "I want you to give me a little money. I have come here to ask you. I want it all for my very own self. I want some money which no one else need know anything about."

"Of course, dear, you shall have money. How much do you want?"

"Well, a good bit. I want to give Jasper a present."

"Your old nurse?"

"Yes. You know it was unkind of Aunt Frances to send her away; mothery wished her to stay with me."

"I know that, Evelyn, and as far as I personally am concerned, I am sorry; but your aunt knows very much more about little girls than I do."

"She does not know half so much about this girl."

"Well, anyhow, dear, it was her wish, and you and I must submit."

"But you are sorry?"

"For some reasons, yes."

"And you would like me to help Jasper?"

"Certainly. Do you know where your nurse is now, Evelyn?"

"I do."

"Where?"

"I would rather not say; only, may I send her some money?"

"That seems reasonable enough," thought the Squire.

"How much do you want?" he asked.

"Would twenty pounds be too much?"

"I think not. It is a good deal, but she was a faithful servant. I will give you twenty pounds for her now."

The Squire rose and took out his check-book.

"Oh, please," said Evelyn, "I want it in gold."

"But how will you send it to her?"

"Never, never mind; I must have it in gold."

"Poor child! She is in earnest," thought the Squire. "Perhaps the woman will come to meet her somewhere. I really cannot see why she should be tabooed from having a short interview with her old nurse. Frances and I differ on this head. Yes, I will let her have the money; the child has a good deal of heart when all is said and done."

So the Squire put two little rolls, neatly made up in brown paper, into Evelyn's hands.

"There," he said; "it is a great deal of money to trust a little girl with, but you shall have it; only you must not ask me for any more."

"Oh, what a darling you are, Uncle Edward! I feel as if I must kiss you again. There! those kisses are full of love. Now I must go. But, oh, I say, WHAT a funny parcel!"

"What parcel, dear?"

"That long parcel on that table."

"It is a gun-case which I have not yet unpacked. Now run away."

CHAPTER XXV.—UNCLE EDWARD.

"But that reminds me. You said I might go out some day to shoot with you."

"On some future day. I do not much care for girls using firearms; and you are so busy now with your school."

"You think, perhaps, that I cannot fire a gun, but I can aim well; I can kill a bird on the wing as neatly as any one. I told Audrey, and she would not believe me. Please—please show me your new gun.

"Not now; I have not looked at it myself yet."

"But you do believe that I can shoot?"

"Oh yes, dear—yes, I suppose so. All the same, I should be sorry to trust you; I do not approve of women carrying firearms. Now leave me, Evelyn; I have a good deal to attend to."

Evelyn went to bed to think over her uncle's words; her disgrace at school; the terrible DÉNOUEMENT which lay before her; the money, which seemed to her to be the only way out, and which would insure her comfort with Jasper wherever Jasper might like to take her; and finally, and by no means least, she meditated over the subject of her uncle's new gun. On the ranch she had often carried a gun of her own; from her earliest days she had been accustomed to regard the women of her family as first-class shots. Her mother had herself taught her how to aim, how to fire, how to make allowance in order to bring her bird down on the wing, and Evelyn had followed out her instructions many times. She felt now that her uncle did not believe her, and the fear that this was the case irritated her beyond words.

"I do not pretend to be learned," thought Evelyn, "and I do not pretend to be good, but there is one thing that I am, and that is a first-rate shot. Uncle Edward might show me his new gun. How little he guesses that I can manage it quite as well as he can himself!"

Two or three days passed without anything special occurring. Evelyn was fairly good at school; it was not, she considered, worth her while any longer to shirk her lessons. She began in spite of herself, and quite against her declared inclination, to have a sort of liking for her books. History was the only lesson which she thoroughly detested. She could not be civil to Miss Thompson, whom she considered her enemy; but to her other teachers she was fairly agreeable, and had already to a certain extent won the hearts of more than one of the girls in her form. She was bright and cheerful, and could say funny things; and as also she brought an unlimited supply of chocolates and other sweetmeats to school, these facts alone insured her being more or less of a favorite. At home she avoided her aunt and Audrey, and evening after evening she went to the stile to have a chat with Jasper.

Jasper never failed to meet her little girl, as she called Evelyn, at their arranged rendezvous. Evelyn managed to slip out without, as she thought, any one noticing her; and the days went by until there was only one day left before Miss Henderson would proclaim to the entire school that Evelyn Wynford was the guilty person who had torn the precious volume of Ruskin.

"When you come for me to-morrow night, Jasper," said Evelyn, "I will go away with you. Are you quite sure that it is safe to take me back to The Priory?"

"Quite, quite safe, darling; hardly a soul knows that I am at The Priory, and certainly no one will suspect that you are there. Besides, the place is all undermined with cellars, and at the worst you and I could hide there together while the house was searched."

"What fun!" cried Evelyn, clapping her hands. "I declare, Jasper, it is almost as good as a fairy story."

"Quite as good, my little love."

"And you will be sure to have a very, very nice supper ready for me to-morrow night?"

"Oh yes, dear; just the supper you like best—chocolate and sweet cakes."

"And you will tuck me up in bed as you used to?"

"Darling, I have put a little white bed close to my own, where you shall sleep."

"Oh Jasper, it will be nice to be with you again! And you are positive Sylvia will not tell?"

"She is sad about you, Evelyn, but she will not tell. I have arranged that."

"And that terrible old man, her father, will he find out?"

"I think not, dear; he has not yet found out about me at any rate."

"Perhaps, Jasper, I had better go back now; it is later than usual."

"Be sure you bring the twenty pounds when you come to-morrow night," said Jasper; "for my funds, what with one thing and another, are getting low."

"Yes, I will bring the money," replied Evelyn.

She returned to the house. No one saw her as she slipped in by the back entrance. She ran up to her room, smoothed her hair, and went down to the drawing-room. Lady Frances and Audrey were alone in the big room. They had been talking together, but instantly became silent when Evelyn entered.

"They have been abusing me, of course," thought the little girl; and she flashed an angry glance first at one and then at the other.

"Evelyn," said her aunt, "have you finished learning your lessons? You know how extremely particular Miss Henderson is that school tasks should be perfectly prepared."

"My lessons are all right, thank you," replied Evelyn in her brusquest voice. She flung herself into a chair and crossed her legs.

"Uncross your legs, my dear; that is a very unlady-like thing to do."

Evelyn muttered something, but did what her aunt told her.

"Do not lean back so much, Evelyn; it is not good style. Do not poke out your chin, either; observe how Audrey sits."

CHAPTER XXV.—UNCLE EDWARD.

"I don't want to observe how Audrey sits," said Evelyn.

Lady Frances colored. She was about to speak, but a glance from her daughter restrained her. Just then Read came into the room. Between Read and Evelyn there was already a silent feud. Read now glanced at the young lady, tossed her head a trifle, and went up to Lady Frances.

"I am very sorry to trouble you, madam," she said, "but if I may see you quite by yourself for a few moments I shall be very much obliged."

"Certainly, Read; go into my boudoir and I will join you there," said her mistress. "I know," added Lady Frances graciously, "that you would not disturb me if you had not something important to say."

"No, madam; I should be very sorry to do so."

Lady Frances and Read now left the room, and Audrey and Evelyn were alone. Audrey uttered a sigh.

"What is the matter, Audrey?" asked her cousin.

"I am thinking of the day after to-morrow," answered Audrey. "The unhappy girl who has kept her secret all this time will be openly denounced. It will be terribly exciting."

"You do not pretend that you pity her!" said Evelyn in a voice of scorn.

"Indeed I do pity her."

"What nonsense! That is not at all your way."

"Why should you say that? It is my way. I pity all people who have done wrong most terribly."

"Then have you ever pitied me since I came to England?"

"Oh yes, Evelyn—oh, indeed I have!"

"Please keep your pity to yourself; I don't want it."

Audrey relapsed into silence.

By and by Lady Frances came back; she was still accompanied by Read.

"What does a servant want in this room?" said Evelyn in her most disagreeable voice.

"Evelyn, come here," said her aunt; "I have something to say to you."

Evelyn went very unwillingly. Read stood a little in the background.

"Evelyn," said Lady Frances, "I have just heard something that surprises me extremely, that pains me inexpressibly; it is true, so there is no use in your denying it, but I must tell you what Read has discovered."

"Read!" cried Evelyn, her voice choking with passion and her face white. "Who believes what a tell-tale-tit of that sort says?"

"You must not be impertinent, my dear. I wish to tell you that Read has found you out. Your maid Jasper has not left this neighborhood, and you, Evelyn—you are naughty enough and daring enough to meet her every night by the stile that leads into the seven-acre meadow. Read observed your absence one night, and followed you herself to-night, and she discovered everything."

A VERY NAUGHTY GIRL

"Did you hear what I was saying to Jasper?" asked Evelyn, turning her white face now and looking full at Read.

"No, Miss Evelyn," replied the maid; "I would not demean myself to listen."

"You would demean yourself to follow," said Evelyn.

"Confess your sin, Evelyn, and do not scold Read," interrupted Lady Frances.

"I have nothing to confess, Aunt Frances."

"But you did it?"

"Certainly I did it."

"You dared to go to meet a woman privately, clandestinely, whom I, your aunt, prohibited the house?"

"I dared to go to meet the woman my mother loved," replied Evelyn, "and I am not a bit ashamed of it; and if I had the chance I would do it again."

"You are a very, very naughty girl. I am more than angry with you. I am pained beyond words. What is to become of you I know not. You are a bad girl; I cannot bear to think that you should be in the same house with Audrey."

"Loving the woman whom my mother loved does not make me a bad girl," replied Evelyn. "But as you do not like to have me in the room, Aunt Frances, I will go away—I will go up-stairs. I think you are very, very unkind to me; I think you have been so from the first."

"Do not dare to say another word to me, miss; go away immediately."

Evelyn left the room. She was half-way up-stairs when she paused.

"What is the use of being good?" she said to herself. "What is the use of ever trying to please anybody? I really did not mean to be naughty when first I came, and if Aunt Frances had been different I might have been different too. What right had she to deprive me of Jasper when mothery said that Jasper was to stay with me? It is Aunt Frances's fault that I am such a bad girl now. Well, thank goodness! I shall not be here much longer; I shall be away this time to-morrow night. The only person I shall be sorry to leave is Uncle Edward. Audrey and I will be going to school early in the morning, and then there will be the fuss and bustle and the getting away before Read sees me. Oh, that dreadful old Read! what can I do to blind her eyes to-morrow night? Throw dust into them in some fashion I must. I will just go and have one word of good-by with Uncle Edward now."

Evelyn ran down the corridor which led to her uncle's room. She tapped at the door. There was no answer. She opened the door softly and peeped in. The room was empty. She was just about to go away again, considerably crestfallen and disappointed, when her eyes fell upon the gun-case. Instantly a sparkle came into her eyes; she went up to the case, and removing the gun, proceeded to examine it. It was made on the newest pattern, and was light and easily carried. It held

CHAPTER XXV.—UNCLE EDWARD.

six chambers, all of which could be most simply and conveniently loaded.

Evelyn knew well how to load a gun, and finding the proper cartridges, now proceeded to enjoy herself by making the gun ready for use. Having loaded it, she returned it to its case.

"I know what I'll do," she thought. "Uncle Edward thinks that I cannot shoot; he thinks that I am not good at any one single thing. But I will show him. I'll go out and shoot two birds on the wing before breakfast to-morrow; whether they are crows or whether they are doves or whether they are game, it does not matter in the least; I'll bring them in and lay them at his feet, and say:

"Here is what your wild niece Evelyn can do; and now you will believe that she has one accomplishment which is not vouchsafed to other girls."

So, having completed her task of putting the gun in absolute readiness for its first essay in the field, she returned the case to its corner and went up-stairs to bed.

CHAPTER XXVI.–TANGLES.

When Audrey and her mother found themselves alone, Lady Frances turned at once to her daughter.

"Audrey," she said, "I feel that I must confide in you."

"What about, mother?" asked Audrey.

"About Evelyn."

"Yes, mother?"

Audrey's face looked anxious and troubled; Lady Frances's scarcely less so.

"The child hates me," said Lady Frances. "What I have done to excite such a feeling is more than I can tell you; from the first I have done my utmost to be kind to her."

"It is difficult to know how best to be kind to Evelyn," said Audrey in a thoughtful voice.

"What do you mean, my dear?"

"I mean, mother, that she is something of a little savage. She has never been brought up with our ideas. Do you think, mother—I scarcely like to say it to one whom I honor and love and respect as I do you—but do you think you understand her?"

"No, I do not," said Lady Frances. "I have never understood her from the first. Your father seems to manage her better."

"Ah, yes," said Audrey; "but then, she belongs to him."

Lady Frances looked annoyed.

"She belongs to us all," she remarked. "She is your first cousin, and my niece, of course, by marriage. Her father was a very dear fellow; how such a daughter could have been given to him is one of those puzzles which will never be unraveled. But now, dear, we must descend from generalities to facts. Something very grave and terrible has occurred. Read did right when she told me about Evelyn's secret visits to Jasper at the stile. You know how from the very first I have distrusted and disliked that woman. You must not suppose, Audrey, that I felt no pain when I turned the woman away after the letter which Evelyn's mother had written to me; but there are times when it is wrong to yield, and I felt that such was the case."

"I knew, my darling mother, that you must have acted from the best of motives," said Audrey.

"I did, my dearest child; I did. Well, Evelyn has managed to meet this woman, and instead of being removed from her influence, is under it to a remarkable and dangerous degree—for the woman, of course, thinks herself wronged, and Evelyn agrees with her. Now, the fact is this, Audrey: I happen to know about that very disagreeable occurrence which took place at Chepstow House."

"What, mother—what?" cried Audrey. "You speak as if you knew something special."

CHAPTER XXVI.—TANGLES.

"I do, Audrey."

"But what, mother?"

Audrey's face turned red; her eyes shone. She went close to her mother, knelt by her, and took her hand.

"Who has spoken to you about it?" she asked.

"Miss Henderson."

"Oh mother! and what did she say?"

"My darling, I am afraid you will be terribly grieved; I can scarcely tell you how upset I am. Audrey, the strongest, the very strongest, circumstantial evidence points to Evelyn as the guilty person."

"Oh mother! Evelyn! But why? Oh, surely, surely whoever accuses poor Evelyn is mistaken!"

"I agreed with you, Audrey; I felt just as indignant as you do when first I heard what Miss Henderson told me; but the more I see of Evelyn the more sure I am that she would be capable of this action, that if the opportunity came she would do this cruel and unjustifiable wrong, and after having done it the unhappy child would try to conceal it."

"But, mother darling, what motive could she have?"

"Well, dear, let me tell you. Miss Henderson seems to be well aware of the entire story. On the first day when Evelyn went to school she was asked during class to read over the reign of Edward I. in the history of England. Evelyn, in her usual pert way which we all know so well, declared that she knew the reign, and while the other girls in her form were busy with their lessons she amused herself looking about her. As it was the first day, Miss Thompson took no notice; but when the girls went into the playground for recess she called Evelyn to her and questioned her with regard to the history. Evelyn's wicked lie was immediately manifest, for she did not know a single word about the reign. Miss Thompson was naturally angry, and desired her to stay in the schoolroom and learn the reign while the other girls were at play. Evelyn was angry, but could not resist. About six o'clock that evening Miss Thompson came into the schoolroom, found Ruskin's SESAME AND LILIES, which she had left there that morning, and took it away with her. She was preparing a lecture out of the book, and did not open it at once. When she did so she perceived, to her horror, that some pages had been torn out. You know, my dear, what followed. You know what a strained and unhappy condition the school is now in."

"Oh yes, mother—yes, I know all that; the only part that is new to me is that Evelyn was kept indoors to learn her history."

"Yes, dear, and that supplies the motive; not to one like you, my Audrey, but to such a perverted, such an unhappy and ignorant child as poor Evelyn, one who has never learnt self-control, one whose passions are ever in the ascendency."

"Oh, poor Evelyn, poor Evelyn!" said Audrey. "But still, mother—still—Oh, I am sure she never did it! She has denied it, mother; whatever she is, she is not a coward. She might have done it in a fit of rage; but if she did she would confess. Why should she wreak her anger on Miss Henderson? Oh, mother darling, there is nothing proved against her!"

"Wait, Audrey; I have not finished my story. Two days passed before Miss Thompson needed to open the history-book which Evelyn had been using; when she did, she found, lying in the pages which commenced the reign of Edward I., some scraps of torn paper, all too evidently torn out of SESAME AND LILIES.

"Mother!"

"It is true, Audrey."

"Who told you this?"

"Miss Henderson."

"Does Miss Henderson believe that Evelyn is guilty?"

"Yes; and so do I."

"Mother, mother, what will happen?"

"Who knows? But Miss Henderson is determined—and, yes, my dear, I must say I agree with her—she is determined to expose Evelyn; she said she would give her a week in which to repent."

"And that week will be up the day after to-morrow," said Audrey.

"Yes, Audrey—yes; there is only to-morrow left."

"Oh mother, how can I bear it?"

"My poor child, it will be dreadful for you."

"Oh mother, why did she come here? I could almost hate her! And yet—no, I do not hate her—no, I do not; I pity her."

"You are an angel! When I think that you, my sweet, will be mixed up in this, and—and injured by it, and brought to low esteem by it, oh, my dearest, what can I say?"

Audrey was silent for a moment. She bent her head and looked down; then she spoke.

"It is a trial," she said, "but I am not to be pitied as Evelyn is to be pitied. Mother darling, there is but one thing to be done."

"What is that, dearest?"

"To get her to repent—to get her to confess between now and the morning after next. Oh mother! leave her to me."

"I will, Audrey. If any one can influence her, you can; you are so brave, so good, so strong!"

"Nay, I have but little influence over her," said Audrey. "Let me think for a few moments, mother."

Audrey sank into a chair and sat silent. Her sweet, pure, high-bred face was turned in profile to her mother. Lady Frances glanced at it, and thought over the circumstances which had brought Evelyn into their midst.

CHAPTER XXVI.–TANGLES.

"To think that that girl should supplant her!" thought the mother; and her anger was so great that she could not keep quiet. She was going out of the room to speak to her husband, but before she reached the door Audrey called her.

"What are you going to do, mother?"

"It is only right that I should tell you, Audrey. An idea has come to me. Evelyn respects your father; if I told him just what I have told you he might induce her to confess."

"No, mother," said Audrey suddenly; "do not let us lower her in his eyes. The strongest possible motive for Evelyn to confess her sin will be that father does not know; that he need never know if she confesses. Do not tell him, please, mother; I have got another thought."

"What is that, my darling?"

"Do you not remember Sylvia–pretty Sylvia?"

"Of course. A dear, bright, fascinating girl!"

"Evelyn is fond of her–fonder of Sylvia than she is of me; perhaps Sylvia could induce her to confess."

"It is a good thought, Audrey. I will ask Sylvia over here to dine to-morrow evening."

"Oh, mother darling, that is too late! May I not send a messenger for her to come in the morning? Oh mother, if she could only come now!"

"No dearest; it is too late to-night."

"But Evelyn ought to see her before she goes to school."

"My dearest, you have both to be at school at nine o'clock."

"Oh, I don't know what is to be done! I do feel that I have very little influence, and Sylvia may have much. Oh dear! oh dear!"

"Audrey, I am almost sorry I have told you; you take it too much to heart."

"Dear mother, you must have told me; I could not have stood the shock, the surprise, unprepared. Oh mother, think of the morning after next! Think of our all standing up in school, and Evelyn, my cousin, being proclaimed guilty! And yet, mother, I ought only to think of Evelyn, and not of myself; but I cannot help thinking of myself–I cannot–I cannot."

"Something must be done to help you, Audrey. Let me think. I will write a line to Miss Henderson and say I am detaining you both till afternoon school. Then, dearest, you can have your talk with Evelyn in the morning, and afterwards Sylvia can see her, and perhaps the unhappy child may be brought to repentance, and may speak to Miss Henderson and confess her sin in the afternoon. That is the best thing. Now go to bed, and do not let the trouble worry you, my sweet; that would indeed be the last straw."

Audrey left the room. But during that night she could not sleep. From side to side of her pillow she tossed; and early in the morning, an

A VERY NAUGHTY GIRL

hour or more before her usual time of rising, she got up. She dressed herself quickly and went in the direction of Evelyn's room. Her idea was to speak to Evelyn there and then before her courage failed her. She opened the door of her cousin's room softly. She expected to see Evelyn, who was very lazy as a rule, sound asleep in bed; but, to her astonishment, the room was empty. Where could she be?

"What can be the matter?" thought Audrey; and in some alarm she ran down-stairs.

The first person she saw was Evelyn, who was making straight for her uncle's room, intending to go out with the well-loaded gun. Evelyn scowled when she saw her cousin, and a look of anger swept over her face.

"What are you doing up so early, Evelyn?" asked Audrey.

"May I ask what are YOU doing up so early," retorted Evelyn.

"I got up early on purpose to talk to you."

"I don't want to talk just now."

"Do come with me, Evelyn—please do. Why should you turn against me and be so disagreeable? Oh, dear! oh dear! I am so terribly sorry for you! Do you know that I was awake all night thinking of you?"

"Then you were very silly," said Evelyn, "for certainly I was not awake thinking of you. What is it you want to say?" she continued.

She recognized that she must give up her sport. How more than provoking! for the next morning she would be no longer at Wynford Castle; she would be under the safe shelter of her beloved Jasper's wing.

"The morning is quite fine," said Audrey; "do come out and let us walk."

Evelyn looked very cross, but finally agreed, and they went out together. Audrey wondered how she should proceed. What could she say to influence Evelyn? In truth, they were not the sort of girls who would ever pull well together. Audrey had been brought up in the strictest school, with the highest sense of honor. Evelyn had been left to grow up at her own sweet will; honorable actions had never appealed to her. Tricks, cheating, smart doings, clever ways, which were not the ways of righteousness, were the ways to which she had been accustomed. It was impossible for her to see things with Audrey's eyes.

"What do you want to say to me?" said Evelyn. "Why do you look so mysterious?"

"I want to say something—something which I must say. Evelyn, do not ask me any questions, but do just listen. You know what is going to happen to-morrow morning at school?"

"Lessons, I suppose," said Evelyn.

"Please don't be silly; you must know what I mean."

"Oh, you allude to the row about that stupid, stupid book. What a fuss! I used to think I liked school, but I don't now. I am sure

CHAPTER XXVI.—TANGLES.

mistresses don't go on in that silly way in Tasmania, for mothery said she loved school. Oh, the fun she had at school! Stolen parties in the attics; suppers brought in clandestinely; lessons shirked! Oh dear! oh dear! she had a time of excitement. But at this school you are all so proper! I do really think you English girls have no spunk and no spirit."

"But I'll tell you what we have," said Audrey; and she turned and faced her cousin. "We have honor; we have truth. We like to work straight, not crooked; we like to do right, not wrong. Yes, we do, and we are the better for it. That is what we English girls are. Don't abuse us, Evelyn, for in your heart of hearts—yes, Evelyn, I repeat it—in your heart of hearts you must long to be one of us."

There was something in Audrey's tone which startled Evelyn.

"How like Uncle Edward you look!" she said; and perhaps she could not have paid her cousin a higher compliment.

The look which for just a moment flitted across the queer little face of the Tasmanian girl upset Audrey. She struggled to retain her composure, but the next moment burst into tears.

"Oh dear!" said Evelyn, who hated people who cried, "what is the matter?"

"You are the matter. Oh, why—WHY did you do it?"

"I do what?" said Evelyn, a little startled, and turning very pale.

"Oh! you know you did it, and—and—— There is Sylvia Leeson coming across the grass. Do let Sylvia speak to you. Oh, you know—you know you did it!"

"What is the matter?" said Sylvia, running up, panting and breathless. "I have been asked to breakfast here. Such fun! I slipped off without father knowing. But are not you two going to school? Why was I asked? Audrey, what are you crying about?"

"About Evelyn. I am awfully unhappy——"

"Have you told, Evelyn?" asked Sylvia breathlessly.

"No," said Evelyn; "and if you do, Sylvia——"

"Sylvia, do you know about this?" cried Audrey.

"About what?" asked Sylvia.

"About the book which got injured at Miss Henderson's school."

Sylvia glanced at Evelyn; then her face flushed, her eyes brightened, and she said emphatically:

"I know; and dear little Evelyn will tell you herself.—Won't you, darling—won't you?"

Evelyn looked from one to the other.

"You are enough, both of you, to drive me mad," she said. "Do you think for a single moment that I am going to speak against myself? I hate you, Sylvia, as much as I ever loved you."

Before either girl could prevent her she slipped away, and flying round the shrubberies, was lost to view.

"Then she did do it?" said Audrey. "She told you?"

Sylvia shut her lips.

"I must not say any more," she answered.

"But, Sylvia, it is no secret. Miss Henderson knows; there is circumstantial evidence. Mother told me last night. Evelyn will be exposed before the whole school."

Now Jasper, for wise reasons, had said nothing to Sylvia of Evelyn's proposed flight to The Priory, and consequently she was unaware that the naughty girl had no intention of exposing herself to public disgrace.

"She must be brought to confess," continued Audrey, "and you must find her and talk to her. You must show her how hopeless and helpless she is. Show her that if she tells, the disgrace will not be quite so awful. Oh, do please get her to tell!"

"I can but try," said Sylvia; "only, somehow," she added, "I have not yet quite fathomed Evelyn."

"But I thought she was fond of you?"

"You see what she said. She did confide something to me, only I must not tell you any more; and she is angry with me because she thinks I have not respected her confidence. Oh, what is to be done? Yes, I will go and have a talk with her. Go in, please, Audrey; you look dead tired."

"Oh! as if anything mattered," said Audrey. "I could almost wish that I were dead; the disgrace is past enduring."

CHAPTER XXVII.—THE STRANGE VISITOR IN THE BACK BEDROOM.

In vain Sylvia pleaded and argued. She brought all her persuasions to bear; she brought all her natural sweetness to the fore. She tried love, with which she was so largely endowed; she tried tact, which had been given to her in full measure; she tried the gentle touch of scorn and sarcasm; finally she tried anger, but for all she said and did she might as well have held her peace. Evelyn put on that stubbornness with which she could encase herself as in armor; nowhere could Sylvia find a crack or a crevice through which her words might pierce the obdurate and naughty little heart. What was to be done? At last she gave up in despair. Audrey met her outside Evelyn's room. Sylvia shook her head.

"Don't question me," she said. "I am very unhappy. I pity you from my heart. I can say nothing; I am bound in honor to say nothing. Poor Evelyn will reap her own punishment."

"If," said Audrey, "you have failed I give up all hope."

After lunch Evelyn and Audrey went back to school. There were a good many classes to be held that afternoon—one for deportment, another for dancing, another for recitation. Evelyn could recite extremely well when she chose. She looked almost pretty when she recited some of the spirited ballads of her native land for the benefit of the school. Her eyes glowed, darkened, and deepened; the pallor of her face was transformed and beautified by a faint blush. There was a heart somewhere within her; as Audrey watched her she was obliged to acknowledge that fact.

"She is thinking of her dead mother now," thought the girl. "Oh, if only that mother had been different we should not be placed in our present terrible position!"

It was the custom of the school for the girls on recitation afternoons to do their pieces in the great hall. Miss Henderson, Miss Lucy, and a few visitors generally came to listen to the recitations. Miss Thompson was the recitation mistress, and right well did she perform her task. If a girl had any dramatic power, if a girl had any talent for seeing behind the story and behind the dream of the poet, Miss Thompson was the one to bring that gift to the surface. Evelyn, who was a dramatist by nature, became like wax in her hands; the way in which she recited that afternoon brought a feeling of astonishment to those who listened to her.

"What remarkable little girl is that?" said a lady of the neighboring town to Miss Henderson.

"She is a Tasmanian and Squire Edward Wynford's niece," replied Miss Henderson; but it was evident that she was not to be drawn out

A VERY NAUGHTY GIRL

on the subject, nor would she allow herself to express any approbation of Evelyn's really remarkable powers.

Audrey's piece, compared with Evelyn's, was tame and wanting in spirit. It was well rendered, it is true, but the ring of passion was absent.

"Really," said the same lady again, "I doubt whether recitations such as Miss Evelyn Wynford has given are good for the school; surely girls ought not to have their minds overexcited with such things!"

Miss Henderson was again silent.

The time passed by, and the close of the day arrived. Just as the girls were putting on their cloaks and hats preparatory to going home, and some were collecting round and praising Evelyn for her remarkable performance of the afternoon, Miss Henderson appeared on the scene. She touched the little girl on the arm.

"One moment," she said.

"What do you want?" said Evelyn, backing.

"To speak to you, my dear."

Audrey gave Evelyn a beseeching look. Perhaps if Audrey had refrained from looking at that moment, Evelyn, excited by her triumph, touched by the plaudits of her companions, might have done what she was expected to do, and what immediately followed need not have taken place. But Evelyn hated Audrey, and if for no other reason but to annoy her she would stand by her guns.

Miss Henderson took her hand, and entered a room adjoining the cloakroom. She closed the door, and said:

"The week is nearly up. You know what will happen to-morrow?"

"Yes," said Evelyn, lowering her eyes.

"You will be present?"

Evelyn was silent.

"I shall see that you are. You must realize already what a pitiable figure you will be, how deep and lasting will be your disgrace. You have just tasted the sweets of success; why should you undergo that which will be said of you to-morrow, that which no English girl can ever forgive? It will not be forgotten in the school that owing to you much enjoyment has been cut short, that owing to you a cloud has rested on the entire place for several days—prizes forgone, liberty curtailed, amusements debarred; and, before and above all these things, the fearful stigma of disgrace resting on every girl at Chepstow House. But even now, Evelyn, there is time; even now, by a full confession, much can be mitigated. You know, my dear, how strong is the case against you. To-morrow morning both Miss Thompson and I proclaim before the entire school what has occurred. You are, in short, as a prisoner at the bar. The school will be the judges; they will declare whether you are innocent or guilty."

"Let me go," said Evelyn. "Why do you torture me? I said I did not do it, and I mean to stick to what I said. Let me go."

CHAPTER XXVII.—THE STRANGE VISITOR IN THE BACK BEDROOM.

"Unhappy child! I shall not be able to retain you in the school after to-morrow morning. But go now—go. God help you!"
Evelyn walked across the hall. Her school companions were still standing about; many wondered why her face was so pale, and asked one another what Miss Henderson had to say in especial to the little girl.
"It cannot be," said Sophie, "that she did it. Why, of course she did not do it; she would have no motive."
"Don't let us talk about it," said her companion. "For my part I rather like Evelyn—there is something so quaint and out-of-the-common about her—only I wish she would not look so angry sometimes."
"But how splendidly she recited that song of the ranch!" said Sophie. "I could see the whole picture. We must not expect her to be quite like ourselves; before she came here she was only a wild little savage."
The governess-cart had come for the two girls. They drove home in silence. Audrey was thinking of the misery of the following morning. Evelyn was planning her escape. She meant to go before dinner. She had asked Jasper to meet her at seven o'clock precisely. She had thought everything out, and that seemed to be the best hour; the family would be in their different rooms dressing. Evelyn would make an excuse to send Read away—indeed, she seldom now required her services, preferring to dress alone. Read would be busy with her mistress and her own young lady, and Evelyn would thus be able to slip away without her prying eyes observing it.
Tea was ready for the girls when they got home. They took it almost without speaking. Evelyn avoided looking at Audrey. Audrey felt that it was now absolutely hopeless to say a word to Evelyn.
"I should just like to bid Uncle Edward good-by," thought the child. "Perhaps I may never come back again. I do not suppose Aunt Frances will ever allow me to live at the Castle again. I should like to kiss Uncle Edward; he is the one person in this house whom I love."
She hesitated between her desire and her frantic wish to be out of reach of danger as soon as possible, but in the end the thought that her uncle might notice something different from usual about her made her afraid of making the attempt. She went up to her room.
"It is not necessary to dress yet," said Audrey, who was going slowly in the direction of the pretty schoolroom.
"No; but I have a slight headache," said Evelyn. "I will lie down for a few minutes before dinner. And, oh! please, Audrey, tell Read I do not want her to come and dress me this evening. I shall put on my white frock, and I know how to fasten it myself."
"All right; I will tell her," replied Audrey.
She did not say any more, but went on her way. Evelyn entered her room. There she packed a few things in a bag; she was not going to take much. In the bottom of the bag she placed for security the two

A VERY NAUGHTY GIRL

little rolls of gold. These she covered over with a stout piece of brown paper; over the brown paper she laid the treasures she most valued. It did not occur to her to take any of the clothes which her Aunt Frances had bought for her.

"I do not need them," she said to herself. "I shall have my own dear old things to wear again. Jasper took my trunks, and they are waiting for me at The Priory. How happy I shall be in a few minutes! I shall have forgotten the awful misery of my life at Castle Wynford. I shall have forgotten that horrid scene which is to take place to-morrow morning. I shall be the old Evelyn again. How astonished Sylvia will be! Whatever Sylvia is, she is true to Jasper; and she will be true to me, and she will not betray me."

The time flew on; soon it was a quarter to seven. Evelyn could see the minute and hour hand of the pretty clock on her mantelpiece. The time seemed to go on leaden wings. She did not dare to stir until a few minutes after the dressing-gong had sounded; then she knew she should find the coast clear. At last seven silvery chimes sounded from the little clock, and a minute later the great gong in the central hall pealed through the house. There was the gentle rustle of ladies' silk dresses as they went to their rooms to dress—for a few visitors had arrived at the Castle that day. Evelyn knew this, and had made her plans accordingly. The family had a good deal to think of; Read would be specially busy. She went to the table where she had put her little bag, caught it up, took a thick shawl on her arm, and prepared to rush down-stairs. She opened the door of her room and peeped out. All was stillness in the corridor. All was stillness in the hall below. She hoped that she could reach the side entrance and get away into the shrubberies without any one seeing her. Cautiously and swiftly she descended the stairs. The stairs were made of white marble, and of course there was no sound. She crossed the big hall and went down by a side corridor. Once she looked back, having a horrible suspicion that some one was watching her. There was no one in sight. She opened the side door, and the next instant had shut it behind her. She gave a gasp of pleasure. She was free; the horrid house would know her no more.

"Not until I go back as mistress and pay them all out," thought the angry little girl. "Never again will I live at Castle Wynford until I am mistress here."

Then she put wings to her feet and began to run. But, alas for Evelyn! the best-laid plans are sometimes upset, and at the moment of greatest security comes the sudden fall. For she had not gone a dozen yards before a hand was laid on her shoulder, and turning round and trying to extricate herself, she saw her Aunt Frances. Lady Frances, who she supposed was safe in her room was standing by her side.

"Evelyn," she said, "what are you doing?"

"Nothing," said Evelyn, trying to wriggle out of her aunt's grasp.

CHAPTER XXVII.—THE STRANGE VISITOR IN THE BACK BEDROOM.

"Then come back to the house with me."

She took the little girl's hand, and they re-entered the house side by side.

"You were running away," said Lady Frances, "but I do not permit that. We will not argue the point; come up-stairs."

She took Evelyn up to her room. There she opened the door and pushed her in.

"Doubtless you can do without dinner as you intended to run away," said Lady Frances. "I will speak to you afterwards; for the present you stay in your room." She locked the door and put the key into her pocket.

The angry child was locked in. To say that Evelyn was wild with passion, despair, and rage is but lightly to express the situation. For a time she was almost speechless; then she looked round her prison. Were there any means of escape? Oh! she would not stand it; she would burst open the door. Alas, alas for her puny strength! the door was of solid oak, firmly fastened, securely locked; it would defy the efforts of twenty little girls of Evelyn's size and age. The window—she would escape by the window! She rushed to it, opened it, and looked out. Evelyn's room was, it is true, on the first floor, but the drop to the ground beneath seemed too much for her. She shuddered as she looked below.

"If I were on the ranch, twenty Aunt Franceses would not keep me," she thought; and then she ran into her sitting-room.

Of late she had scarcely ever used her sitting-room, but now she remembered it. The windows here were French; they looked on the flower-garden. To drop down here would not perhaps be so difficult; the ground at least would be soft. Evelyn wondered if she might venture; but she had once seen, long ago in Tasmania, a black woman try to escape. She had heard the thud of the woman's body as it alighted on the ground, and the shriek which followed. This woman had been found and brought back to the house, and had suffered for weeks from a badly-broken leg. Evelyn now remembered that thud, and that broken leg, and the shriek of the victim. It would be worse than folly to injure herself. But, oh, was it not maddening? Jasper would be waiting for her—Jasper with her big heart and her great black eyes and her affectionate manner; and the little white bed would be made, and the delicious chocolate in preparation; and the fun and the delightful escapade and the daring adventure must all be at an end. But they should not—no, no, they should not!

"What a fool I am!" thought Evelyn. "Why should I not make a rope and descend in that way? Aunt Frances has locked me in, but she does not know how daring is the nature of Evelyn Wynford. I inherit it from my darling mothery; I will not allow myself to be defeated."

A VERY NAUGHTY GIRL

Her courage and her spirits revived when she thought of the rope. She must wait, however, at least until half-past seven. The great gong sounded once more. Evelyn rushed to her door, and heard the rustle of the silken dresses of the ladies as they descended. She had her eye at the keyhole, and fancied that she detected the hated form of her aunt robed in ruby velvet. A slim young figure in white also softly descended.

"My cousin Audrey," thought the girl. "Oh dear! oh dear! and they leave me here, locked up like a rat in a trap. They leave me here, and I am out of everything. Oh, I cannot, will not stand it!"

She ran to her bed, tore off the sheets, took a pair of scissors, and cut them into strips. She had all the ways and quick knowledge of a girl from the wilds. She knew how to make a knot which would hold. Soon her rope was ready. It was quite strong enough to bear her light weight. She fastened it to a heavy article of furniture just inside the French windows of her sitting-room, and then dropping her little bag to the ground below, she herself swiftly descended.

"Free! free!" she murmured. "Free in spite of her! She will see how I have gone. Oh, won't she rage? What fun! It is almost worth the misery of the last half-hour to have escaped as I have done."

There was no one now to watch the little culprit as she stole across the grass. She ran up to the stile where Jasper was still waiting for her.

"My darling," said Jasper, "how late you are! I was just going back; I had given you up."

"Kiss me, Jasper," said Evelyn. "Hug me and love me and carry me a bit of the way in your strong arms; and, oh! be quick—be very quick—for we must hide, you and I, where no one can ever, ever find us. Oh Jasper, Jasper, I have had such a time!"

It was not Jasper's way to say much in moments of emergency. She took Evelyn up, wrapped her warm fur cloak well round the little girl, and proceeded as quickly as she could in the direction of The Priory. Evelyn laid her head on her faithful nurse's shoulder, and a ray of warmth and comfort visited her miserable little soul.

"Oh, I am lost but for you!" she murmured once or twice. "How I hate England! How I hate Aunt Frances! How I hate the horrid, horrid school, and even Audrey! But I love you, darling, darling Jasper, and I am happy once more."

"You are not lost with me, my little white Eve," said Jasper. "You are safe with me; and I tell you what it is, my sweet, you and I will part no more."

"We never, never will," said the little girl with fervor; and she clasped Jasper still more tightly round the neck.

But notwithstanding all Jasper's love and good-will, the little figure began to grow heavy, and the way seemed twice as long as usual; and when Evelyn begged and implored of her nurse to hurry, hurry, hurry,

CHAPTER XXVII.–THE STRANGE VISITOR IN THE BACK BEDROOM.

poor Jasper's heart began to beat in great thumps, and finally she paused, and said with panting breath:

"I must drop you to the ground, my dearie, and you must run beside me, for I have lost my breath, pet, and I cannot carry you any farther."

"Oh, how selfish I am!" said Evelyn at once. "Yes, of course I will run, Jasper. I can walk quite well now. I have got over my first fright. The great thing of all is to hurry. And you are certain, certain sure they will not look for me at The Priory?"

"Well, now, darling, how could they? Nobody but Sylvia knows that I live at The Priory, and why should they think that you had gone there? No; it is the police they will question, and the village they will go to, and the railway maybe. But it is fun to think of the fine chase we are giving them, and all to no purpose."

Evelyn laughed, and the two, holding each other's hands, continued on their way. By and by they reached the back entrance to The Priory. Jasper had left the gate a little ajar. Pilot came up to show attentions; he began to growl at Evelyn, but Jasper laid her hand on his big forehead.

"A friend, good dog! A little friend, Pilot," was Jasper's remark; and then Pilot wagged his tail and allowed his friend Jasper—to whom he was much attached, as she furnished him with unlimited chicken-bones—to go to the house. Two or three minutes later Evelyn found herself established in Jasper's snug, pretty little bedroom. There the fire blazed; supper was in course of preparation. Evelyn flung herself down on a chair and panted slightly.

"So this is where you live?" she said.

"Yes, my darling, this is where I live."

"And where is Sylvia?" asked Evelyn.

"She is having supper with her father at the present moment."

"Oh! I should like to see her. How excited and astonished she will be! She won't tell—you are sure of that, Jasper?"

"Tell! Sylvia tell!" said Jasper. "Not quite, my dearie."

"Well, I should like to see her."

"She'll be here presently."

"You have not told that I was coming?"

"No, darling; I thought it best not."

"That is famous, Jasper; and do you know, I am quite hungry, so you might get something to eat without delay."

"You did not by any chance forget the money?" said Jasper, looking anxiously at Evelyn.

"Oh no; it is in my little black bag; you had better take it while you think of it. It is in two rolls; Uncle Edward gave it to me. It is all gold—gold sovereigns; and there are twenty of them."

"Are not you a darling, a duck, and all the rest!" said Jasper, much relieved at this information. "I would not worry you for the money,

A VERY NAUGHTY GIRL

darling," she continued as she bustled about and set the milk on to boil for Evelyn's favorite beverage, "but that my own funds are getting seriously low. You never knew such a state as we live in here. But we have fun, darling; and we shall have all the more fun now that you have come."

Evelyn leant back in her chair without replying. She had lived through a good deal that day, and she was tired and glad to rest. She felt secure. She was hungry, too; and it was nice to be petted by Jasper. She watched the preparations for the chocolate, and when it was made she sipped it eagerly, and munched a sponge-cake, and tried to believe that she was the happiest little girl in the world. But, oh! what ailed her? How was it that she could not quite forget the horrid days at the Castle, and the dreadful days at school, and Audrey's face, and Lady Frances's manner, and—last but not least—dear, sweet, kind Uncle Edward?

"And I never proved to him that I could shoot a bird on the wing," she thought. "What a pity—what a sad pity! He will find the gun loaded, and how astonished he will be! And he will never, never know that it was his Evelyn loaded it and left it ready. Oh dear! I am sorry that I am not likely to see Uncle Edward for a long time again. I am sorry that Uncle Edward will be angry; I do not mind about any one else, but I am sorry about him."

Just then there came the sound of a high-pitched and sweet voice in the kitchen outside.

"There is Sylvia," said Jasper. "I am going to tell her now, and to bring her in."

She went into the outside kitchen. Sylvia, in her shabbiest dress, with a pinched, cold look on her face, was standing by the embers of the fire.

"Oh Jasper," she said eagerly, "I do not know what to make of my father to-night! He has evidently had bad news by the post to-day—something about his last investments. I never saw him so low or so irritable, and he was quite cross about the nice little hash you made for his supper. He says that he will cut down the fuel-supply, and that I am not to have big fires for cooking; and, worst of all, Jasper, he threatens to come into the kitchen to see for himself how I manage. Do you know, I feel quite frightened to-night. He is very strange in his manner, and suspicious; and he looks so cold, too. No fire will he allow in the sitting-room. He gets worse and worse."

"Well, darling," said Jasper as cheerfully as she could, "this is an old story, is it not? He did eat his hash, when all is said and done."

"Yes; but I don't like his manner. And you know he discovered about the boxes in the box-room."

"That is over and done with too," said Jasper. "He cannot say much about that; he can only puzzle and wonder, but it would take him a long time to find out the truth."

CHAPTER XXVII.—THE STRANGE VISITOR IN THE BACK BEDROOM.

"I don't like his way," repeated Sylvia.

"And perhaps you don't like my way either, Sylvia," said a strange voice; and Sylvia uttered a scream, for Evelyn stood before her.

"Evelyn!" cried the girl. "Where have you come from? Oh, what is the matter? Oh, I do declare my head is going round!"

She clasped her hands to her forehead in absolute bewilderment. Jasper went and locked the kitchen door.

"Now we are safe," she said; "and you two had best go into the bedroom. Yes, you had, for when he comes along it is the wisest plan for him to find the kitchen locked and the place in darkness. He will never think of my bedroom; and, indeed, when the curtains are drawn and the shutters shut you cannot get a blink of light from the outside, however hard you try."

"Come, Sylvia," said Evelyn. She took Sylvia's hand and dragged her into the bedroom.

"But why have you come, Evelyn? Why is it?" said poor Sylvia, in great distress and alarm.

"You will have to welcome me whether you like it or not," said Evelyn; "and what is more, you will have to be true to me. I came here because I have run away—run away from the school and the fuss and the disgrace of to-morrow—run away from horrid Aunt Frances and from the horrid Castle; and I have come here to dear old Jasper; and I have brought my own money, so you need not be at any expense. And if you tell you will—— But, oh, Sylvia, you will not tell?"

"But this is terrible!" said Sylvia. "I don't understand—I cannot understand."

"Sit down, Miss Sylvia, dearie," said Jasper, "and I will try to explain." Sylvia sank down on the side of the little white bed.

"Now I know why you were getting this ready," she said. "You would not explain to me, and I thought perhaps it was for me. Oh dear! oh dear!"

"I longed to tell you, but I dared not," said Jasper. "Would I let my sweet little lady die or be disgraced? That is not in me. She will hide here with me for a bit, and afterwards—it will come all right afterwards, my dear Miss Sylvia. Why, there, darlings! I love you both. And see what I have been planning. I mean to go up-stairs to-night and sleep in your room, Miss Sylvia. Yes, darling; and you and Miss Evelyn can sleep together here. The supper is all ready, and I have had as much as I want. I mean to go quickly; and then if your father comes along and rattles at the kitchen door he'll get no answer, and if he peers through the keyhole, the place will be black as night. Then, being made up of suspicions, poor man, he'll tramp up-stairs and he'll thunder at your door; but it will be locked, and after a time I'll answer him in your voice from the heart of the big bed, and all his suspicions will melt away like snow when the sun shines on it. That is all, Miss

A VERY NAUGHTY GIRL

Sylvia; and I mean to do it, and at once, too; for if we were so careful and chary and anxious before, we must be twice as careful and twice as chary now that I have got the precious little Eve to look after."

Jasper's plan was carried out to the letter. Sylvia did not like it, but at the same time she did not know how to oppose it; and when Evelyn put her arms round her neck and was soft and gentle—she who was so hard with most, and so difficult to manage—and when she pleaded with tears in her big brown eyes and a pathetic look on her white face, Sylvia yielded for the present. Whatever happened, she would not betray her.

CHAPTER XXVIII.—THE ROOM WITH THE LIGHT THAT FLICKERED.

Now, all might have gone well for the little conspirators but for Evelyn herself. But when the girls, tired with talking, tired with the spirit of adventure, had lain down—Sylvia in Jasper's bed, and Evelyn in the new little white couch which had been got so lovingly ready for her—Sylvia, tired out, soon fell asleep; but Evelyn could not rest. She was pleased, excited, relieved, but at the same time she had a curious sense of disappointment about her. Her heart beat fast; she wondered what was happening. It seemed to her that in this tiny room at the back of the kitchen she was in a sort of prison. The sense of being in prison was anything but pleasant to this child of a free country and of an untrained mother. She slipped softly out of bed, and going to the window, unbarred the heavy shutters and looked out.

There was a moon in the sky, and the garden stood in streaks of bright light, and of dense shadow where the thick yew-hedge shut away the cold rays of the moon. Evelyn's white little face was pressed against the pane. Pilot stalked up and down outside, now and then baying to the moon, now and then uttering a suspicious bark, but he never glanced in the direction of the window out of which Evelyn looked. To the right of the window lay the hens' run and hen-house which have already been mentioned in these pages. Evelyn knew nothing about them, however; she thought the view ugly and uninteresting. She disliked the thick yew-hedge and the gnarled old yew-tree, and grumbling under her breath, she turned from the window, having quite forgotten to close the shutters. She got into bed now and fell asleep, little knowing what mischief she had done.

For it was on that very same night that Mr. Leeson determined, not to bury his bags of gold, but to dig them up. He was in a weak and trembling condition, and what he considered the most terrible misfortune had overpowered him, for the large sums which he had lately invested in the Kilcolman Gold-mines had been irretrievably lost; the gold-mines were nothing more nor less than a huge fraud, and all the shareholders had lost their money. The daily papers were full of the fraudulent scheme, and indignation was rife against the promoters of the company. But little cared Mr. Leeson for that; one fact alone concerned him. He, who grudged a penny to give his only child warmth and comfort, had by one fell blow lost thousands of pounds. He was almost like a man bereft of his senses. When Sylvia had left him that evening he had stood for some time in the cold and desolate parlor; then he sat down and began to think. His money was invested in more than one apparently promising speculation. He meant to call it all in—to collect it all and leave the country. He would not trust another sovereign in any bank in the kingdom; he would guard his own money; above all things, he would guard his precious savings. He had saved during his residence at The Priory something over twelve hundred pounds. This money, which really represented income, not capital, had been taken from what ought to have been spent on the necessaries of life. More and more had he saved, until a penny saved was more valuable in his eyes than any virtue under the sun; and as he saved and added sovereign to sovereign, he buried his money in canvas bags in the garden. But the time had come now to dig up his gold and fly. There were three trunks in the box-room; he would divide the money between the three. They were strong, covered with cow-hide, old-fashioned, safe to endure even such a weight as was to be put into them. He had made all his plans. He meant to take Sylvia, leave The Priory, and go. What further savings he could effect in a foreign land he knew not; he only wanted to be up and doing. This night, just when the moon set, would be the very time for his purpose. He was anxious—very anxious—about those fresh trunks which had been put into the attic; there was something also about Sylvia which aroused his suspicions. He felt certain that she was not quite so open with him as formerly. Those suppers were too good, too delicate, too tasty to be eaten without suspicion. At the best she was burning too much fuel. He would go round to the kitchen this very night and see for himself that the fire was out—dead out. Why should Sylvia warm herself by the kitchen fire while he shivered fireless and almost candleless in the desolate parlor? Soon after ten o'clock, therefore, he started on his rounds. He went through room after room, looking into each; he had never been so restless. He felt that a great and terrible task lay before him, and so bewildered was his mind, so much was his balance shaken, that he thought more of the twelve hundred pounds which he had saved than of the thousands which he had lost by foolish investment. The desolate rooms in the old Priory were all as they had ever been—scarcely any furniture in some, no furniture at all in others; they were bare and bleak and ugly. He went to the kitchen; the door was locked. He shook it and called aloud; there was no answer.

"The child has gone to bed," he said to himself. "That is well."

He stooped down and tried to look through the keyhole; only darkness met his gaze. He turned and shambled up-stairs. He turned the handle of Sylvia's door. How wise had been Jasper when she had guessed that the master of the house would do just what he did do!

"Sylvia!" he called aloud—"Sylvia!"

"Yes, father," said a voice which seemed to be quite the voice of his daughter.

"Are you in bed?"

"Yes. Do you want me?"

"No; stay where you are. Good night."

CHAPTER XXVIII.–THE ROOM WITH THE LIGHT THAT FLICKERED.

"Good night," answered the pretended Sylvia.

But Mr. Leeson, as he went down-stairs, did not hear the stifled laughter which was smothered in the pillows. He waited until the moon was on the wane, and then, armed with the necessary implements, went into the garden. He would certainly remove half the bags that night; the remainder might wait until to-morrow.

He reached the garden; he arrived at the spot where his treasure was buried, and then he stood still for a moment, and looked around him. Everything seemed all right—silent as the grave—still as death. It was a windless night; the moon would very soon set and there would be darkness. He wanted darkness for his purpose. Pilot came shuffling up.

"Good dog! guard—guard. Good dog!" said his master.

Pilot had been trained to know what this meant, and he went immediately and stood within a foot or two of the main entrance. Mr. Leeson did not know that a gate at the back entrance was no longer firmly secured and chained, as he imagined it to be. He thought himself safe, and began to work.

He had dug up six of the bags, and there were six more yet to be unearthed, when, suddenly raising his head, he saw a light in a window on the ground floor. It was a very faint light, and seemed to come and go.

He was much puzzled. His heart beat strangely; suspicion visited him. Had any one seen him? If so he was lost. He dared not wait another moment; he took two of the bags of gold and dragged them as best he could into the house. He went out again to fetch another two, and yet another two. He put the six canvas bags in the empty hall, and then returning to the garden, he pressed down the earth and covered it with gravel, and tried to make it look as if no one had been there—as if no one had disturbed it. But he was trembling all over, and as he did so he looked again at the flickering, broken light which came dimly, like something gray and uncertain, from within the room.

He went on tiptoe softly, very softly, up to the window and peered in. He could not see much—nothing, in fact, except one thing. The room had a fire. That was enough for him.

Furious anger shook the man to his depths. He hurried into the house.

CHAPTER XXIX.—WHAT COULD IT MEAN?

Anger gave Mr. Leeson a false strength. He put the canvas bags of gold into a large cupboard in the parlor; he locked the door and put the key into his pocket. Then he went gingerly and on tiptoe to another cupboard, and took down out of the midst of an array of dirty empty bottles one which contained a very little brandy. He kept this brandy here so that no one should guess at its existence. He poured himself out about a thimbleful of the potent spirit and drank it off. He then returned the bottle to its place, and fumbling in a lower shelf, collected some implements together. With these he went out into the open air.

He now approached the window where the light shone—the faint, dim light which flickered against the blind and seemed almost to go out, and then shone once more. Slowly and dexterously he cut, with a diamond which he had brought for the purpose, a square of glass out of the lower pane. He put the glass on the ground, and slipping in his hand, pushed back the bolt. All his movements were quiet. He said "Ah!" once or twice under his breath. When he had gently and very softly lifted the sash, he took a handkerchief from his pocket and wiped away some drops which stood on his forehead. Then he said "Ah!" once more, and slipped softly, deftly, and quietly into the room. He had made no noise whatsoever. The young sleepers never moved. He stood in the fire-lit, and in his opinion lavishly furnished, room. Here was a small white bed and an occupant; here a larger bed and another occupant. He crept on tiptoe towards the two beds. He bent down over the little occupant of the smaller bed.

A girl—a stranger! A girl with long, fair hair, and light lashes lying on a white cheek. A curious-looking girl! She moaned once or twice in her sleep. He did not want to awaken her.

He looked towards the other bed, in which lay Sylvia, pretty, debonair, rosy in her happy, warm slumber. She had flung one arm outside the counterpane. Her lips parted; she uttered the words:

"Darling father! Poor, poor father!"

The man who listened started back as though something had struck him.

Sylvia in that bed—Sylvia who had spoken to him not two hours ago up-stairs? What did it mean? What could it mean? And who was this stranger? And what did the fire mean, and all the furniture? A carpet on the floor, too! A carpet on his floor—his! And a fire which he had never warranted in his grate, and beds which he had never ordered in his room! Oh! was it not enough to strike a man mad with fury? And yet again! what was this? A table and the remains of supper! Good living, warmth, luxuries, under the roof of the man who was fireless and cold and, as he himself fondly and foolishly believed, a beggar!

CHAPTER XXIX.—WHAT COULD IT MEAN?

He stood absolutely dumb. He would not awaken the sleepers. A strange sensation visited him. He was determined not to give way to his passions; he was determined, before he said a word to Sylvia, to regain his self-control.

"Once I said bitter things to her mother; I will not err in that direction any more," he said to himself. "And in her sleep she called me 'Father' and 'Poor father.' But all the same I shall cast her away. She is no longer my Sylvia. I disown her; I disinherit her. She goes out into the cold. She is ruining her father. She has deceived me; she shall never be anything to me again. Paw! how I hate her!"

He went to the window, got out just as he had got in, drew down the sash, and stepped softly across the dark lawn.

He was very cold now, and he felt faint; the effect of the tiny supply of brandy which he had administered to himself had worn off. He went into his desolate parlor. How cold it was! He thought of the big fire in the bedroom which he had left. How poor and desolate was this room by contrast! What a miserable bed he reposed on at night—absolutely not enough blankets—but Sylvia lay like a bird in its nest, so warm, so snug! Oh! how bad she was!

"Her mother was never as bad as that," he muttered to himself. "She was extravagant, but she was not like Sylvia. She never willingly deceived me. Sylvia to have a strange and unknown girl—a stranger—in the house! All my suspicions are verified. My doubts are certainties. God help me! I am a miserable old man."

He cowered down, and the icy cold of the room struck through his bones. He looked at the grate, and observed that a fire had been laid there.

"Sylvia did that," he said to himself. "The little minx did not like to feel that she was so warm and I so cold, so she laid the fire; she thought that I would indulge myself. I! But am I not suffering for her? While she lies in the lap of luxury I die of cold and hunger, and all for her. But I will do it no longer. I will light the fire; I will have a feast; I will eat and drink and be merry, and forget that I had a daughter."

So the unfortunate man, half-mad with bewilderment and the grief of his recent losses, lit a blazing fire, and going to his cupboard, took out his brandy and drank what was left in the bottle. He was warm now, and his pulse beat more quickly. He remembered his six bags of gold, and the other six bags in the garden, and he resolved that if necessary he would fly without Sylvia. Sylvia could stay behind. If she managed to have such luxuries without his aid, she could go on having them; he would leave her a trifle—yes, a trifle—and save the rest for himself, and be no longer tortured by an unworthy and deceitful daughter. But as he thought these things he became more and more puzzled. The Sylvia lying on that bed was undoubtedly his daughter;

A VERY NAUGHTY GIRL

but his daughter had spoken to him from her own room at a reasonable hour—between ten and eleven o'clock—that same night. How could there be two Sylvias?

"The mystery thickens," he muttered to himself. "This is more than I can stand. I will ferret the thing out—yes, and to the very bottom. Those trunks in the attic! I suppose they belong to that ugly child. That voice in Sylvia's room! Well, of course it was Sylvia's voice; but what about the other Sylvia down-stairs? I must see into this matter without delay."

He went up-stairs and found himself outside Sylvia's door. He turned the handle, but it was locked. There was a light in the room, doubtless caused by another fire. He looked through the keyhole; the door was locked from within, for the key was in the lock.

More and more remarkable! How could Sylvia lock the door from within if she was not in the room? Really the matter was enough to daze any man. Suddenly he made up his mind. It was now five o'clock in the morning; in a short time the day would break. Sylvia was an early riser. If Sylvia or any one else was in that room he would wait on the threshold to confront that person. Oh, of course it was Sylvia; she had slipped back again and was in bed, and thought he would never discover her. How astonished she would be when she saw him seated outside her door!

So Mr. Leeson fetched a broken-down chair from his own bedroom, placed it softly just outside the door of the room where Jasper was reposing, and prepared himself to watch. He was far too excited to sleep, and the hours dragged slowly on. There was an old eight-day clock in the hall, and it struck solemnly hour after hour. Six o'clock—seven o'clock. Sylvia rose soon after seven. He waited now impatiently. The days were beginning to lengthen, and it was light—not full daylight, but nearly so. He heard a stir in the room.

"Ha, ha, Miss Sylvia!" he said to himself, "I shall catch you, take you by the hand, bring you down to my parlor, tell you exactly what I think of——Hullo! she is making a good deal of noise. How strong she is! How she bounded out of bed!"

He listened impatiently. His heart warmed now to the work which lay before him. He was, on the whole, enjoying himself at the thought of discovering to Sylvia how black he thought her iniquities.

"No child of my own any more!" he said to himself. "'Poor father,' indeed! 'Darling father, forsooth!' No, no, Sylvia; acts speak louder than words, and you were convicted out of your own mouth, my daughter."

Jasper dressed with despatch. She washed; she arranged her toilet. She came to the door; she opened it. Mr. Leeson looked up.

Jasper fell back.

"Merciful heavens!" cried the woman; and then Mr. Leeson grasped her hand and dragged her out of the room.

CHAPTER XXIX.—WHAT COULD IT MEAN?

"Who are you, woman?" he said. "How dare you come into my house? What are you doing in my daughter's room?"

"Ah, Mr. Leeson," said Jasper quietly, "discovered at last. Well, sir, and I am not sorry."

"But who are you? What are you? What are you doing in my daughter's room?"

"Will you come down to the parlor with me, Mr. Leeson, or shall I explain here?"

"You do not stir a step from this place until you tell me."

"Then I will, sir—I will. I have been living in this house for the last six weeks. During that time I have paid Miss Sylvia, and she has had money enough to keep the breath of life within her. Be thankful that I came, Mr. Leeson, for you owe me much, and I owe you nothing. Ah! do you recognize me now? The gipsy—forsooth!—the gipsy who gave you a recipe for making the old hen tender! Ha, ha! I laugh as I thought never to laugh again when I recall that day."

Mr. Leeson stood cold and white, looking full at Jasper. Suddenly a great dizziness took possession of him; he stretched out his hand wildly.

"There is something wrong with me," he said. "I don't think I am well."

"Poor old gentleman!" said Jasper—"no wonder!" and her voice became mild. "The shock of it all, and the confusion! Sakes alive! I am not going to take you into that icy bedroom of yours. Lean on me. There now, sir. You have not lost a penny by me; you have saved, on the contrary, and I have kept your daughter alive, and I have given you the best food, made out of the tenderest chickens, out of my own money, mark you—out of my own money—for weeks and weeks. Come down-stairs, sir; come and I will get you a bit of breakfast."

"I—cannot—see," muttered Mr. Leeson again.

"Well then, sir, I suppose you can feel. Anyhow, here is a good, strong right arm. Lean on it—all your weight if you like. Now then, we will get down-stairs."

Mr. Leeson was past resistance. Jasper pulled his shaky old hand through her arm, and half-carried, half-dragged him down to the parlor. There she put him in a big armchair near the fire, and was bustling out of the room to get breakfast when he called her back.

"So you really are the woman who had the recipe for making old hens tender?"

"Bless you, Mr. Leeson!—bless you!—yes, I am the woman."

"You will let me buy it from you?"

"Certainly—yes," replied Jasper, not quite knowing whether to laugh or to cry. "But I am going to get you some breakfast now."

"And who is the other girl?"

A VERY NAUGHTY GIRL

"Does he know about her too?" thought Jasper. "What can have happened in the night?"

"If you mean my dear little Miss Eve, why, no one has a better right to be here, for she belongs to me and I pay for her—yes, every penny; and, for the matter of that, she only came last night. But do not fash yourself now, my good sir; you are past thought, I take it, and you want a hearty meal."

Jasper bustled away; Mr. Leeson lay back in his chair. Was the world turning upside down? What had happened? Oh, if only he could feel well! If only that giddiness would leave him! What was the matter? He had been so well and so fierce and so strong a few hours ago, and now—now even his anger was slipping away from him. He had felt quite comforted when he leaned on Jasper's strong arm; and when she pushed him into the armchair and wrapped an old blanket round him, he had enjoyed it rather than otherwise. Oh! he ought to be nearly mad with rage; and yet somehow—somehow he was not.

CHAPTER XXX.—THE LOADED GUN.

Now, it so happened that the fuss and confusion incident on Evelyn's departure had penetrated to every individual in the Castle with the exception of the Squire; but the Squire had been absent all day on business. He had been attending a very important meeting in a neighboring town, and, as his custom was, told his wife that he should probably not return until the early morning. When this was the case the door opening into his private apartments was left on the latch. He could himself open it with his latch-key and let himself in, go to bed in a small room prepared for the purpose, and not disturb the rest of the family. Lady Frances had many times during the previous evening lamented her husband's absence, but when twelve o'clock came and the police who had been sent to search for Evelyn could nowhere find the little girl, and when the different servants had searched the house in vain, and all that one woman could think of had been done, Lady Frances, feeling uncomfortable, but also convinced in her own mind that Evelyn and Jasper were quite safe and snug somewhere, resolved to go to bed.

"It is no use, Audrey," she said to her daughter; "you have cried yourself out of recognition. My dear child, you must go to bed now, and to sleep. That naughty, naughty girl is not worth our all being ill."

"But, oh, mother! what has happened to her?"

"She is with Jasper, of course."

"But suppose she is not, mother?"

"I do not suppose what is not the case, Audrey. She is beyond doubt with that pernicious woman, and as far as I am concerned I wash my hands of her."

"And—the disgrace to-morrow?" said poor Audrey.

"My darling, you at least shall not be subjected to it. If I could find Evelyn I would take her myself to the school, and make her stand up before the scholars and tell them all that she had done; or if she refused I would tell for her. But as she is not here you are not going to be disgraced, my precious. I shall write a line to Miss Henderson telling her that the guilty party has flown, and that you are far too distressed to go to school; and I shall beg her to take any steps she thinks best. Really and truly that girl has made the place too hot to live in; I shall ask your father to take us abroad for the winter."

"But surely, mother, you will not allow poor little Evelyn to get quite lost; you will try to find her?"

"Oh, my dear! have I not been trying? Do not say any more to me about her to-night. I am really so irritated that I may say something I shall be sorry for afterwards."

A VERY NAUGHTY GIRL

So Audrey went to bed, and being young, she soon dropped asleep. Lady Frances, being dead tired, also slept; and the Squire, who knew nothing of all the fuss and trouble, came in at an early hour in the morning.

He lay down to sleep, and awoke after a short slumber. He then got up, dressed, and went into his grounds.

Lady Frances and Audrey were at breakfast—Lady Frances very pale, and Audrey with traces of her violent weeping the night before still on her face—when a servant burst in great terror and excitement into the room.

"Oh, your ladyship," he exclaimed, "the Squire is lying in the copse badly shot with his own gun! One of the grooms is with him, and Jones has gone for the doctor, and I came at once to tell your ladyship."

Poor Lady Frances in her agony scarcely knew what she was doing. Audrey asked a frenzied question, and soon the two were bending over the stricken man. The Squire was shot badly in the side. A new fowling-piece lay a yard or two away.

"How did it happen?" said Lady Frances. "What can it mean?"

Audrey knelt by her father, took his icy-cold hand in hers, and held it to her lips. Was he dead?

As he lay there the young girl for the first time in all her life learned how passionately, how dearly she loved him. What would life be without him? In some ways she was nearer to her mother than to her father, but just now, as he lay looking like death itself, he was all in all to her.

"Oh, when will the doctor come?" said Lady Frances, raising her haggard face. "Oh, he is bleeding to death—he is bleeding to death!"

With all her knowledge—and it was considerable—with all her common-sense, on which she prided herself, Lady Frances knew very little about illness and still less about wounds. She did not know how to stop the bleeding, and it was well the doctor, a bright-faced young man from the neighboring village, was soon on the spot. He examined the wounds, looked at the gun, did what was necessary to stop the immediate bleeding, and soon the Squire was carried on a hastily improvised litter back to his stately home.

An hour ago in the prime of life, in the prime of strength; now, for all his terrified wife and daughter could know, he was already in the shadow of death.

"Will he die, doctor?" asked Audrey.

The young doctor looked at her pitifully.

"I cannot tell," he replied; "it depends upon how far the bullet has penetrated. It is unfortunate that he should have been shot in such a dangerous part of the body. How did it happen?"

A groom now came up and told a hasty tale.

CHAPTER XXX.—THE LOADED GUN.

"The Squire called me this morning," he said, "and told me to go into his study and bring him out his new fowling-piece, which had been sent from London a few days ago. I brought it just as it was. He took it without noticing it much. I was about to turn round and say to him, 'It is at full cock—perhaps you don't know, sir,' but I thought, of course, he had loaded it and prepared it himself; and the next minute he was climbing a hedge. I heard a report, and he was lying just where you found him."

The question which immediately followed this recital was, "Who had loaded the gun?"

Another doctor was summoned, and another telegraphed for from London, and great was the agitation and misery. By and by Audrey found herself alone. She could scarcely understand her own sensations. In the first place, she was absolutely useless. Her mother was absorbed in the sickroom; the servants were all occupied—even Read was engaged as temporary nurse until a trained one should arrive. Poor Audrey put on her hat and went out.

"If only my dear Miss Sinclair were here!" she thought. "Even if Evelyn were here it would be better than nothing. Oh, no wonder we quite forget Evelyn in a time of anguish like the present!"

Then a fearful thought stabbed her to the heart.

"If anything happens——" She could not get her lips to form the word she really thought of. Once again she used the conventional phrase:

"If anything happens, Evelyn will be mistress here."

She looked wildly around her.

"Oh! I must find some one; I must speak to some one," she thought. "I will go to Sylvia; it is no great distance to The Priory. I will go over there at once."

She walked quickly. She was glad of the exercise—of any excuse to keep moving. She soon reached The Priory, and was just about to put her hand on the latch to open the big gates when a girl appeared on the other side—a girl with a white face, somewhat sullen in outline, with big brown eyes, and a quantity of fair hair falling over her shoulders. Even in the midst of her agitation Audrey gave a gasp.

"Evelyn!" she said.

"I am not going with you," said Evelyn. She backed away, and a look of apprehension crossed her face. "Why have you come here? You never come to The Priory. What are you doing here? Go away. You need not think you will have anything to do with me in the future. I know it is all up with me. I suppose you have come from the school to—to torture me!"

"Don't, Evelyn—don't," said Audrey. "Oh, the misery you caused us last night! But that is nothing to what has happened now. Listen, and forget yourself for a minute."

Poor Audrey tottered forward; her composure gave way. The next moment her head was on her cousin's shoulder; she was sobbing as if her heart would break.

"Why, how strange you are!" said Evelyn, distressed and slightly softened, but, all the same, much annoyed at what she believed would frustrate all her plans. For things had been going so well! The poor, silly old man who lived at The Priory was too ill to take any notice. She and Sylvia could do as they pleased. Jasper was Mr. Leeson's nurse. Mr. Leeson was delirious and talking wild nonsense. Evelyn was in a scene of excitement; she was petted and made much of. Why did Audrey come to remind her of that world from which she had fled?

"I suppose it was rather bad this morning at school," she said. "I can imagine what a fuss they kicked up—what a shindy—all about nothing! But there! yes, of course, I do not mind saying now that I did do it. I was sorry afterwards; I would not have done it if I had known—if I had guessed that everybody would be so terribly miserable. But you do not suppose—you do not suppose, Audrey, that I, who am to be the owner of Castle Wynford some day——"

But at these words Audrey gave a piercing cry:

"Some day! Oh, Evelyn, it may be to-day!"

"What do you mean?" said Evelyn, her face turning very white. She pushed Audrey, who was a good deal taller than her cousin, away and looked up at her. Audrey had now ceased crying; she wiped the tears from her cheeks.

"I must tell you," she said. "It is my father. He shot himself by accident this morning. His new gun from London was loaded. I suppose he did not know it; anyhow, he knocked the gun against something and it went off, and—he is at death's door."

"What—do—you say?" asked Evelyn.

A complete change had come over her. Her eyes looked dim and yet wild. She took Audrey by the arm and shook her.

"The gun from London loaded, and it went off, and—— Is he hurt much—much? Speak, Audrey—speak!"

She took her cousin now and shook her frantically.

"Speak!" she said. "You are driving me mad!"

"What is the matter with you, Evelyn?"

"Speak! Is he—hurt—much?"

"Much!" said Audrey. "The doctor does not know whether he will ever recover. Oh, what have I done to you?"

"Nothing," said Evelyn. "Get out of my way."

Like a wild creature she darted from her cousin, and, fast and fleet as her feet could carry her, rushed back to Castle Wynford.

It took a good deal to touch a heart like Evelyn's, but it was touched at last; nay, more, it was wounded; it was struck with a blow so deep, so sudden, so appalling, that the bewildered child reeled as she ran. Her eyes grew dark with emotion. She was past tears; she was almost

CHAPTER XXX.—THE LOADED GUN.

past words. By and by, breathless, scared, bewildered, carried completely out of herself, she entered the Castle. There was no one about, but a doctor's brougham stood before the principal entrance. Evelyn looked wildly around her. She knew her uncle's room. She ran up-stairs. Without waiting for any one to answer, she burst open the door. The room was empty.

"He must be very badly hurt," she whispered to herself. "He must be in his little room on the ground floor."

She went down-stairs again. She ran down the corridor where often, when in her best moments, she had gone to talk to him, to pet him, to love him. She entered the sitting-room where the gun had been. A great shudder passed through her frame as she saw the empty case. She went straight through the sitting-room, and, unannounced, undesired, unwished-for, entered the bedroom.

There were doctors round the bed; Lady Frances was standing by the head; and a man was lying there, very still and quiet, with his eyes shut and a peaceful smile on his face.

"He is dead," thought Evelyn—"he is dead!" She gave a gasp, and the next instant lay in an unconscious heap on the floor.

When the unhappy child came to herself she was lying on a sofa in the sitting-room. A doctor was bending over her.

"Now you are better," he said. "You did very wrong to come into the bedroom. You must lie still; you must not make a fuss."

"I remember everything," said Evelyn. "It was I who did it. It was I who killed him. Don't—don't keep me. I must sit up; I must speak. Will he die? If he dies I shall have killed him. You understand, I—I shall have done it!"

The doctor looked disturbed and distressed. Was this poor little girl mad? Who was she? He had heard of an heiress from Australia: could this be the child? But surely her brain had given way under the extreme pressure and shock!

"Lie still, my dear," he said gently; and he put his hand on the excited child's forehead.

"I will be good if you will help me," said the girl; and she took both his hands in hers and raised her burning eyes to his face.

"I will do anything in my power."

"Don't you see what it means to me?—and I must be with him. Is he dead?"

"No, no."

"Is he in great danger?"

"I will tell you, if you are good, after the doctor from London comes."

"But I did it."

"Excuse me, miss—I do not know your name—you are talking nonsense."

A VERY NAUGHTY GIRL

"Let me explain. Oh! there never was such a wicked girl; I do not mind saying it now. I loaded the gun just to show him that I could shoot a bird on the wing, and—and I forgot all about it; I forgot I had left the gun loaded. Oh, how can I ever forgive myself?"

The doctor asked her a few more questions. He tried to soothe her. He then said if she would stay where she was he would bring her the very first news from the London doctor. The case was not hopeless, he assured her; but there was danger—grave danger—and any shock would bring on hemorrhage, and hemorrhage would be fatal.

The little girl listened to him, and as she listened a new and wonderful strength was given to her. At that instant Evelyn Wynford ceased to be a child. She was never a child any more. The suffering and the shock had been too mighty; they had done for her what perhaps nothing else could ever do—they had awakened her slumbering soul.

How she lived through the remainder of that day she could never tell to any one. No one saw her in the Squire's sitting-room. No one wanted the room; no one went near it. Audrey was back again at the Castle, comforting her mother and trying to help her. When she spoke of Evelyn, Lady Frances shuddered.

"Don't mention her," she said. "She had the impertinence to rush into the room; but she also had the grace to——"

"What, mother?"

"She was really fond of her uncle, Audrey; I always said so. She fainted—poor, miserable girl—when she saw the state he was in."

But Lady Frances did not know of Evelyn's confession to the young doctor; nor did Dr. Watson tell any one.

It was late and the day had passed into night when the doctor came in and sat down by Evelyn's side.

"Now," he said, "you have been good, and have kept your word, and have obliterated yourself."

She did not ask him the meaning of the word, although she did not understand it. She looked at him with the most pathetic face he had ever seen.

"Speak," she said. "Will he live?"

"Dr. Harland thinks so, and he is the very best authority in the world. He hopes in a day or two to remove the pellets which have done the mischief. The danger, as I have already told you, lies in renewed hemorrhage; but that I hope we can prevent. Now, are you going to be a very good girl?"

"What can I do?" asked Evelyn. "Can I go to him and stay with him?"

"I wonder," said the doctor—"and yet," he added, "I scarcely like to propose it. There is a nurse there; your aunt is worn out. I will see what I can do."

"If I could do that it would save me," said Evelyn. "There never, never has been quite such a naughty girl; and I—I did it—oh! not meaning to hurt him, but I did it. Oh! it would save me if I might sit by him."

CHAPTER XXX.–THE LOADED GUN.

"I will see," said the doctor.

He felt strangely interested in this queer, erratic, lost-looking child. He went back again to the sickroom. The Squire was conscious. He was lying in comparative ease on his bed; a trained nurse was within reach.

"Nurse," said the doctor.

The woman went with him across the room.

"I am going to stay here to-night."

"Yes, sir; I am glad to hear it."

"It is quite understood that Lady Frances is to have her night's rest?"

"Her ladyship is quite worn out, sir. She has gone away to her room. She will rest until two in the morning, when she will come down-stairs and help me to watch by the patient."

"Then I will sit with him until two o'clock," said the doctor. "At two o'clock I will lie down in the Squire's sitting-room, where I can be within call. Now, I want to make a request."

"Yes, sir."

"I am particularly anxious that a little girl who is in very great trouble, but who has learnt self-control, should come in and sit in the armchair by the Squire's side. She will not speak, but will sit there. Is there any objection?"

"Is it the child, sir, who fainted when she came into the room to-day?"

"Yes; she was almost mad, poor little soul; but I think she is all right now, and she has learnt her lesson. Nurse, can you manage it?"

"It must be as you please, sir."

"Then I will risk it," said the doctor.

He went back to Evelyn, and said a few words to her.

"You must wash your face," he said, "and tidy yourself; and you must have a good meal."

Evelyn shook her head.

"If you do not do exactly what I tell you I cannot help you."

"Very well; I will eat and eat until you tell me to stop," she answered.

"Go, and be quick, then," said the doctor, "for we are arranging things for the night."

So Evelyn went, and returned in a few minutes; then the doctor took her hand and led her into the sickroom, and she sat by the side of the patient.

The room was very still—not a sound, not a movement. The sick man slept; Evelyn, with her eyes wide open, sat, not daring to move a finger. What she thought of her past life during that time no one knows; but that soul within her was coming more and more to the surface. It was a strong soul, although it had been so long asleep, and already new desires, unselfish and beautiful, were awakening in the child. Between twelve and one that night the Squire opened his eyes and saw a little girl, with a white face and eyes big and dark, seated close to him.

He smiled, and his hand just went out a quarter of an inch to Evelyn. She saw the movement, and immediately her own small fingers clasped his. She bent down and kissed his hand.

"Uncle Edward, do not speak," she said. "It was I who loaded the gun. You must get well, Uncle Edward, or I shall die."

He did not answer in any words, but his eyes smiled at her; and the next moment she had sunk back in her chair, relieved to her heart's core. Her eyes closed; she slept.

CHAPTER XXXI.—FOR UNCLE EDWARD'S SAKE.

The Squire was a shade better the next morning; but Mr. Leeson, not two miles away, lay at the point of death. Fever had claimed him for its prey, and he continued to be wildly delirious, and did not know in the least what he was doing. Thus two men, each unknown to the other, but who widely influenced the characters of this story, lay within the Great Shadow.

Evelyn Wynford continued to efface herself. This was the first time in her whole life she had ever done so; but when Lady Frances appeared, punctual to the hour, to take her place at her husband's side, the little girl glided from the room.

It was early on the following morning, when the mistress of the Castle was standing for a few bewildered moments in her sitting-room, her hand pressed to her forehead, her eyes looking across the landscape, tears dimming their brightness, that a child rushed into her presence.

"Go away, Evelyn," she said. "I cannot speak to you."

"Tell me one thing," said Evelyn; "is he better?"

"Yes."

"Is he out of danger?"

"The doctors think so."

"Then, Aunt Frances, I can thank God; and what is more, I—even I, who am such an awfully naughty girl—can love God."

"I don't like cant," said Lady Frances; and she turned away with a scornful expression on her lips.

Evelyn sprang to her, clutched both her hands, and said excitedly:

"Listen; you must. I have something to say. It was I who did it!"

"You, Evelyn—you!"

Lady Frances pushed the child from her, and moved a step away. There was such a look of horror on her face that Evelyn at another moment must have recoiled from it; but nothing could daunt her now in this hour of intense repentance.

"I did it," she repeated—"oh, not meaning to do it! I will tell you; you must listen. Oh, I have been so—so wicked, so—so naughty, so stubborn, so selfish! I see myself at last; and there never, never was such a horrid girl before. Aunt Frances, you shall listen. I loaded the gun, for I meant to go out and shoot some birds on the wing. Uncle Edward doubted that I could do it, and I wanted to prove to him that I could; but I was prevented from going, and I forgot about the gun; and the night before last I ran away. I ran to Jasper. When you locked me up in my room I got out of my sitting-room window."

"I know all that," said Lady Frances.

A VERY NAUGHTY GIRL

"I went to Jasper, and Jasper took me to The Priory—to Sylvia's home. Jasper has been staying in the house with Sylvia for a long time, and I went to Sylvia and to Jasper, and I hid there. Audrey came yesterday morning and told me what had happened; and, oh! I thought my heart would break. But Uncle Edward has forgiven me."

"What! Have you dared to see him?"

"The doctor gave me leave. I stayed with him half last night, until you came at two o'clock; and I told Uncle Edward, and he smiled. He has forgiven me. Oh! I love him better than any one in all the world; I could just die for him. And, Aunt Frances, I did tear the book, and I did behave shockingly at school; and I will go straight to Miss Henderson and tell her, and I will do everything—everything you wish, if only you will let me stay in the house with Uncle Edward. For somehow—somehow," continued Evelyn in a whisper, her voice turning husky and almost dying away, "I think Uncle Edward has made religion and GOD possible to me."

As Evelyn said the last words she staggered against the table, deadly white. She put one hand on a chair to steady herself, and looked up with pathetic eyes at her aunt.

What was there in that scared, bewildered, and yet resolved face which for the first time since she had seen it touched Lady Frances?

"Evelyn," she said, "you ask me to forgive you. What you have said has shocked me very much, but your manner of saying it has opened my eyes. If you have done wrong, doubtless I am not blameless I never showed you——"

"Neither sympathy nor understanding," said Evelyn. "I might have been different had you been different. But please—please, do anything with me now—anything—only let me stay for Uncle Edward's sake."

Lady Frances sat down.

"I am a mother," she said, "and I am not without feeling, and not without sympathy, and not without understanding."

And then she opened her arms. Evelyn gave a bewildered cry; the next moment she was folded in their embrace.

"Oh, can I believe it?" she sobbed.

Thus Evelyn Wynford found the Better Part, and from that moment, although she had struggles and difficulties and trials, she was in the very best sense of the word a new creature; for Love had sought her out, and Love can lead one by steep ascents on to the peaks of self-denial, unselfishness, truth, and honor.

Sylvia's father, after a mighty struggle with severe illness, came back again slowly, sadly to the shores of life; and Sylvia managed him and loved him, and he declared that never to his dying day could he do without Jasper, who had nursed him through his terrible illness. The instincts of a miser had almost died out during his illness, and he was willing that Sylvia should spend as much money as was necessary to secure good food and the comforts of life.

CHAPTER XXXI.–FOR UNCLE EDWARD'S SAKE.

The Squire got slowly better, and presently quite well; and when another New Year dawned upon the world, and once again the Wynfords of Wynford Castle kept open house, Sylvia was there, and also Mr. Leeson; and all the characters in this story met under the same roof. Evelyn clung fast to her uncle's hand. Audrey glanced at her cousin, and then she looked at Sylvia, and said in a low voice:
"Never was any one so changed; and, do you know, since the accident she has never once spoken of being the heiress. I believe if any thing happened to father Evelyn would die."

THE END.

A VERY NAUGHTY GIRL

A Very Naughty Girl Historical Context

During the period this book was originally written, the world was a very different place. The events of the time produced an impact on the authorship, style and content of this work. In order for you the reader to better appreciate and connect with this book, it is therefore important to have some context on world events during this timeframe. To this end, we have included a detailed events calendar for the *20th* century for your reference.

Please give consideration in particular to the years around *1901*, the year in which this work was first published.

Disclaimer: Some scenes throughout history may not be suitable for children, for example, in relation to war or violence. Please use your own discretion before reading this section to your child or allowing your child to read it.

1901 With terrible labour conditions and Europe's nationalism vs imperialism, a new century begins. Imperialism was promoted by Europe's nobility and the Church. Emperor Franz Joseph of Austria-Hungary was a moral man.
1902 Lenin, the Russian Marxist, celebrates his 32nd birthday. What Is to Be Done, his new book, was released in May. In it, he accuses Eduard Bernstein, 52, his socialist elder, of forsaking Marx's scientific socialism. Bernstein is attempting to modernise Marxism by using failed predictions. Lenin is unwavering and sees no failures. Western Agricultural Contracting Company (WACC) was founded in 1903 by California growers. WACC was accused by the Japanese-Mexican Labor Association (JMLA) of cutting wages on purpose. WACC allegedly forced workers to pay double commissions and purchase goods at inflated prices, according to JMLA.
1904 A British navy strike was feared by German naval and military attachés in London. The general population was unaware of the situation.
1905 Because "our youngsters were not placed in any position where their perspectives may be impacted by pupils of the Mongolian race," the San Francisco School Board has moved Japanese children to the city's only Asian school.

A VERY NAUGHTY GIRL

1906 In the United States, Doubleday released Upton Sinclair's masterwork The Jungle. The plot revolves around a diligent immigrant family attempting to achieve the "American Dream." The book exposes meatpacking industry deception and fraud. Despite corporate lobbyists' efforts to weaken it, legislation featuring serious government inspections and limits was approved. The watered down socialist message irritated Sinclair.

1907 The decision by the Japanese to disband the Korean army caused a revolt within the army, which the Japanese met with violence.

1908 The Hoover Company set to manufacture James M. Spangler's new upright portable vacuum cleaner in the United States.

A proposed federal income tax statute is approved by President Taft and his Attorney General in 1909.

1910 Slavery has been legal in China for over 3000 years, but it was now declared illegal.

1911 Albert Einstein enrols at Karl-Ferdinand University in Prague. He taught mechanics and kinetic heat theory during the summer semester.

To protect US interests, American forces occupy Tientsin, China, in 1912. A contingent will be stationed there until 1938.

The Constitution was amended in 1913 to allow Congress "power to levy and collect taxes on incomes, from whatever source derived, without regard to distribution among the states, census or enumeration."

The heir to the Austro-Hungarian monarchy and Inspector General of the armed forces, Archduke Franz Ferdinand, travels to Bosnia without the usual security against assassins on June 28th, 1914. The event that follows is widely regarded as having precipitated the outbreak of World War I. Before Gavrilo Princip, a Bosnian Serb, shot him and his wife to death in Sarajevo, Bosnia, Ferdinand states that everything is in God's hands. The elderly Habsburg monarch Franz Joseph is relieved. Ferdinand's succession was something he despised.

1914 The Ludlow Massacre occurred. A tent colony of 1,200 striking miners, was destroyed by the Colorado National Guard.

1915 A newly constructed vacuum tube amplifier is used to make the first coast-to-coast phone call (New York City to San Francisco).

The Royal Army Medical Corps performed the first successful blood transfusion in 1916.

1917 Mexico opposes the United States, while Germany has sent the Zimmermann Telegram, advocating the restoration of border states stolen from Mexico after the US-Mexican War. The text of the telegram intercepted by the British is released by the US government.

A VERY NAUGHTY GIRL HISTORICAL CONTEXT

1918 With the Sedition Act of 1918, the US Congress extended the 1917 Espionage Act.
On November 11, 1918, after more than four years of savage fighting and the loss of millions of lives, the World War One armistice is signed at Le Francport near Compiègne. The war on land, sea, and air between the Allies and their last surviving opponent, Germany, came to an end when the cannons on the Western Front fell silent. The ceasefire between Germany and the Allies was the first step toward ending World War One, despite the fact that fighting continued elsewhere. People assemble from all over the world, from Germany to the United States, for the most raucous celebration ever. General Pershing is disgruntled because he had wanted to take the battle to Germany.
1919 A peace conference to end World War I is held in Paris. 27 countries were in attendance, but Germany wasn't one of them. Senators in the United States vote against joining the League of Nations in 1920. Article X of the League Covenant, which mandated aid to a member who had been attacked from outside, was criticised. Warren G. Harding was elected as the 29th President of the United States in 1921. "We now find them both secure," he says, referring to liberty and culture. "The business cycle is clearly moving forward," he added. "I hope Congress and the Administration will support every reasonable government measure to smooth the resumption and stimulate future development."
1922 Joseph Stalin is named General Secretary of the Communist Party of the Soviet Union, a post created by Lenin at Stalin's insistence.
1923 The US pulls its last troops out of Germany, leaving the Ehren Breitstein Fortress unoccupied, which the French rapidly take over.
1924 A constitution is ratified by the Soviet Congress. It was a pact that merged three countries into one: Belorussia, Ukraine, and Transcaucasus.
1925 The "Monkey Trial" in Tennessee came to an end. John T. Scopes was found guilty of breaking state law by teaching evolution. Scopes was fined $100, but the verdict was overturned on a technicality.
1926 The pound is overvalued and on the gold standard. Coal exports were declining, and mine owners wanted to cut salaries. Unemployment is on the rise. In London, a BBC radio drama depicting a workers' revolution provokes panic.
1927 The first transatlantic radio phone contact was made between New York and London.
1928 In Buenos Aires, another politically unsuccessful bomb attack against Italian fascism occurred. 22 peiople were injured and 43 died.

A VERY NAUGHTY GIRL

1929 The Litvinov Protocol is signed in Moscow by the Soviet Union, Poland, Estonia, Romania and Latvia.

1930 To his fascist blackshirts, Mussolini declared, "Words were magnificent, but weapons, machine guns, ships, and aeroplanes were more beautiful." (Smoke from Humans)

Poland's persecution of Germans in Upper Silesia is condemned by the League of Nations in 1931.

1932 The Stimson Doctrine is on the rise in Manchuria: non-recognition of territorial changes imposed by force.

1933 Oxford University students debate whether "this House will ever fight for king and country." Yes, was the verdict. Universities in the United States shared this sentiment.

1934 The USSR is concerned about a resurgent Germany. It has extended its non-aggression pact with Poland and started a major military buildup.

1935 Civil planes are not allowed to overfly the White House

1936 Sweden has been resurrected from the ashes. Since 1929, its industrial production has doubled, and unemployment has dropped to 5%. The unemployment rate in the United States is around 15%, which is half of what it was in 1932.

1937 "I know some of you think I should be harder on Hitler than I am," Mr. Baldwin stated, "but have you contemplated the potential of a bomb on your breakfast tables?"

Adolf Hitler was appointed High Commander of Germany in 1938. (Oberkommando).

Hitler believed that the United Kingdom and France will not go to war, but World War II breaks out in Europe at dawn on September 1, 1939. Germany marches into Poland with a vengeance. Hitler proclaims, "Our adversaries are pitiful creatures. They were in Munich when I saw them." The Poles fought hard, but in terms of soldiers and machines, they were seriously outmanned, particularly in the air. The United Kingdom and France declared war on Germany on September 3, 1939, but supplied no significant assistance to Poland.

1939 "The Jewish race in Europe will be exterminated," Hitler declared in the Reichstag if "international Jewish financiers" succeed in reigniting World War II. Delegates to the Reichstag applaud.

1940 Navrenty Beria, the current NKVD chief, puts former NKVD leader Nicholai Yezhov on trial. Beria encourages Yezhov to confess in order to save Stalin. Yezhov respectfully declines.

5000 British troops land in Greece in 1941. Goebbels writes in his diary: "His colleagues and he wish for peace. Late. The game has to be finished."

1942 Japan declares war on the Netherlands and sends military forces to Indonesia and Borneo. Japan attacks New Guinea.

A VERY NAUGHTY GIRL HISTORICAL CONTEXT

Roosevelt, Churchill, Henri Giraud, and Charles De Gaulle agreed at a ten-day summit in Casablanca that the war must conclude with the unconditional surrender of all enemy governments.

1944 DNA, the nucleic acid that contains genetic instructions necessary for the birth and life of all known living species, was discovered by an American medical researcher named Oswald Avery (1877-1955).

1945 On the island of Luzon, 531 American POWs are liberated by 100 US forces and over 400 Filipino guerrillas. One US soldier and 26 rebels are killed.

On May 8, 1945, a week after Hitler committed suicide, the Allies acknowledged Germany's surrender.

On May 8, 1945, Winston Churchill announced VE Day. This day marks the end of World War II in Europe.

To commemorate the end of WWII, street celebrations were held throughout the United Kingdom.

Despite the fact that the war in the Far East was officially concluded, more people died in fighting.

Japan did not surrender. The war in the Far East persisted for a few more months.

On August 15, 1945 Japan readily accepted the Allied terms and surrendered after atomic bombs were dropped. Victory over Japan (VJ) Day is the name given to this day.

The official surrender documents were not signed until September 2nd. The official surrender was held on the USS Missouri in Tokyo Bay on September 2, 1945, six years and one day after the Germans invaded Poland. The Second World War came to a close.

1946 "Mr. Churchill today stands in the position of a war firebrand," Stalin tells the Soviet people.

1947 The US accused Poland's Provisional Government of "failing to carry out its solemn commitments" to hold free and fair elections in accordance with the Yalta and Potsdam Agreements.

The Czechoslovak parliament ordered a report on the politicisation of the police from the Interior Minister, a communist.

1949 Cardinal Mindszenty was imprisoned in Hungary for the rest of his life for treason. He "acknowledged" his wrongdoing. More individuals came to believe in the depravity of "Communist" governments.

1950 Senator Joe McCarthy of Wisconsin claims the US State Department contained 205 communists.

Ridgway's men retook Soeul in the Korean War and pushed against Chinese and North Koreans. The mood in Washington regarding the outcome of the war was said to be improving.

1952 Senator Robert Taft proposed ending diplomatic relations with the Soviet Union while campaigning for President.

A VERY NAUGHTY GIRL

Egypt's premier, Mohammed Naguib, expresses his goal to "liberate Palestine" in 1953, causing concern among Israelis.

1954 China's GDP is growing at a rate of 15% per year after one year of its five-year industrialisation plan. In China, a 14-year transformation from family farms to collectives is underway. Armed Egyptians detonated bombs near an Israeli hamlet ten kilometres from the Egyptian/Gaza armistice line, killing a young woman and wounding 18.

1956 All privately owned enterprises in China were put into state-ownership.

1957 Jacques Duclos, a leader of the French Communist Party, opposed "dangerous" tendencies. Duclos was a supporter of the Soviet Union's foreign policy collaboration. The Communist Party of the United States opposes the Communist Party of the Soviet Union.

1958 Venezualan coup d'etat. Military officers take command alongside civilians. Perez Jimenez and his pals board a plane bound for Miami.

1959 The Dalai Lama's palace was under assault from Chinese mortars. The Dalai Lama emerges from his palace six hours later, disguised as a soldier and carrying a weapon draped over his shoulder.

1960 The National Association of Broadcasters has vowed to punish anyone who accepts money for playing music recordings over the radio, following a controversy in the United States.

1961 Eisenhower warned of the rising domination of a military-industrial complex amid concerns about military spending and an arms race.

In Berlin in 1962, 'Bridge of Spies' Russian spy, Abel, was traded for Francis Gary Powers, a former U-2 pilot.

1963 In his inaugural address, Alabama Governor George Wallace says, "Segregation today, tomorrow, and forever."

In the Panama Canal Zone in 1964, US high school students flout a flag-flying ban. A fight breaks out between students from the United States and Panama. Riots against the United States erupt. Twenty-one Panamanians and four US servicemen are killed.

1965 For the 1964 'Mississippi Burning' murders of Schwerner, Goodman, and Chaney, a federal grand jury in Mississippi charged 18 persons.

1966 Julian Bond, a young black man who opposed the Vietnam War, is denied a seat in the Georgia legislature.

Governor Ronald Reagan meets with FBI agents in 1967 to discuss radicals in Berkeley.

In 1968, in the Vietnam war, US forces fought back against Giap's assault. The Viet Cong suffers a significant defeat.

A VERY NAUGHTY GIRL HISTORICAL CONTEXT

1969 In eleven days, an offshore oil well off the coast of Santa Barbara spilled 200,000 gallons of oil over 800 square miles of sea and 35 miles of coastline. California's inhabitants were enraged.
1970 The greatest philosopher of the twentieth century, Bertrand Russell, died at the age of 97.
1971 Edward Heath's Britain recognises the Amin authority in Uganda. To destroy Obote's allies and intellectuals, Amin established the "State Research Bureau." Military leaders who refused to back the coup were executed.
1972 People in Dublin set fire to the British Embassy in response to the 'Bloody Sunday' tragedy in Derry. Many British-owned businesses in Ireland were set on fire. West Berlin's British Yacht Club is blasted also.
1973 Lyndon B Johnson died four years after stepping down from the presidency.
1974 Patricia Hearst is claimed by the Symbionese Liberation Army, led by General Cinque.
1975 Jane Fonda filed a $2.8 million lawsuit against the US government, alleging civil rights breaches. The CIA intercepted her foreign mail, according to the Department of Justice.
Patty Hearst was found guilty of robbery by an American court in 1976.
1977 Jimmy Carter succeeds Gerald Ford as the 39th President of the United States. "A new beginning," he remarked, "a new devotion within our Government, and a new spirit among us all."
1978 Sweden is the first country to impose a ban on aerosol sprays that could deplete the ozone layer.
Ayatollah Khomeini was allowed to return to Iran by Prime Minister Bakhtiar in 1979. Khomeini, who wanted all foreigners out of Iran, is greeted by millions.
1980 In Afghanistan, the Kamal administration announced it invited Soviet soldiers in "in light of Afghanistan's opponents' ongoing aggressive conduct."
1981 Ronald Reagan was sworn in as the 44th President of the United States. "A strong, robust, expanding economy that supports equal opportunity for all Americans, free of bigotry or discrimination," the president promised.
1982 Colonel Gaddafi of Libya refers to President Ronald Reagan as a "terrorist" and a "destructive" figure.
1983 The Federal Reserve Board's Paul Volcker keeps interest rates at 13% to combat inflation.
1984 Officials in China revealed plans to buy $1 billion worth of Western technology in order to speed up bureaucratic processes and attract foreign investment.

1985 The eight-day convention of the Chinese Writers' Association closed with a declaration of "democracy and freedom."
In 1986, Spain and Portugal joined the EEC, which would later become the EU.
1987 Margaret Thatcher is in the Soviet Union on a peace mission. Her appearances gather enormous audiences of friendly people who surprise and defy security.
In the Iran-Contra affair, Lieutenant Colonel Oliver North and Vice Admiral John Poindexter were accused of conspiring to defraud the US in 1988.
1989 In Paraguay, Alfredo Stroessner's 35-year dictatorship came to an end.
A McDonald's restaurant opened in Moscow in 1990.
1991 The United Nations deadline for Iraqi disengagement from occupied Kuwait expires, allowing Operation Desert Storm to begin.
1992 Slovenia and Croatia were recognised as sovereign entities by the European Community.
1993 Iraq permits UN weapons inspectors to fly into the country.
1994 In Mexico the EZLN seize control of five Chiapas municipalities and march on Mexico City.
President Bill Clinton proclaimed a national emergency in 1995 and extended a $20 billion loan to Mexico without Congress approval.
1996 The Irish Republican Army is irritated that Sinn Féin's political branch or party is not participating in the peace talks with Britain. In London's Canary Wharf District, an IRA one-ton bomb explodes, killing two people, injuring 39 others, and bringing down a six-storey building.
1997 President Bill Clinton made it illegal for the federal government to fund cloning research.
1998 Human cloning was banned in 19 European nations.
1999 China's government-imposed restrictions on internet use, particularly at Internet cafes.
2000 President Clinton signed the Bill to permanently normalize trade relations with China.

This concludes the historical context.

Thank you for your interest in our publications. Please don't forget to check out our other books and leave a review if you enjoyed this book.

The edits and layout of this print version are Copyright © 2022 by Wombrook Publishing
www.wombrookpublishing.com

Printed in Great Britain
by Amazon